THE APOTHECARY'S POISON

GLASS AND STEELE, BOOK #3

C.J. ARCHER

WWW.CJARCHER.COM

CHAPTER 1

LONDON, SPRING 1890

"This is it!" Matt folded the newspaper and slapped it down on the table beside his untouched plate of bacon, eggs and toast. He stabbed his finger at a brief article near the bottom of the page. "This is the breakthrough we need. Eat up, India. After breakfast, we're going to the hospital."

"Which hospital?" Duke asked, rising. "What's happened?"

Willie and Cyclops crowded around Matt and peered at the newspaper. I couldn't see over Cyclops's brawny shoulder to read it.

"What's the breakthrough?" I asked.

Cyclops picked up the paper. Willie caught the edge to hold it still, her lips moving as she read.

Cyclops whistled. "Could be," he said. "Could be what we've been looking for."

Willie let go of the paper, looped her arms around her cousin and hugged him. Matt hugged her back. He was trying hard to contain his smile, but he lost the fight and grinned. His gaze connected with mine over the top of Willie's head.

I tried to read the paper, but Duke took it from Cyclops and out of my view. I'd only managed to read the headline and journalist's byline: MEDICAL MIRACLE AT LONDON HOSPITAL, by Oscar Barrett.

"God damn," Duke murmured as he read.

"Will someone tell me what it's about?" I asked, only just managing not to stamp my foot. "Is there evidence of a magical doctor?"

"Possibly," Matt said. "If the article is accurate."

"Why wouldn't it be accurate?" Willie asked, returning to her chair and her breakfast of sausages and bacon.

"Because newspaper men like to sensationalize." Matt also sat, and the rest of us followed suit.

I finally managed to grab the newspaper and read the article. According to Oscar Barrett, a patient at the London Hospital had been declared dead upon arrival by one doctor, only to sit up after being tended to by another. According to a witness, the patient then asked for an ale to slake his "devil of a thirst." A representative for the hospital said the first doctor made a mistake. The reporter, however, insisted the witness was reliable and that the patient had presented with no pulse and wasn't breathing when Dr. Hale "worked his magic."

"An interesting last line," I said.

"That isn't the first time that reporter has used it," Matt said. "That's the third piece I've read by Oscar Barrett in *The Weekly Gazette* where he uses the exact same phrase."

How curious. "Dr. Hale," I said, setting the newspaper down beside my plate. "That name seems a little familiar, but I can't place it." I re-read the article then pored over it a third time. I felt Matt's gaze upon me but didn't glance up. I didn't want to face him in case he read the doubt on my face. In the end, he guessed anyway.

"India?" he urged. "You don't seem very enthusiastic."

I was about to tell him why but changed my mind. From his tone, I guessed he had the same doubts too. Expressing them didn't make them disappear or change the course of what we must do next. I cut the top off my boiled egg. "The sooner we finish breakfast, the sooner we can go to the hospital and verify the claim ourselves."

Matt's elderly aunt entered the dining room, putting an end to the discussion of Dr. Hale's medical miracle. While she knew that Matt was ill, she didn't know the magical nature of it. Few did. That was how it must remain.

"What a lovely morning," she said, pouring herself a cup of tea at the sideboard. "India, will you walk with me today?"

"I have errands to run with Matt," I said. "Perhaps Willie can accompany you."

Willie and Miss Glass shot me matching withering glares.

"I can't," Willie said. "I've got errands to run too."

"No you don't," Duke said, sitting back with a smile. "We're free all day."

"Then *you* go."

"I will, if Miss Glass can put up with my company."

Miss Glass nibbled the edge of her toast. "Gladly. Your company is always welcome, Duke. Yours too, Cyclops."

Willie dropped her fork on the plate, making Miss Glass jump. "And my company?"

"Is tolerable."

"Fine. If you insist that I come, Letty, I will."

A short, charged silence was only broken by Miss Glass's resigned sigh. "Only if you refrain from smoking."

"Christ," Willie muttered, stabbing a sausage with her fork. "It's bad enough you order me about in here, you got to do it outside, too?"

"It's for your own good. Smoking is a disgusting habit. I don't suppose you'll change into a dress?"

"No!"

"Then you'll have to walk several paces behind."

Willie dropped her fork again and a sausage rolled off the plate and onto the floor. "I ain't the goddamned maid."

Miss Glass winced. "Do you have to use such vulgar language?"

"Goddamned ain't a cuss word. Not like fu—"

"Willie!" Matt pinned her with a glare and she pressed her lips together. "Aunt, let Willie walk alongside you."

Willie picked up another sausage from her plate with her fingers and bit off the end, all while shooting Miss Glass a triumphant look.

"You are family, after all," he went on.

Willie choked and spat out the half-eaten sausage.

"We are *not* blood related," Miss Glass said. "That's an important distinction."

"Sure is," Willie said.

Miss Glass sighed. "Very well, she can walk with me."

"Why, thank you, Princess." Willie frowned and studied her sausage. "How did I get talked into that?"

I smiled into my teacup and refrained from telling her that she was jealous of the attention Miss Glass gave Duke and Cyclops lately. Ever since the appointment of staff at number sixteen Park Street, Miss Glass had begun to treat them more as friends than servants. This was the first time they would step out in her company, however. The very public display of acceptance between the two rough American men and a genteel English lady was quite a statement. She might appear to be a conformist, but a rebellious streak ran through her. She broke the rules when she wanted to, in her own subtle way.

I looked at Matt and caught him smiling into his teacup too. He winked at me, clearly pleased with how they were all getting along. Despite Willie's scowl, she seemed to want to be included in the party and his aunt made no more complaints. Indeed, she didn't even wrinkle her nose when Willie picked the fallen sausage off the floor and bit off the tip.

Thirty minutes later, Matt and I climbed into the brougham and Bryce drove us to the Whitechapel Road hospital at a bracing pace. An uncomfortable five-minute silence felt as if it stretched twice as long until Matt finally broke it.

"Dr. Hale may not be magical," he said. "This could be a wild goose chase."

"But we have to know for certain," I finished for him. "There is hope, Matt. As you said at breakfast, this could be a breakthrough."

Two weeks ago, during our investigation into the disappearance of a magical mapmaker, we'd discovered the timepiece magician Matt sought, known only as Chronos, was most likely living in London under the name Pierre DuPont. After a brief glimpse of DuPont at the clock factory where he worked, he'd fled. We'd not seen him since and decided to change direction in our search. Instead of looking all over London for DuPont, without any clue where to begin, we hoped to find him by seeking out the thing he wanted most— a magical doctor.

Chronos had spent years looking for a magical doctor whose skills he could combine with his own. He'd found that doctor in an American backwater, and they'd experimented on Matt after he was shot. The experiment had saved Matt's life, but the doctor had regretted his actions afterward and refused to perform such magic again. Chronos, however, had been enthused by the results and was eager to continue experimenting. With Dr. Parsons refusing, and later dying, Chronos needed another magical doctor.

Matt had suggested that if Chronos was indeed in London, under the name DuPont, it was possible he'd finally found another doctor magician here. We'd spent the next two weeks visiting all the hospitals, both in search of a doctor with rare skill and for a man who fit the description of Chronos. We'd not had any luck with either.

The *Weekly Gazette* article was the first indication that our theory might hold water. It seemed as though London harbored a doctor magician after all.

"We didn't speak to Dr. Hale last time we inquired at the London Hospital," I said. "Perhaps questioning him directly will yield results."

Matt absently patted the breast pocket where he kept his magic watch tucked away. He looked quite healthy today, although it was still early and he'd already yawned twice since leaving the house. Yet no matter how ill or tired he appeared, he was still the most handsome man I'd ever laid eyes on. "We have to be delicate."

"And not mention my own magic, not even to encourage him to open up."

Matt watched me closely. "Is that a promise?"

"It is. I plan to be careful, from now on."

He leaned forward and sandwiched my hand between both of his. The gesture sent a thrill through me, even though our gloves prohibited contact. "The murder of Daniel Gibbons frightened you."

"It served as a timely warning. He was killed because of his magic."

"He was killed by a rival, jealous of his skill, who thought he was doing something his guild wanted. Since you're not a practicing watchmaker, you won't have the same problem."

"Matt, it was you who warned me to keep my magic a secret. Are you now telling me not to hide it?"

He sat back. "I'm simply trying to allay your fears."

"But you still think it best to keep it quiet?"

"I do."

"As do I." I sighed. "For now. I reserve the right to tell someone if I think they ought to know."

"And you must use it if you are in danger." He nodded at my reticule sitting in my lap.

I closed my fingers around the pouch. The familiar shape of my watch inside was a comfort. It had saved my life once, as had a clock I'd tinkered with. Apparently my magic was strong, but I didn't know how to wield it with spells, and I certainly couldn't fix Matt's watch. I hoped Chronos could teach me.

An elderly porter met us in the hospital reception room. "You don't look poorly," he said, eyeing us up and down. "Are you visiting? Visiting hour is four to five in the afternoon."

"We want to speak to Dr. Hale," Matt said.

The porter clicked his tongue and muttered something about demanding toffs before hailing a nurse who entered from a side door. She drew us aside as the porter dealt with a man cradling his arm against his chest.

"Is he in surgery?" Matt asked when the nurse said Dr. Hale wasn't available.

"He's not a surgeon," she said crisply. "He's a physician. He's on his rounds now. He won't be long, if you'd like to take a seat."

"I read about the doctor in this morning's paper," Matt told her. "Did you see the article?"

The nurse rolled her eyes. "Dr. Hale made sure that I did. He made sure we all saw it. Is that why you're here?" Her face softened as she regarded Matt. "To have him perform a miracle for you? I *knew* this would happen. I told him it would. Mark my words, you'll be the first of many through those doors today, hoping for a *medical miracle*." She spat out the two words as if they tasted sour. "The reporter shouldn't have written that, and Dr. Hale should have had more care."

"In not letting anyone see him perform his miracle?"

"In not letting the reporter think he performed a miracle and saved that fellow's life. Oh, sir. You haven't gone and got your hopes up, have you?"

Matt went still. "Are you implying he didn't save that patient?"

"He died again, shortly afterward. Or...not *again*, not *really*. He died for the first time, since he couldn't have been dead before, could he? The dead don't come back to life for a few minutes—only to die a second time—do they?"

"He's dead," Matt said flatly.

The nurse nodded. Matt lowered his head and crushed the brim of his hat in his hand. My mind turned with possibilities and questions. It wasn't so much that the patient was now dead that intrigued me, but the fact that he'd been alive for a few minutes *between* his two deaths, if that were indeed what had happened.

"Start at the beginning," I urged the nurse. "Who was the patient and what was his condition?"

She folded her arms. "I'm not at liberty to divulge patient information. But, sir, madam, I want to urge you not to put any stock in that reporter's claims. There was no miracle here." She leaned forward, glanced toward the door, and lowered her voice. "Dr. Hale's just a jumped up apothecary, so the other doctors say. He certainly didn't cure anyone of anything. That patient's well and truly dead, now. I am sorry if you came here hoping the doctor would help you. If you tell me what ails you, I'll send for the appropriate doctor, one who specializes in your type of complaint."

"We want to speak to Dr. Hale," Matt said tightly. "We'll wait."

She sighed. "Very well. I'll have one of the nurses send for him." She indicated two empty chairs near where the porter stood by the door. "I'm afraid you'll have to wait out here. Patients are directed through to either the men's or women's reception room, but since you're not patients, you have to remain here."

Another patient entered, a bloody cloth tied around his head. He eyed us as if we were intruders, not supposed to be there. The London Hospital was located in the heart of the city's roughest areas. Patients were working class at best. It wasn't a hospital for the likes of Matt, or even me. I felt conspicuous in my best blue and cream day dress and smart hat with its blue satin ribbon.

We didn't have to wait long before a white-coated man greeted us, smiling broadly. He was much younger than I expected, perhaps in his late twenties, with thick brown hair that flopped over his forehead, and spectacles perched on a Roman nose. His features were a little familiar but I couldn't place him.

He extended a slender hand to Matt without breaking his smile. "I'm Dr. Hale. You wanted to see me about the medical miracle? Are you a reporter?"

"I am," Matt said, without pause. "My name is Matthew Glass and this is Miss Steele, my partner."

Partner! I wished he'd apprised me of the plan before he launched into it with both feet. He might be good at playing roles but I was not. I needed to prepare.

"Partner?" Dr. Hale said. "That's odd for a reporter to work in teams. And with a woman, no less."

"I'm more of an assistant, really," I said.

"It's as much her article as it will be mine," Matt countered.

Dr. Hale clicked his heels together and nodded at me. "Well, how intriguing and utterly delightful for me. It's a pleasure to meet you both. Shall we talk in my office?"

He led us up the stairs, past a desk staffed by a nurse who greeted Dr. Hale with a benign smile. "Keep up the good work, Nurse Benedict," he said.

"It's Nurse Barnaby," she said.

"This way, Mr. Glass, Miss Steele. Ah, Dr. Wiley." Dr. Hale hailed an elderly man with a quick step and eyes that narrowed upon seeing Hale. "These two reporters from the, er..."

"*The Times*," Matt said.

"*The Times!*" Dr. Hale's step faltered. "My, my, I had no idea. Did you hear that, Dr. Wiley? They're from *The Times!*"

"I heard," Dr. Wiley bit off.

"These two reporters from *The Times* wish to speak to me about my medical miracle. Perhaps you ought to join us, since you played a role." Dr. Hale leaned toward us. "My esteemed colleague originally declared the patient deceased on arrival."

"A mistake," Dr. Wiley said, his cheeks reddening. "Clearly."

"Or was it?" Dr. Hale winked.

Wiley heaved a sigh, as if he'd heard Hale tell the story a dozen times. "This is no joking matter. Does Dr. Ritter know you're speaking to reporters?"

"Bah!" Hale laughed and waved a hand in dismissal. "He'll thank me when he hears of it."

"I doubt it. I seem to recall him forbidding you to mention it publicly."

"Think of the publicity the hospital will receive. In *The Times*, no less."

"You're walking a thin line, Hale. You have been warned, sir," Wiley said to Matt. "I urge you not to believe a thing he tells you. If you want the real story, ask myself or Dr. Ritter."

"Always scare-mongering," Hale said with a conspiratorial wink at me. "Come, Miss Steele, Mr. Glass, let's begin. You must be itching to know the details."

Dr. Wiley hurried off, shaking his head. He glanced back and quickened his step before disappearing through a door.

Dr. Hale led us into a bare wood-paneled office. He shut a book that lay open on the desk and placed it inside his top drawer. It was the only book in the office, although a bookcase took up an entire wall. Instead of books, however, each shelf contained a row of cream ceramic jars, all labeled in Latin. I recognized the language but lacked the education to read it.

"Dr. Wiley is a trifle embarrassed," Hale said apologetically. "He's the most experienced doctor here, aside from our principal, Dr. Ritter, of course." He sat behind the desk chair and indicated we should sit too. "Dr. Wiley declared the patient deceased and when I brought him back to life, the good doctor almost fainted." Hale laughed. "One of the nurses had to steer him to a vacant bed."

"And was he dead?" Matt asked bluntly.

Dr. Hale regarded Matt then me. "You look startled, Miss Steele. Indeed, you look as if you weren't expecting your colleague to ask that question without preamble."

"Mr. Glass is full of surprises," I said rather lamely. But he was right—I hadn't expected Matt's directness, particularly when Hale could be a link to Chronos. We needed him, but Matt looked as if he wanted to wipe Hale's smirk from his face with his fist. Perhaps it was frustration at coming so close only to find the man we needed was rather obnoxious.

"Dr. Hale, we're very busy, as I'm sure you are too," Matt said. "We'd like to get to the bottom of this mystery as soon as possible. If no miracle was performed then I'm afraid we're wasting our time." He began to rise. "Miss Steele?"

"Wait!" Hale indicated Matt should sit again. "You're not wasting your time. It's just that...I've been warned not to speak of it, you see." He glanced at the door.

"By Dr. Ritter, the principal?"

"And others."

"Why? What are you afraid will happen?"

11

"It's not me who is afraid of the consequences, Mr. Glass. I'm rather excited about this development, as it happens. It's they who are afraid—Dr. Ritter, Dr. Wiley, and...others." He clasped his hands on the desk and pointed a finger at Matt. "I think you and I are of like mind, Mr. Glass, along with Mr. Barratt, of course."

"The reporter for *The Weekly Gazette?*" I asked.

He nodded. "Yet even he only alluded to it in his article, despite implying he would tell the truth. He didn't even print my statement."

"Allude to what?" Matt asked.

"Ah." He sat back with a smile too slick to trust. "You want me to say it first, do you? Well then. I suppose I will. Magic, Mr. Glass. It exists, and *I* am a magician." He spread out his hands like a messiah welcoming his disciples. "Neither of you look surprised."

"We've heard of magic," Matt said. "But few speak openly about it."

"They've been ordered not to."

"As have you, by your own account, and yet you do."

His smile turned smug. "This breakthrough is bigger than Dr. Ritter or anyone else. Bigger than this hospital and the guilds. It can't be swept under the carpet. It should be celebrated. What I did two days ago is a miracle, just like the newspaper claimed. No one has ever brought a dead man back to life."

"But he's not alive," I said. "He's dead."

Hale's smile slipped. "I'll work on extending the magic so that it lasts longer. But it was a solid first step."

"And how will you extend it?" I asked.

Hale's nostrils flared. "I can't give away my secrets. If you print my ideas, another magician might steal them."

I tried to think of a way to incorporate a question about

time magic without revealing myself and what we knew but could think of none.

"Was he already dead?" Matt asked. "Or simply on the brink of death?"

Hale laughed. "It depends on whom you ask. Dr. Wiley swears that he was dead, but one of the nurses said she saw his chest rise with a breath."

"And what do you say?"

"In all honesty, I cannot be certain. But it changes nothing. My magic—"

"How can you not be certain?" Matt asked. "You're a physician."

Dr. Hale's smile returned, harder than before. "I didn't check. I know, I know, it was a mistake, but I believed Dr. Wiley without question. He's very experienced."

"And old," Matt said. "And a nurse claimed the patient breathed. You should have checked."

Hale's mouth worked but no words came out. He looked as if he would reach across the desk and strangle Matt to keep him quiet. "The fact is," he eventually said, "whether the patient was already dead or almost dead, I brought him to full recovery for a few minutes. Alas, it didn't last. But think of the implications, Mr. Glass. Think of what it could mean."

"I am," Matt said heavily. "I think of nothing *but* the implications."

"If I could perfect the cure, make it last longer..." He left the sentence unfinished, but his smile had returned. "But there's no way to do so."

I looked to Matt but he shook his head slightly. He didn't want me to reveal what we knew about combining time magic with types. I agreed with him, for now. We should not reveal our knowledge until we knew we could trust Hale. He may have lied about this entire scenario for the attention.

"I'm very excited by your interest," Hale went on. "*The*

Weekly Gazette is one thing, but *The Times* is quite another. Your reach is incredible and the paper's reputation beyond question. If you report on magic, and state that it exists, then you will be believed." He got up and began pacing back and forth in front of his window, as if he couldn't be still. "This is an exciting development and quite unexpected. I think the world is ready to believe. People *want* magic to exist. They're tired of their mundane lives. They want to break the monotony. Magic can do that." He snapped his fingers and pointed at Matt. "Speak to Oscar Barratt. He might be able to enlighten you on some other magical cases. I believe I wasn't the first magician he reported on."

The more he spoke, the more I found myself believing him. He might be arrogant, and a little irritating, but he did speak in earnest. He was a magician. I was certain of it.

My heart did a little skip in my chest. If this man was a magical doctor, then Chronos might be aware of his existence and perhaps have been here. I was about to ask Hale when Matt suddenly sat forward. He'd had his doubts about Hale's story, but I suspected he now thought the same as me.

"Do you know a man named Pierre DuPont?" he asked, the words spilling from his lips in a rush.

Hale shook his head. "Is he a reporter with an interest in magic, too?"

"He also goes by the name Chronos."

Surprise flickered across Hale's face. "The old clock-maker? He came here some time ago. He never told me his real name. DuPont sounds like a French name, but that Chronos fellow didn't have an accent."

My breath caught in my throat. We'd thought the name and accent were part of a disguise, but to hear Hale confirm it was a relief. And to think he'd met Chronos! It was more than I'd hoped for.

"What does he look like?" Matt asked. His features

schooled, but the flush in his cheeks gave away his excitement.

"White hair, elderly but rather sprightly for his age." Hale leaned forward and glanced at each of us in turn. "He's a magician." He leaned back again. "But I see that you both knew that already."

The knuckles on Matt's fisted hand turned whiter. "Do you know where we can find him?"

"Yes."

"Where?" both Matt and I blurted out.

CHAPTER 2

"*W*hy the sudden interest in Chronos?" The pout could be heard in Hale's voice, if not seen on his face. "I thought it was me you wanted to interview for your story."

"We do," I said, before Matt could dismiss him and ruin not only our chances of finding Chronos but having Hale help us once we did find him. Although Dr. Parsons, the original magical doctor, had claimed the problem was with Matt's timepiece, not his body, it was possible he'd been mistaken. Perhaps both magicians were required to work together after all.

"Then don't you want to know the details of how I cured the patient?" Hale asked, indicating his bookcase full of jars.

"Of course we do," I said, summoning some patience from goodness knew where. Matt's body had gone rigid, as if he were trying to contain himself. "But we're interested in all magic, and we've heard about Chronos. May we have his address, please?"

"Oh, I don't know where he lives," Hale said, "only the name of a tavern where he drinks. He told me if I ever came across a magical doctor that I was to contact him at the Cross Keys on High Holborn."

Matt stood. "Thank you, Doctor." He checked his pocket watch—not his magical one—and headed for the door. "India?" he said when he realized I hadn't followed.

But I couldn't take my gaze off Dr. Hale. "What did he mean if you 'came across a magical doctor?' *You* are a magical doctor."

"Ah, you made the same mistake as Chronos."

Matt stalked back to me and leaned his knuckles on the desk. "You told us you're magical."

"I am. But I'm an apothecary, not a doctor. Well, I *am* a physician by profession, but my magic is with medicines." He indicated the jars again. "Do you understand the difference?"

Matt lowered his head. He must have thought the same as me—that if we required both a doctor and horology magician, we had at least found the former. But we had not.

I stood and touched his arm. "Was Chronos disappointed when he found out?"

"Furious," Hale said. "He ranted and raved. He even picked up one of my jars, and was about to throw it at the wall, until I wrestled it off him. I managed to calm him down and explain the difference between my profession and my magic. My work is not in the same field as my magic, although they're related."

I wagged my finger at him. "I know where I've heard your name now! You're Dr. Hale of Dr. Hale's Cure All." We used to keep a bottle of his medicine in our kitchen. It soothed some headaches but cured little else, despite its claim. "But if you don't work as an apothecary, why is your name on the bottle?"

"It's common practice for actual doctors to lend their name to medicines. It makes them more authentic in the public's eyes, you see, and that helps sales. A pharmacist friend asked me to give my name to his cure-all, and I readily agreed. Most of those medicines are his." He nodded at the jars. "Some are my own, once infused with magic—which no longer works, alas. I had one in my pocket when that patient came in." He opened his drawer and pulled out a small brown bottle stoppered with a cork. "I saw him gasp his last breath —or perhaps it was simply *a* breath—so I whispered my spell into the bottle and trickled some of the medicine into his mouth."

"The article didn't mention medicine," I said heavily.

"An oversight on Barratt's part. Unfortunately, the medicine only gave the patient a few more minutes of life. I had hoped for days or even weeks. Imagine the attention then!" He returned the bottle to his drawer. "You both look as disappointed as Chronos when he learned my magic is in medicines and not actual doctoring."

I glanced at Matt. He didn't look disappointed; he looked eager to get away.

"Apothecary magic is just as interesting and important as any other," Hale said defensively.

"A magical doctor can cure a man with nothing more than his hands," Matt said with a speaking glance at the jars.

Hale sniffed and crossed his arms. "Yes. Well. As a physician, I am able to cure people of their illnesses too—sometimes forever—whereas the effects of magic are fleeting, whether performed by a doctor or apothecary. Besides, magical doctors are rare, apparently."

"You've never come across any?" Matt asked.

"No."

"You've never suspected any of your colleagues of being magical? Have any performed feats of doctoring too extraordinary to be explained away?"

"No. As I said, magic is rare, and the sort of magician you're looking for is the rarest form, according to Chronos.

Not even he knew if one exists. Of course, I wouldn't expect artless like you two to understand."

"We're learning," I said.

"Anyway, it was nice to see that my magic still works, since I don't use it often, and even more satisfying to have it come to Barratt's attention. Sales of Dr. Hale's Cure All will increase dramatically as a result of the article, I expect. My friend will be pleased."

"Are all the Cure-All bottles infused with magic?" Matt asked.

He hesitated. "Just my own medicines." Again, he indicated the stack of shelves with its bottles of all shapes and sizes. I did not see a Cure-All among them, except for his personal bottle that he slipped back into the desk drawer.

"Come, India," Matt said. "We've got work to do."

Hale thrust out his hand, and Matt shook it and thanked him. "It was a pleasure to meet you both," Hale said. "Be sure and let me know when *The Times* will run the article so I can tell all my friends and the staff here. They'll enjoy reading it, I'm sure."

Matt went to open the office door only to have it wrenched open from the other side. Dr. Wiley stood there with another man of advanced years who sported a dense gray beard and matching eyebrows that crashed together in a severe frown. They stood aside to allow us to pass.

"You're from *The Times*, are you?" asked the older man.

Matt nodded and kept walking.

"Do you carry a letter of introduction from your editor?"

Matt stopped. "I don't usually need one."

The man looked Matt over then straightened his spine and squared his shoulders. He was still a much less impressive figure than Matt. "Then how can we be certain you are who you say you are?"

"We don't have time for this," Matt growled.

"What did you say your name was?"

"It's Glass," Dr. Hale said, joining us in the doorway. "And this is Miss Steele. Dr. Ritter, they're genuine, I assure you."

Dr. Ritter was the principal doctor at the hospital and therefore the chief of staff. He was Dr. Hale's superior. "Your assurance is meaningless, Hale."

Hale blinked rapidly behind his spectacles. "Pardon?"

Ritter pushed past me and into the office. Wiley scampered after him. "Pack your things and leave," Ritter said as Wiley closed the door. "You no longer work here."

"B-but I can't just leave." Hale cried. "What about my patients?"

I held my hand up to Matt, who stood a few feet away, his fingers tapping against his thigh. I pressed my ear to the closed door and could just make out Ritter's furious words.

"You have embarrassed this hospital for the last time! You're a disgrace to your profession, and I've had enough! The article was the last straw! Going public with such a fanciful, ludicrous claim of miracles...it's beyond the pale! Take your medicines and leave before I throw you out myself."

The door opened and I hurried away, but their voices filtered out through the gap.

"You can't do this to me!" Hale cried. "I'm too important to—"

"Too important? Ha! You're nothing but an apothecary trying his hand at doctoring. Your skills as a physician are moderate, at best. Go back to being a pharmacist, Hale. If you can get employment, that is."

"What is that supposed to mean?"

"It means I've contacted the Apothecary's Guild and told them to watch out for you. They were *very* interested in the stunt you pulled here and your ridiculous claims of magic and miracles. I doubt they want a crackpot in their midst either."

The last thing I heard as we hurried along the corridor was Hale's protest. "I am not a crackpot! I am a magician surrounded by artless idiots."

Neither Matt nor I spoke until we reached our carriage. "The Cross Keys on High Holborn," Matt directed Bryce. He'd barely had time to settle on the seat opposite me when the coach lurched forward.

"It's unlikely Chronos will be there at this hour," I said, checking my watch. It was only ten forty-five.

"I'm not getting my hopes up that he'll be there at all." Matt's bright, clear eyes told a different story, however. He looked invigorated, healthier and more alert than I'd seen him in weeks. His health had grown progressively worse since I'd met him, his need to use his watch more frequent. No one had mentioned it, but I could sense everyone's worry.

"I think you're allowed to get your hopes up, Matt. This is the closest we've come to finding Chronos. I almost whooped like Willie when Hale confirmed he'd spoken to him." I wanted to reach across the gap and touch his knee, his hand, *something* to show him how relieved I was, because mere words didn't seem enough.

But I did not. Respectable women weren't raised to touch men, even if they could be considered friends. I'd never even held hands with Eddie, the man I'd once called my fiancé.

"We have to be prepared for him to run off when he sees us," Matt said with a shake of his head. "God knows why he ran when we saw him at the factory."

"You stand by the door at the Cross Keys, and I'll go inside. If I see the fellow who called himself DuPont, I'll signal to you. I think it's safe to assume that DuPont and Chronos are one and the same."

"What would I do without you, India?"

I rolled my eyes. "My plan is hardly clever. You were probably about to suggest the same thing yourself."

He grinned, proving me right. I smiled back, enjoying the sight of him in a positive mood. "Allow me to praise you every now and again. You deserve it," he said. "You did, after all, charm Dr. Hale, whereas I wanted to knock his head off, on more than one occasion."

"You weren't the only one, by the sound of it. First Chronos himself, after discovering Hale was an apothecary magician not a doctor, and then Dr. Ritter."

"And probably Dr. Wiley too, since Hale enjoyed reminding him that he declared that patient dead when he clearly wasn't."

"I would have dismissed Hale, too, if I were Ritter," I said. "He reminded me of something slimy you find at the bottom of a pond."

He laughed softly. "You can't dismiss someone for that. You can dismiss him for negligence or negatively affecting the reputation of the hospital. I don't know what Hale thought he was trying to achieve by using his magic on that patient and then talking about it to Barratt. He's a fool, and now he's paying for it."

"Or is he?"

He frowned. "What do you mean?"

"Perhaps he wanted to bring publicity to Dr. Hale's Cure All medicine. Having his name in the paper beneath the headline Medical Miracle will bring some attention to it, even though the medicine itself wasn't mentioned. He said himself that sales will increase."

"Perhaps. But he has also attracted the attention of the Apothecary's Guild and found himself unemployed. If he gets a percentage of sales from the Cure All then he might still consider it worthwhile, but if he was paid a set sum to have his name on the label, what good did it do?"

"Whatever happens to him," I said, "thank God for Hale, his magic, and his arrogance. Now we know where to find Chronos."

"Not to mention thanks to Oscar Barratt the reporter."

I'd wondered about Barratt and his interest in magic. It might be worth talking to him to find out if he knew of any timepiece magicians. Then again, if we found Chronos it wouldn't matter. We only needed the one.

High Holborn wasn't far from Worthey's clock factory in Clerkenwell where we'd seen DuPont. The Cross Keys looked as if it had sat in the same position for centuries, its wooden façade and small paned windows inviting passersby in for a quiet ale. I clamped my hand to my hat to keep it in place as I tipped my head back and looked up. The bold gold writing against the black paint glinted in the sunlight, but it didn't hold my attention for long.

"It's no wonder Chronos drinks here," I said.

Matt followed my gaze to the large clock jutting out from the center of the building, one floor up. He smiled and opened the door for me. "Be discreet."

I touched the brim of my hat to hide as much of my face as possible and entered. Matt stood just inside the door beside the umbrella stand, his own hat pulled low at the front.

A polished bar ran most of the room's length. Bottles, barrels and glasses behind it and a bartender who looked at me as if a woman had never walked into his establishment before. Empty tables and chairs occupied the other side of the room, and beside those were secluded booths that weren't visible from the front door. I quickly checked each one and returned to Matt.

"There are only six drinkers at the moment," I said. "None

are DuPont. I still think you should check, just in case DuPont and Chronos are not the same man."

He nodded at the barman as he passed and looked into each of the booths. With a shake of his head at me, he approached the barman. They exchanged words and Matt reached into his pocket and passed him some money. The barman pocketed it and nodded.

Matt joined me and placed my hand in the crook of his arm. He steered me toward the coach and cheerfully asked Bryce to take us home. Matt's eyes sparkled with humor and hope amid the dark circles of tiredness. We may not have found Chronos, but we were close. We both felt it.

"What did the barman say?" I asked as I climbed into the cabin, my hand in Matt's as he assisted me up the step.

"That a man known only as Chronos drinks there occasionally. He fits the description."

I clapped my hands. "We have him, Matt! We've found him."

He closed the door but hadn't sat as the coach lurched forward. He would have tumbled into me if he hadn't pressed one hand to the ceiling and the other to the wall behind my head. The angle brought him very close to me, his chest just inches from my face.

I looked up at the same time that he looked down. His face softened and his smile slipped. The hand on the ceiling moved to my shoulder, the thumb stroking the underside of my jaw.

I swallowed, hoping for his kiss, waiting for it, *aching* for it. His eyes turned smoky and his lips parted. He moved closer, closer until he filled my view, scrambling my senses.

"India," he murmured, his voice thick, "when I am healed—"

We turned a corner and he lost his balance. Before I could even take a proper breath, Matt was sitting on the seat opposite me. He stared out the window, his profile uncompromising, as if we'd not just shared a charged moment.

"Are you all right, Matt?"

"Fine." He cleared his throat and tore his gaze away to look at me. "You?"

"Also fine, thank you." I clutched my reticule tighter and waited for him to continue his speech, but he did not. "You were saying?"

He stroked the crease cutting through his forehead until it cleared. "My behavior just now was unforgivable. I apologize. I...I don't know what came over me."

I hoped it was the same thing that had come over me, but it didn't seem so. He showed no signs of desire—no flushed cheeks, no quickening of his breath, and no eagerness to be close to me again. He wouldn't even look at me directly. The sting of his rejection brought tears to my eyes. I studied my reticule in my lap until I'd composed myself. I looked up, only to see that he'd been watching me.

My cheeks warmed yet he remained unmoved. "Did you pay the barman to notify you if Chronos returns?" I asked, determined not to let him see how he'd affected me.

He nodded. "I asked him to attempt to find out where Chronos lived and to also send someone to fetch me immediately. Apparently Chronos drinks there once a week, sometimes twice, always alone. He paid the innkeeper to tell him when someone asked after him. He uses the staff as a sort of messaging service."

"But if the innkeeper tells Chronos about us, he might run away again."

"That's why I paid the innkeeper more than Chronos is paying him."

I blew out a measured breath. "Let's hope he's greedy enough to sell his services to the highest bidder."

Bristow met us at the front door just as the ebony and

brass clock in the entrance hall ticked over to eleven-fifty. "You have visitors, sir. Lady Rycroft and the Misses Glass."

"All of them?" Matt asked, handing Bristow his hat.

"All of them."

"Is my Aunt Letitia with them?"

"Yes, sir."

Matt glanced past me through the open drawing room door. Hope Glass, the youngest, waved and smiled. Her two sisters, on the sofa beside her, pretended not to notice us. Matt's two aunts weren't visible from where we stood, and I couldn't see Willie, Cyclops or Duke.

"Shall we, India?" Matt asked.

It would seem I couldn't get out of it. Nor did it seem like Matt wanted to make his excuses. Perhaps it was too late for that, now that we'd been spotted, but I didn't expect him to *want* to join them. His aunt and cousins had called twice in the last two weeks, and he'd sat with them. His uncle hadn't visited, and I didn't expect him to after Matt almost thrashed him in his own home. Matt's Aunt Beatrice looked as if she'd rather bite off her own tongue than chat with either of us, but her desire to see one of her daughters wed her husband's heir outweighed her distaste for the American and his unimportant assistant.

"Pssst." Willie hissed from the staircase and signaled us to approach her. She did not step off the bottom step, as if it offered sanctuary from a potentially horrid fate.

"Not joining your cousins in the drawing room?" I asked with mock innocence.

She pulled a face. "Those little twits ain't *my* cousins and you know it, India Steele."

"Coward."

"Clever, more like. I don't have to put up with 'em." She gave me a smug look. "Do you?"

She had me there.

"How did it go at the hospital?" she asked Matt.

"Positively," he said. "We'll talk later."

She screwed up her nose and nodded at the drawing room. "You seem eager to get in."

"I don't think all of my cousins are silly twits, Willie."

"Don't you go getting any ideas about that Hope," she warned. "Englishwomen don't do so well in the California sun."

"I have no plans on taking anyone back to America."

"And Letty don't like her," she went on, as if he hadn't spoken. "I trust your aunt's opinion more than I trust yours. Men get turned too easily by a pretty face and fine figure."

I tended to agree with her; not so much by the pretty face observation but her faith in Miss Glass's opinion. From what I'd seen of Hope Glass, she wasn't always the sweet girl she pretended to be. She was very aware of her appeal to men and, I suspected, knew how to manipulate them. I felt a little cruel for thinking such a thing when I had no proof of it. Perhaps I'd put too much stock in what Miss Glass thought of her niece.

Or perhaps I was jealous. Matt certainly seemed keen to see her. He was already striding toward the drawing room. He waited at the door for me to catch up and allowed me to walk ahead of him.

"There you are," Lady Rycroft said as we entered. "We've been waiting an age for you, Matthew."

"An age," Miss Glass echoed with a glare at her nephew. "They arrived shortly after we returned from our walk. Willemina, Cyclops and Duke scattered, of course."

"You didn't honestly expect them to have tea with us," Lady Rycroft said with a flare of her nostrils. "The girl may be Matthew's relative, but she's rougher than a navvy. And the men!" She shuddered. "That dark one with the eye patch looks like a convict."

I waited for Matt to say something in Cyclops's defense, but he simply sat on the piano stool while I occupied the chair beside Miss Glass.

"Mama," Hope whined.

"I think the eye patch lends a dashing quality," the middle sister, Charity, said. She wasn't as pretty as Hope, or as witty, but she seemed to have the strongest sense of adventure of all three. At least she could hold a conversation. The eldest, Patience, was very shy and rarely lifted her gaze from her lap. "It makes him look like a pirate," Charity went on. "Pirates are *so* romantic."

Hope rolled her eyes. "You do say the silliest things, sometimes."

"Cyclops is rather sweet," Miss Glass said. "I like him."

"As do I," I chimed in.

Matt gave me a small smile, but no one else paid me any attention. I continued anyway.

"And he most certainly is not an outlaw."

Matt shifted his weight. I frowned at him but he didn't meet my gaze.

"India, pour yourselves tea," Miss Glass said. "Now that Matthew is here, I'm sure my sister-in-law will stay a little longer."

I did as told and handed a cup to Matt. He looked even more tired, and I feared he needed to use his watch. He would not hurry this visit along, however. He was much too proud to reveal his exhaustion, even to family.

"We have news, Matthew," Lady Rycroft said with a triumphant smile that lifted her dour features. "Patience is getting married in the summer at Rycroft. If you're still in the country, you will be invited."

"Congratulations," Matt said to Patience. "I'm very pleased for you."

She managed to lift her chin long enough to murmur her thanks and blush profusely.

"Who is the lucky fellow?"

"A baron by the name of Cox," Lady Rycroft said.

"Widowed last year," Charity added with a sly smile. "He has four small children *all* the way up at the Cox's Yorkshire estate. Oh yes, he's *quite* a catch for our *oldest* sister."

Patience's chin lowered further.

"Don't be so waspish," Hope scolded.

Charity sniffed, in perfect imitation of her mother, and turned away from her younger sister.

"One down, two to go," Hope said more cheerfully. "It's a start."

Her mother clicked her tongue. "Really, Hope. There's no need for sarcasm."

"Does Lord Cox have brothers?" Miss Glass asked. "Or eligible friends? Hope is quite correct in that we have to find suitable husbands for her and Charity. You cannot put any store in Matthew choosing one of them, Beatrice."

"Exactly," Matt said, not for the first time. "I have no intention of marrying anyone at the moment."

"So you keep insisting," Lady Rycroft said, picking up her teacup. "But all men must marry, Matthew. You are no exception. It makes sense to choose a girl already familiar with the house and estate."

Conversations with Lady Rycroft always circled back to Matt marrying one of her daughters, sooner or later. Usually he managed to change the subject without too much fuss, but this time he looked impatient. I wanted to remind him that it was he who'd quite willingly entered the drawing room.

"Tell me what you've been up to today, Matt," Hope said before the tension stretched to breaking point.

He smiled at her in relief. "India and I had business affairs to attend to."

"Poor Miss Steele, traipsing hither and thither, following you about the city. I do hope you rewarded her with a little treat."

"You seem to have me confused with a lapdog," I said before Matt could respond.

Hope blinked at my snippy impertinence. Lady Rycroft's lips pinched, deepening the grooves drooping from her mouth to chin. "Really, Letitia, you ought to control your companion's tongue."

"As you ought to control your daughter's," Miss Glass shot back.

"Hope said nothing wrong."

"Indeed," Hope said, hand against her chest. "If I offended you, Miss Steele, I am truly sorry. I had no intention of being cruel. I wasn't thinking. So silly of me. I feel utterly mortified to have caused you any pain."

Somehow she'd managed to make me look like the fool for taking offence when none was intended. At least I had Miss Glass on my side—and Charity. She rolled her eyes at her sister, clearly unconvinced by her apology.

"Matt, you believe me, don't you?" Hope asked, her brow furrowed prettily.

"My opinion doesn't matter," he said. Before anyone could respond, he pushed to his feet. "If you'll all excuse me, I have work affairs that need my attention. India, I'll require your assistance."

Thank goodness for that. I finished my tea and followed him out of the drawing room and up the stairs.

"I'm beginning to see what Aunt Letitia means about Hope," he said. "Pity. I thought she was the interesting one."

We had just reached the landing when Hope called to us from the entrance hall below. She lifted her skirts and approached, her sister Charity two steps behind. Her mother, Patience and Miss Glass waited at the base of the stairs.

"Miss Steele," Hope said, joining us on the landing, "I wanted to apologize again. I didn't think my words through, and I meant no offence. I know you may not believe that, but it's the truth." She caught my hand. "I like you very much and admire you greatly."

"Me?"

"Yes, you. You're composed and poised, and I doubt you ever say or do foolish things."

I eyed Matt sideways but he did not tell her some of the foolish things I'd said and done. "Not always," I told her.

"I wish I was more like you."

Beside her, Charity rolled her eyes again, but stopped when she caught sight of Duke and Cyclops standing at the top of the stairs. "Mr. Cyclops!" she said, touching her hair. "What a pleasant surprise. Are you joining us for tea?"

Cyclops looked to Duke. Duke merely shrugged.

"We're leaving, Charity." Hope took her sister's arm in a firm grip. "Miss Steele, please tell me you forgive me or I shan't sleep a wink."

"I forgive you," I said. What else could I say? I didn't think her apology entirely sincere, but it would make me look ungrateful to say so. "Thank you for your apology."

She bobbed me a small curtsy and wrenched her sister's arm to drag her back down the stairs. Charity shot Cyclops a smile. His eye widened and he retreated out of sight. Duke's broad face broke into a grin.

Matt and I continued up the stairs and headed into the sitting room, a cozier space than the drawing room, reserved for members of the household rather than visitors.

"They gone?" Willie asked, sitting sideways in a chair, her legs draped over the arm.

"Leaving now," Matt said as Duke and Cyclops joined us.

"Finally." She swung her feet to the floor and leaned

forward, elbows on knees. "So what happened at the hospital?"

Matt told them what Hale had revealed and how he'd convinced the innkeeper at the Cross Keys to inform us when Chronos returned.

"Well, God damn," Willie murmured. Cyclops grinned and Duke slapped his knee and *whooped*.

"So we wait," Cyclops said, still smiling.

Matt nodded. "We wait."

"I'm tired of waiting," Willie groaned. "We got nothing to do but go for walks and have tea with your mad relatives."

"You ain't mad," Duke said. "Just eccentric."

Willie pulled a face at him and he chuckled.

"Would you like me to dismiss the servants and you can do their duties instead?" Matt asked.

She slumped into the chair and crossed her arms.

"We're getting closer, Willie," I said. "In the meantime, you need a hobby."

"I had a hobby. Y'all won't let me play poker no more."

"Gambling was costing you a fortune," Matt told her. "So how was your walk this morning? I see you and Aunt Letitia managed not to kill one other."

"It was fine until we came home and found your other aunt and cousins waiting for us," Duke said. "We disappeared up here."

"Not that we were wanted in the drawing room," Cyclops added.

"*You* were wanted." Duke winked at him. "Miss Charity Glass couldn't stop staring. Careful, Cyclops, or you'll find yourself hitched to an English rose."

Cyclops's big shoulders shook with his silent chuckle. "She's not for the likes of me," he said, without a hint of disappointment or resentment.

"Ain't nothing wrong with American roses," Willie muttered.

"True," Duke said. "But you got to watch out for the thorns."

Duke and Cyclops laughed. Willie gestured rudely with her fingers.

"I'm retiring until luncheon," Matt announced. "India, do you have a moment?"

I walked with him up the stairs, curious as to why he needed to speak to me alone. "If this is about Hope, it's all right, Matt. I've been called worse than a lapdog."

"To be fair, she didn't call you a lapdog. She merely implied it. And I tend to believe her when she said it wasn't intentional."

My step slowed, and he matched his pace to mine. "You like her," I said flatly.

He cocked his head to the side. "I'm not sure what you mean."

"She's pretty and clever, so it's understandable." She was young, too. The perfect age to catch a man's eye.

We stopped outside the door to his rooms and he turned to face me. "India, you've got it all wrong. I have no intention of marrying her."

"That's not what I said or meant. I know you won't marry until you're cured, but that doesn't mean you can't like her." I folded my arms to chase away the sudden chill. "I'm sorry, I've overstepped. It's none of my affair." I turned to go but he caught my arm, only to suddenly let it go again.

He folded his arms and tucked his hands away. "You're right," he said quietly. "I do like her. She doesn't enjoy the situation we've been thrust into any more than I do, yet she deflects the awkwardness with humor. But liking her company for an hour or two a week doesn't mean I want to spend my life with her. Can you not see the difference?"

"I suppose." I shook my head, wanting to shake off the conversation altogether. Hope may be able to deflect awkwardness with humor, but I couldn't. "Is that what you wanted to discuss with me?"

He laughed softly. "Hardly." He sobered and cleared his throat. "I want to apologize again for what happened in the carriage."

"You don't have to."

"I do. It's not like me to take advantage of a woman alone. I feel terrible."

"You look terrible, but that's the tiredness. Go and rest and think nothing more about what happened. Indeed, nothing happened. Besides, I'd already forgotten it." I didn't wait to see or hear his reaction. I turned and walked away so he couldn't see that I'd lied. Because I hadn't forgotten it. How could I? He'd almost kissed me.

THE FOLLOWING MORNING, Matt and I prepared to visit the office of *The Weekly Gazette* to speak to Oscar Barratt about magic and magicians. We did not get out of the house, however. As we put on gloves and hats in the entrance hall, a firm knock rapped on the door.

Bristow opened it to Commissioner Munro from Scotland Yard. Two police constables stood either side of him. It was not a social call, then.

"Commissioner," Matt said, eyeing the constables. "To what do we owe this visit?"

Munro's moustache dipped with the flattening of his lips. "I'm afraid I've come to arrest you for the murder of Dr. Hale."

CHAPTER 3

"*M*urder!" Matt bellowed.

"Arrest him!" I blurted out, moving in front of Matt. "No, you cannot! He hasn't murdered anyone."

"India," Matt said gently. "He said he has come to arrest me, not that he will." He arched his brows at the commissioner. "Isn't that why you've come in person, Munro?"

The commissioner hesitated then nodded once. "May we come in? We don't wish to alarm your neighbors."

"My neighbors are used to me being arrested," Matt said, standing aside.

Munro's already stern countenance darkened further. "That was a misunderstanding."

"Will you come into the drawing room?" I said, leading the way before Matt said something he regretted.

"What's going on?" Willie asked from the staircase. "What's he doing here? What's happened?"

"Dr. Hale is dead," Matt told her. "Munro wants to talk to us since we saw Hale yesterday."

"Lucky you did or—" Willie sucked in her top lip then released it with a *pop*. "Never mind."

"Perhaps keep Miss Glass away until the commissioner has left," I told her. She nodded and hurried back up the stairs.

Munro ordered his constables to remain outside the drawing room, and Matt shut the door on them. I was itching to find out more about Dr. Hale, but politeness and concern dictated that I ask how the commissioner was coping with his son's death. It had only been two weeks since discovering his illegitimate son had been murdered by a fellow mapmaker's apprentice.

"I am well," was all he said.

"And the boy's mother?"

"I haven't seen her since the funeral." When neither I nor Matt filled the ensuing silence, he added, "She won't get over Daniel's death. I have my work, but she has nothing."

And no one, I might have added, but I did not. Munro was still married to his wife, although whether she knew about Daniel, I didn't know.

"To the matter at hand," Munro said with military abruptness. "The detective inspector in charge of the case wanted to have you arrested. I told him I would speak to you first. I owe you that, Glass, considering...our history."

"Thank you," Matt said cautiously.

"Do you mean there is still a chance he will be arrested?" I asked. "But he didn't kill anyone! Why would he murder Dr. Hale? It's absurd. Your inspector is incompetent. Is it Nunce from Vine Street?"

Matt rested his hand over mine, and I swallowed the rest of my questions and retorts. Hysteria would not help. I did, however, clutch his fingers. I wanted him to know that I wouldn't abandon him, no matter what Munro did.

"Miss Steele, you seem to be under the impression that I am here to question Mr. Glass only. You, too, are under suspicion."

I swallowed heavily and bit my tongue.

Matt's grip tightened. "You'd better explain your reasoning," he growled.

Munro clasped his hands over his stomach and eased back in the armchair. "You two went to see Hale yesterday."

"So?"

"You impersonated reporters from *The Times*."

"You need more than that, Munro."

"You, Mr. Glass, have excellent knowledge of poisons, and Dr. Hale was poisoned."

I sucked in a breath and blinked at Matt. How much did he know about poisons? It was difficult to tell from his face. "That doesn't mean he would murder Dr. Hale," I said.

"My detective inspector thinks otherwise. At the very least, it justifies this interrogation."

"Who told you I am knowledgeable about poisons?" Matt asked. His tone was idle but the rigidity of his body implied otherwise.

Munro steepled his thumbs. "That isn't important."

"It is to me."

"Where were you last night?" Munro asked.

"Here, all night."

"I can vouch for him," I said quickly.

Munro's gaze dipped to my hand, linked with Matt's.

Matt withdrew. "She means we were together in the sitting room until ten, along with my friends, cousin and aunt. They and the servants can testify that neither I nor India went anywhere."

"And after ten?"

"I went to bed, alone. You'll have to take my word as a gentleman that I didn't sneak out during the night and murder anyone."

Munro's "Hmmm" gave nothing away and did not reassure me in the least. "Why did you visit Hale yesterday? Why pretend to be reporters?"

"That's a private matter."

Munro waited, but Matt remained silent. The two men eyed one another, neither looking away, but it was Munro who spoke first. "You're not helping your cause, Glass. Tell me why you were there yesterday."

Matt still did not speak. Munro's nostrils flared but he let the silence drag and drag. It was a technique used by some to force the other person to talk. It didn't work on Matt but it did on me.

"We read an article in *The Weekly Gazette* about a medical miracle Hale performed on a patient and hoped he could perform a similar miracle for us. Mr. Glass is ill, you see, and has been told by American doctors that there is no cure."

Matt jerked around to face me, and I felt the full force of his ire. I lifted my chin. I did not regret telling Munro. This was not a time for his pride to dictate actions.

"You don't look ill," Munro said.

"We wanted to speak to Dr. Hale impartially," I told Munro. "We wanted to get a sense of how the miracle had been performed before we informed him of Matt's illness. That's why we pretended to be reporters."

"And what did you learn?" Munro asked.

"That the patient he saved probably wasn't dead but did, in fact, die soon afterward."

"So my men also discovered. No miracle was performed. Your visit was wasted."

It was far from being a waste from our point of view. We had a way to meet Chronos now, thanks to Hale. Thank goodness we'd spoken to him before his demise.

Munro rose. "Thank you for being honest with me, Miss Steele, and I'm sorry to have alarmed you. We must consider all possibilities, and when I heard a man named Glass had visited Hale yesterday with his assistant, a Miss Steele, my curiosity was piqued."

"Curiosity or suspicion?" Matt pressed.

Munro ignored the question.

"If you hadn't learned that I knew about poisons, you would not have come," Matt said. Again, Munro didn't answer. "I've never mentioned my interest in chemistry to you."

"I like to thoroughly check the people who work for me," Munro finally said. "You are no exception, despite the task you and Miss Steele recently performed for me." He slapped his hands behind his back. "I hope you understand, Glass. I'm sure you would do the same."

"My sources of information are always known to me. I trust them implicitly. I don't trust information passed on by strangers of unknown reputation."

I suddenly realized what Matt was referring to. The commissioner had learned about Matt's interest in chemistry from someone who wanted to besmirch his reputation: Sheriff Payne. It *had* to be him. Payne had already visited Munro and tried to discredit Matt once. Thank goodness Munro hadn't taken the malicious sheriff's word at face value.

"Thank you for coming here personally, sir," I said. "We appreciate your effort to discover the truth."

"I'll inform my detective that he must look elsewhere for suspects. He's young and enthusiastic, so I'm sure he'll uncover something soon enough."

"Is it wise to leave a young man in charge of a murder case?" Matt asked.

Munro bristled. "Are you questioning my methods?"

"Perhaps I can help him," Matt went on. "Guide him down the right path, that sort of thing."

"That would be a conflict of interest."

"Only if I were guilty, which I am not."

Munro grunted. "I'll keep your offer in mind."

He opened the door and his constables fell into step behind him.

Matt touched my shoulder and mouthed, "Ask him questions." Did he not think Munro would answer him but would say more to me?

"How was Hale poisoned?" I asked, thinking quickly. "Was it in his food?"

"That's not yet clear," Munro said, without breaking stride. "Although there was a bottle of his Cure-All found near the body, its contents spilled over his paperwork."

"Where was he found?"

"The hospital, in his office, sitting at his desk. The type of poison is not known. The signs on the body don't match any that we know."

"Hale was an apothecary," Matt said. "He might have made his own poison."

"And swallowed it accidentally or deliberately?" Munro nodded slowly. "It's possible."

Matt signaled that I should keep asking more questions, but Bristow was already opening the front door.

"He was found at his desk at the hospital," I said, "but he was dismissed from his position, just as we left."

"He was given until the end of the day," Munro said. "At five, when Dr. Ritter realized no one had seen Hale leave, he checked the office and found him dead."

"How awful for him."

"He sees dead people every day," Munro said with bland indifference. "I doubt the sight of one more affected him."

Yes, but it was someone he knew, someone he worked with. "Does Dr. Hale have next of kin?" I asked.

Matt nodded, satisfied with my question.

"None that we are aware of. We're not yet sure who inherits or if there was a will at all."

"Did he have enemies? Aside from Dr. Wiley, perhaps."

Munro halted on the doorstep. His constables stopped too, like automaton with rusty mechanisms. "Wiley?"

"You don't know about him?" Matt said, all innocence. "Are you sure you don't require my assistance?"

Munro frowned. "Good day, Mr. Glass, Miss Steele."

Bristow shut the door and Matt stared at it. "We need to investigate this. I'm not leaving our freedom in the hands of a young but enthusiastic detective. It's a recipe for wrongful arrest."

"I quite agree." But I had a more pressing concern and needed to clear the air. I waited for Bristow to melt away toward the back of the house before speaking. "Matt, I'm sorry I told him about your illness, but I couldn't see any way out of it."

He sighed. "Neither could I, but…"

"But you'd still prefer he didn't know."

"I prefer no one to know, India. Not even you." He smiled gently, softening the sting of his words. "But I understand why you told him, and I don't blame you."

"I should hope not." I picked up my skirts and marched up the stairs. He quickly caught up to me.

"Why?"

"Because I am not to blame for your pride, Matt. You don't like people knowing because you don't like to appear weak."

"Name any man who does."

"Don't get snippy with me for pointing out your fault. It's only a minor one, after all, and you have few others of note, if any."

"I'm thoroughly relieved," he muttered.

I stopped on the landing. "Now you're upset."

"I am not."

"And you're acting like a child."

He frowned. "I think *you* are upset with *me*."

"Why would I be upset with you?"

"For what happened in the carriage yesterday."

"Not at all. I'd forgotten about it, to be honest." I continued up the stairs. He didn't follow until I was half way up.

"*I* hadn't forgotten," he said quietly.

We found the others in the sitting room, playing cards. Willie discarded her hand upon our entry, but the others continued.

"Does he want you to investigate the murder?" Duke asked, discarding two cards and accepting another two from Cyclops.

Matt shook his head. "Where's my aunt?"

"In her parlor writing correspondence," Willie said. "Matt, what's wrong? You don't look so good. Do you need your watch already?"

"No," he growled. "And will everyone stop talking about my health."

"I was only askin'. You've got a temper this morning."

Matt stood by the fireplace where a low fire warmed the room. "Munro didn't come to ask for my help in finding out who murdered Hale. He came to question us about our involvement in Hale's murder."

Willie jumped up. "Question or arrest?" She stalked off to the door, hands on hips, only to stop and slam it shut.

"He hasn't arrested them, Willie." Cyclops nodded at us. "They're still here."

"I've a mind to chase him down and tell him what's what. He suspected you, and after everything you did for him, too!"

"What did we do for him?" Matt shot back. "His son died."

"That ain't your fault. If it weren't for you and India, the body would never have been found."

Matt dragged his hand through his hair and scrubbed the back of his neck. "That's why he came here personally. He gave us the benefit of the doubt—"

"Benefit of the doubt!" Willie threw her hands in the air and let them fall on her hips. "Why would he think you had anything to do with murdering Hale?"

"If you let him finish," Duke said, "maybe he'd tell us."

I sat on the sofa and patted the seat beside me. "You'll wear out the carpet with all that pacing, Willie. Come and sit with me, and Matt will tell you what happened."

"Don't leave out no details," she told him, sitting dutifully.

Matt told them why the police suspected us. "The commissioner's been talking to Payne," he finished. "Or his detective has. It must be he who put the notion in his head that I know about poisons."

Willie once again shot to her feet. "If I knew where that low-down dog was staying I'd go there and blow his brains out."

"And make matters worse for Matt," I told her.

"Sit down, Willie," Duke snapped. "And stop going off half-cocked. Just listen, for once."

She did not sit but stood by Matt, arms crossed, and glared daggers at Duke as if it were his fault that Matt was in this predicament. Poor Duke merely sighed.

"You've got a plan to clear your name," Cyclops said, a smile flirting with his lips. "You're going to find the real killer."

"I'm going to try," Matt said.

"How?" I asked.

"I don't know, yet, but I'm not leaving my fate to a young and enthusiastic detective who may be influenced by Payne."

"I agree," I said. "So let's think about this. Where should we start? Get our hands on the poisoned bottle of Cure-All, speak to Dr. Ritter or Wiley, and perhaps the nurses? Sometimes you learn more from the lower orders than you do from those in charge."

Matt drummed his fingers on the mantelpiece, nodding slowly. "Cyclops, Duke and Willie, see what you can learn at the hospital. There must be gossip about Hale's death."

"How?" Duke asked. "None of us have medical knowledge. We can't pretend to be doctors."

"One of you go in as a patient," I said. "And the other two as concerned friends."

Duke squared up to Cyclops. "All right. Punch me in the jaw." He cricked his neck from side to side. "I'm ready."

"I'll do it!" Willie pushed off from the mantel, but Matt caught her arm.

"Or you could just feign illness," he said.

"Spoil sport."

"What will you two do?" Cyclops asked.

"Visit Oscar Barratt, the author of the article about Hale's medical miracle," Matt said. "Now we have something else to ask him—does he know who would want to murder Dr. Hale?"

THE OFFICE of *The Weekly Gazette* was as close to the headquarters of most of London's influential newspapers on Fleet Street as it could be without actually being on Fleet Street. We drove past the grand buildings of *The Evening Standard* and *The Daily Telegraph* and into a lane that looked like Fleet Street's rubbish dump. Sheets of newspaper flapped and rolled in the swirling breeze, piling up in doorways and against lamp posts. Where Fleet Street bustled with activity, and rightly earned its reputation as the heart of the London news scene, Lower Mire Lane felt as if it clung to its more sophisticated brother's coattails by its dirty fingernails. A freshly painted red sign above the *The Weekly Gazette's* door was a bright spot in an otherwise drab, deserted street.

We had decided to use our real names and tell Oscar Barratt about our interest in magic, since we were quite sure he was aware magic existed. His articles, when analyzed with that in mind, certainly pointed in that direction. Matt hadn't forbidden me to mention my own magic, and I suspected he wanted to decide for himself if Barratt was a threat first. As did I.

We asked a spotty faced lad in the outer office if Mr. Barratt was available and gave him our names.

"What do you want to speak to him about?" he asked, sounding bored. Perhaps people walked in off the street all the time and asked to speak to a journalist. Or perhaps he simply disliked his job.

"Dr. Hale's murder," Matt said.

The youth's eyes lit up and he raced through a door behind a desk as if our arrival was the most exciting thing to happen to him all week.

"That got quite a response," I said.

"Salacious news always does, and *The Weekly Gazette* is one of the worst offenders," Matt said.

"You dislike it? But I thought you enjoyed reading it. You buy it every week."

"I buy almost every newspaper and journal I can get my hands on. You never know when something interesting crops up, as it did in yesterday's edition. I might read it, but I don't like the sensationalist nature of the reporting. It wouldn't surprise me if half of it were made up. At the very least, pertinent facts get left out or distorted."

"Like the fact that Dr. Hale's miracle patient wasn't dead and he used a medicine?"

"Precisely." He picked up a copy of the latest edition from

the desk and flipped through the pages.

I sighed.

He looked up from the paper. "Is something wrong?"

"I don't read the newspapers much, but I've always considered them factual, to the best of the reporter's ability. It's a little disconcerting to think they're not. I'll never believe another thing I read in the papers again. Mr. Barratt has gone down considerably in my estimation."

The door behind the desk burst open and a man strode through. His cheeks were slightly flushed and his breathing uneven. "I'm sorry to keep you waiting," he said. "I raced to get here from the back room." He thrust out his hand to Matt. "Oscar Barratt, at your service."

Mr. Barratt spoke with the accent of an educated London gentleman but without the rounded vowels of Miss Glass's peers. He was about my age, or a little older, which surprised me. I'd expected a man of middle age with a lot of experience under his belt. He was handsome too, with dark brown hair, smooth skin, and a short goatee beard. Deep brown eyes missed nothing as he gave Matt the once over and then turned his attention to me. He smiled and shook my hand firmly, as if I were his equal. It was refreshing.

"My name is Matthew Glass," Matt said, "and this is Miss Steele.

"Glass and Steele! I know those names. You were involved in discovering the body of the mapmaker's apprentice. And Miss Steele, you were influential in the capture of the Dark Rider several weeks ago."

"You've heard of us," I said, rather stupidly. Who would have thought that I'd become a well-known figure?

"I read about you in the newspapers but did not report on the incidents myself. I'm delighted to meet you—and a little in awe. You are quite remarkable, Miss Steele. Quite remarkable."

My face flamed, and I wished he wouldn't look at me with such bright eyes and a curious smile. "Oh," I murmured. "Thank you, but my role wasn't important."

"Nonsense," Matt spat out. "It was very important on both occasions. Now, to the matter at hand. We want to ask you about your article in the latest edition of the *Gazette*." He pointed to the page open on the desk. "You do know that Dr. Hale has been murdered?"

Barratt nodded. "I heard."

"How did you hear?"

The front door opened and a man pushing a trolley laden with large packages wrapped in brown paper entered. The opening of the door triggered a little bell above it. The spotty lad emerged from the back room.

"Come with me to my office," Barratt said to us. "It's quieter there when the press isn't running."

"You print the *Gazette* here?" Matt asked as we passed through the door into a large chamber piled with more bundles. Some were open, revealing stacks of blank paper.

"In the cellar." Barratt waved at a door behind a man who did not look up from his desk. "You can't talk in here when the press is running. It operates mostly at night, though, ready for the morning's delivery, and only once a week. I was just down there talking to my editor and the paper's head compositor." He led us through another door, along a short corridor, and into a small office. A large map of London directly opposite the desk provided an interesting change to the stack of newspapers, piles of books, and torn articles pinned to a cork board. "You're lucky you caught me," Barratt said. "I was about to head out and see what I can learn about Hale's death. I just heard of it myself."

"How?" Matt asked again.

Barratt hesitated, as if surprised by Matt's intensity. "Through one of my informants at the hospital."

"You have informants at the hospital?"

Barratt gave him a curious little smile. "Of course."

"But you're a reporter, not a policeman," I said.

Barratt's smile widened. "We reporters also want to find the truth, Miss Steele."

"Is that so?" I studiously kept my gaze on him so as not to glance at Matt. "That's very noble of you."

Barratt gave a little bow. "Thank you. You're the first person to ever call a journalist noble in my hearing. Please tell me you believe that and aren't merely saying it because you want something from me."

"Oh, I, er…"

He winked and didn't look at all disheartened. "It's all right, Miss Steele. I have a thick skin. So tell me, do you have information regarding Dr. Hale's death?"

"If we had information about the murder we'd go to the police," Matt said. "We want to discuss another matter which may or may not be tied to Hale's death."

Barratt indicated the chairs. "Then you'd better sit."

Matt held out the chair for me. "We were going to speak with you before Dr. Hale's death," I told Barratt. "You see, yesterday we read your article about Hale's medical miracle and decided to find out for ourselves whether it was true or not."

"Why wouldn't it be true?" Barratt asked, spreading out his hands.

"Journalists have been known to sensationalize reports to sell more papers."

"I don't."

Matt grunted. "Don't play the innocent with us, Mr. Barratt. You're no different."

Why was Matt being so cross with him? We needed Barratt to answer our questions.

"What Mr. Glass is trying to say," I said, "is that we learned

48

you withheld some facts from your story. For instance, the patient probably *wasn't* dead at the time, and Dr. Hale used a medicine. It was not a miracle."

Barratt didn't look at all concerned that he'd been caught out. He simply nodded. "The witness I spoke to swore that the patient was dead when Hale tended to him. Another witness had said that he wasn't, but couldn't be completely sure, so I decided not to pursue that route. I was on deadline, you see, and the story had to be filed to get it to print in time. As to Dr. Hale using a medicine, I included that point in my story. My editor took it out without my knowledge. I wish he hadn't, but he's my employer and can do as he pleases."

"That's not fair," I said. "It's your name in the byline, not his. He shouldn't be allowed."

Barratt merely shrugged. "I must try to report the truth as I see it, Miss Steele. It's my editor's job to sell more newspapers. Sometimes that means he changes parts, here and there, to make the story more interesting to the public. Now, may I ask you a question?" He directed this to Matt, not me. "Why were you so interested in Dr. Hale's medical miracle?"

I bit the inside of my cheek and glanced sideways at Matt. I couldn't imagine him admitting to Barratt that he was ill.

"We're interested in magic." Matt's words dropped heavily into the silence.

I sucked in a breath and held it.

Barratt had also seemed to stop breathing. "Go on." He had not scoffed, laughed or denied the existence of magic. This man knew. I was certain of it now.

"You've written a few articles that allude to magical events," Matt said.

"Only in vague terms."

"Dr. Hale's so-called miracle was the latest."

"And?" Barratt prompted.

"Why?" Matt pressed. "What are you trying to achieve?"

Barratt stood and came round the desk. He perched on the edge near Matt and folded his arms over his chest. For a moment, I thought he did it to intimidate and force Matt to withdraw his question, but then he answered. "I want to draw people out. People with an interest in magic, like yourselves, who are looking for signs that magic exists. My reports act as those signs."

"Again," Matt said, his voice a low growl, "why?"

Barratt unfolded his arms, knocking a stack of papers piled on his desk. They fluttered to the floor near Matt's feet. One fell between Matt and me. Matt picked some up and handed them back to Barratt.

"Well?" Matt asked. "Tell us what interest you have in drawing out people curious about magic."

Barratt stared at the papers in his hand. A small frown appeared between his brows. He glanced at Matt, glanced at the papers again, and sighed. Perhaps the one he needed was the one that had fallen between Matt and me. I picked it up only to let it go again with a gasp.

The paper was warm. The room, however, was cool.

"India?" Matt asked. "What's the matter?"

Barratt watched me with an intensity that I'd only ever seen on Matt's face before. It was as if the world had closed in and it was only he and I in the room.

"Miss Steele?" he asked, his voice barely above a whisper. "What is it?"

I picked up the paper again. This time the warmth infused me, gently washing up my arm. It was magical heat, the kind that responded to my magic. "You're a magician." The words tumbled out before I thought them through; before I realized what conclusion he would come to. I quickly dropped the paper on the desk then tucked my hand into my skirt folds.

Barratt's gaze followed it then lifted to my face. "Yes, Miss Steele. I am. And I see from your reaction that you are too."

CHAPTER 4

"*I* have some magical ability," I said before Matt could stop me. Before I could stop myself. I *wanted* to tell Barratt but fear might cripple me if I let it. "Timepieces," I added.

Mr. Barratt smiled, a genuine, heartfelt smile. "Thank you for telling me, Miss Steele. I can see that you're concerned about imparting such personal information to a stranger."

"With good reason," Matt said. "If it's mentioned outside this room, you'll be receiving another visit from me. With much less civility."

Barratt held up his hands in surrender. "I can see that you're very protective of her."

That seemed to diffuse Matt's temper somewhat. He tapped his finger on the paper I'd picked up. "You're a paper magician?"

"Ink. Miss Steele felt the warmth of the ink magic, not the paper."

"What does ink magic achieve?"

Barratt sat down and pulled a piece of blank paper to him then dipped his pen in the inkwell. He began to write. 'Watch

51

these words, Miss Steele' he wrote. 'They're remarkable words for a remarkable woman.'

"Nothing's happening," Matt growled.

Barratt began to recite poetic words in another language. I couldn't understand them, but they sounded dreamlike when spoken in such a rich, modular voice. They mesmerized me.

Until the words lifted off the page.

I sat back and stared. The words rose from the paper as if they were leaves caught in a breeze. The letters swirled in the air, keeping position within their word and sentence so that they looked like twirling ribbons.

"Beautiful." I reached out and when Barratt merely moved some papers to the side of his desk without warning me to stop, I touched one.

The ink broke and the sentences collapsed, splashing over my fingers, the desk surface and some of the papers. "Oh! I'm so sorry," I said.

Barratt smiled and handed me a cloth from his desk drawer. "It's quite all right, Miss Steele."

"That was lovely," I said, wiping the cloth over my gloves. "Not just how the words floated, but the spell you cast, too. It's pure poetry. I could listen to you recite it for hours."

He chuckled. "You flatter me."

When I realized how my gushing sounded, I swallowed the rest of my praise. That was not the message I wanted to convey to him.

"Pretty indeed," Matt said with that low growl still in his voice. "But what use is it?"

"The floating is not very useful, but it does make an impact." Barratt grinned, and Matt scowled more. "I know another spell that dries the ink faster so that I don't smudge it. I still write longhand, you see. A few of my colleagues have switched to mechanical writing, using a typing machine, but

I prefer this way." He shrugged, palms up. "It's not the most useful magic, unfortunately. My family have manufactured ink for generations. They make the finest ink in the world. My brother runs the company now, and I decided to make my own way, outside the family business." He took the cloth from me and mopped up the splashed ink. "But I was unable to get away from ink. It calls me, you see. I feel compelled to be near it. You understand, Miss Steele."

"Yes," I said quietly. "Yes, I do."

"My father told me there's a spell to make the ink magician write faster, but he didn't know it. No one does, anymore. Ever since magicians stopped openly practicing their magic, they lost touch with one another and no longer shared spells. Some magicians went into hiding and stopped practicing altogether, others only taught their children basic spells, afraid the guilds would find out about them if they did anything too elaborate. And so the art of magic has been lost. I find this a tragedy. Don't you, Miss Steele?"

"I…I am uncertain how I feel. I've only recently discovered my magic, you see. I know no spells. My father was artless and never told me about it. I don't know how many generations I need to go back in order to discover which ancestor I inherited this from."

His frown deepened with every word I spoke. "I'm sorry for you. Perhaps we can work together to learn more about your magic. I'm afraid I don't know any timepiece magicians, but you never know when one will come out of the woodwork. As you two have done today."

"Is that why you're reporting on magic?" Matt asked. "To draw magicians to you?"

Barratt nodded. "I want to create a safe community for us, a place where we can once again discuss our magic and practice where no one fears us."

"As the guild members fear us," I said.

"You've had run-ins with guilds?" He cocked his head to the side. "I have a suspicion that the young mapmaker who was found murdered was magical."

Matt nodded. "Killed by a jealous rival."

"Do you think the guild master put him up to it? I've heard rumors that the guild members used to kill magicians, centuries ago, hence the need for magicians to remain secret. Rumors only, of course."

"We've heard those rumors too," I said. It was deeply troubling, if true.

"The Mapmaker's Guild master orchestrated the kidnapping but not the murder," Matt said. "It's possible the Watchmaker's Guild master was also behind the apprentice's kidnapping. The murderer acted alone, however."

Barratt glanced at me. "The Watchmaker's Guild have caused problems for you, Miss Steele?"

"They would not let me into the guild," I told him. "My father tried to convince them, before his death, but they refused. Once he was gone, I couldn't get work." I did not mention the role Eddie Hardacre, my fiancé at the time, played. The less I thought about him the better. "None of the guild members would employ me. Indeed, they all seemed wary of me. They never told me why, but I suspected it was because they learned about my magic somehow."

"How did *you* discover it?"

"It was pointed out to me that I have a knack for fixing watches and clocks. Matt knew a little about magic and suggested that I could be magical. From there, I learned about the warm residue left by magic. Much of what I learned came from the mapmaker's apprentice's family and a suspect in the case." I did not tell him that my watch and a clock had saved my life, nor did I mention how combining my magic with another's could extend the time for that magic, as it had done with Matt's watch. Some things were best left unspoken on a first meeting.

"Fascinating," Barratt said. "I'm so glad you came today, Miss Steele. May I call upon you to discuss your experiences further? Perhaps, if I can gather more magicians, we can all meet."

I glanced at Matt only to see him already staring at me, dark and forbidding shadows in his eyes. Did he not want me to meet other magicians? Was he worried about having magicians call on us at his home? Perhaps he worried that his aunt would find out something that would confuse her frail mind.

"I'll call on you when I am ready," I said to Mr. Barratt.

He glanced at Matt too and sighed. "I'm glad my article worked," he said. "It's a pity Hale died before we could speak to him further about his magic."

"More than a pity for Hale and his family," Matt said.

"He had no family. I asked him that when we met, because I was curious about his magic. His parents died when he was young and a grandfather raised him. It was he who taught him about his apothecary magic."

"Do you know who inherits his estate?" Matt asked.

Barratt shook his head. "Not a clue. You sound as if you want to discover who killed him. Is this a new venture for the two of you, after your previous investigative successes?"

"No," I said at the same time that Matt said, "Yes."

Barratt laughed softly. "Whatever your reasons, I'll try to help if I can." He leaned forward. "As long as I am the only reporter you speak to once you learn who killed Hale."

"*If* we learn who killed him," I said.

"Mr. Glass?" Barratt asked. "Do you promise?"

"That'll depend on how helpful you are to us," Matt said.

"That's only fair. What else do you wish to know about Hale?"

"Did you speak to Dr. Wiley at all?"

"The doctor who declared the patient dead? Not at all, but we did pass him in the corridor as Hale walked with me. If looks could kill, he would certainly be a suspect."

"What about Dr. Ritter, the principal?"

"I didn't meet him. Hale did imply that the hospital board wouldn't be happy with his story making it into the newspapers, but he laughed it off. He mentioned no names."

"Was Hale eager for you to mention his magic in the article?" I asked.

Barratt nodded. "He thought gathering all the London magicians together was a good idea. He doesn't—didn't—want magic to disappear from the world altogether, even rather useless magic, like mine. He thought my articles were as good a way as any to draw magicians out." He rubbed his forehead. "I still can't believe he's gone. He was the only openly magical person I'd met."

"He had nothing to fear," I said. "Since he didn't work as an apothecary, he didn't need the guild's approval."

"Even I have to be careful to keep my magic secret from the guilds," Barratt admitted. "If the Inkmaker's Guild learned about me, they would trace my magic back to my family and throw them out of the guild."

"And they'd have to give up their business," I said quietly. No guild membership meant no license to create and sell. It was the law. "Hale had no family so it was not a concern for him."

"The English system of guilds is archaic and unfair," Matt said. "It should be changed. Any man and woman should be allowed to manufacture goods or own shops, not just guild members."

"Spoken like a foreigner," Barratt said with a humorless laugh. "There is a lot at stake here. The guilds will hold onto their power with every breath in their body, and they have friends in parliament who will not change the law. I'm afraid it's not going away." His eyes flashed as he picked up the pen and dipped it into the inkwell. He wrote something on the paper in front of him. "Unless the public demands it, of course. Then parliamentarians will have to take notice."

"Is that what you're trying to ultimately achieve?" Matt asked. "Public attention?"

"Very slowly and carefully, Mr. Glass. Perhaps one day the public will embrace magic again, but we need to reintroduce it in such a way that they're not afraid of us. The first step is to bring it into their consciousness."

"Through newspaper reports," I said.

"Through newspaper reports that show the good magic can do."

"You're not going to show the negative?" Matt asked. "Editing out the facts again?"

Barratt passed me a blank piece of paper. "Hold this, please, Miss Steele. You are correct, Mr. Glass, I have only written about the positive aspects of magic, but that's only because I haven't been presented with any negative. All the harm has come from the artless in their persecution of magicians." He smiled at me then began his melodic chant.

The fresh words rose from his page and floated through the air, dancing rhythmically, coiling, rising and dipping to the music of his spell. Then finally the words settled on the page I held flat on my palms.

"'Twenty-four Lowther Street, Chelsea,'" I read.

"My home," he said. "I live alone. Please visit me anytime —there or here. I'll be happy to discuss magic with you, Miss Steele. Or, indeed, anything you'd like."

"That is very kind of you, Mr. Barratt. Very kind indeed." I folded the page and tucked it into my reticule.

Matt scrubbed his jaw then stood. "We should go, India."

"But I have more questions." I turned to Barratt. "It

doesn't sound like Dr. Hale would have killed himself. Not if he was making those plans with you. Is that your conclusion too?"

"It is," Barratt said. "He was enthusiastic about the future. You think he took his own life?"

"It's a possibility, but one I also dismiss. He didn't seem like the type. Nor do I think he put the poison into the bottle of Cure-All by accident. Why would he be using poisons, in his profession, anyway?"

His brow furrowed in thought. "You need to learn more about it."

"Thank you, Mr. Barratt," Matt said tightly. "We know what we have to do next."

"We do?" I asked, rising.

Matt thanked Barratt who in turn took my hand and bowed over it. "You're most welcome," Barratt said to me, even though I hadn't been the one to address him.

He escorted us back out to the outer office. Matt opened the door but paused. He looked as if he were warring with himself over something, then finally gave in. "If you hear of any watch or doctor magicians, contact us at sixteen Park Street, Mayfair," he said in a low voice. "I'll pay you for your troubles, of course."

Barratt blinked. "You don't have to pay me. I'll be glad to help. But why doctors, Mr. Glass? Watchmakers I under-stand. Miss Steele wishes to learn more about her magic. But a doctor?"

"Goodbye, Mr. Barratt," Matt said, opening the door wider for me.

We climbed into the coach and Matt ordered Bryce to return home.

"Well," I said, waving at Barratt through the window as we drove off. "That was very enlightening. I'm so glad we spoke to him. Thank you for suggesting it."

His features relaxed for the first time since meeting Barratt. He almost smiled. "I'm glad you're happy, India. It makes up for enduring his presence."

"Enduring? Whatever do you mean? I thought he was very pleasant."

"Of course you would. He was flirting with you."

"He was not!"

He arched his brows.

I couldn't tell whether Barratt's flirtations bothered him or not. Was it too much to ask that he be a little jealous of another man showing interest in me? "Is that why you were so fierce with Mr. Barratt?" I asked. "Because he was flirtatious?"

Matt simply looked out the window and my heart dipped. "He's a suspect in Hale's murder."

"Nonsense," I blurted out.

He slowly turned to face me, his jaw once again rigid. "We can't rule him out, India."

"Why not? What reason would he have to kill Hale?"

"I haven't yet thought of a motive. He did speak with Hale recently, and wrote about him. As I said, let's not rule him out yet."

I shook my head. "He is no murderer. He was very nice to us."

"He was nice to *you*, India. He was merely polite to me. I think he'd prefer to talk to you without me present."

I opened and closed my mouth without saying anything. The words wouldn't come out.

"Don't forget he left out important facts from his article about Hale," he went on. "I don't believe it was all his editor's fault."

"If you don't like him, why did you give him your address?" I said. "Clearly you don't want him to come calling."

He swallowed and looked down at his hands. "If he meets

a watch magician in the course of his work then I do want him to come calling. I want him to tell you where to find another like you. I know you're lonely."

I bit back my snippy retort. He seemed quite forlorn all of a sudden. "I'm not lonely, Matt. Not since I met you and your friends. And the only timepiece magician I wish to meet is Chronos, so he can fix your watch."

His gaze met mine and he offered up a weak smile. "Then perhaps Barratt can send him our way, if he meets him."

"I doubt Mr. Barratt will meet him," I said with a sigh. "Chronos is not keen on revealing himself. He would stay far away from journalists."

Matt closed his eyes and tipped his head back. He rested for the remainder of the journey home.

Matt wouldn't be still that afternoon as we waited for Duke, Willie and Cyclops to return from the hospital. He paced the length of the sitting room until his aunt ordered him to leave.

"Go for a short walk to calm down before our guests arrive," she said.

That made Matt stop in his tracks. "Guests? Not my cousins again."

"You don't wish to see Hope Glass?" I asked, trying to tease him and raise a smile. It fell flat and he merely narrowed his gaze at me.

"Not at the moment," he hedged. "Why?"

I lifted a shoulder and returned to reading the letter from my friend Catherine Mason. She wished to call upon me, and I couldn't be happier. Calling on her had become difficult ever since her parents had become worried about their daughter associating with someone the Watchmaker's Guild disliked. I didn't want to make their situation any more awkward for them than it already was.

"Mrs. Haviland and her daughter, Oriel," Miss Glass said.

Matt groaned. "Again? Aunt, I told you why I cannot marry anyone, and if I could, Oriel Haviland would not be my choice."

She peered over her reading spectacles at him. "Oriel Haviland is coming because I specifically wanted her mother's presence. She and Lady Abbington are friends, and since I hardly know the countess, I thought it prudent to invite a mutual acquaintance."

"Ah, yes, the eligible widow," Matt said flatly. "The one you think is more suitable for me than Oriel."

"She does have a mind of her own, and she is very comely."

"Even so, my health hasn't changed. I won't marry anyone while I'm ill."

"You'll find a cure soon." She returned to her own correspondence, open on her lap. "Didn't you visit the hospital yesterday and speak to that clever doctor, the one who performed a miracle?"

"You don't miss much, do you?" he said with half a smile and a shake of his head.

"People tend to underestimate women of a certain age. Or just women in general." She winked at me.

I was happy to see that her mind was sharp today. It had been a few days since she'd rambled nonsensically about a knight riding a white horse and confused Matt with his father. Those occurrences seemed to be growing rarer, but they still happened and worried us all, particularly Matt.

"Do I have to be here for your callers?" Matt asked, drumming his fingers on the mantel.

"Yes," she said, without looking up.

"I don't know if I'll be good company."

"You're always good company, Matthew, particularly where the fairer sex are concerned. They find you charming. Isn't that right, India?"

We certainly did. "Quite so," I managed to say.

Matt's fingers stopped their drumming momentarily as he watched me from beneath lowered lashes. I returned to Catherine's letter, my face heating, and Matt's fingers resumed their impatient rhythm.

Miss Glass put her letter down with a click of her tongue. "Will you cease that infernal tapping!"

"Let's go for a walk, Matt," I said quickly. "You seem to need to be out and about."

He nodded.

"No!" his aunt cried. "Stay here, Matthew."

"But it was your suggestion that I go for a walk," he said.

"I meant for you to go alone, to clear your head. You can't do that if you walk with someone else." She shot me an apologetic look. "I do like you, India, dear, but you can chatter too much sometimes."

"She does not, Aunt. India's words are always measured." He put his hand out to me. "Let's go while the sun's out."

Miss Glass looked pained. "You must be careful, India. You and Matthew are spending far too much time together lately. People will talk."

"She's my assistant, and that is the end of it." He stretched out his fingers. "India?"

"Don't be too concerned, Miss Glass," I said, forcing a smile into my voice. "Nobody of consequence will connect Matt and me in that way. I'm much too old and plain, for one thing."

The sudden dampening of her eyes surprised me. "Oh, India, when it comes to men, you are as naive as a girl half your age. I hope you don't take my meddling to mean that there is not a man for you. There is." The unspoken words 'Just not Matthew' hung in the air between us.

I swallowed past the lump in my throat. "I understand perfectly." I took Matt's hand and allowed him to lead me out of the sitting room as a gentleman would lead a lady onto the dance floor.

"I no longer know what to say to her," he said as we headed down the stairs. "She's not listening to me. And to be so rude to you, too. It's unforgivable."

"She wasn't rude," I said. "At least, that wasn't her intention. I thought she was quite sympathetic."

"You're far too kind to her."

It was she who was kind to me, accepting me as her companion when I was nothing more than a shop girl. But I wanted the discussion to end so didn't say as much to Matt.

We collected gloves and hats from Bristow and headed to Hyde Park. It was busy for a weekday. The late spring sunshine brought the Mayfair ladies out for a stroll, as well as nannies pushing perambulators and governesses trying to keep their active charges in check. There were few men about so Matt stood out, particularly with his height. He received several appraising glances from passersby and either genuinely didn't notice or pretended not to.

The fashionable set usually came out after five and drove slowly along Carriage Drive in an open barouche or on horseback on Rotten Row. I much preferred the quiet of the early afternoon.

"It's been some time since I've come to Hyde Park at this time of year," I said. "I'd forgotten how lovely it is. The air is almost clear here today."

"You need to get out of London more, India. This air is not clear."

I laughed and lifted my face to the sunshine, only to catch him looking at me with a serious expression. I didn't want to be serious. I wanted to pick up my skirts and deviate from the path. I wanted to run through the grass and chase butterflies. These last few weeks had been tense, watching Matt's health deteriorate and with our investigation into poor Daniel Gibbons' death. I wanted to put all that behind us.

"My aunt was right about one thing," he said, quietly. "You're neither old nor plain."

I focused forward again. "Can we end this discussion, please I don't wish to talk about it."

"Very well." But after several steps and a taut silence, he said, "Is that what you really think?"

"Don't, Matt. It's a lovely day. Let's not spoil it."

"Eddie Hardacre has a lot to answer for," he muttered.

"It's hardly his fault that I'm unwed at twenty-seven."

"Perhaps you're just waiting for the right man. As I have been waiting for the right woman."

"I hope the right woman is someone from your aunt's set or I pity you. She'll be very upset if it's not."

"Can we change the subject?"

"So it's very well for *you* to want to change the subject, is it?"

"You've been known to continue a discussion well after I want it ended." His smile banished the grim set to his mouth and the shadows in his eyes. He seemed genuinely happy at that moment.

I nudged him with my elbow. "What's a safe topic? Not our current investigation, since we can be overheard, and not our relationships with non-existent paramours."

"There's always the weather. You English seem obsessed with it."

"Or you can tell me why you didn't defend Cyclops's reputation yesterday when your cousins referred to him as a pirate."

"I'd like to, but I won't. His past is his story to tell, not mine. I hope you understand."

"I do, Matt, and I respect your silence. Very well, the weather it is."

We didn't talk about the weather much at all. Instead, he asked me questions about enterprise, trade and manufacturing in England. I answered as best as I could, which felt woefully inadequate. He probably knew more than me, considering how much of his day he spent reading the newspaper.

"Why this interest?" I asked as we slowly returned to Park Lane.

"I'm thinking of expanding my investments here."

"Then you need a man of business to advise you properly, not an assistant with little knowledge outside the watch-making industry."

"I prefer to do it myself rather than employ a man of business. My lawyer will suffice for the contracts, but you can advise me on more than you know."

"Such as?"

"Such as, what do you think of the fudge I had Mrs. Potter make?"

"What has fudge got to do with anything?"

"I might invest in manufacturing it. It's very popular in America, and I doubt English tastes are all that different."

"In that case, I liked it very much. You're very enterprising for a man—" I bit my tongue and kept my gaze directly ahead.

"For a man with my condition?"

"I...I'm sorry, Matt. I didn't mean to bring up your health."

He sighed. "It's all right. I didn't mean to snap at you. I just wish you wouldn't consider my health something that should hold me back. It doesn't. At least, I don't want it to."

I tightened my grip on his arm. His muscles flexed then

relaxed. "Then why are you letting it hold you back in marriage negotiations?"

His step slowed. "That's different."

"It shouldn't be."

"India, I can't saddle a wife to me while I'm ill. A husband should be able to protect his loved ones. I don't know how much longer I'll even have my strength."

The pain in his voice clawed at my heart. He hated how his exhaustion made him weak, and I hated that he thought it made him less of a man. "I disagree. A woman who loves you would be happy to have you as her husband even for a few days."

"You're too kind," he muttered. "But on this we will have to differ."

We returned to the house to find that the Havilands and Lady Abbington had arrived in our absence. Matt waited for me as I handed my hat to Bristow.

"After you," he said.

I shook my head. "Not this time. They're your guests. I am…" Superfluous, I wanted to say. "I am a little tired," I said instead. Indeed I was. Tired of seeing women vying for his attention, tired of seeing him charm them without even trying, tired of wishing I were eligible enough to be a contender for his heart.

A small dent appeared between his brows. "Very well."

I read in my rooms until Matt knocked on my door an hour and a half later. His face was the color of ash, yet it was only a few hours since he'd last used his watch.

"Feeling better?" he asked.

I nodded and reached up to cup his cheek but checked myself and fidgeted with my hair instead. "Are the others back yet?"

He shook his head. "If they don't come home soon, I'm going to the hospital."

"How was the famous Lady Abbington?" I asked.

"It's hard to say. She couldn't get many words in. Mrs. Haviland dominated the conversation."

"I heard someone play the piano very well."

"That was Oriel Haviland, urged by her mother. Between the two of them, I hardly got to know Lady Abbington."

"Then brace yourself for another visit from her—without the Havilands, next time. Your aunt won't give up that easily."

He smiled, but it didn't chase the exhaustion from his eyes.

"Go and rest, Matt."

He nodded. "I wanted to see if you were all right first."

I folded my arms to hold myself as still as possible. "Why wouldn't I be?"

"I'm not sure. You seemed…unlike yourself, earlier."

I shrugged, unsure how to answer him. I didn't want him knowing how I truly felt about him. I wasn't even sure what I felt anyway. All I knew was that I liked spending time with him and I worried about his future. Sometimes it worried me sick.

Mrs. Bristow appeared behind Matt, and Matt stood aside to let the housekeeper pass. She held out a tray to me. On it was a covered platter.

"Miss Glass asked me to bring you these," she said, lifting the platter lid.

Two plump cream puffs the size of my fist sat on a plate, a light dusting of powdered sugar on top. "I adore cream puffs," I said. "Were these left over from the afternoon tea?"

"We didn't have cream puffs," Matt said, sounding put out.

"Miss Glass asked Mrs. Potter to make them while you went for your walk," Mrs. Bristow said. "She asked for cream puffs especially because they are your favorite."

"I wonder why your aunt would have Mrs. Potter make them just for me," I said to Matt.

"She feels guilty for earlier." He laid his hand on the doorknob. "Enjoy your cream puffs, India. I'll see you at dinner, if those don't spoil your appetite."

I ate my cream puffs by the window, looking out across the rooftops. My fourth floor bedroom gave me an excellent view of the city and the sky. It was bluer than it had been in months, no matter what Matt said. I smiled and silently thanked the good fortune that had sent me to a place where people respected and protected me. I didn't have to worry about my next meal, or if I would even have a roof over my head, as I had after my father died.

No matter what Miss Glass feared, I wouldn't jeopardize what I had now for Matt's attention. I wouldn't tell him how I felt and risk his rejection and her ire. I liked the life I lived at number sixteen Park Street too much.

* * *

CYCLOPS, Duke and Willie returned in time to dine with us. Matt looked refreshed, and his aunt ate in her own chambers. I'd gone to see her just before the dinner gong sounded to thank her for the cream puffs.

She'd looked at me blankly and said, "What cream puffs? I don't eat the things. Too fattening. You know that, Veronica."

I smiled sadly and closed her door, wondering who Veronica was.

"What did you discover?" Matt asked as soon as Bristow ushered out the footman and closed the door, leaving the five of us alone in the dining room.

"What makes you think we found anything out?" Willie said, spooning beans onto her plate.

"Duke's face."

Duke schooled his features—or tried to. He simply ended

up with one eyebrow sitting above the other and his cheeks sucked in.

Willie shook her head. "That's why you lose at poker, Duke. Your face can be read like a book."

"Ha!" he barked. "Then you must struggle. You ain't read a whole book in years."

Matt appealed to Cyclops. "Well?"

"It's not what we found out," Cyclops said, "but what we found." He opened the flap of his jacket and pulled a bottle from his inside pocket. He passed it across the table to Matt. "That's the bottle which contained the poison."

"You stole it!" I cried. "Cyclops!"

"Needs must, India," the big man said.

Matt removed the stopper. "Are you sure this is the bottle found next to Hale's body?"

Duke nodded. "It was guarded by a constable and all."

"The police are using the hospital equipment and a doctor to analyze it," Cyclops said.

"In the basement," Willie said, helping herself to the beef. "There were three of them and the doctor down there. It weren't easy to get past them, but Cyclops is good." She flashed him a grin.

Cyclops glanced at me then concentrated on his potatoes.

Matt sniffed the bottle then sniffed it again. "I can't detect any poisonous odors, but there are several that don't have a smell. India, you've used Dr. Hale's Cure-All before." He passed the bottle to me. "Is that what it usually smells like?"

I took it and sniffed, then drew the bottle away from my nose. Far away. "My god," I said on a breath.

"What is it?" He took the bottle off me and sniffed again. "What did you smell?"

"It wasn't the smell," I told them. "It was the warmth emanating from inside. Magical warmth."

CHAPTER 5

"Y ou sure?" Willie asked, reaching across the table for the bottle.

Matt passed it to her. "Is the glass itself warm?"

I shook my head. "It definitely came from inside. Matt, whatever was in that bottle had a spell put on it. If the contents of the bottle were magic then it can only mean that an apothecary magician is the murderer."

Willie handed the bottle to Duke who sniffed, and then he handed it to Cyclops who also smelled it.

"Is this how Cure-All is supposed to smell?" Cyclops asked me.

"As far as I can recall," I said. "We can easily find another bottle and compare. Mrs. Bristow might have one."

Matt rose and tugged on the bell pull. A moment later Bristow entered and Matt asked him to fetch a bottle of Cure-All if his wife kept any. The butler left without batting an eyelid at the request.

"Could it be anyone other than an apothecary magician?"

Duke asked. "Could a spell have been placed on another liquid, like water, and that slipped into the bottle?"

"Ain't no such thing as a water magician," Willie said.

"How do you know?"

"Because magic is in things that can be created. Watches, maps, medicines."

"McArdle was a gold magician. Gold ain't created."

"McArdle couldn't use his magic on gold still in its raw form," Matt told him, "only gold worked by a goldsmith."

"Like them Roman coins," Willie said, shoveling beans into her mouth.

"Beer," Duke said, "or wine. Those are created. If that kind of magician exists, they could have poured it into the bottle."

Cyclops lifted his glass of wine. "We would have smelled beer or wine in the bottle."

Bristow returned and handed the Cure-All to Matt before leaving again. Matt smelled both bottles then passed them to me.

"They smell the same," I said, passing the bottles to Cyclops. "One thing we must remember is that the magic may already have vanished, no matter how it came to be in there."

Everyone smelled both bottles and we all agreed they had the same scent. That didn't mean that a minute amount of magic-infused liquid couldn't have dripped in.

"Ink," Matt blurted out. "Ink is a liquid."

"Matt," I chided. "Mr. Barratt isn't a murderer."

"Barratt flirted with her," he told the others, as if that explained my point of view.

"He was charming," I said, "but I'm being perfectly objective. He had no reason to kill Hale."

"That we know of yet."

"I think India's right," Cyclops said. "I don't think he's the poisoner."

"How can you know that?" Willie asked, no longer paying any attention to her food.

He held up both bottles. "Since the contents of these smell the same, it's unlikely another substance was introduced, particularly one as noticeable as ink." He tipped a drop of each onto the tablecloth. They were both clear. Ink would have changed the color. "The magician must know how to turn the original medicine into poison. I ain't an expert, but I'd wager only an apothecary can do that."

Matt stabbed a slice of beef with his fork. "You are probably right. But aside from Hale himself, we know of no other apothecary magicians."

"Then we'll have to find one," I said. "We should start with Dr. Hale's business partner."

"Agreed. We'll visit tomorrow morning." Matt studied one of the bottles. "There's an address at the bottom of the label: The Pitt Medicine Company, 167 New Bond Street. You and I will go, India. Cyclops, you'd better return the bottle to the hospital. The artless policemen and doctor won't find anything in it, but we should do the right thing."

Cyclops looked at the bottles, side by side in front of Matt. "Which one's which?"

I picked them both up and placed my hand over the openings. "This one contains the magic poison." I handed the bottle to Cyclops. "I'll return the other to Mrs. Bristow."

"You coming with me back to the hospital?" Cyclops asked Willie. "We'll go tonight."

"You can count on it," she said. "Ain't nothing to do here except teach Letty how to play poker."

Matt narrowed his gaze at her. "Do *not* teach my aunt to play poker."

Willie flashed him a smile and tucked into her food.

I cornered Cyclops outside his room before he, Duke and Willie returned to the hospital. They'd decided to go late, when only a skeleton staff remained to take care of patients overnight.

"Everything all right?" he asked with a frown. "Something wrong with Matt?"

"Nothing like that," I reassured him. "I want to know how you're going to return the bottle to the hospital."

He leaned one shoulder against the wall near the door and crossed his arms. The poorly lit corridor made his good eye seem darker, his face graver. "Is that all?"

I bit the inside of my cheek. "Ye-es."

"You don't want to know how I got past three constables and a doctor to steal that bottle?"

"Well, now that you mention it, I did wonder."

"It weren't too hard. Willie and Duke distracted them and I took the bottle."

"How did Willie and Duke distract them? For that matter, how did you know the bottle was in the basement at all?"

"One of the nurses was partial to a bit of ready."

"You bribed her?"

"Bribery's better than throwing punches."

He had a point.

"She told us the bottle was in the laboratory in the basement and who was watching it. The three of us acted like orderlies and went down. No one stopped us. Orderlies are like servants."

"Invisible?"

He nodded. "Once down there, Willie acted like a madwoman. She created a scene, babbling, frothing at the mouth, and the like. Two of the constables chased her. While they were gone, Duke and I put out the lamps. Ain't no windows down there to let in the light. The other constable came out to investigate. Willie's carrying on lured him further away. Duke and I went inside the laboratory, pretended to be orderlies and asked the doctor about a delivery. He didn't know what we were talking about, so he had to find the paperwork. When his back was turned, I slipped the bottle of Cure-All he'd been testing into my pocket and we walked out. Willie joined us on the stairs."

I stared at him, stunned by their brazen theft. "Any number of things could have gone wrong. What if the constables hadn't chased Willie? What if the doctor had ordered you to leave without checking his paperwork?"

He lifted one broad shoulder. "We would have changed tactic, tried something different. There were three of us and four of them. Two were as scrawny as a corn stalk. They wouldn't have put up much of a fight."

"You would have thrown punches after all?"

"We wouldn't have hurt any of them too bad."

I was quite impressed that they'd managed to steal the bottle without anyone getting hurt but the lengths they would have gone to worried me. "What about putting it back tonight?" I asked.

"It won't be so hard. The laboratory will be dark and no one will be about down there."

"It'll be locked."

"A locked door never stopped me before. Or Duke, or Willie."

"Or Matt," I added. "Did you learn these skills from Matt's outlaw relatives?"

"*They* learned that way." He pushed off from the wall. "My education didn't come from my family. It came from being chased all over Nevada by lawmen."

A chill crept down my spine but I didn't shiver or show a sign that his words affected me. I didn't want him to think I feared him, because I did not. He was a good man, and lawmen weren't always honest. Sheriff Payne had proved that.

The brow above his good eye lifted. "Are you going to ask why they chased me?"

"I feel like I'm intruding on your privacy," I said carefully.

He chuckled. "You English are too polite. How do you find out anything about anyone?"

"We gossip about them behind their back."

His rumbling laugh eased my mind. I laughed too.

"I'll tell you another time," he said. "For now, I have a bottle of Dr. Hale's Cure-All to return to a hospital."

* * *

THE PITT MEDICINE COMPANY'S shop in New Bond Street had more than ten times the jars and bottles on its shelves than Dr. Hale housed in his office. The labels of some claimed miraculous cures for all sorts of ailments, from headaches to bowel problems and everything in between. There was a surprising number for feminine complaints. If even half worked, the world would be a pain-free place, but having used some in the past, I knew few performed as well as their labels boasted. Pharmacists shouldn't be allowed to get away with such falsehoods.

It wasn't the medicines, ointments and creams that drew my attention, however. It was the long case clock standing by the door like a guard, its pendulum swinging ponderously back and forth. Its rhythm called me, and I went to inspect it. With a frown, I pulled my watch out of my reticule. The clock was three minutes behind.

Matt also had no interest in the medicines. He couldn't tear himself away from the large glass jars on the table containing curiosities suspended in fluid. He bent to inspect a collection of jars, one containing a yellow snake coiled in on itself, another with a claw from an indeterminate beast, and another with the skeletal remains of a rodent-like creature.

I turned away and smiled at the bespectacled man behind the counter where a pyramid of Dr. Hale's Cure-All rose higher than his head. "Good morning. Are you Mr. Pitt?"

"Indeed, I am, madam." He smiled and pushed his spectacles up his nose. He didn't look like a man who'd just lost his business partner. He was mid-thirties with a pleasant if somewhat pale face and eyes of such a light blue that they almost blended into the surrounding whites. "How may I help you and your husband?"

"We're not married," I said. "Mr. Glass is a private inquiry agent, and I'm his assistant." Matt and I had discussed our roles in the carriage and decided a formal approach would work better in this instance, considering all the questions we had.

"Partner," Matt said, tearing himself away from the curiosities. "Miss Steele is my partner, not my assistant. It's a recent promotion and she's not yet used to it."

Mr. Pitt looked as surprised as I felt, although I tried to keep a benignly professional countenance. "Investigators?" Mr. Pitt said. "Is this to do with Jonathon's death?"

"Dr. Hale's, yes."

"I've already spoken to the police. I have nothing more to add."

"Perhaps we'll have different questions," Matt went on, unperturbed.

Pitt returned to unpacking empty jars from a wooden box on the counter. "Do you work for the guild?"

"Which guild?"

"The Apothecary's. Who else?"

"I'm just checking that we're on the same page, Mr. Pitt." Matt's voice was all patience and civility, and Mr. Pitt looked a little ashamed of his own belligerent tone. "We don't work for the guild," Matt went on. "Our employer wishes to remain anonymous, however."

He paused in his task. "Anonymous? Why?"

"It's someone with an interest in seeing justice served. Someone who doesn't have faith in Scotland Yard."

"I see," Mr. Pitt said carefully. "You have me intrigued, Mr. Glass, but as long as it's not the guild, I'll do my best to answer your questions."

Why did he not like the guild making inquiries?

"Do you know who Dr. Hale's heirs are?" Matt asked.

"I do, as it happens." He gave us a flat-lipped humorless smile. "It's me."

"You?" I blurted out. "Does he not have any family?"

Mr. Pitt shook his head. "Not even distant relatives."

"You were close to him?"

"Not really, although he dined at my house, from time to time. My wife felt sorry for him, you see, and she asked him to join us once a week. She thought he was lonely, although I don't think he was. He just didn't care to make friends, and he never married. He never showed any interest. Jonathon was…odd. It wasn't that people disliked him; they simply didn't warm to him. I was the closest thing to a friend he had, so I suppose that's why he left it all to me." He held up a finger. "So he told me, anyway, when he made out his will three years ago. It's entirely possible he made another one since and gave his fortune to someone else. I'll discover tomorrow, when the will is read at his lawyer's office. My presence has been requested."

He sounded very matter-of-fact, without a hint of sorrow for Hale's passing. If this man was the closest thing to a friend that the doctor had, it was rather sad.

"Before your investigative brain begins to pin the murder on me," Mr. Pitt said, "may I point out that I was nowhere near the hospital that day. I am also already wealthy, thanks to the success of my Cure-All." He nodded at the pyramid. "I have no need of Jonathon's money."

"*Your* Cure-All?" Matt plucked a jar from the top and made a show of inspecting it. "Dr. Hale's name is on the label."

Mr. Pitt's nostrils flared. He gave Matt a cool smile. "I created it and asked him to put his name to it. Dr. Hale's Cure-All sounded better than Pitt's Cure-All. Hale and hearty and all that. Pitt conjures up pock marks."

"Not to mention that it seems as though a doctor has endorsed it," Matt said.

"A doctor *has* endorsed it. I can tell from your accent that you're not English, Mr. Glass, but I can assure you, my Cure-All has an excellent reputation here. Have you used it, Miss Steele?"

"I have," I said. "I've found it of great benefit for all sorts of ailments." Perhaps that last was a little too effusive, but it certainly made Mr. Pitt smile. I'd rather have him on our side through a little flattery than not at all.

"Excellent. I am so pleased to hear it. My wife swears by it. She says it settles the children to sleep when they're restless with an ache or pain, and it works wonders on the complaints that the fairer sex suffer."

"Quite," I said tightly.

"So, you see, Jonathon's death is causing my business problems." He glanced at the clock and shook his head. I was about to mention that it ran slow when he said, "It's midmorning, and I haven't had a single customer. They stop out the front to ogle and whisper then move on without entering. I'll wring the neck of the murderer if I find him. He's ruining me."

He'd more than ruined Dr. Hale, but I didn't point that out.

"Is that because the newspapers revealed the poison was in a bottle of Cure-All?" Matt asked.

Mr. Pitt nodded. "Bloody irresponsible of them, if you ask me, and quite unnecessary."

A customer looked as if she were about to enter, but her companion shook her head, pointed at the bottles on the counter, and said something that made the first lady gasp. They bustled away.

"I will weather this setback," Mr. Pitt said, resembling a general addressing his troops. "I'll change the name of it, if I must, although it will be costly to re-do the labels."

"Not to mention a shame," I said. "For the memory of Dr. Hale, I mean."

"Of course."

"Did Dr. Hale have any enemies?" Matt asked. "Anyone who would want to see him dead?"

"Perhaps," he hedged. "I don't like telling you this, but I know I must. I've already told the police. Jonathon mentioned an incident that happened two weeks ago. A man threatened him, you see. Someone we're both acquainted with, an apothecary. His name is Oakshot. He was the husband of one of Jonathon's patients who sadly passed away. He accused Jonathon of administering too much morphine. She was petite, and morphine is dangerous if the incorrect dose is given to an already ill patient. One must be careful."

"Why did Oakshot suspect Dr. Hale administered the incorrect amount?" Matt asked.

"Jonathon thinks—thought—one of the other doctors put it into Oakshot's head. The other doctors at the hospital have been against him ever since his appointment to the staff. Physicians and surgeons look down on apothecaries, you see. They consider us little better than herbalists." He rolled his eyes.

"But Dr. Hale was a qualified physician," I said.

"Indeed. He went to Oxford and completed his medical training at St. George's Hospital. But his background as an apothecary rankled with them. He could never quite shake it off. It never bothered him, though. He was quite ambivalent to the opinions of others, until Oakshot accused him of killing his wife. Jonathon was deeply upset by it." He picked up a cloth and began slowly polishing the counter, even though the surface gleamed.

"Forgive me, Mr. Pitt," I said, "but I must ask. *Did* Dr. Hale give Mrs. Oakshot the wrong amount of morphine? Was that why he was upset? Because he felt guilty?"

Mr. Pitt stopped polishing. "While Jonathon didn't admit as much to me, I think you may be right. It was impossible to prove or disprove, but he certainly seemed as if he were second guessing himself after Oakshot's accusation."

"What did the hospital do?" Matt asked.

"Nothing, as far as I know."

"Does Mr. Oakshot have a shop?"

"He manufactures medicines but has no retail outlet himself. His products are distributed to many pharmacies throughout England." He pointed to shelves lined with medicine jars on our right. "Many of those are manufactured by Oakshot's."

"Does he have his own cure-all?" Matt asked.

I frowned. Was he implying that Oakshot's motive for killing Dr. Hale could have been two-fold—revenge for his wife's death *and* eliminating a business rival whose name graced another medicine's label?

"Of course. Every pharmacist worth his salt has his own cure-all."

"What sort of reputation does Oakshot have within the industry?" Matt asked.

"Excellent. He's the largest manufacturer of medicines in

London with a reputation the rest of us envy. You can see for yourselves, if you like. His factory is located in Hackney Wick. "

Matt approached the counter. "An envious reputation? Do you mean to say his medicines work exceptionally well?"

I approached the counter too, eager to gauge Mr. Pitt's reaction.

He glanced at each of us in turn and cleared his throat. "What are you implying, Mr. Glass?"

Matt pressed his palms on the counter. "Are Oakshot's medicines as good as Dr. Hale's?"

Mr. Pitt leaned away. He glanced past me to the door again then leaned forward. "Are you asking what I think you're asking?" he said, voice low.

"Is Mr. Oakshot a magical apothecary, like Dr. Hale was?"

Mr. Pitt sucked in a breath between his teeth. "H-how do you know? *What* do you know?"

"We know that Dr. Hale could infuse magic into his medicines, but the magic didn't last for long. He admitted it to us when we spoke to him after that newspaper article appeared in *The Weekly Gazette*."

"He admitted it to you?" he blurted out. "Was he mad?"

"He trusted us," I said.

Matt shot me a glare and gave a small shake of his head.

"We know about magicians, you see," I said. "The article directed us to him." It was the only response I could think of that didn't give away my magic.

Mr. Pitt pressed his lips together. "I feared it would act as a signpost for anyone hunting out magic. Jonathon didn't care. He was pleased." He shook his head. "Fool. I warned him that it was a bad idea, that people who feared magicians might come after him, but he wouldn't listen."

"We're not those sort of people," I assured him. "We have

an interest in magic, but that's only because we want to know more about it. We're curious."

"Much of our work involves magic, one way or another," Matt said. "We're thinking of making it a specialty within our agency."

I blinked at him. He sounded sincere. Then again, he'd proven to be a marvelous actor.

"And you read about Jonathon in the article." Mr. Pitt shook his head. "That reporter has a lot to answer for. His reporting was irresponsible. Have you spoken to him?"

Matt nodded. "Do you know of anyone who would attack Hale because he was magical?"

Mr. Pitt sighed. "Other apothecaries, perhaps, out of jealousy. The guild members, too, for the same reason. The guilds don't like magicians, you see. They're afraid it puts the artless members out of business."

"Artless?" I asked idly.

"A word Jonathon used for those without magic."

"Why would the guild be worried about Dr. Hale if he wasn't a practicing apothecary?" Matt asked. "He posed no threat to any of them."

"I don't know, Mr. Glass. Some of them have an irrational fear, you see, and think any good apothecary is magical. Oakshot himself has had visits from them."

"Do you think he's a magician?"

Mr. Pitt shrugged one shoulder.

"Have you had run-ins with the guild, Mr. Pitt?" I asked.

He indicated the pyramid of Cure-All. "There were rumblings when we released this, and Jonathon and I were questioned by the guild master. Nothing came of it. Jonathon didn't use his magic in it. He said it was rather useless since it didn't last."

"It can last weeks," I said. "Perhaps even months."

"So we've heard," Matt said quickly. "But Miss Steele is

right. If Hale put magic in your Cure-All it could work for a brief time afterward. It might be enough to give it a reputation as a wonder medicine."

"I see your point, but there is a flaw in your theory. Jonathon simply put his name to it. He didn't create it. I did. Alone."

The silence that followed thickened, our unspoken question hanging suspended like the curiosities in the jars of fluid.

"No, I am *not* magical," he finally said. He directed his fierce gaze first at Matt then at me.

I realized that I had a way of telling if he spoke the truth or not. I took a bottle of Cure-All off the pyramid, opened it and smelled. No warmth. I did the same for other bottles, taking random ones off shelves and pretending to smell while actually trying to detect magical warmth. Mr. Pitt watched me for a while then must have dismissed my actions as harmless. He turned back to Matt.

"What concerns me," Mr. Pitt said, "is how did the poison get into Jonathon's Cure-All in the first place?"

"A good question," Matt said. "The thing is, Dr. Hale suffered none of the symptoms from any known poison. It also had no smell or color."

"That is unusual. Are you sure?"

Matt nodded. "We believe a magic poison was added to the bottle."

Mr. Pitt's already pale face whitened further. The blue veins stood out on his forehead and throat, and his mouth worked but no words came out for several seconds. "How do you know?" he muttered.

"We have our methods," Matt said.

Mr. Pitt shook his head. "No, I don't believe it. He wouldn't kill himself."

"We weren't suggesting that," I said.

Mr. Pitt turned sharply to me.

"The question is," Matt said, "do you know any other apothecary magicians?"

"That's what you think?" Mr. Pitt scrunched the cloth still in his hand and wiped the counter in a slow arc. He took his time answering. "I have my suspicions, but I'm not certain. And no, I will not name the man I suspect. It wouldn't be fair."

"We wish him no harm," Matt said. "We just want to question him."

"I can't do it. I'm sorry. If the guild gets wind of it, they'll persecute him. He could lose his license, and the man has children to provide for."

Not children *and* a wife? Could he have omitted that point because the man was now a widower? Like Mr. Oakshot?

"Do you have any further questions?" Mr. Pitt asked.

"Just one," Matt said. "The journalist for *The Weekly Gazette* told us that Dr. Hale talked to him freely about his magic. If he feared the guild, why would he do that?"

"That's the problem. Jonathon didn't fear the guild, because he was not a practicing apothecary—and because he was a fool. His head was completely turned by that journalist. Bloody irresponsible, pardon my language, Miss Steele."

"I don't understand," I said, giving up on detecting for magical warmth. "What do you mean, 'his head was turned?'"

"The reporter fellow had the grand idea that magicians and artless could live peacefully together, without fear or jealousy. I tried to tell him otherwise, but Jonathon wouldn't listen to me. The reporter got in his ear, telling him how wonderful life could be if everyone got along." He clicked his tongue. "That fellow ought to be ashamed of himself for bringing attention to magic. Who knows, he may have inadvertently caused Jonathon's death by writing that article about his 'medical miracle.'"

I bristled. "You can't blame the victim for being murdered. It's entirely the murderer's fault."

"I'm not blaming the victim, Miss Steele. I'm blaming that reporter. It's the magicians he writes about who are the victims, not him."

I stamped down on my temper, not entirely sure why I was so angry. Oscar Barratt had noble intentions. Intentions that he must now set aside until the murderer was found. In a way, he *was* a victim.

"Thank you, Mr. Pitt," Matt said. "We'll purchase a bottle of Cure-All then leave you alone. My housekeeper's stock is low."

I returned to the clock while Mr. Pitt wrapped up a bottle for Matt. I opened the glass casing and corrected the minute hand.

"Thank you, Miss Steele," Mr. Pitt said, looking up from his wrapping. "I have to adjust it every day, but I forgot this morning, what with all the newspaper reports on Jonathon's death to read."

"Every day?" I asked. "It must need fixing. Do you want me to have a look?"

"You know about clocks?"

"My father used to own a shop."

"We don't have time." Matt scooped up the wrapped bottle from the counter before Mr. Pitt could hand it to him. "Thank you, Mr. Pitt. You've been helpful." He opened the door for me and waited with an arched look.

I sighed, closed the clock casing, and exited the shop. "It wouldn't have taken long," I told him as I passed.

Matt continued to hold the door open for a gentleman using a silver-topped walking stick. His carriage waited behind ours.

"Good morning, my lord," Mr. Pitt greeted him.

I was pleased to see that Mr. Pitt hadn't lost everyone's custom. Or perhaps the lord hadn't read the papers yet.

I climbed into the coach while Matt gave Bryce the address to Mr. Oakshot's factory, then he sat opposite me. He regarded me with a slight frown. "You feel compelled to fix clocks and watches, don't you?"

"I don't like seeing time running slow, if that's what you mean."

"You *need* to fix them, to handle them."

"Are you going to take my watch away from me again and turn all the clocks around?" I clutched my reticule tighter. "It was somewhat amusing the first time, but you proved your point. There's no need to do it again."

He smiled crookedly. "No, India, I'm not."

Even so, I did not loosen my grip. "What do you think of Pitt?"

"Intelligent, cautious, perhaps not telling us the entire truth," he said.

"Why do you think that?"

"He had smooth answers for every question."

A bubble of laughter rose up my throat. "Oh, Matt, if that were a crime, you would be under arrest every day. You are the smoothest man I've ever met."

"I'm utterly sincere," he protested.

"Having ready, smooth answers to everything doesn't make you *insincere*. The same for Mr. Pitt. I think you're mistaken about him. I think he's simply not all that upset by Dr. Hale's death, but I don't think he had any part in it. I believe him when he says he's not magical. I detected no warmth in any of his medicines whatsoever. And besides, he had more to lose than gain from Dr. Hale's death. No one will touch his Cure-All, now that the newspapers have revealed it was the murder weapon, of sorts. He'll lose business."

Matt removed his hat and dragged his hand through his hair, ruffling it. For a brief moment, he didn't look at all like the gentleman he usually presented but more like the outlaw his mother's family wanted him to be. But then he smoothed down his hair and replaced his hat back on his head. I sighed. Both versions of Matt were utterly, devastatingly handsome, and very much forbidden to me.

"I think we should visit the Apothecary's Guild," he said. "We might learn something from them, although probably not through direct questions."

"We have quite a list of people to visit now. We won't get time until tomorrow if we still want to talk to Dr. Wiley and Ritter today."

"And I must return home at midday and in the evening to rest," he bit off. "Yes, I know. No need to remind me."

"I wasn't. Don't speak to me like that."

He winced and rubbed his forehead. "Sorry, India. You're right, and I spoke out of turn. I'm not myself lately."

I bit the inside of my cheek. "I'm sorry, too, Matt. There was no need for me to snap back at you. I don't feel like myself lately, either. I don't know why."

* * *

BLACK SMOKE BILLOWED from the chimney stacks of Mr. Oakshot's factory and joined the miasma spewing from the surrounding factories to blanket Hackney Wick. Soot settled on our clothing in the short walk from the carriage to the red brick building, and I pressed my handkerchief to my nose in an attempt to block out the stench of burning coal and God knew what else.

We found Mr. Oakshot in an office on the first level,

standing with his hands at his back before a large window that overlooked the factory floor below. He turned when Matt cleared his throat.

"Good morning," Matt said, hand extended. "My name is Matthew Glass and this is my partner, Miss Steele."

Mr. Oakshot looked like a man in need of a rest. He was about forty and, like Matt, exhaustion pulled his features tight and shadowed red-rimmed eyes. He gave Matt's hand a firm shake. "Your accent has a hint of American," he said. "Are you looking to distribute my medicines in your country?"

"Actually, we're private inquiry agents investigating the death of Dr. Hale."

Mr. Oakshot whipped his hand back and fisted it at his side. "Get out!" he barked. "I don't want to hear his name uttered within my hearing."

"It'll just take a moment of your time," Matt said. "We have a few questions we'd like to—"

Mr. Oakshot stepped up to Matt, toe to toe, and bared his teeth. "Get. Out. Of. My. Sight."

"But—

Mr. Oakshot grabbed hold of Matt's jacket lapels and swung his fist.

CHAPTER 6

*M*att blocked Mr. Oakshot's fist with his forearm. Mr. Oakshot swung again and Matt caught his wrist.

"Not in front of Miss Steele," Matt said with far more calm than I felt.

Mr. Oakshot pulled free of Matt's grip and straightened his waistcoat and tie. He did not try to hit out again, but Matt's stance remained tense, poised to fight.

"We're deeply sorry to hear about your wife's death," I said, my heart hammering against my ribcage. Mr. Oakshot turned to me, his dark hazel eyes boring into me, challenging. "You have our sincerest condolences. We understand that Dr. Hale believed he may have given your wife the incorrect dose of morphine."

The ferocity dissolved from his eyes at my sympathetic tone. He heaved in a shaky breath. "Hale believed that, did he? That's not what he told me." He turned back to the window, his shoulders stooped, hands loose at his sides. He was the picture of a dejected, defeated man.

Matt nodded at me, urging me to continue. I joined Mr.

Oakshot at the window. Below us, workmen dressed in over-alls fed furnaces that heated large cauldrons of liquid. Steam rose in drifts and swirled among the rafters. The factory hands wiped their brows between stirring the cauldrons and tipping in ingredients. At the far end, men filled bottles at a long table while another two pasted labels onto bottles before they were packed into boxes. It was a busy factory.

"Tell us what happened that day at the hospital?" I asked.

Mr. Oakshot crossed his arms, resting them on his paunch. "She'd been ill for some time. A tumor in her stomach, so the doctors said. They couldn't cure her. My medicines..." he choked out. "My medicines couldn't cure her either, only ease her pain for a short time. She felt wretched that day—the day she died. She'd hardly slept because of the pain, and she couldn't keep anything down. I took her to the hospital, and Hale assured me he'd take care of her. It was a busy day. There were lots of patients coming in and not enough staff. They wouldn't let me stay with my wife, so I went for a walk. When I got back..." He cleared his throat. "When I got back, she had passed." He bowed his head and closed his eyes.

I touched his arm. "Who told you that Dr. Hale might have made a mistake with the morphine dose?"

He removed a handkerchief from his pocket and wiped his nose. "The doctor in charge."

"Dr. Ritter?"

He nodded. "He didn't outright admit it. He just said that Hale's mind wasn't on the task, that he had to tend to lots of patients that day, and he'd made the same mistake once before, although that patient survived. He said Hale had limited experience compared to the other doctors and that he—Ritter—would have words with him to get to the bottom of it."

"Do you know if he did?"

"I never found out. I went straight to Hale's office myself and told him what I thought of him. No one tried to stop me then, but they came when they heard the shouting." He stared down at the factory floor, and his body relaxed a little. He seemed to take comfort in the pattern of activity, from filling the cauldrons through to packing bottles into boxes. He must have looked upon that scene every day for years.

"I don't regret it," he went on. "Even though he's dead now, and you shouldn't speak ill of the dead, I don't regret confronting him."

I looked to Matt to see if he wanted to take over questioning, but he gave his head half a shake, which I took to mean he wanted me to continue. "You knew Dr. Hale personally, since he was an apothecary before he became a physician," I said.

Mr. Oakshot nodded. "He was a good apothecary, so when he gave it all up to become a doctor, I was surprised."

"How good was he?"

His back stiffened. "One of the best in London. Why?"

"There are strange rumors about him."

"What kind of rumors?"

"The journalist who reported on the medical miracle he recently performed implied he was a magician."

Mr. Oakshot's eyes briefly flared, and his gaze flicked to Matt then back to me. He swallowed heavily. "You've been reading too many fairytales, Miss Steele. There's no such thing as magic. Those rumors are the product of fertile minds trying to sell more newspapers."

"You think the journalist made it up?"

"What other explanation is there for such nonsense? Dr. Hale was a great apothecary who gave up his business to become a doctor. Like me, he got to be great through hard work and a talent for chemistry. There's no secret to success, Miss Steele. No magic."

"Thank you for confirming that," I said. There was no point in pressing him further. Unlike Mr. Pitt, Mr. Oakshot would not admit the existence of magic to us. "Are you an active member of the Apothecary's Guild?" I asked instead.

"I'm on the Court of Assistants."

The Court of Assistants was the inner sanctum of any guild. Its members awarded prizes, issued pensions to infirm members or widows, and oversaw guild finances and memberships. If someone in the Apothecary's Guild knew Dr. Hale was a magician, then Mr. Oakshot would likely also know. I was quite sure someone at the guild knew—or at least suspected.

His elevated position in the guild settled it for me—I would not tell him that I was magical, or that we even knew that Dr. Hale was poisoned by magic-infused medicine. The risk was too great.

But what about Mr. Oakshot himself? Was he a magician, as Mr. Pitt implied, and had managed to keep it a secret from the rest of the guild members?

I glanced around the office. Glasses and a decanter sat on the sideboard and a tall bookcase held herbal books, not medicines as Pitt's apothecary's shop did. What appeared to be a recipe book lay open on the desk with a mortar and pestle beside it and a collection of dark red berries, seeds and roots in a bowl. I counted only five bottles and three pots on the desk, all with the distinctive Oakshot labels of a leafy oak tree. Why did he have them in here and not on the factory floor? Had he been placing spells on their contents? Or on the raw ingredients?

"May I?" I asked, picking up a bottle of stomach bitters and removing the cork stopper. "Juniper?"

"Among other things." He closed the recipe book and glanced at Matt behind me.

I replaced the stopper and picked up another bottle to smell it too. Like the first, I sensed no magical warmth.

Mr. Oakshot watched me intently, a frown striking across his forehead. He looked as if he would ask me what I was doing when I reached for the third bottle, but Matt distracted him.

"Do you go down to the factory floor yourself?" Matt asked.

"Occasionally, but my presence is largely unnecessary," Mr. Oakshot said. "My foreman oversees the work. I remain up here, managing the orders as well as creating new medicines, from time to time."

"You still keep your hand in, even after building this empire?" Matt indicated the window and the factory below.

"It may be an empire in England, Mr. Glass, but I haven't yet conquered the rest of the world. My wife and I planned to establish a factory on the continent." He trailed his fingers across the polished wooden surface of the desk. "All that has been put on hold, now. It may never happen."

"Why not? You're still young, and think of what you would leave to your children."

Mr. Oakshot sighed. "I simply don't have the energy at the moment."

"Perhaps one day."

"Perhaps."

I picked up the last pot and made a show of smelling the greyish cream inside. It was not warm.

"I have to ask another question about Dr. Hale," Matt said quietly. He waited until Mr. Oakshot nodded before continuing. "Where were you the day he died?"

"I've told the police this already," Mr. Oakshot said. "I was here. My foreman can vouch for me."

"All day?"

"I stepped out briefly to go home and see that my children were well cared for. I went nowhere near the hospital. I'd said my piece to Hale and wanted to avoid that place and him."

"Did you know he was poisoned?" Matt asked.

"I read it in this morning's newspaper. The poison was most likely in the bottle of Cure-All that he kept in his desk." He *humphed* a humorless laugh. "I find that particularly satisfying."

"Why?"

"Because his Cure-All outsold mine ever since it came onto the market. Its enormous sales have profited both Hale and Pitt. But just today, orders of my Cure-All rose dramatically. I suspect the trend to continue as pharmacies around the country find they can't give away Dr. Hale's Cure-All anymore." His eyes gleamed and the twist of his lips made me shiver. "As I said, it's very satisfying."

"Because you believe it's revenge for your wife's death," Matt said.

"Not entirely. Dr. Hale's own death extinguished my anger toward him for my wife's. The satisfaction I speak of is not personal, it's business. My Cure-All used to be the top selling medicine until his went on the market. I've been trying to claw back my share ever since, but to no avail. His Cure-All became more and more popular. Until today. Today, I win."

There was no mistaking the bitterness in his tone and the undercurrent of deep satisfaction too. He had every reason to want Dr. Hale dead, both personally and professionally. He had just rocketed to the top of my list of suspects.

I returned the last pot to the desk. "You said *his* Cure-All. Mr. Pitt claims *he* created it, and that Dr. Hale simply lent his name to it. You don't believe that?"

He sat at his desk and made a great show of rearranging

things. "I wouldn't know. Those two kept to themselves. They never told anyone what was in their Cure-All."

"Dr. Hale was no longer a member of the Apothecary's Guild," Matt said. "Is Mr. Pitt an active member?"

"Yes. He only goes to the hall when it's compulsory. He doesn't join us for dinners or meetings. Now, unless you have any more questions directly related to Dr. Hale's death, I'll have to ask you to leave. I'm very busy."

"Thank you," Matt said. "You've been very helpful."

Mr. Oakshot sat back and clasped his hands over his stomach. "I'm sorry about before. I was…overset."

"We understand," I said.

"What will you do if you discover who murdered him?"

"Tell the police," Matt said.

"I hope I get to shake the killer's hand before he hangs."

I hurried out with Matt, Mr. Oakshot's macabre words ringing in my ears. "I know he's grieving, but there's something sinister about his reaction to Hale's death," I said as Matt assisted me into the carriage.

He folded up the step and directed Bryce to drive us home. "We should allow him some liberties," Matt said, settling opposite me. "It seems as though he loved his wife very much. I think I'd be just as angry toward Hale if his incompetence led to the death of someone I loved."

I watched him closely and he regarded me levelly in turn, as if daring me to challenge his opinion. "Would you kill him, though?"

"For incompetence? No."

But would Matt kill a man who'd deliberately murdered his loved one? "If Mr. Oakshot is a magician, he hides it very well. There was no warmth in the bottles on his desk."

"He might have infused other medicines with magic, just not those," he said.

"The workmen on the factory floor would wonder why he removed bottles to his office."

"Not if he did it after they'd all departed for the day."

He had a point and I conceded it with a nod. "We can't dismiss him, but I can't imagine he'd be on the Court of Assistants for the guild if he was magical."

"It could be the perfect place to hide, right there in plain sight. I've done it before, many times."

"You have? How intriguing. Tell me more."

He smiled. "You have a thirst for knowledge about my past."

"That's because you've told me so little. Any information I can get is a little piece of the puzzle I didn't have before."

"So I'm a puzzle, now."

"You always have been, Matt, and you know it."

He tipped his head back and laughed. "And here I thought you had my measure. You seem to know what I'm thinking, most of the time. So what is it you want to know?"

"Tell me about hiding in plain sight, for starters. Was it when you were an outlaw in your grandfather's gang or after you left and began working for the law?"

"Both. There's not much to tell. When the lawmen came looking for us, I pretended to be an innocent bystander and gave them directions to my grandfather's men—in the opposite direction to where they'd actually gone. And later, when I worked on the right side of the law, I would pretend to be my grandfather's lackey to dupe the outlaws he associated with. It worked for a time, until word got out. After that, I had to lay low. I kept my distance from my grandfather and his posse."

"Was that when you became friends with Duke and Cyclops?"

He nodded. "Duke had been Willie's friend for a long time, and he became mine too while she harbored me. I met

Cyclops one night when we were both sleeping rough." He smiled. "I came across his camp, but it appeared to be vacated so I helped myself to the food left behind. Little did I know that he'd heard me coming and had hidden so he could ambush me."

"And did he ambush you?"

"Yes. He tried to kill me, but I managed to explain that I wasn't his enemy before he beat me senseless."

"You talked him out of attacking you? Why am I not surprised?"

"Only after I got in a few good punches of my own, thank you. He didn't completely overpower me, although it wasn't easy. We fought for so long we both reached the point of exhaustion and we simply couldn't go on. So it was a win by mutual surrender. It was several minutes before I'd regained my breath enough to talk to him."

Despite his somewhat whimsical retelling, I suspected it had been a frightening time. Cyclops was a giant. Matt may have a more athletic frame, but if Cyclops had him in his grasp, it would be difficult to get out.

We arrived home and Matt retired to his rooms once Duke reassured him that the bottle had been returned to the hospital without anyone getting caught. They'd paid a nurse to say she'd come across it among the linen. Matt left it to me to tell them how our interviews had gone and to field their questions. All discussion came to an abrupt end when Miss Glass entered the sitting room. Bristow and the footman, a blond youth named Peter, followed her, carrying trays.

"A light luncheon," Miss Glass announced. "I don't wish to spoil my appetite for this evening."

"This evening?" we all echoed.

"My dinner party." She looked to me. "Did I not mention it?"

"No," Willie grumbled. "You did not. Does that mean we

got to be prisoners in our own rooms so your guests don't see us?"

Miss Glass plucked a sandwich off the platter. "Thank you, Bristow, that will be all. Be sure and see that the Spode is ready for tonight."

"Mr. Glass doesn't have Spode, ma'am," the butler intoned.

"No Spode?" She clicked her tongue. "That will have to change. India, make a note to purchase a set of Spode for Matthew."

I blinked slowly. "I'll add it to my list of tasks for when this investigation is complete." What more could I say? I supposed, as his assistant, it was my job to buy him a set of Spode. Or was I a partner now? And what did that even mean?

"Do your best, Bristow. No Spode," Miss Glass said on a sigh as the butler and footman left. "What is the world coming to?"

Willie picked up a sandwich and pulled the layers of bread apart to inspect the filling. "What in God's name is so special about Spode?"

"You wouldn't understand the need for fine china, Willie."

Willie pulled out the slice of cucumber in her sandwich, opened her mouth, and dropped the slice in. "You're right there," she said, munching. "China breaks too easy. Tin, now, that'll last an age. It even looks better with a few dents."

Miss Glass wrinkled her nose. "You'd better not ruin dinner for Matthew," she warned. "I worked tirelessly to insure Lady Abbington could come tonight. There have been a flurry of letters back and forth."

"Lady Abbington," I echoed dully. "But she was just here for tea only yesterday."

"Matthew didn't speak to her much, thanks to Mrs. Haviland's excessive chatter. I haven't invited the Havilands this time, so he can talk to Lady Abbington as much as he likes."

"You're inviting Lady Abbington on her own?"

"Nonsense. That would be odd. I've invited Richard, Beatrice and their daughters."

"Lord and Lady Rycroft! But I thought you didn't want Matt to marry any of their girls."

"Matt ain't going to like it," Willie sang.

Either Miss Glass didn't hear her or she chose to ignore her. "Lady Abbington is an elegant, serene woman and full of spirit. Next to her, my nieces will seem plain and witless."

"They don't need to be in the same room for that," Willie said.

"Not to you and me, Willemina, but Matthew is different. He's a man."

Duke and Cyclops exchanged glances. They looked as if they'd rather be elsewhere.

"Matt ain't interested in the Glass girls." Willie glanced at me, her mouth stretched into a thin line. "And you know it, Letty."

"It's best to be safe rather than sorry. I have a theory." Miss Glass glanced at the door and leaned forward. "The more Matthew sees them, the sooner he'll reach the same conclusion that we all have. They're horrid girls without a brain between them."

"Hope seems smart," Duke chimed in. "And nice."

Miss Glass and Willie glared at him. I may have, too. He appealed to Cyclops. Cyclops bit into his sandwich and studied the floor.

"Is that all?" I asked. "Or will there be other guests?"

"Four more," Miss Glass muttered into her sandwich.

"More eligible girls?" Willie asked with a laugh. "Poor Matt. He's under siege."

"Two women and two men. The women are not eligible as far as Matthew's concerned."

Willie rolled her eyes at me and smiled. "They beneath him?"

"One is not suitable, no." Miss Glass's gaze flicked to me then back to the platter of sandwiches. My chest tightened. "The other is his cousin."

"More goddamned cousins!" Willie shook her head. "This one been kept in the attic, eh?" She laughed so hard she snorted and choked on her sandwich. She coughed and wiped her sleeve over her mouth only to stop. Her laughter ceased. She stared at Miss Glass. "Oh, no, you don't, Letty. I ain't going to sit through some hoity toity dinner."

"I don't particularly like the idea either, but I've decided it's necessary."

"Why me?"

"It's not just you, Willie," I said. "Miss Glass mentioned four guests." I nodded at Duke and Cyclops.

Duke groaned. Willie burst out laughing. "Well, that's all good then. If I have to suffer then so do all of you."

"But I haven't got a dinner suit," Duke whined.

"Borrow one of Matthew's," Miss Glass said. "Cyclops?"

Cyclops held up his hands in surrender. "I have a suit. Thank you for including me, Miss Glass. I'm looking forward to my first English dinner party."

"Traitor," Willie muttered.

"Good man." Miss Glass touched her finger to the corner of her eye. "Do you have a patch in a color other than black? It would help if you looked less like a pirate."

"He can't not look frightening," Willie told her. "If the ladies get scared, that's their own silly fault for jumping to wrong conclusions without getting to know him first."

"I quite agree, but that's not why I asked. I'm concerned that Charity will like it a little too much. She thinks pirates are romantic and it wouldn't surprise me if she flirted with Cyclops."

"Don't want her running off with Cyclops and ruining the family reputation, eh?"

"It's not her or the Glass reputation I'm worried about. It's Cyclops. I do like you, Cyclops dear," she said to the big man. "I won't inflict one of my nieces on you if I can avoid it. Don't worry, you won't be seated next to her."

It was another two hours before Matt joined us. He finished the sandwiches while we informed him about the dinner arrangements. He refused to attend at first, until his aunt told him that we were all invited.

"All of them?" he asked, looking dubiously at Willie.

"All of them," Miss Glass said.

"Then I'll allow it, but in future, I need more warning."

Matt and I prepared to head out to the hospital to speak with Dr. Ritter and Dr. Wiley when a detective inspector from Scotland Yard called upon us. He was alone. If it weren't for this fact, I would have been concerned that he'd come to arrest Matt.

"May we speak, Mr. Glass?" Detective Inspector Brockwell asked.

"We can speak here," Matt said, indicating the entrance hall in which we stood.

"Somewhere more private." Brockwell looked past Matt to the main staircase where Duke stood, arms crossed over his chest, eyes narrowed. He looked as if he would bundle the detective out if he so much as even whispered the word arrest.

"The drawing room," Matt said. "Do you mind if my assistant, Miss Steele, joins us?"

"As you wish."

I placed Brockwell in his early-thirties, quite young for such an elevated position within the police force. He sat in an armchair and scratched one of his bushy sideburns. He waited until we were both seated before drawing in a deep breath and beginning.

"I've received a complaint about you, Mr. Glass." He enunciated each word with unhurried precision, so that the consonants had the effect of puncturing the sentence.

"A complaint about what?" Matt asked, not at all ruffled. "And from whom?"

"About your visit to a certain person involved in the Hale case. There's no need to name names."

"Speak with Commissioner Munro," Matt said. "I have his permission to investigate."

Brockwell paused, but whether pauses were simply part of his plodding manner, or it was a sign of his uncertainty, I couldn't be sure. "The commissioner didn't mention this to me."

Matt sat calmly, waiting for the inspector to go on. Neither man seemed unnerved by the taut silence, but my nerves jangled. I closed my fist tight and dug my nails into my palm to distract me.

"I don't know why Munro would allow you to interfere when you are also a suspect," Brockwell eventually said.

"You don't need to know," Matt shot back.

"I beg to differ." Brockwell got up and strolled idly around the room, inspecting objects, pictures, and his reflection in the mirror above the mantel. He scratched his sideburn again.

Matt relaxed into the armchair. How could he remain so calm?

"The thing is," Brockwell finally said, "I've heard all about you, Mr. Glass."

"Heard what?" Matt said, matching Brockwell's idle tone. His body, however, went rigid.

"That your past in America has been checkered, to put it mildly."

Oh no. If Commissioner Munro hadn't said anything, it must have been Sheriff Payne, hoping to ruin Matt's reputation and raise Brockwell's suspicions.

"Munro already knows about my past," Matt said. "He's communicated with lawmen from the States to confirm that I work for them from time to time."

"Yes, but I have it on good authority that Commissioner Munro and your American contacts don't know the half of what you've done. The illegal half, that is."

Matt stood and strolled over to Brockwell. He was considerably taller and broader across the shoulders, but Brockwell didn't back away. He met Matt's gaze with his own direct one. "I'd wager, Detective, that you are the one who doesn't know the half of it. Don't believe everything Sheriff Payne tells you."

Surprise flickered across Brockwell's face before his features flattened again. "I never take anyone at face value, Mr. Glass. I'm aware that a charming exterior can hide the most villainous nature. Even the most well-to-do families have secrets."

That was most certainly a reference to Matt and his well-to-do English relatives. The man was shameless.

"This is outrageous," I said, springing to my feet. "You come here and insult Mr. Glass, who has been nothing but helpful to your police force. Do not forget that he has solved two crimes for your organization."

"I believe you solved the first of those, Miss Steele," Brockwell said, a hint of amusement in his voice. That only riled me more.

"There you go again, Detective, jumping to conclusions when you don't have all the information. Mr. Glass was very much involved in solving the case of the Dark Rider, but he allowed me to take the credit so I could claim the reward." I had the great satisfaction of seeing Brockwell look uncertain.

"The sheriff wants you to think Matt is corrupt, and yet it is he who is corrupt. While that cannot be proved, it doesn't mean it's not true. Until such a time that it is proved, you ought to follow your commissioner's example and give Matt the benefit of the doubt. Now, kindly leave."

I strode to the door and stood by it, waiting for Brockwell. With a glance at Matt first, he joined me.

"My apologies for upsetting you, Miss Steele," he said with a short bow.

"It's not me you ought to be apologizing to."

He offered a tight smile but no apology to Matt. "The fact remains that you are hindering my investigation by speaking to one of my suspects."

"How is that hindering?" Matt asked. "In fact, if we compared answers, we might learn something."

Brockwell seemed to consider this but shook his head. "I'll do it on my own."

"There's no need to work alone. Together, we can find the murderer faster."

"I work perfectly well on my own, Mr. Glass. I haven't reached the rank of detective inspector by sharing my results with others."

What an arrogant man! And a fool, at that. I shook my head at Matt, wanting him to know that I thought it pointless to press Brockwell further.

"While I have Munro's authority to investigate, I will continue to question whomever I like," Matt said. "Is that clear?"

"Crystal," Brockwell bit off. "Good day, Miss Steele."

He marched past me and accepted his hat from Bristow. Willie and Duke stood guard by the open front door and watched him leave. Brockwell descended the steps slowly and passed the brougham, with Bryce in the driver's seat, waiting for us. Duke slammed the door closed.

"What did that turd want?" Willie asked.

"To tell me to stop investigating." To Bristow, Matt said, "My hat, please. India, our visit to the hospital will have to wait. I'm going to call upon Commissioner Munro."

"Alone?" I asked.

He nodded. "Duke, Willie, find Cyclops. I want the three of you to go in search of Sheriff Payne."

Duke and Willie exchanged glances. "Where do we start?" Duke asked.

"I have no idea." Matt slapped his hat on his head and pulled on his gloves and Bristow opened the door. Matt turned to me. His hard features relaxed somewhat.

"Are you sure you don't want me to come with you to speak to Munro?" I asked.

"It's not necessary. I don't think we'll get to the hospital at all today. Why not visit Miss Mason while I'm out?"

I watched him go then listened to Duke, Willie and Cyclops in the library as they planned their search for Payne. Matt had set them an impossible task, yet none whined, not even Willie. With my help, they drew up a list of hotels, but no one considered them a viable possibility. If Payne found himself in London for some time, he would have secured cheaper lodgings, perhaps in a private house. If that were the case, he'd be extremely difficult to find.

"Do you want me to help?" I asked.

"The three of us will be enough for today," Cyclops assured me. "You take the afternoon off, like Matt suggested. We can drive you to Miss Mason's, if you like, then continue on our way."

"I think it's wise if I stay away from the Masons for a little while. Could you drive me to the Cross Keys instead? I'd like to have a drink."

"You shouldn't go alone," Duke said. "All sorts find themselves in taverns."

"The Cross Keys is respectable enough, and it's the middle of the afternoon. Thank you for your concern, Duke, but I'll be fine."

Willie clamped her hand on my shoulder. "Good for you, India. I reckon it's a good idea."

* * *

I SPENT an hour at the Cross Keys, sitting in a booth and watching people come and go. No one bothered me. The man I knew as DuPont didn't enter, although I hadn't really held any hopes that he would. According to the innkeeper, who remembered me from my first visit, Chronos hadn't returned at all, and he restated his promise to notify Matt if he did.

I caught an omnibus back to Park Street, but it was slow progress thanks to the late afternoon traffic. Matt walked in soon after me. I told him where I'd been, and he told me how his meeting with Munro went.

"As well as can be expected," he said with a sigh. "He said he'll speak to Brockwell."

The clock on the library mantel chimed six. "I'd best get ready for dinner," I said. "Your aunt went up a half hour ago. The others should be back soon."

"Before you do." He reached into his inside jacket pocket and pulled out a small package. He handed it to me. "I went shopping after seeing Munro, and I bought you something to wear tonight."

I stared at the parcel wrapped in brown paper. "Why are you giving me gifts?"

"Can I not give my friend a gift from time to time?"

"No!"

He smiled, and it was wonderfully mischievous. It made

me happy to see him in a good mood, despite today's setback with Brockwell. "Just open it, India."

I unwrapped the paper then lifted the lid on the box. Nestled on a bed of royal blue velvet was a silver brooch in the shape of a winged dragon. Its bright green eyes sparkled. Were they paste or real emeralds? I wasn't experienced in gems to know the difference and I didn't want to seem greedy by asking.

"It's beautiful," I said on a breath. "It'll look lovely pinned to my sage and ivory gown. I don't wish to seem ungrateful, Matt, but why are you giving this to me?"

"Because I left without thanking you for standing up to Brockwell on my behalf. I want you to know it was appreciated." He nodded at the box. "Dragons are fierce, and so are you when you want to be."

"A simple thanks would have sufficed."

"Why make a simple gesture when a grand one is possible? Do you like it?"

"Very much so. Thank you."

He smiled and a slight blush crept over his cheeks. "It was a choice between that dragon, a beetle and a butterfly. I didn't think butterflies or beetles particularly fierce."

"Clearly you've never met a stink bug."

* * *

LORD AND LADY RYCROFT and their daughters were the first to arrive. We'd seen little of Lord Rycroft since the first meeting between Matt and his uncle. On that occasion, Matt had almost thrashed Lord Rycroft after he threw out some insults that Matt took offence to. His frosty greeting would indicate that he hadn't forgiven his nephew.

Matt, however, greeted his uncle politely, along with his aunt and cousins. We gathered in the drawing room for drinks and conversation but it was terribly stilted. Lord and Lady Rycroft could barely even look at Willie, Duke and Cyclops. It was as if they could pretend that Matt's friends and poor relation weren't present if they ignored them. I fared little better, receiving only a cool greeting from both.

Their daughters weren't quite so rude, and I made a point of asking Patience questions about her wedding. She warmed to me after a few minutes and shyly showed me her engagement ring.

"It's lovely," I said.

"As is your brooch." She nodded at the dragon pinned to my dress. "Is it a family heirloom?"

"Goodness, no. My family heirlooms consist entirely of timepieces. Your cousin gave me this just today."

Hope had been talking to Matt but suddenly swiveled to face me. Her gaze fell to the brooch. "How sweet," she declared. "Look at those emerald eyes."

Charity, sitting on my other side, leaned in to inspect the brooch. "Are they real emeralds?"

"Of course they damn well are," Willie snapped. "If you knew Matt better, you'd know he don't like fakes." She shot Hope a wicked smile. "Of any type."

Hope bristled, and Matt quickly engaged her in conversation again.

"Don't mind my sisters, Miss Steele," Patience whispered. "They're jealous that Matthew is giving you his attention."

I glanced at Matt. He seemed to be giving Hope all his attention at the moment. "Thank you, Patience. You're very kind. Your future husband is a very lucky man. I hope he knows it."

She broke into a grin, improving her otherwise plain features and brightening her eyes. She wasn't pretty, particularly compared to her sisters, but I was beginning to enjoy her company. I'd much rather be seated next to her than either Charity or Hope.

We talked some more about her wedding while Miss Glass tried to engage her brother and sister-in-law in conversation, only to receive scowls and curt answers from Lord Rycroft. Lady Rycroft was too distracted by Matt and Hope to speak to anyone. Willie and Duke had to fend for themselves while Cyclops found himself cornered, quite literally, by Charity Glass. She stood indecently close and blinked up at him with exuberant innocence. His one eye watched her warily, as if he expected her to attack him at any moment.

Brisk footsteps approaching the drawing room provided a welcome distraction from the tension in the air, and we all turned to greet Lady Abbington. But it was not Lady Abbington who entered.

It was Sheriff Payne.

CHAPTER 7

*M*att sprang to his feet and marched up to Payne. "What do you want?" he said, a thread of steel running through his voice.

"India," his aunt whispered. "It's that awful man again."

"He barged right past me, Mr. Glass," Bristow said, looking agitated.

"What's the meaning of this?" Lord Rycroft demanded in a petulant manner unique to the ruling class. "Who is this upstart?"

Duke cracked his knuckles and Cyclops extricated himself from the corner. He stood beside Matt. Willie, who'd not changed out of men's clothes, muttered something about leaving her Colt in her room. I went to stand beside Miss Glass. Her trembling hand touched mine.

Payne licked his lips. "You *cur*."

"Get out before I thrash you," Matt barked.

"You'd dare to thrash a man of the law?"

"You're not the law here."

"Girls!" Lady Rycroft cried, flapping her arms about as if she were directing traffic. "Girls, to me!" But none of her daughters moved. They were riveted to the drama playing out before them.

"I'm glad you've got visitors," Payne said, his thin mouth stretching into a thinner smile. "I want them to hear about your thieving family back home."

"This *is* my family," Matt said, almost sounding amused. "And they already know about my American side. Believe me, they're quite disgusted by my past. Nothing you say will make it worse."

A sheen of sweat broke out on Payne's high forehead beneath his hat brim. Matt's nonchalance was getting to him. "You sure about that? They know the particulars?" The more he spoke, the thicker his American accent became and the less confident he sounded.

"You're angry at me for speaking to Munro," Matt said, the steeliness back in his voice. "I understand. It's frustrating being thwarted at every turn."

"I ain't thwarted, Glass. Not in the least." Payne snickered. His eyes flashed and he planted his feet a little apart, as if settling himself in for a long stay. "Want me to tell them something they don't know?"

"Duke, Cyclops, help Bristow show Sheriff Payne to the door."

"Sheriff?" Lord Rycroft's bellow startled Miss Glass. He squared up to Matt, getting between him and Payne, although they were taller and easily peered over his head. "Matthew, I demand to know what's going on."

"Shut it," Willie snapped. "This ain't your affair."

Rycroft's jowls wobbled in indignation, proving that he couldn't entirely ignore Willie and the others, no matter how much he pretended to.

"I'll see you swing, Glass," Payne snarled. "Be it here or back home, makes no difference to me."

Miss Glass gasped and pressed a hand to her chest. One

of the Glass girls whimpered while their mother flapped a handkerchief in front of her face.

"*Do* something, Richard," she begged her husband. But Lord Rycroft merely glared down his nose at Payne with righteous indignation and said nothing.

Duke and Cyclops grabbed Payne by the arms and hauled him backward, dragging his heels on the carpet. His feet scrabbled for purchase and he tried to struggle free, but could not. His hat fell off and Bristow picked it up. They got him to the door when the clock on the mantel chimed. Payne glanced at it and blinked.

Then, as if the chime triggered something, his anger vanished. His brittle, harsh chuckle filled the silence. "I know your secret," he blurted out as they dragged him from the room. "I know you need your watch. I know what it does."

Oh no.

"How do you know?" Willie snapped.

Matt's hand whipped out and grasped her arm. He must have squeezed hard because she winced.

Payne's protests finally quieted, and the front door opened and closed. A strained silence followed in which no one seemed to know what to do or say. Lord Rycroft finally broke it.

"Come, Beatrice, we're leaving."

"No," Matt said. "Stay. He's gone now. You have nothing to fear, Uncle."

"Afraid of some crackpot American?" He snorted and puffed out his chest. "Hardly. Beatrice, the choice is yours."

Lady Rycroft blinked back tears and looked at each of her daughters, although her gaze settled longest on Hope.

"Let's stay, Mama," Hope said. "I'm sure he won't come back now he's said his piece."

That settled it, and there was no more discussion of leaving. Lady Abbington arrived seven minutes later, blissfully unaware of the drama that preceded her. She sailed into the drawing room with all the serenity and grace that Miss Glass claimed she possessed. I quickly learned that she had not overstated Lady Abbington's charms or beauty. Her fair hair had been elegantly arranged with a string of pearls woven through it, and her deep violet gown showed off a tiny waist and creamy skin at her throat.

But it was the confidence with which she held herself that caught my attention. After introductions, she easily fell into conversation with both of Matt's aunts and his uncle, none of whom mentioned Payne's visit. Matt stood with them, part of the conversation yet not contributing, and hardly glancing Lady Abbington's way. His mind was elsewhere. On Payne, no doubt. He absently touched his breast pocket where he kept the watch, proving my point.

I could tell from Willie, Duke and Cyclops's silences that they thought about Payne too. I wished we could all discuss his accusation, but that would have to wait. For now, I was left with troubled thoughts flitting through my head. Surely Payne couldn't possibly know about Matt's watch—not for certain. He must have been guessing, based on what he'd witnessed a few weeks ago when he'd spied Matt using his watch in the carriage, early one evening. Whether he knew magic was involved, I couldn't be sure, but he did seem to presume the watch was important to Matt.

The dinner gong finally sounded, and we headed into the dining room. Miss Glass blamed the odd numbers and balance of genders on her nieces being present, something which made her sister-in-law bristle and Hope dismiss with laughter.

She stopped laughing, however, when she saw that she was seated at one end of the dining table and Matt at the other. Her mother pursed her lips and looked as if she would protest the arrangement when Charity piped up.

"Do swap seats with me, Hope," she said from where she sat on Matt's side. "You know I can't abide being so near the fireplace."

"The fire has been extinguished," Miss Glass told her.

"But I still don't like sitting near fireplaces, Aunt Letitia. It's the mantelpieces, you know." Charity didn't wait for a response but simply moved to the opposite end of the table.

Hope tried to smile and pretend not to be embarrassed but the candlelight picked out her blush. Dipping her head, she walked calmly to her sister's vacated chair and sat.

At first I thought Charity had conspired to help her sister sit near Matt and then I realized that Hope had been next to Cyclops. Charity smiled at him as she sank onto Hope's vacated chair.

"Wasn't it thrilling when that sheriff fellow intruded?" she said quietly. Sitting on Cyclops's other side, I could hear her perfectly. "You were so brave, Mr. Cyclops, and so strong. Just like a pirate."

He swallowed and signaled to Bristow to fill his wine glass.

I bit my lip to stop myself smiling. It felt good to find something to smile about this evening, although I doubted Cyclops would appreciate it. I looked up and caught Matt watching me, one eyebrow raised in question. I slid my eyes sideways to indicate that I smiled at Cyclops's predicament. He must have understood because he smirked too. Both Hope and Lady Abbington noticed our silent communication.

"What did the sheriff want?" Charity asked. "And what did he mean, Cousin Matthew needs his watch?"

"Who knows?" Cyclops said. "Your father's right; he's soft in the head."

I wondered if Matt was enduring similar questions down his end of the table. Hope appeared to carry much of the conversation, distracting Matt from Lady Abbington on his other side. She, however, couldn't keep her gaze off him and eventually managed to steal his attention away from Hope.

But not for long. "Hope, dear," Lady Rycroft said loudly from across the table. "Tell Matthew about Rycroft and how it looks so lovely in the summer. Oh, and tell him how many horses your father keeps in the stables."

The room fell silent.

Hope's eyes fluttered closed and she drew in a deep breath, as if fortifying herself. Then she began to tell Matt how the lake glistened in the sunshine and was perfect for picnics or boating.

"All of it will be Matthew's one day," Lady Rycroft said to Lady Abbington, again, loud enough for everyone to hear. "He's going to cast my poor girls out of their home unless he marries one of them."

"Mama," Hope said on a groan.

Patience dipped her head, but not before I saw her cheeks flush crimson.

"Don't be so dramatic, Beatrice," Miss Glass said with a shake of her head. To Lady Abbington, she added, "My sister-in-law likes to exaggerate. Patience is to be wed soon, and I'm quite sure offers will be made to Charity and Hope shortly too. Particularly Hope. Men seem to like her. And, of course, my nephew insists on marrying for love." The unspoken message that he hadn't fallen in love with his cousins hung in the air.

Lady Rycroft stared at Miss Glass as if she couldn't quite believe her own sister-in-law had publicly thwarted her. Then she appealed to her husband.

Lord Rycroft attacked his soup with vigor, slurping spoonful after spoonful so he couldn't talk.

"Matthew is quite the romantic," Miss Glass went on,

seemingly oblivious to the tension she'd caused. "Where do you stand on the notion of marrying for love, Marianne?"

Lady Abbington seemed caught off guard for a brief moment, but quickly recovered. "I think it a very noble idea, and certainly romantic, but it's not always practical."

"Precisely," Lady Rycroft said. "Love may be well and good for the lower classes, but not us."

"I do think it possible on rare occasions," Lady Abbington went on. "Marrying for love works best where both halves of the union bring something equal to the marriage and no one benefits more than the other. That way neither husband nor wife feels as though they were taken advantage of, and love can run its course."

"Very wise, Marianne," Miss Glass said. "Don't you agree, Matthew?"

"Indeed," he said. "Speaking of marriage, tell us about your fiancé, Patience."

Patience spoke quietly yet enthusiastically about Lord Cox, and even more enthusiastically about his four children. It was clear that she adored them and was relishing becoming an instant mother upon her marriage to their father.

"There," Miss Glass said when she paused, "now that is a love match."

"Because it is equal," Lady Abbington noted. "Congratulations, Patience, you seem to have secured a rare opportunity. I hope your sisters are as fortunate. And you, Miss Steele, Miss Willie?"

"I ain't marrying," Willie declared. "I ain't going to be no man's slave, at his beck and call."

Charity snorted into her wine glass.

"Miss Steele?" Lady Abbington asked. "What do you think about marrying for love?"

"I agree with you," I said. "A happy marriage based on

love can only succeed between equals, but not for the reasons you state, in my opinion. When two people are in love, neither will feel as though they were taken advantage of, because both *did* bring something equal to the union —love."

She conceded this point with a small shrug. Even that was elegantly effortless. "But?"

Matt set down his knife and fork and regarded me intently.

"But there are rarely just two people to consider in a marriage," I went on. "There are obligations, particularly for the party with the least to gain, and the futures of other family members must be taken into account."

"Quite so," Lady Rycroft said with an arched look at her sister-in-law.

I studiously avoided looking at Miss Glass. She would feel that I'd betrayed her. It was Matt, however, who spoke up.

"I disagree, India. One should not consider the opinions of family when it comes to marriage. That way leads to unhappiness for both parties."

"I'm not advocating that people who despise one another should marry," I said. "Not at all. But I do think love cannot last against external forces, not in the long term. It's too much pressure, particularly for the party whose station was raised by an advantageous marriage. She—or he—would feel guilt eventually, and that might poison the love felt in the beginning."

"Well said." Lady Abbington applauded lightly.

"I believe there must be a balance between feeling and obligation," I clarified.

"As do I. Mr. Glass? What do you say?"

Matt studied me with a brief yet intense gaze. Then he picked up his knife and fork. "I say we change the topic."

"I agree." Willie signaled to Bristow to fill her wine glass.

"There ain't no such thing as love, anyway. It's something poets made up in the old days to get under ladies' skirts."

"Willimena!" Miss Glass scolded.

The grooves drooping from Lady Rycroft's mouth deepened, and she shook her head. "Close your ears to such crassness, girls."

Both Hope and Charity appeared to be trying not to laugh, but Patience's face flamed. Willie looked as if she would shoot back a retort, but I shook my head at her, and she closed her mouth again with a roll of her eyes.

Lord Rycroft saluted her with his glass. "Never thought I would agree with an American woman who dresses like a man and sounds like she just crawled out of the gutter, but I do."

"Well," Lady Rycroft said with forced cheerfulness. "We'll be traveling soon to Rycroft for the wedding, and I cannot wait to go home. I do miss my friends and neighbors there. So few come to London, nowadays. Have you found that, Marianne?"

Lady Abbington and Lady Rycroft fell into a discussion about the London social scene, leaving Hope to occupy Matt's attention. I was sure Lady Rycroft angled it that way on purpose.

The dinner seemed to last an age and then it felt like another age as we ladies waited in the drawing room for the men to rejoin us. Conversations were stilted, and to make matters worse, Willie had gone with the men. I had no ally. I got up to inspect the clock on the mantel. It ran perfectly on time, but perhaps I ought to check the mechanisms anyway. If nothing else, it was something to do.

The gentlemen and Willie rejoined us then, but only briefly. Miss Glass, who'd been perfectly fine all night, called Matt by his father's name, and begged him to stay home or their father would grow angry.

Charity snickered behind her hand.

"Stop it, Letitia," Lord Rycroft hissed at his sister. "You're making a fool of yourself."

She didn't seem to hear him.

"Come with me, Miss Glass," I said, taking her by the elbow. She leaned heavily on me, but she was so frail that I bore her weight easily. I helped her up the stairs then sent for her maid.

When Polly arrived, I went to my own room, not the drawing room. I wouldn't be missed and I found the entire evening so frustrating. My nerves needed to do something calming. I sat at my desk and opened the housing on my watch. It was working perfectly fine but tinkering with it made me feel a little better.

Someone knocked lightly on my door fifteen minutes later. I opened it to Matt, his hair disheveled as if he'd run his hands through it over and over. The whites of his eyes sported tiny red webs and his skin looked pale in the light of his lamp.

"They're gone," he said simply.

"All of them? Already?"

He nodded. "That was a trying evening. I don't blame you for not returning, but prepare for Willie's ire. She thinks you abandoned her."

That made me smile. "You sound as though you didn't enjoy yourself."

He simply tilted his head to the side.

"And it was all for you, too," I said. "You didn't enjoy Lady Abbington's company?"

He lifted one shoulder. "She seems pleasant."

"Lady Rycroft will be happy to hear you describe her as merely pleasant. Her conniving worked."

"I think it was Charity's conniving to sit next to Cyclops that started the evening off on an...interesting note."

"How is he?"

"Recovering with a stiff drink in the drawing room. Want to join us? We were about to talk about Payne, but I thought you should be there."

I didn't want to leave my watch with its innards on my desk so I scooped them up, and the watch too, and followed him downstairs to the drawing room.

"O-ho!" Willie cried, hand on hip. "The prodigal daughter returns."

"Take her with you, next time," Duke begged me. "She grumbled the second you left and didn't let up until all the guests departed."

"How is Miss Glass?" Cyclops asked.

"I left her in Polly's hands. Hopefully a rest will do her good." I glanced at Matt and almost told him that a rest would do him good too, but I refrained. I didn't want to feel the heat of his glare.

"So what do you think Payne meant?" Duke asked as he poured brandy into glasses at the sideboard. "Do you think he knows?"

"Not about magic," I said, spreading the pieces of my watch out on my lap. "He couldn't possibly." I shook my head as Duke offered me a glass.

"I agree," Matt said quietly. "Even if he's spoken to Abercrombie and Hardacre about me, they don't know my watch is magical. No one does, except us."

"And Chronos," Cyclops said. "But Payne won't know about him."

"So he can't possibly know the particulars," I said. "All he does know is what he witnessed that day when you used your watch in the carriage."

"That holding my watch makes my veins turn purple," Matt finished.

"There. It's settled. He was bluffing. It's something you

Americans are good at."

"It's all the poker," Willie said with a nod. "Damn it, I wish I had my gun on me when he burst in. I wouldn't have killed him," she protested when we all glared at her. "Just made it so the bullet grazed him."

Duke swirled his brandy around the glass. "And frightened the ladies half to death."

"Maybe it would have sent them away." She sounded as if she were storing up that piece of information for a future dinner party.

I bent into the lamplight and slotted the final spring back into place. "Payne seemed rattled enough without the need for your Colt, Willie." I looked up to see Matt watching me. Or, rather, watching what I was doing.

"He didn't like that Matt spoke to Munro about him," Cyclops said. "He probably wasn't expecting Munro to give Matt the benefit of the doubt."

"Because Payne doesn't know that Daniel Gibbons was Munro's son," Willie said. "Thank God for that."

Matt dug his forefinger and thumb into his eyes. I cleared my throat and his hand dropped away. I screwed the housing shut on the back of my watch and closed my fist around it then arched my brows at him.

He pulled his watch out of his inside pocket and tipped his head back. The watch glowed, pulsing as if it were alive, and purple light flowed along his veins, disappearing into his hair. A moment later, he returned the watch to his pocket and his veins stopped glowing. His gray pallor had been banished, but he still looked tired.

The others must have agreed because they all decided at once that it was time for bed. Duke finished his brandy and Willie bade everyone goodnight. I got up to follow her, but Matt grabbed my hand as I passed.

"Stay," he murmured.

Cyclops narrowed his gaze at me. "Just for a moment," I told both him and Matt. "I'm too tired to stay up long."

Cyclops shut the door, leaving Matt and me alone.

"Is everything all right?" I asked.

"I'm not sure." Matt stood and gently took my hand. He opened my fisted fingers to reveal my watch. "Is something wrong with it?"

"No."

He palmed my hand. My breath hitched and his warmth seeped through my skin. Magical warmth, I realized with a start. My magic was responding to the magic his watch injected into his body. "Then why did you pull it apart?" he asked.

"I don't really know. I simply felt like it. Tonight was... frustrating, and working on timepieces soothes me."

"I see."

I studied the watch on my palm. "I think it's the methodical and precise nature of the work. It occupies my mind as well as my hands. Although I know my watch so well now, I could probably do it without thinking." I forced myself to stop rambling. "Was there anything else you wanted to talk to me about?"

His thumb caressed mine, the stroke slow and languid. It was a motion that ought to soothe, but it sent my heart into a frenzy. I still could not look up at his face.

"India, what you said at dinner about marriage—"

I whipped my hand away and placed both behind my back. "Let's not discuss it. We'll just have to agree to disagree on this score."

"For now."

"What does that mean? You can't change my mind, and I can't change yours."

"We'll discuss it later, when the time is more relevant."

"Relevant to what?"

He strode to the door and opened it for me. "Goodnight, India."

"You can't refuse to answer me, Matt. That's not fair. Particularly when *you* asked *me* to stay behind."

"You're right. I actually wanted to tell you that I'm sorry how tonight turned out. Next time, with more warning, we'll both have a chance to make our excuses."

I laughed. "If you think your aunt will let you get out of it, you're sorely mistaken. I, however, am irrelevant to her purposes. I might enjoy a night out at the theater with the others instead. Something amusing, perhaps even bawdy. Willie would love that."

I walked off and he followed me, grabbing a lamp off the table. "You would not only abandon me to the ladies but you would take all my allies with you?"

I nodded and headed up the stairs. "That way you can get to know Lady Abbington properly. And Hope too, of course."

He pressed his lips together and remained silent until we arrived at my room. I reached for the doorknob but his hand beat mine. His face drew close. His eyes gleamed in the light from the lamp.

"I wish I knew what you thought about that, India," he murmured, his voice rich and low, "but I find myself at a loss to read your mind for once."

My throat went dry. I tried to swallow but it didn't help. "I'm so glad I'm not entirely predictable and dull," I quipped, hoping he couldn't see the heat in my cheeks and the desire in my eyes.

One side of his mouth kicked up. "You are anything but dull. I find you utterly fascinating."

Oh my. I tried to think of something witty to say but my mind went completely blank.

He opened the door, bringing his face even closer to mine. His breath ruffled my hair. "Goodnight, India."

"Goodnight, Matt. Sleep well."

* * *

DR. RITTER REFUSED to see us until Matt told him that his journalist friend would write a negative piece on the hospital's negligence in their treatment of Mrs. Oakshot.

"The power of the newspapers," Matt whispered to me as a nurse led us through to Dr. Ritter's office.

The office was twice the size of Dr. Hale's. His bookshelves were covered with books and journals, rather than medicine bottles, and a portrait of the queen looked down upon his bald head as he sat behind his desk.

He did not shake Matt's hand or welcome us, but he stood to greet us with his knuckles pressed to the desk surface. "Mrs. Oakshot's death was an unfortunate mistake committed by Dr. Hale," he said in a loud voice. "It's not the hospital's fault, and your friend should not report otherwise. Do you hear?"

"We only want to ask questions," Matt said. "If you agreed to see us we wouldn't have needed to resort to desperate measures."

"Is it that Barratt fellow from *The Weekly Gazette*? It wouldn't surprise me. He writes some liberal nonsense."

"Why did you tell Mr. Oakshot that Dr. Hale gave Mrs. Oakshot the incorrect dose of morphine?"

Dr. Ritter straightened slowly, the bluster gone from his manner. "I didn't *tell* him anything."

"You implied, so Mr. Oakshot claims."

"That discussion was private and none of your affair." He sat and studied the papers laid out on his desk. "Please leave. I'm busy."

"You had no right to tell him that," I said. "He was a grieving man, looking for someone to blame."

"And he found someone. No harm was done, Miss Steele."

"No harm! He is a suspect in the murder of Dr. Hale, and if he is found guilty, it is your fault. Can you live with yourself if his children become orphans?"

"Get out," he snarled.

Matt caught my elbow. Perhaps he was afraid I would leap across the desk and slap Dr. Ritter, or perhaps he simply didn't want to leave yet. "The thing is, Dr. Ritter, you are a suspect too."

"I beg your pardon!" he spluttered.

"You had access to Dr. Hale's bottle of Cure-All, you're a doctor so have knowledge of medicines and poisons, and you argued with Dr. Hale before his death."

"I did not argue with him, I dismissed him from his position. He accepted my decision."

"Did he?" Matt said. "Or did he threaten you, and you realized you needed to silence him?"

"Threaten me with what?"

Matt shrugged. "I'm sure he could find something that the newspapers would be interested to report on."

Dr. Ritter's lips pressed together so hard they turned white. "Get. Out!"

Matt steered me toward the door and we exited in a hurry.

"We didn't learn anything," I said, "but I do feel better. He ought to know the damage he has potentially caused by telling Mr. Oakshot about Dr. Hale's incompetence."

"I agree," Matt said. "Dr. Wiley!" he called as the doctor entered the corridor ahead. "May we have a word?"

Dr. Wiley glanced past us, then behind him. He looked as if he wanted to turn and walk off, but he remained. He even managed a tentative smile.

"It's Miss Steele and Mr. Glass, isn't it?" he said. "Are you here for medical reasons?"

"Nothing like that," Matt said. "We're helping the police with their investigation into Dr. Hale's death." Matt made it sound as if we were doing it officially. The changed tactic worked better than the previous one. Dr. Wiley didn't argue and nor did he try to escape.

"You want to question me further?" He grasped his clipboard to his chest. "Detective Inspector Brockwell has already questioned me thoroughly. I don't have anything more to add." A nurse bustled past and he watched her until she was out of earshot then he leaned toward us. "I had nothing to do with Hale's death. I'm not even convinced it was murder. He probably did it to himself."

"Why would he do that?" Matt asked.

"Out of guilt for his part in a patient's death, or shame for losing his job here. Or, if you are looking for someone else to blame, you should investigate the widower of that patient, a Mr. Oakshot. He was extremely aggressive toward Dr. Hale after his wife's death." He held up a finger. "I've just thought of another who was angry with Hale."

"Who?" I asked.

"A fellow by the name of Clark from the Apothecary's Guild."

I sucked in a breath. Murder and magic seemed to always lead to the guilds. "But Dr. Hale was no longer a part of that guild," I said. "He wasn't a practicing apothecary anymore."

"Nevertheless, Mr. Clark was here not long after you that day, as it happens. He spoke to Hale in his office and did not look at all happy when he came out. One of the nurses heard raised voices but couldn't hear the actual exchange."

"Was Dr. Hale seen alive after Mr. Clark left?"

Dr. Wiley nodded. "I spoke to him myself. We had to discuss his patients, you see, since I would take over many of them until a replacement could be employed. I told the police all this."

"And they will appreciate you repeating it for me," Matt said. "Can you tell us where you were after your meeting with Dr. Hale?"

He bristled. "I was with a patient until six then I went home."

"Can anyone verify that?"

"My signature on the patient's medical chart. I signed it and wrote the time just before I left. Ask the nurse at the desk to show it to you. Tell her I authorized it."

"Thank you, Dr. Wiley."

He continued on his way along the corridor and we headed in the other direction. "What do you think of the fellow named Clark from the Apothecary's Guild speaking to Hale?" I said quietly.

"I think we must visit him next. But first, let's confirm Wiley's story."

I left it to Matt to ask the nurse on duty for any charts Dr. Wiley had signed the afternoon of Hale's death. He was good at that sort of thing and she agreeably fetched them for us. We pored over the paperwork and confirmed that Wiley signed a patient's chart at five minutes to six.

"Wait a moment," I said, studying the list of names and times. "There's a signature after his written at five forty-five. Shouldn't these notes be in chronological order? Someone seeing the patient before him should have signed above Wiley not below."

Matt posed this question to the nurse and she confirmed it with a frown. "That's my signature," she said. "I don't lie, sir, I promise you, but I don't look at the times that were signed above mine unless I need to give the patient medicine at a regular interval." She tapped the line on the chart where she'd signed. "I just checked his pulse."

"Dr. Wiley must have read the clock incorrectly," Matt said gently. "Nothing to worry about."

"That must be it." Her mouth twisted to the side and her frown deepened.

"Did you also see a man named Clark talk to Dr. Hale in his office that afternoon?"

"I did, sir. He left Dr. Hale's office with a black look in his eyes, muttering under his breath."

"What about?"

"I only caught a few words. Something about talking to that reporter fellow. That's all I heard."

Matt thanked her and we headed out of the hospital to our waiting carriage.

"So Wiley wasn't with the patient when he claimed he was and he deliberately lied about it," I said.

"It would appear so. The question is, why?"

"And what else has he lied about?"

"Do you know where the Apothecary's Guild hall is?" Matt asked Bryce.

"Aye, sir, it's in Black Friars Lane."

"Drive us there now."

Twenty minutes later we arrived at the guild hall's grand colonnaded entrance. The obligatory coat of arms above the closed arched doors depicted a golden man with bow and arrow in hand, the sun's rays radiating from his head. Unicorns crouched on either side of him.

"Why the unicorns?" I asked Matt as we waited for his knock to be answered.

"I don't know, but I think the figure is Apollo, the Greek god of medicine, among other things."

"If I had a coat of arms, I'd like unicorns on it, too. They're so much more impressive than horses."

He laughed softly but schooled his features when the door opened. A liveried porter welcomed us through to the courtyard beyond. The building rose three levels high on all sides of the courtyard with a staircase at the back leading up to a door. A youth lounged against a lamp post in the center of the yard, an open book in hand.

"We're looking for Mr. Clark," Matt said to the porter. "We believe he's a member here."

"He's the guild master, sir," the footman said.

"Is he here at the moment?"

"He is, sir, but I'm afraid he's busy. Would you like to wait?"

"We would."

"And you are?"

"Mr. and Mrs. Wild. My American-based company wishes to discuss the potential supply of medicines from the guild. I was given Mr. Clark's name by an associate."

The porter's eyes lit up. "I'm sure Mr. Clark will be available to talk to you very soon." He called out to the youth. "Cartwright, show Mr. and Mrs. Wild to the parlor."

Cartwright tucked his book under his arm and smiled. He couldn't have been more than eighteen with his slender build and tuft of pale hair struggling to make an impact on his chin. He led the way to the staircase with long, purposeful strides until Matt asked him to slow down, for my sake.

I glared at him to show that I was perfectly capable of keeping up and he winked at me.

"My apologies, Mrs. Wild," the lad said. "Mr. Clark says I'm always in a hurry too."

"Are you his apprentice?" Matt asked.

"I am *an* apprentice, but not his."

"Is he a good fellow?"

Cartwright narrowed his gaze at Matt as he opened the door at the top of the steps. "He's an excellent apothecary. He oversees production of the medicines here."

"The guild produces its own on the premises?"

"Yes, sir, in the cellar. We supply to some large organizations, including the Royal Navy, Army and the East India

Company. Mr. Clark oversees it all. Your company will be in good hands, sir."

"I'll take that on board when making my decision. I haven't decided if I want to go with Oakshot's, or perhaps even a smaller company, like Pitt's."

"Sir, I would caution you not to go with either."

"Why?"

"Mr. Pitt's operation is not equipped for a large international order. While his reputation is fair, and he has a loyal base of customers, he's simply not set up for mass production. And while Mr. Oakshot is considered to be an excellent apothecary…well, there's something not quite right about him, sir." He indicated a door and we entered, but he did not.

"What do you mean?" Matt asked.

"It's hard to say, but Mr. Clark doesn't like Mr. Oakshot, and if Mr. Clark doesn't like someone, there's a good reason. I'll go and tell Mr. Clark you're here, shall I?"

"Yes, of course. Oh, just one thing. I seem to have broken my watch." Matt patted his jacket at his chest. What was he up to? "Do you know a good watch repairer?"

"You could ask at the Watchmaker's Guild hall, sir. It's in Warwick Lane, not far from here."

"Do you know the master there?"

"It's a Mr. Abercrombie."

"You've met him?"

"Several times. He sometimes dines here with Mr. Clark." With a jerky nod, the lad hurried off.

"Very cleverly done, Matt," I said.

"Thank you," he said. "So it seems we have a connection between the two guilds."

"It may mean nothing." If it meant nothing, why did my heart pound and my head spin with possibilities?

"Or it may mean they exchange information about certain topics. Magic, for instance. I'm glad we used assumed names."

He inspected the floor-to-ceiling glass cabinet of medicine jars while I stood by the long case clock. It had a lovely gold face, with black hands and numerals, and a gold lock. I wondered if the key was kept nearby.

"You want to open it up, don't you?" Matt murmured, suddenly standing behind me.

"I thought you were inspecting those jars."

"There are only so many medicine labels one can read before growing bored." He removed a glove and touched the lock. "Shall we look for the key?"

"The porter probably has it. He looked very responsible and not the sort to leave a long case clock unlocked. Anyone could come along and tamper with it."

"You may not believe this, India, but there are very few people who would tamper with a clock. We don't all want to dissect them."

A small man entered, his steps quick and neat. Slender fingers did up his jacket buttons then smoothed an errant strand of hair into place. He sported a cleanly shaved face and sky blue eyes that darted between me and Matt. He shook Matt's hand and introduced himself as Mr. Josiah Clark the guild master.

"Please take a seat," he said. "Let's see what I can do for you, Mr. Wild. Cartwright tells me you own a company in America. What is it your company does?"

"Actually, I have a confession to make," Matt said. "I told your porter and apprentice that so I could meet you."

Mr. Clark's face fell. He glanced at the door. Matt rose and shut it then sat again.

"Mrs. Wild and I are private inquiry agents helping the police in their investigation into Dr. Hale's death."

Mr. Clark shot to his feet. "Get out."

"Sit down, Mr. Clark, or I'll be inclined to tell Detective Inspector Brockwell that you were not helpful and that perhaps he should look into your operation here."

"My operation! There is nothing illegal going on here."

"No doubt Brockwell told you that Dr. Hale was murdered."

"I haven't spoken to the police, and nor do I expect to."

Matt glanced at me.

"I've done nothing wrong, Mr. Wild, if that's what your name really is."

"You had an argument with Dr. Hale on the day of his death," Matt said. "What did you argue about?"

"That is none of your affair!"

"Mr. Clark, you don't seem to realize, but I will report your reluctance to cooperate to Detective Inspector Brockwell. He won't look kindly upon your silence. If you truly have nothing to hide, then just tell the truth."

Mr. Clark looked longingly at the door then sighed. He sat again. "Dr. Hale's name appeared in the newspapers that morning. He'd reportedly performed a medical miracle. I wanted to know more about it, how he'd brought that patient back to life, that sort of thing."

"And what did you learn?"

"That he didn't perform any sort of miracle. The patient was still alive at the time he administered the medicine."

"So if that was all, why did you argue with him?"

Mr. Clark swallowed and his gaze darted to the door again. "He's defaming the good name of the guild through his ridiculous claims."

"But the guild was never mentioned in the article, and he's not even a member anymore."

"He was stripped of his membership that day, as it happens. We called a special meeting and voted him out."

"That day?" I echoed. "Because of the article?"

Mr. Clark lifted one shoulder and let it drop.

"Or because of his magic?" Matt said.

Mr. Clark paled and his eyes became huge. "H-how…wh-what do you mean?"

"Don't pretend you know nothing about magic. You knew Hale was an apothecary magician, and you were glad when he became a doctor. But then you read that article in *The Weekly Gazette* and you became worried that Hale was telling people about magic. After speaking to him, you realized he wanted to bring magic into the open through articles like the one Mr. Barratt wrote. That worried you, didn't it? Because if the public learnt that some medicines can be infused with magic, they'd only want to go to those pharmacists, not the artless ones like yourself."

Every word acted like a shove to Mr. Clark's chest, pushing him further back in his armchair until it looked as if it would swallow him. "He had to be stopped!"

Matt leaned forward, his eyes bright. I could hardly believe it myself—the Apothecary's Guild master was admitting to knowing about magic.

"What Hale wanted to achieve was madness. Sheer madness," Mr. Clark said in a high voice. "The public can't find out. Thousands of pharmacists around the country would lose their customers."

"So you killed him," Matt said.

"No!" Mr. Clark leapt up, and Matt stood too. "Of course not. I told him to cease talking to reporters, particularly that Barratt fellow." He shook his finger at Matt. "If you're looking for a murderer, you should investigate *him*."

"Why?" I asked.

"Because Hale said Barratt was desperate for magicians to tell him about their magic, and Hale felt as if he couldn't get out of it." Mr. Clark spoke quickly, the words tripping over themselves as they tumbled from his lips. "Perhaps he told

Barratt that he no longer wanted to be mentioned in his articles and Barratt became furious."

"That's ridiculous," I said.

"Dr. Hale was alive when I left the hospital," he said. "I do know that much."

I thought Matt would question him about his connection to Abercrombie, but he did not. "Good day, Mr. Clark. Thank you for your time."

We left, walking quickly down the steps and through the courtyard to the entrance where the porter let us out with a smile.

"Home," Matt said to Bryce, climbing into the cabin behind me. "So what do you think, India? Is Clark guilty?"

"I'm not sure, but I'm highly suspicious. Thank goodness we didn't tell him our names, because I'm sure he'll mention this visit to Abercrombie."

"If he tells Abercrombie an American and Englishwoman visited to discuss magic, Abercrombie will work it out."

I clutched my reticule tighter.

"Stay close to me, India."

I nodded. "It'll be all right, though. Abercrombie simply organized one kidnapping. He hasn't…"

"Killed anyone?" he finished for me. "Not that we know of."

We traveled in silence until we were almost at Park Street. My mind was on the link between Abercrombie and Clark, but Matt's had wandered in a different direction, going by his next statement.

"We now know that Oakshot is one of the best apothecaries," he said. "It could be an indication that he's a magician."

The coach slowed, and Matt alighted first to fold the step down for me. He held out his hand, and I was about to take it when a small boy walked past, very close, and bumped against him.

Matt remained balanced but he turned quickly to confront the lad, only for the boy to stumble into him again.

"Are you unwell?" Matt asked him.

The boy tucked his hands beneath his armpits, shrugged, and ran off.

"Is he all right?" I asked, craning my neck to see. "He looked half starved."

"Bloody hell!" Matt growled. "He stole my watch!"

CHAPTER 8

*M*att sprinted after the lad.

"Thief!" I shouted. "Stop that boy!" But the two ladies strolling down Park Street merely shuffled aside as the lad passed, not so much as lifting a foot to trip him.

The boy disappeared around the corner with Matt several paces behind. Too far behind. He would not be able to catch a nimble boy who could disappear into a crowd or slip through an open window. A heavy weight settled in my stomach. If Matt couldn't catch him and retrieve his watch...

Bristow joined me on the pavement. "Miss Steele? Is something wrong?"

"A pickpocket stole Matt's watch."

"I saw him! He's been waiting nearby for an hour."

"Waiting where?"

"He started in this very spot until I moved him on. He went only as far the neighbor's." He shook his head. "I should have got him to clear off altogether."

If only he had.

"It was as if he was waiting here on purpose," Bristow said.

Waiting for Matt. The lad had been paid by someone to steal Matt's magic watch. My stomach churned at the thought.

"Please have luncheon ready for Mr. Glass's return," I said to Bristow. "He'll be back soon."

Did I believe it? I wasn't sure. I hoped and prayed, but the knot of dread in my chest tightened with every passing second. If Matt didn't get his watch back, he would sicken and die.

Bristow climbed the steps and Bryce drove off. I considered ordering him to chase down the thief, but a small child could go places a coach could not.

A chilly breeze whipped down the street. I shivered and hugged myself. Pedestrians passed me. Time ticked slowly by.

And finally I saw Matt rounding the corner ahead. I ran to him and met him half way. He looked worried. The knot in my stomach tightened more.

"Matt!" I grasped him by the shoulders and searched his face. He looked exhausted but not anxious.

"I caught him," he said "but let him keep the watch."

My mouth dropped open.

"It was my regular watch, India, not my other one."

I patted his jacket at his chest and felt the reassuring lump of his magic watch, safely tucked in the inside pocket. My eyes fluttered closed and I sucked in a shaky breath.

"The only way a pickpocket could get that one is if I'm unconscious," Matt said. "That's why I keep it in a buttoned down pocket. India, are you all right?" He took my hand. "You look pale."

"I thought it was your other one," I said weakly. "And when you disappeared, I thought you might never catch him and… I think you know where my thoughts ran after that."

He tucked my hand into the crook of his arm and steered

me toward the house. I was grateful for his steadying presence. "I'm sorry I didn't clarify before chasing after him. The reason I took so long is because I questioned the boy thoroughly before letting him go."

"You let him go *and* you let him keep your watch."

"He's a child, India. I couldn't turn him over to the constables. He needs the money that watch will bring more than I need the watch."

I sighed. "I know. But I think he was after your other one. Bristow said the boy's been here for some time."

He nodded. "He told me he was paid by a gentleman to wait for me then steal my watch. If it had been a random event, I would have dismissed it, but he blurted out about the gentleman as soon as I caught him."

"Did he describe him to you?"

"He said it was just a gentleman who looked like any other. Neither old nor young, tall nor short, fat nor thin. He had no distinguishing marks that the boy can recall, and no accent."

"So it's not Payne."

"Or Payne disguised his accent, or perhaps paid someone else to approach the boy. That's what he does, removes himself as far as possible from the scene of the crime and everyone connected to it. That's how he gets away with it, by disassociating himself, so that when his name is linked, he can call those intermediaries liars."

I tightened my grip on his arm. "It may not have been Payne."

"I can't think of anyone else who suspects my watch is important."

"Chronos knows. He doesn't want to speak to you, so perhaps he wants to remove the watch from you altogether, for reasons not yet clear to us. And then there's Abercrombie. When he ordered those thugs to kidnap you to stop you meeting Mirth at the bank, he left the watch with you, so he knows it's important."

"But not that it keeps me alive. He doesn't know it's anything other than a regular watch with sentimental value. If he didn't want it then, he wouldn't want it now. My money's still on Payne."

Matt plodded up the front steps to the house and suppressed a yawn as Bristow took his hat. We ate a quick luncheon with his aunt before he retired to his rooms for a much needed rest. Miss Glass and I sat quietly talking as we did our needlepoint. My nerves had calmed somewhat, after the shock of the theft, but at least our conversation kept my thoughts from wandering in that direction overmuch. If they had, I might feel worried all over again.

"Veronica," Miss Glass said to me after an hour sitting together, "when will Harry be back?"

I set my embroidery hoop down on the seat beside me and rose. I took her hands in mine and smiled. "Soon," I told her. "Now, let me take you to your room. You need a rest."

She touched her temple. "I do feel a little tired." Miss Glass's episodes of confusion occurred when she was either tired or overwrought. She usually seemed better after a nap.

I returned to the sitting room after sending Miss Glass's maid up to her mistress, but I was soon disturbed by the arrival of a visitor.

"Mr. Barratt! What a surprise," I said, greeting him.

"Not an unpleasant one, I hope," the journalist said.

"Not at all, but I'm afraid Mr. Glass is indisposed at the moment."

"Then I'll speak with you alone." His eyes shone with good humor. "What a happy outcome for me."

I smiled and indicated he should sit. "Bring tea, please, Bristow."

The butler left and Mr. Barratt sat on the armchair. "I

wasn't expecting to see you here, Miss Steele. Shouldn't you be with Mr. Glass, attending to business matters in his office?"

I hadn't said that Matt was attending to business matters, or that he was in his office. Mr. Barratt was fishing. While I wouldn't tell him Matt was resting, I had no qualms telling him about our domestic arrangements. "I live here," I said. "I act as companion to Matt's aunt when he has no need of me."

"Indeed? So you see a great deal of him?"

"It's unavoidable."

"Even in a house this size?"

I laughed. "There are only six bedrooms, not including the servants' bedchambers in the attic. Not at all large, compared to some."

He laughed too. "Not in my world, Miss Steele."

"Nor mine. It's quite a difference to the rooms above my father's watch and clock shop. After his death, I needed employment, and Matt needed an assistant. It worked out perfectly for me. Considering I had no experience as anyone's assistant except my father's, I'm not sure he got the same benefit from the arrangement as I did."

"I beg to differ," he said warmly. "I think he did very well out of the arrangement. Very well indeed. He does, after all, get to enjoy your company every day."

My face heated, and I tried to laugh off his flattery, but I felt his gaze on me. It was unnerving; not because I felt embarrassed by his flattery but because I liked it.

"Tell me about yourself," he said after an awkward pause. "I'd like to get to know you better."

"Why?"

"Because I like you, and that's what people do when they like one another."

"Oh. Yes. Of course." I sounded like an unsophisticated oaf.

"And you're a magician and I've met so few."

"Shhh." I glanced at the door just as Bristow entered, carrying a tray. He deposited it on a table and I poured the tea. "There's not much to tell," I said to Mr. Barratt after Bristow left. "My mother died when I was young, and my father passed just over a month ago. I've been around watches my entire life and helped him in the shop whenever I could."

"You said he was artless and you never knew you were a magician until recently. It must have come as a surprise."

He had no idea how much. When my watch had saved me, I thought I was going mad and imagining things. "Tell me, Mr. Barratt, does your magic manifest itself in ways other than the one you showed me at the *Gazette* office?"

He set his cup down and gave me his full attention. "What do you mean?"

How much should I tell him? How much could I trust him? If I wanted answers, I had to, at least a little. "What I'm going to tell you cannot be repeated to a soul. Do you understand? I don't want to read about it in your newspaper tomorrow morning."

He uncrossed his legs and leaned forward, fixing me with a curious gaze. "I promise to keep your secret, Miss Steele."

I took a sip then set down my cup too. The slight delay seemed to irk him but he did not try to rush me. "My watch saved my life once, as did a clock I worked on."

"Saved your life how?"

"I threw the clock at an assailant. It wasn't a very good throw, and would have missed him, but the clock deviated from its course and hit his head."

He sat back again, somewhat deflated. "Perhaps your aim is better than you think."

"My watch jumped out of my reticule and wrapped its

chain around the Dark Rider's wrist when he attacked me. It caused him to convulse violently."

He sat forward again and cocked his head to the side. "Jumped out?"

"Of its own accord, yes. I know it sounds odd, but I swear it happened.

"I believe you. Did you order it to...act on your behalf?"

I shook my head. "I wouldn't know how."

"Did you say anything to it? Anything at all?"

"No. It was as if it knew."

He scrubbed a hand across his jaw and studied the middle distance. "Remarkable."

"You know more about magic and magicians than anyone," I said. "Have you heard of this sort of thing happening to others?"

"No. Never. Those I have met use simple spells to work simple magic, most of which is useless—and temporary. I've heard of previous generations wielding stronger spells. No spell at all, however...that's new and very intriguing. You're special, Miss Steele."

"Is special a polite word for odd?"

He smiled. "Not on this occasion. Having a clock and watch both save you is a benefit. You're fortunate. I wonder how it works. I mean, why you? Why can't I summon ink and make it splash in someone's eyes, for example?"

"Has your life ever been in danger?"

"No."

"Perhaps that's why. Perhaps it only works when there is a threat."

He considered this for a moment then shook his head. "My father died when a runaway coach knocked him over as he crossed the road. He was an ink magician too and had a sample bottle in his pocket. It didn't save him."

"Oh. I'm sorry."

"It's quite all right, Miss Steele, but I think it disproves your theory and proves mine. You *are* special. The question is, why?"

Why indeed. "I know so little about my grandparents or great-grandparents, so perhaps I inherited it from one of them. I wish I knew more about this magic and where it came from. Not knowing is terribly frustrating."

"I can imagine." He moved to sit beside me on the sofa, so close that our knees almost touched. "There must be some people still alive who knew your grandparents. Could you speak to them?"

"About magic?" I shook my head. "It's not a good idea to bring it up with the artless."

"Why not?"

"Because they'll assume I'm asking because I've inherited my magic, and they'll fear me or despise me since they're afraid of losing customers."

"I'm not advocating drawing it to the public's attention, just a few friends."

"Aren't you? Isn't that what this meeting is about?"

He narrowed his eyes. "What do you mean?"

"You want me to help you bring magic into the open, whether through your newspapers or simply by discussing it with people. Well, Mr. Barratt?" I pressed when he didn't answer. "Isn't that true?"

He blew out a measured breath, taking his time to answer. "The cause is important to me," he said carefully. "I do want to bring magic into the open. But I sincerely wish to see you learn more about your magic, not to help me, but to help yourself. I know how frustrating it must be for you. I can't imagine not knowing where my magic came from and not being able to discuss it with like-minded magicians." He placed his hand over mine.

I stared down at it. I ought to withdraw, but I didn't want

to. "Thank you for understanding," I said. "It means a lot to me. I have no magical friends, you see, and—"

A shadow blocked the light from the doorway. I looked up to see Matt standing there, looking disheveled from his rest and startled at seeing a visitor. His gaze rose from our linked hands to my face. His jaw hardened.

"Barratt," he growled. "What are you doing here?"

I snatched my hand away.

"I came to see you," Mr. Barratt said, rising. "I've been enjoying tea with Miss Steele while you completed your business. We've been discussing her magic."

Matt strode in and stood by the fireplace. "*Your* magic, India?"

I knew from his glare that he didn't want me to talk about it with Mr. Barratt. But, despite his profession, I believed the journalist would keep my secret and only release it if I gave permission.

I poured tea for Matt and held it out to him. "Yes, my magic." I heard the hard tone in my voice and didn't regret it. He couldn't order me about on this. "It's nice to talk to other magicians about it," I added, softer. He accepted the cup but I did not let it go immediately. I held on until his gaze connected with mine again.

He lifted his chin in a nod, and I allowed him to take the cup and saucer.

"There are things only another magician can understand," Mr. Barratt said cheerfully. "Miss Steele needs a friend to talk to about it from time to time, that's all."

"And you are now that friend," Matt said tightly.

Mr. Barratt smiled.

Time to change the subject before the tension in the air stretched more. "Now that you're here, Matt, perhaps Mr. Barratt can tell us a little more about his discussion with Dr. Hale."

"Excellent idea," Matt said with far more eagerness than the situation warranted. "According to our source, Dr. Hale claimed you badgered him into talking about his magic."

"Badgered? I did no such thing. He willingly spoke to me. He thought my articles were a good way to draw out more magicians."

"That's not what we were told. Did he tell you he'd changed his mind, perhaps? Did you fight about it?"

I tried to catch Matt's eye but he would not look at me. No doubt he knew he'd find himself on the sharp end of my glare and didn't want to be spiked.

"Who is your source?" Mr. Barratt asked.

"Just answer the question," Matt said.

"Your source has it wrong. Dr. Hale and I spoke again after the newspaper article ran that morning—"

"You mean on the day he died. Why didn't you tell us you spoke to him then, too?"

"It wasn't relevant," Mr. Barratt said, his voice laced with steel. "As I was saying, we spoke about his concerns, and I assured him that the articles were vague enough that the artless would think nothing of it. In fact, we agreed that the articles were important—that finding more magicians was important—with the aim of one day going public. Like me, he was tired of hiding his magic."

"Acceptance isn't going to happen overnight," Matt said. "Getting the word out to the public will cause years of unrest between the artless and magicians. Perhaps even decades. The artless are afraid of losing their businesses, their liveli-hoods, and they're not going to sit idly by and allow magi-cians to take everything from them. You live in a fantasy world if you think that."

"I admit some adjustments will be necessary," Mr. Barratt said. "But they can be made. The country isn't overrun with magicians, for one thing. There will still be opportunities for the artless and their businesses to succeed."

"I wish I shared your enthusiasm and optimism. I truly do. I want India to be able to discuss her magic without fear of recrimination, but I've seen the worst of humanity, and I have little faith in magicians and the artless living harmoniously together. If keeping magic a secret means she is safe, then that's what I advocate, no matter how much it frustrates you—or her. Frustration is a small price to pay for one's life."

He did not look at me, but I felt as though he spoke directly to me. I'd always understood his need for secrecy, but to hear his voice rasp with earnestness as he told Mr. Barratt his reasons drove it home.

"I cannot argue with your position, Mr. Glass," Mr. Barratt said. "I would very much like to keep Miss Steele safe too."

Matt stiffened.

"But this is beyond her, or me, or any single magician," Mr. Barratt went on. "This is not about today or tomorrow, or even next year or ten years from now. What I want will change the lives of the next generation of magicians and the generation after that. I'd like my grandchildren to live openly and harmoniously among the artless without fear."

"You seem to have missed my point. What I'm trying to tell you is that there may not be any grandchildren of magicians because *this* generation will be wiped out."

Mr. Barratt stilled. I hardly dared to breathe. Hearing it put so baldly shocked me, although I couldn't say why. Perhaps because I didn't truly believe such a thing could happen. Matt, however, did. That mattered. It mattered very much.

"You have a lower opinion of your fellow man than I do, Mr. Glass," Mr. Barratt said.

"Perhaps because I've seen more of the lowest form of man than you."

"Having reported on the Ripper murders, I respectfully disagree." He looked as if he was about to say something else to Matt, but instead turned to me. He once again covered my hand with his. "We're frightening Miss Steele."

I withdrew my hand. "A little heated discussion doesn't frighten me," I assured him.

"You are made of stern stuff. You're braver than most females I've met." He smiled. "Another point of uniqueness in your favor."

"You ought to meet Matt's cousin, Willie. I'm weak compared to her."

"Hardly," Matt muttered. "Was there a reason for your visit, Barratt, or did you simply stop by to drink tea with India?"

"I came to warn you both that Detective Inspector Brockwell from Scotland Yard questioned me about you, among other things."

"Thank you for the warning," Matt said. "His questions are merely form."

"What sort of questions?" I asked.

"How well I knew you, mostly. He mentioned you were ill, Mr. Glass, and that's why you claimed to be interested in Hale and his medical miracle. Nothing serious, I hope."

"No," Matt bit off.

"Thank you for stopping by, Mr. Barratt," I said quickly. "It was good of you to warn us."

He stood and took my hand. "Thank you for the discussion and tea. It was most enjoyable, at least for a little while."

Behind him, I caught Matt rolling his eyes.

"I'll see you out," I said.

I walked him to the door, and Matt followed. Mr. Barratt

climbed into a waiting coach and gave the driver orders. He waved as the coach rolled away.

"He can afford to keep his own horse and conveyance," I said. "That's surprising for a journalist."

"Family money," Matt said. "His brother is one of the most successful ink producers in the country, remember?" He shut the front door and indicated I should walk ahead of him back to the sitting room. This time, Matt sat and sipped his tea. "What did he say to you before I came in?"

"We were discussing my family and where my magic came from." I considered stopping there, but I knew I'd feel guilty for withholding the most important detail. "Now...don't get mad."

He set the teacup down with a clank and glared at me.

"I told him about my watch saving my life."

He took two deep breaths, letting the last one out slowly. "It's your choice to tell him that if you wish."

"I know. Of course it is. But I knew you wouldn't like it."

He picked up the cup and sipped his tea. Mine had gone cold. We ought to have some cake, too. That would keep our mouths full and stop us from saying things we regretted, and by the time we'd finished eating, he might be calmer.

But without cake, I ended up saying what was on my mind. "Don't be angry with me, Matt."

"I'm not."

"You are. Your features are hard, and you can't even look at me."

He looked at me and his jaw softened but not his eyes. "I'm not mad at you, I'm mad at him. I don't like him, and I don't like his ideas. They're reckless."

I couldn't argue with him, not when he had my safety in mind. Besides, part of me agreed with him. The other part of me agreed with Oscar Barratt, but I wouldn't let on as much.

I refilled both our teacups. "Let's focus on the matters at

hand and not Mr. Barratt's ideas. We have two tasks and two tasks only. Find Chronos and find Dr. Hale's murderer to clear your name."

"There's been no word from The Cross Keys," he said. "As to Dr. Hale, I'm at a loss. We have several suspects but no good leads."

"We could speak with Abercrombie and find out what he told Mr. Clark of the Apothecary's Guild."

"He won't tell us."

"Then we should concentrate on finding out which of our apothecaries is a magician. That's all we know for certain about our murderer."

"Agreed. A little spying is in order. But first, this afternoon, would you like to help me pick out a new watch?"

My heart rose, and I couldn't stop the smile creeping over my face. "Yes, please. We could visit the Masons. I'd like to give Mr. Mason your custom. Although he might get in trouble from the guild if Abercrombie finds out I visited. I don't want to cause him any difficulties. On the other hand, every respectable watchmaker in London knows who and what I am now. None will want me in their shop." I slumped back in the chair with a deep sigh. "Perhaps I shouldn't go at all."

"Since we questioned all of the prominent watchmakers, I don't think it matters if I go alone. They'll remember me anyway and may refuse to serve me."

"You are very distinctive."

"It's the accent."

"No, Matt, it's not."

He frowned. "What is it then?"

I was considering whether to tell him he was too handsome to be so easily forgotten when Bristow announced another visitor, my friend, Catherine Mason.

"What a lovely surprise," I said, kissing her cheek. "Bristow, please bring a fresh pot of tea. And some cake."

Catherine smiled shyly at Matt as he greeted her. The last time she'd visited me, he'd been absent, as had the others. We exchanged small talk until the tea and cake arrived, by which time I realized she had something to tell me. Perhaps Matt's presence held her back.

"Catherine, is something wrong?" I prompted. "Is it your Mr. Wilcox problem?"

"Good lord, no," she said. "I spoke to Mr. Wilcox about our unsuitability, and I haven't seen him since. I think I may have hurt his feelings a little."

"Better hurt them a little now rather than a lot later."

"You're so wise, India."

"She is indeed," Matt said, setting down his teacup. "Perhaps I should leave you two ladies to talk alone."

"Please stay." Catherine put down her cup too. "It might be best if you hear this as well."

She had me intrigued now. "What is it, Catherine? What's happened?"

"Mr. Abercrombie continues to visit my father regularly. More than ever, in fact. I try to listen in whenever I can."

"Please be careful, Catherine," I said. "Don't let them catch you."

She frowned. "That's the odd thing. Your name comes up in what is sometimes a heated discussion and *you* tell *me* to be careful." She settled her very blue, very piercing gaze on me. She'd never looked at me so fiercely before. It was unnerving. "I think it's time you tell me what's going on."

I glanced at Matt. He gave his head a slight shake.

"Stop treating me like a child," Catherine snapped. "You're my friend, India, and I know you're in trouble. I want to help you, but I can't if I am kept in the dark."

She was right. She might be silly on occasion but she had

a good heart and had matured in recent months. "It's a lot to comprehend," I began. "And you might not believe me at first."

"India," Matt warned.

"We can trust her, Matt. What does it matter, anyway? The entire guild seems to know. She's bound to find out sooner or later, and I'd rather she learned it from me first."

He rubbed his forehead and nodded. "I suppose you're right."

"Catherine, do you believe in magic?"

She stared at me, her mouth ajar. "Is this a joke?"

"I'm very serious. Magic exists, although it's rare. Magicians specialize in certain creative fields and can infuse their magic into their creations using spells. We recently met an ink magician who can make ink float off one page onto another. We've also met map magicians who can create the most elaborate yet accurate maps, and a gold magician who had forgotten the art of multiplying gold but could feel ancient magic in golden objects."

She spluttered a laugh but it died on her lips. "And you're telling me you're a magician?"

I nodded. "Of timepieces. That's why I'm so good at fixing watches and clocks."

"You're good because your father taught you well. You understand even the most complicated mechanisms because you're clever, not because of…magic."

"I don't know any spells," I went on. "My father kept my ability a secret from me, and I was led to believe that I was clever, as you suggest. But that doesn't explain it all. I have a strong affinity with timepieces. I can fix most and make them incredibly accurate." I didn't tell her how my watch had saved my life, or how time magic and medical magic were combined in Matt's watch. She wasn't ready to hear *that*.

"India! This is..." She shook her head over and over, but at least she was no longer laughing off my explanation.

"It's shocking, I know," I said. "You'll need time to think it through."

She took several seconds to consider my claim and did not so much as laugh or call me a fool.

"Let's say you're not talking utter nonsense," she said carefully. "What does it have to do with Abercrombie and the guild? Why does he dislike you? If you're a magician then shouldn't he be celebrating your achievements? *You* ought to be guild master."

"He and the guild members are frightened. They're not magicians, and they're worried that if magicians are allowed to own shops, customers will flock to them for their fine pieces. It's not just the Watchmaker's Guild that's afraid, but the other guilds too. There seems to be a loose agreement between all the guilds to bar magicians to protect their businesses. That's why I wasn't accepted into the Watchmaker's Guild and granted a license. No license, no shop."

"I thought it was because you were a woman." She sounded numb, but at least she wasn't denying it altogether.

"Has Abercrombie been telling your father to keep you away from me?" I asked.

"Actually no, not anymore. My father has urged me not to visit you, but Abercrombie has recently changed his tune. He now wants me to come here, but to spy on you."

"Spy on me! For what purpose?"

She shrugged. "I don't know. India, he dislikes and distrusts you."

"Because I have the ability to ruin his business and ruin the guild's reputation and importance. But I have no interest in having a shop, Catherine. None at all. Watch and clockmakers like your father have nothing to worry about there.

Tell your father that. In fact, tell Mr. Abercrombie when next he visits."

"I don't think it wise," Matt said. "It's better for her if she pretends innocence."

"Fiddlesticks," Catherine said with a sniff. "I'm tired of everyone thinking me naive and silly. I'm going to at least tell Father, and he can decide whether to tell Mr. Abercrombie or not."

"I think that's a good compromise," I said.

Cyclops walked in and paused in the doorway when he spotted Catherine. "My apologies," he said. "I didn't know you had company."

"I don't think you two have properly met," I said. "Cyclops, this is my friend, Catherine Mason."

Cyclops bowed and she gave him a small curtsy before sitting again. "I noticed you through your father's shop window," he said.

"You noticed me?" Catherine's pale cheeks flushed pink. "When you were Mr. Glass's coachman?"

"He's not my coachman anymore," Matt assured her. "That was a temporary arrangement that couldn't be helped. Cyclops is a good friend."

"Then I'm pleased to finally meet you properly, Mr. Cyclops."

"Bailey," Cyclops said.

"Pardon?"

"My name's Nate Bailey." He fingered the edge of his eye patch. "Cyclops is what they called me after I got this. But I'd like it if you called me by my proper name, Miss Mason."

"Yes, of course."

Matt's brow furrowed. "Do you want all of us to stop calling you Cyclops now?"

"Just Miss Mason." Cyclops's gaze flickered to her then

away. "It doesn't seem right that she should call me that, somehow."

"Why?"

"I agree," I said to save Cyclops from answering him.

Matt looked from me to Cyclops to Catherine then back to Cyclops. Then he smiled into his teacup. "I see."

"I gave up looking for...your colleague, Matt," Cyclops said. "It's impossible in a city this large without a place to begin."

Matt nodded. "I suspect Willie and Duke will be back soon, too. Come and join us."

"You've returned at an opportune moment," I said, pouring tea into a spare cup for Cyclops. "We've just finished telling Catherine about my magic and explaining why that means the guild members fear me. I think she should tell her father about me. What do you think?"

He accepted the cup and sat a little awkwardly on the sofa. Usually he sprawled, as did Duke and Willie, but this time he sat with his back straight and his legs tucked in, not stretched out in front of him. I hoped Catherine appreciated the fine figure he cut for her benefit. He did ruin the effect a little by wrapping his fingers around the teacup rather than holding it by the delicate handle. To be fair, it would have looked like a sausage trying to fit through the eye of a needle.

"I think Miss Mason can trust her parents but no one else," he said. "You accept the existence of magic, Miss Mason?"

"I...I suppose." She wrinkled her nose. "It is rather fanciful, but since I know India isn't the fanciful type, I must believe her."

"I think that's a fair assessment of her character."

"Is magic unique to England, or are there magicians in America, Mr. Bailey?"

"We have magicians back home. It took me some time to

accept they were real. I didn't trust too many folk back then, and I didn't know Matt all that well, so believing in magic was like taking a leap off a cliff. I soon learned the truth of it. Saw some of it work with my own eyes."

"Really?" Catherine's gaze studied every inch of Cyclops's face, and I rather suspected he liked it. He was certainly chattier than I'd ever known him to be. "Tell me more about your home. What's America like?"

"I can't speak for all of it, but it can be a wild place where Matt and I come from. It ain't somewhere that fair ladies like yourself should visit, Miss Mason."

She eyed him over her teacup. "And what about ladies seeking adventure?"

He chuckled, the deep rich sound filling the room. Catherine smiled back. "Those will find it interesting enough but may wish they were home safe in their English beds if they ever witness a gunfight or saloon brawl."

"Oh, I don't know. I think that rather depends on how adventurous she is."

Matt looked all at sea as he watched Catherine flirting with his friend and Cyclops enjoying it. It seemed he hadn't expected it. But then, he didn't know her like I did. Catherine may seem sweet, with her pretty face and big eyes, but she had a wicked streak and sought adventure whenever she could—which wasn't often, under her mother's watchful eye. I suspected she would like to travel to America, or anywhere, before she settled down with a husband. *If* she settled down at all.

We talked more about America and magic again, and the discussion returned to Abercrombie and the guild's determination to spy on me.

"Perhaps Catherine could report back to them," I said, as an idea occurred to me. "But she could pass on false information."

Both Cyclops and Matt shook their heads but gave no explanation for their disagreement. They were being such *men* about the whole thing, and I appealed to Catherine for her opinion. But she shook her head too.

"Without my father's agreement, it's pointless," she said. "He won't allow it, and I don't want to go behind his back. What if *you* confront Abercrombie?"

"I've tried that, and he either chases me away or orders someone to escort me out of his shop," I said.

"I think it's an excellent idea," Matt said. "I've decided to confront him about his meetings with Clark from the Apothecary's Guild. This way we kill two birds with one stone." He checked the clock on the mantel. "We'll go now, India, if you don't mind."

"You want me to come with you?"

"Of course. He won't dare pull the same stunt he did last time we visited his shop, and your presence may even irk him enough that he gives more information than he should. Besides, who else will tell me if he's trying to sell me a good watch or a bad one?"

"I think you'll rattle him well and good," Catherine said. "Is Mr. Bailey going with you?"

"He's not required. Perhaps you two can get to know one another a little better in our absence."

"That's not a good idea," Cyclops said, rising.

"Nonsense." Matt pressed his friend's shoulder until Cyclops sat again. "Miss Mason seems in no hurry to leave."

"Indeed I'm not," she said. "I'd like to get to know you better, Mr. Bailey. I'd like that very much."

CHAPTER 9

*T*he last time I'd been to Abercrombie's Fine Watches and Clocks on Oxford Street, I'd been chased by vigilantes after Mr. Abercrombie accused me of stealing one of his watches. Although I knew Matt was right, and Abercrombie wouldn't dare do such a thing again now that he knew what Matt was capable of, I was still anxious as we headed into the shop. I expected our reception to be frosty, at the very least.

I was right.

Abercrombie spied us immediately and rushed forward before any of his four staff could greet us. He glared at me over the pince nez perched precariously on the tip of his nose. "What do you want?" he hissed under his breath. "State your business then leave without creating a scene."

The wicked gleam in Matt's eyes gave me fair warning of his plans, but I suspected Mr. Abercrombie didn't see it coming. "Now, now, Mr. Abercrombie," Matt said loudly enough that the other customers could hear. "You must put that misunderstanding behind you. It must be difficult to admit that you were wrong to accuse Miss Steele of theft, but

157

she holds no grudges. Or are you still upset that the police questioned you about your involvement in Daniel Gibbons's murder?"

The sound of several gasps momentarily drowned out the ticking of dozens of clocks. The customers watched the scene playing out before them openly instead of with surreptitious sideways glances. Two customers even left. The staff stopped serving and stared at their master in disbelief.

Mr. Abercrombie's oiled mustache wriggled, worm-like, above his lip. He looked as if he wanted to thrash Matt. Part of me wished he would try, simply so I could see Matt thrash him instead. "Perhaps you'd like to join me out the back." Mr. Abercrombie did not wait for an answer but marched off.

Matt didn't follow, so I remained at his side. He held his elbow out to me. "I'm here to purchase a watch," he said idly. "What do you think of that one, Miss Steele?" he asked, pointing to an elegant enamel faced watch with a calendar.

"Does it have tourbillon regulator?" I asked the assistant behind the counter. "No? What about a karrusel?"

"Er…" He looked to Mr. Abercrombie.

Mr. Abercrombie shooed him out of the way. "So you wish to play this silly game," he said to us when we were alone. "Very well, let's play." He drew the watch out from the glass cabinet and laid it on the counter in front of Matt.

Matt didn't even look at it. "I hear you're asking young women to spy on us now."

Mr. Abercrombie's head jerked up.

"That's low, even by your standards," Matt went on.

"I, I…" Abercrombie licked his lips. "I don't know what you mean."

I could not believe Matt would be so blatant, and yet I wanted to applaud him. It was the best—and perhaps only— way to get Abercrombie to leave us alone; to make him think we were always one step ahead.

"Don't play the fool with me," Matt growled, voice low. "Mason himself has not tattled but not everyone in the household is loyal to you. I have an idea. Let's cut out the middleman and I'll report directly to you, beginning now."

"You're mad," Mr. Abercrombie said.

Matt leaned his knuckles on the counter. Abercrombie took a step back, putting distance and the counter between them. "I'm damned furious," Matt said. "As anyone would be after being kidnapped and kept prisoner for several hours."

Mr. Abercrombie swallowed heavily and stepped back again, knocking the clocks on the wall behind him. One slipped to the side and the cuckoo popped out, grazing Abercrombie's ear.

"I've been looking forward to this first meeting with you," Matt said. "I want you to know that I harbor no ill feelings."

"I...I don't know what you're talking about. That wasn't me."

Matt grunted a harsh laugh. "I know it was you, even if I have no proof."

"You have no proof because I didn't—"

Matt slammed his fist down on the counter. The remaining customers hurried out, and the staff kept their distance. I wasn't sure whether to take Matt's arm and urge him to calm down or let his anger ride itself out.

"Who told you about India's magic?" Matt asked in a harsh whisper.

Of all the questions I thought he'd say, that was not on the list. I held my breath and forced myself to look unruffled as Mr. Abercrombie's gaze fell on me.

"Wh-what do you mean?" he asked.

"Again, you're playing the fool." The chill in Matt's tone sent a shiver down *my* spine. "Don't."

Abercrombie removed his pince nez. "Eddie Hardacre told me."

"Eddie!" I cried. "How did he know?"

"Your father told him."

My father? But why? How could he tell someone else but not me? I blinked back the tears burning my eyes. I refused to cry in front of Abercrombie.

"To keep you safe," Matt said quietly, guessing the direction of my thoughts. "He knew he was dying and thought Hardacre would protect you after he was gone."

"Instead, Eddie betrayed me." I placed my palms on the counter to steady myself.

Matt placed his hand over mine.

"We must choose our friends wisely, Miss Steele," Mr. Abercrombie said with a lift of his chin. "Clearly you have a problem in that regard."

Matt removed his hand. "You know a Mr. Clark from the Apothecary's Guild," he said.

"What has that got to do with anything?"

"It has a great deal to do with magic, the guilds, and—"

Abercrombie rushed toward the counter. "Be quiet," he hissed. "Lower your voice."

Matt's mouth twisted into a sinister sneer. It was at these moments, when anger overtook him, that I felt I didn't know him at all. It may only ever be directed at the deserving, like Abercrombie, but it chilled me nevertheless. "What are you and Clark plotting?" he growled.

"Nothing! For God's sake, man. Josiah Clark is merely a friend of mine. Occasionally we dine together at my guild's hall or his. There's nothing mysterious in that, and we are certainly not plotting against...people like Miss Steele."

"Just like you didn't plot with the master of the Mapmaker's Guild to kidnap Daniel Gibbons?"

Abercrombie stiffened. "The police questioned me and let me go. Duffield, the master of that guild, worked alone."

That was a lie, but neither we nor the police could prove it.

Matt made a great show of inspecting more watches in the glass cabinet. No customers remained in the shop, only staff. If nothing else, we'd succeeded in costing Abercrombie some business today.

"On second thoughts," Matt said, "I've changed my mind. I won't purchase one of your watches. Your collection is far too provincial for my tastes. I think I'll take my custom elsewhere."

He tucked my hand into the crook of his arm and we left the shop together.

"He's rattled," Matt said as we settled in the carriage.

"But what do you think he's up to with Mr. Clark? Another kidnapping? Hale's murder? If so, perhaps we shouldn't have poked the bees' nest like that."

"Whatever it is, he'll be more likely to abandon his plans now that he knows we're watching him."

"That's what you wanted to achieve in there?"

"Short of actually extracting his plans from him, yes. I doubted he would simply tell us what he was plotting. Not unless I beat it out of him."

"Then thank goodness his staff remained," I said, only half joking.

"It wasn't his staff who kept me in check." He watched me from beneath heavy lids then turned to look out the window. Anger hung over him like a storm cloud the rest of the way home.

Duke and Willie had returned to the house a few minutes before us, and Catherine was gone. I wanted to ask Cyclops if he'd enjoyed her company much longer after we'd departed but did not get the chance.

"Cyclops, with me," Matt ordered, striding past Willie coming down the staircase. "I need a sparring partner."

Cyclops and Duke exchanged glances but it was Willie who spoke. "Sparring! What in damnation did you do to him, India?"

"We went to see Abercrombie," I said.

"Ah. That explains it."

"It does, rather."

Cyclops rolled up his shirtsleeve and went to follow Matt.

"Don't go in too hard," I told him. "Remember he's not well."

"Don't let him hear you say that," Cyclops said.

"Besides," Duke said, "Matt can take anything Cyclops can throw at him, even when he ain't well."

"If I was a different sort of man, I'd take offense at that." Cyclops slapped Duke on the shoulder and raced up the stairs, taking two at a time.

"I'm going to watch," Willie said. "Coming, India?"

"No, thank you. Watching two men punching one another is not my idea of a pleasant afternoon."

"Right you are. It ain't meant to be pleasant. It's about raw strength and manly pride. It's damned good to watch."

"Be sure Miss Glass doesn't catch wind of it," I called after her as she ran up the stairs. Duke followed and I retired to my own rooms to freshen up and consider whether we'd made a mistake in visiting Abercrombie.

In the end, I couldn't decide. I conceded that Matt may have a point. Abercrombie and Clark might abandon their plan, if they had one, now that they knew we were watching them.

Or they might hasten it. Or come after us to silence us.

* * *

I WENT in search of Miss Glass but was distracted from my quest by the grunts and Willie's occasional cheer coming from the drawing room. A little peek at the men sparring would do no harm. Perhaps Willie was right and boxing wasn't such a bloodthirsty sport after all. Queensberry's Rules had helped it become more respectable and less violent, so my father had told me, and the nobility flocked to matches. Only the men, of course. Women were strictly forbidden. Yet another reason to see what all the fuss was about and prove, if only to myself, that my constitution couldn't be described as delicate.

I opened the door and peered through the gap. They'd moved the furniture out of the way to create a large space in which Matt and Cyclops circled one another, fists raised. They were not fighting under Queensberry's Rules. I didn't know much about the code, but I did know gloves must be worn. Both Matt and Cyclops merely had strips of white cloth wrapped around their knuckles. It couldn't possibly offer enough protection.

Cyclops jabbed with his left then followed it with his right in quick succession. Matt dodged both, but only just, then went in low, catching Cyclops unawares. He hit Cyclops in the stomach. The big man grunted but got in a punch of his own to Matt's body before he managed to dance out of the way. I suspected they'd both pulled back so as not to hurt the other. I'd seen Matt fell men with his fists, and I suspected Cyclops was capable too, yet neither looked to be in pain.

"Go on, Matt," Willie jeered. She sat on the back of an armchair, her booted feet on the seat. Miss Glass would have a fit if she saw. "You can do better than that."

"Willie," Duke growled, "not today. Look at him. He can hardly stand."

Surely he exaggerated. Matt was avoiding most of Cyclops's punches well. I tried to get a better look at his face, but he had his back to me. His body seemed alert and his reactions quick.

Willie, sitting where she could see Matt's face, frowned. "Matt," she called to her cousin, "that's enough. You stop now."

Matt ignored her and threw another punch at Cyclops, but Cyclops swayed backward and it missed him.

I maneuvered around the furniture and joined Duke and Willie to get a better look at Matt. My movement caught his attention, distracting him from the fight. Cyclops's fist connected with Matt's face with a sickening thud.

I cringed, and Cyclops caught Matt's shoulder to steady him.

"Why didn't you get out of the way?" he said.

Willie leapt off the chair. "Miss Uptight over here distracted him with her halo." She inspected Matt's face. "That's going to show up nice and black later. Better start thinking of an explanation that won't give your aunt a conniption."

"I'm sorry," I said, touching his cheek gently. "I thought you wouldn't see me if I was quiet."

"You were quiet," he said, "but no less distracting."

"Oh, Matt," I said on a sigh. "Look at you." It wasn't just the bruise beginning to form beneath the eye but the unhealthy pallor and exhaustion etched into the lines slicing across his forehead. "Where is your watch?"

I moved off toward the jacket slung over the back of the sofa but he caught my arm. "Not yet, India. I'll use it later so it lasts me through the night."

The fact that he had to control its use worried me. "All right. But you should freshen up. One look at you and Miss Glass will know what you've been up to."

"After we get the room back to order."

We returned the furniture to its usual state and Matt retired to his rooms. Cyclops sat on the sofa with a groan and I sat beside him.

"Sherry, India?" Duke asked from the sideboard.

"Yes, please." I turned to Cyclops. "Did Catherine stay long after we left?"

"A good half hour at least," he said, extending his arm and stretching out his fingers.

"What did you talk about?"

"America, mostly. She had a lot of questions."

I smiled and accepted the glass of sherry from Duke. He handed Cyclops a brandy. "She's got a curious spirit."

"Aye, she's the adventuring type." He smirked into his glass.

"Why are you smiling like that?" I asked, unable to stop smiling myself.

"No reason. She took me by surprise."

"Ah. You were expecting a demure English rose."

"From the look of her, aye. She seemed like the sort that likes to wear pretty dresses and gossip all day."

I laughed. "Oh, Cyclops, you've been duped by her pale beauty and youthfulness. I assure you, Catherine is as robust as they come, in spirit if not in body. She may like to wear pretty dresses, and will pass on juicy gossip as much as the next person, but she's more than that."

He held up his hand. "I admit I judged her before I got to know her. Guilty as charged, ma'am."

"I'm glad you got to know the real Catherine. She's quite a character, although she's prone to romanticism. Men fall in love with her too easily, you see, and she falls for their flattery without getting to know them well first. It usually ends in heartache—theirs, not hers."

He cradled his glass in his hands as if he were warming them on a teacup. "I can see how that would cause you to worry about her."

"Only when the man in question is unsuitable, whether because of his nature or hers." I sidled closer and lowered my voice. "In your case, however, I think it would be a good match. You're both—"

"Stop there, India. Miss Mason is not for the likes of me."

"You can't know that yet. It's much too soon. Why not get to know her better and then judge."

He shook his head and downed the rest of his brandy. "She's not for people like me," he said again.

"Cyclops, if you're referring to the difference in your skin colors then I'm compelled to point out that it wouldn't matter to her and shouldn't to you, not if you truly like one another."

"It'll matter to her family."

As much as I liked Mr. and Mrs. Mason, I knew he was right, but only to a point. "It would at first, but if you made their daughter happy, they'd come to accept you in time. They're good people. Anyway, we're getting ahead of ourselves. You don't know one another well enough yet to decide if there's anything between you."

"Aye, agreed, but it's not just that."

"Then what is it? You're a good man, kind, loyal, and I'd wager you can turn your hand to anything. How could anyone possibly find fault in you?"

"You don't know everything about me, India."

I settled back in the sofa and regarded the unscathed half of his profile. He had bold cheekbones, smooth skin, and a soulful eye, but the patch and scar marred the handsomeness and even gave him a sinister appearance, if one didn't know his nature.

"I know you were being hunted by the law back in America," I said. "I don't know why, and it doesn't matter to me what they think you did, and it won't matter to Catherine either. You must be innocent or Matt wouldn't be your friend."

"It would matter if she—or any Englishwoman—came back home with me." He shifted his weight. "You've got it wrong anyway. By the time I left California to come here with Matt, I wasn't being hunted by lawmen no more. Only my employer was still after me."

"What for?" I bit my lip and winced. "Sorry, it's none of my business. You don't have to answer that."

He gave a half-hearted chuckle. "I don't blame you for wanting to know, India. You done well not to pry before now."

"It hasn't been easy. Sorry."

"You English apologize a lot."

"Sorry."

We both laughed.

"There's not much to tell," Cyclops went on. "I was over-seer at a mine in Nevada. I worked my way up over five years and had a lot of respect for my employer and he for me. But when he died suddenly, and his son took over, everything changed. Skillitt, his name was. He tried to cut costs wher-ever he could. I went along with his new methods for a time, but when he told me to order cheap weaker timbers to shore up the shafts, I refused."

"Weaker timbers could mean shafts might collapse?" I asked.

"Aye, and men would lose their lives. I quit and went to work at another mine. But a week later, a shaft at Skillitt's collapsed, sure enough. Mr. Skillitt blamed me, said I was the one who ordered the weaker timbers without his knowledge. He set the law onto me and I was arrested, tried and sentenced to hang."

"Oh my god."

"I escaped on the way back to the jailhouse after the trial. I didn't know where I was running to, I just kept on going. For five months, I lived off the land or stole if my hunting failed, but I never stayed in one place for long. I wound up in California, and that's when Matt found me."

"Hiding out," I said, remembering the story Matt had told me. "You fought before both giving up."

The side of his mouth lifted. "Toughest fighter I ever met, and he a gentleman and all. Took me by surprise when he opened his mouth and educated words fell out."

I could well imagine it. Matt didn't fit into a neat mold. "Did the Californian lawmen not care what you'd done in Nevada?"

"They cared all right, but Matt sorted it out. After I told him what happened, he arranged for the best lawyer to look into my case. I was re-tried back in Nevada, in my absence, and my name was cleared. But Mr. Skillitt was furious because my defense blamed him. He was never brought to justice, on account of his fortune and influence, but his reputation never recovered. He lost some business and friends out of it, and he hated me."

"So he sent men after you?"

He nodded. "Usually word got to me before they did, and Matt hid me well enough, but I had to stay alert. Skillitt's still after me. So you see, I couldn't take a woman back with me. Not to that life."

"It sounds to me like you shouldn't go back at all. It's much safer here for you."

He lifted one shoulder. "America is my home."

"People make new homes elsewhere all the time. You already have at least one friend here."

"If you mean you, then I ain't convinced you're going to stay here. You might decide to try America."

"I have no reason to move."

"Don't you?" he asked slyly.

"No."

"The weather's warmer."

"That's hardly a convincing argument. I'm used to the cold and damp. Besides, summer is always just around the corner."

"Aye, but I'm hoping we won't be here for the summer." He cast a longing gaze at the door through which Matt had exited. "I don't think he'll last to see it if we don't fix his watch."

* * *

THERE WAS NOTHING FOR IT. We had to resort to spying on our suspects. We'd achieved very little through interrogating them, so it was time for more underhanded methods.

After breakfast, Matt assigned Cyclops to watch Mr. Pitt, Duke to watch Mr. Clark, and himself to spy on Mr. Oakshot. Willie protested that she had nothing to do, and didn't want to sit around sipping tea with Miss Glass and me until she died of boredom, so Matt allowed her to go to the London Hospital to try to learn anything useful about Wiley and Ritter.

"I could help too," I said. "I could check all the medicines for any that feel magically warm. When I find one, I simply ask a nurse who handled it last."

"You'll slow me down or get caught," Willie declared. "You ain't coming."

"Why would I get caught?"

"You're too distinctive."

"I am not. I'm the sort of woman who blends into the background. I hardly ever get noticed by anyone."

Willie snorted. Matt, Duke and Cyclops politely and diplomatically disagreed with me.

"Besides," I said, "if either of us is going to get noticed, it's you in your men's clothing."

"India's got a point," Duke said to Willie. "You're like a lighthouse beacon. Ships see you a mile offshore."

"And avoid me?" She stamped her hands on her hips and settled her feet apart. "Is that what you're implying? That men change course when they see me?"

He held up his hands in surrender. "You said it, not me."

"Willie's right," Matt said. "You're not going, India. You can't just wander into their dispensary and ask nurses who handled the medicines."

"I don't plan on wandering in," I said, placing my hands on my hips as Willie had done. "I plan on tricking my way in."

"No. You'll get in Willie's way."

"Ha!" Willie shot me a triumphant look.

"Don't get cocky," I snapped. "He's only refusing because he's protecting me. He thinks I can't take care of myself."

"You can't," Willie and Duke both said. She winked at him. He frowned back at her and apologized to me.

"You can't, India," he said. "Sorry, but it's the truth."

"I can take care of myself, thank you very much," I said snippily. "I have a mouth and a brain. I can talk my way out of a situation. If Willie is cornered, she'll shoot her way out. My method is far more civil and involves no bloodshed." I spun round and marched out of Matt's study only to have him grasp me by the arm and stop me in the corridor.

"You're mad with me," he said.

I rounded on him. "I understand your point, Matt, but I think you're wrong. I'm not delicate, so stop treating me as if I were a snowflake that'll melt at the first sign of heat."

His grip tightened ever so slightly before letting me go. "You're forgetting one vital thing."

"That I'm a woman, and Willie is…whatever she is?"

That almost coaxed a smile from him, but his lips quickly flattened again. "The main reason you shouldn't go to the hospital is because you're known; not only by Wiley and

Ritter but several nurses have seen you too. You couldn't possibly sneak about. And before you try telling me nobody notices you, I'd like you to know that I vehemently and categorically deny that claim."

"I...I'm not sure what to say to that." I may not have known what to say but my face certainly knew how to react. It blushed to the roots of my hair.

"Say, 'Thank you, Matt, I agree with you.'"

I arched my brows at him. "Now you're being silly."

"Say 'I'm lovely.'"

"I will not."

"Go on, it's easy. 'I'm very pretty. I have a lovely face and figure. In fact, my figure is more than lovely, it's—'"

"Matthew?" Miss Glass emerged from her bedroom, her lips pinched in horror. "Why are you telling India that your face and figure are lovely?"

Matt and I laughed.

"Never mind, Aunt," he said. "If you'll both excuse me, I have to get ready to go out for the day."

"Is India going with you?" she asked.

"Yes," I said as Matt said, "No."

"Good. India and I shall pay a call on our friends, the Mortimers."

It sounded as good a plan as any, since I wasn't allowed to spy. The Mortimers were nice people anyway, and I liked their company very much. It would be a pleasant outing.

Miss Glass and I left in the brougham mid-morning and returned before luncheon. Bristow met us at the door and took our hats and coats as Bryce drove off to the mews. A man I hadn't seen approach climbed the steps and touched the brim of his hat in greeting. He was broad shouldered but not tall, with short stubby fingers. He wore no gloves and his gray tie had been done up in a rather slap-dash fashion. The rest of his clothing was good quality, and clean, but simple.

"Good morning," he said to Bristow in a cockney accent. "Are you Mr. Glass?"

Bristow sniffed. "Mr. Glass does not open his own door. I am the butler." I'd never heard him put on airs before, and I almost burst out laughing.

But the look on the stranger's face stopped me. The veins on his temples and neck bulged and I had the feeling he was holding himself back from either shouting or attacking Bristow.

"Is Mr. Glass in?" the man snapped.

"He is not," Bristow said. "May I leave him a message?"

"Or can I help you?" I asked. "I'm his assistant."

"Miss Steele?" the fellow said. How did he know my name? "In that case, you can." He jerked his head at Bristow. "Haven't you got some butlering to do?"

Bristow's nostrils flared.

"Bristow is perfectly all right where he is," I cut in before the butler could attempt to force the fellow out. I suspected he would not win that contest. The stranger looked rather solid.

He glanced up the staircase behind me and toward the sitting room door where Miss Glass had retreated. Was he looking for other residents? Others who may try to toss him out?

I did not have a good feeling about this. "Who are you and what do you want?" I demanded.

"It doesn't matter who I am or who I work for. I ain't asking, Miss Steele, I'm telling you. Stop your investigation."

All the air sucked out of my body, leaving me feeling weak and at sea. "Pardon?" I whispered.

"You heard me. Tell Mr. Glass to stop investigating Hale's death. It ain't nothing to do with you."

Bristow edged between the man and me. "Get out or I'll summon the constables."

The man touched the brim of his hat. "Be sure and tell Mr. Glass, ma'am. My employer is serious on this matter. Deadly serious."

My heart thudded even as my blood chilled. We'd been warned off the investigation into Daniel Gibbons's murder too. That time, it had been Abercrombie's doing. Had he sent this man? The similarities were too close to ignore.

"Who employs you?" I pressed. "Who wants us to stop? And why?"

He turned and headed down the steps, his gait unhurried. He had not come in a conveyance so walked up the street. In a moment of madness, I removed my hat.

"A coat, Bristow. And a parasol. Hurry!"

"You're going to follow him? Is that wise?"

"Perhaps not, but it is necessary." I shoved my hat into his chest. "Go!"

He rushed into the cloak room and came back with my blue coat, a parasol and the footman. "Take Peter," Bristow said. He helped me into my coat and handed me the parasol. "Do as Miss Steele says, and see that no harm comes to her," he ordered Peter.

I ran out, not waiting to see if the footman followed. The stranger disappeared around the corner into Aldford Street. I ran after him, Peter alongside me, and breathed a sigh of relief when I spotted the stranger crossing Park Lane. He glanced over his shoulder, but I ducked behind the parasol.

"Act naturally," I told Peter.

The Hyde Park walking path was not too busy and the man was easy to spot with his stocky stature. He glanced around again and must have been satisfied that he had not been followed because he didn't check again.

His slow, steady pace took him out of the park at Hyde Park Corner and into Grosvenor Crescent, Belgravia. Like Mayfair, Belgravia was an area of extraordinary wealth.

Impressive mansions graced the curved streets overlooking a lush garden square. I'd been here quite recently with Matt. In fact, the closer we drew to Belgrave Square, the more certain I became that the man was heading toward the exact same house. When he knocked on the front door and was let in by a butler I recognized, I knew we had the connection we needed.

The house belonged to Lord Coyle.

The notion thrilled and chilled me in equal measure. Lord Coyle kept a private collection of magical objects. He'd purchased a magical globe from the Mapmaker's Guild in a clandestine exchange with the globe's creator. He was no stranger to magic.

But how was he connected to Dr. Hale? And why did he not want us to investigate Hale's murder?

"Come, Peter," I said. "Let's return home."

As I said it, the door opened again. I gasped as a different man emerged from the house.

It was Oscar Barratt.

CHAPTER 10

*M*att returned alone at lunch time. I waited until after his rest before telling him about the stranger's warning. As expected, he was livid, but he restrained himself well enough and only thumped his desk once.

"That's not all," I said. "I followed him to—"

"You followed him!" he exploded. "Are you mad? He could have attacked you."

"I had both Peter and my watch with me, and it was broad daylight."

"Even so."

"Even so, stop protesting and listen. Peter and I followed him to Lord Coyle's house in Belgravia."

He stared at me, open-mouthed. "That is an interesting development," he eventually said, sounding calmer. "What's Lord Coyle's got to do with any of this?"

"He collects magical things. Perhaps he bought one of Hale's medicines to add to his collection. But why kill him? It doesn't make sense."

"Perhaps Hale wouldn't sell him anything so Coyle killed him in anger." He studied the desk surface, lost in thought.

I tried thinking of a way to tell him the rest of my news without piquing his suspicious nature, but I couldn't. There was no way to avoid it. He had to be told. "That's not all," I said. "A few minutes after that man went into Coyle's house, another came out. Oscar Barratt."

"Barratt! Well, well. So he's involved in this after all." He looked rather pleased about it, too.

"It may mean nothing. He could have other business with Coyle."

He leaned back in the chair and regarded me. "India, you can't possibly continue to defend him after this discovery. There's a direct link between Barratt and Coyle, and Coyle sent someone to threaten you."

"An *indirect* link. And I'm not defending him. I'm keeping an open mind."

It was a long time before he spoke again, and I thought that was the end of it until he said, "Why do you defend him? Why won't you accept that he's a suspect in Hale's murder?"

"I...I don't know."

He rubbed his thumb along the chair arm as if he were trying to scrub a mark off the leather. The movement occupied his attention. "Is it because you feel...a connection to him?"

"I suppose that could be it. We're both magicians."

"But that's the only similarity between you." He finally looked at me and I was shocked to see that he already seemed exhausted, and yet he'd only just woken from a nap.

"His family are in trade, like mine," I said, not really thinking about what I was saying. I wanted to ask him why he looked so awful, but his odd mood put me off.

"He's from a wealthy family," he said. "Yours are middle class."

"Thank you for pointing that out."

"That didn't come out right." He rubbed his forehead. "India, what I'm trying to say is, don't be taken in by Barratt's charms. I know his type. They only befriend people who can help them achieve their goals. They use people. I don't want you to get hurt."

"Thank you for your concern," I said, more harshly than I intended, "but I'm quite capable of determining who is a true friend and who is merely acting the role."

"You thought I was the Dark Rider," he pointed out. "And that Dorchester was innocent."

I leapt to my feet in what must have looked like petulance, but I didn't care. Matt's words stung; not because he'd judged me harshly, but because he was right. "You forgot to mention Eddie."

He winced and closed his eyes. "India, I'm sorry. That was cruel. I shouldn't have said it."

"Perhaps I needed to hear it. Perhaps I *am* too trusting of Barratt." I turned to leave, not wanting him to see the tears pooling in my eyes. I felt like a fool.

He reached the door before me and caught me by the shoulders. He dipped his head to look into my face, forcing me to lower my chin to keep him from seeing my eyes. "I've upset you. Damn it. I'm an idiot, India. You have every right to be angry with me. So go ahead. Say something about me that irritates or upsets you."

"Wh-what do you mean?"

"Point out my faults. It'll make you feel better and put us back on even ground."

My chin wobbled, to my absolute horror. "How can I when I can't find fault with you?"

"You can. I speak out of turn, for one thing. Anything else?"

Why couldn't he stop being nice? It was making me want to cry.

"India," he murmured gently, "I'm sorry I hurt you. I shouldn't have said those things."

"But I *am* a terrible judge of character," I spluttered. I couldn't hold back the tears anymore. They flowed out of me, along with all the frustration and humiliation I'd felt after Eddie ended our engagement. I prided myself on being clever and yet I'd been thoroughly duped by him.

Matt drew me into his arms and tucked my head beneath his chin. He felt warm and solid and safe. I wanted to remain there; I wished with every piece of me that I could be held by him like this whenever I wanted. But I could not, and that made me cry more.

"What Eddie did is not your fault, it's his," Matt said, massaging my neck. "Dorchester too. Forget them. Trusting the wrong person happens to the best of us. I'd rather be like you, and believe everyone is good on first meeting, than suspect everyone is bad. You're a positive, trusting person, India, and it's part of the reason I admire you."

The more he massaged my neck, the more my tears dried. But I did not move away. Now that I'd stopped crying I could hear his heartbeat. It kept rapid time but was rhythmic and reassuring. Surely such a strong heart couldn't fail. Surely he wouldn't die without the watch.

Matt gently drew me away. He wiped the pads of his thumbs across my cheeks and kissed my forehead. His lips lingered and for a moment I thought—hoped—he would tilt my head back and kiss me on the mouth.

But instead he stepped away with a sigh. He pulled a handkerchief from his pocket and handed it to me. "Will you be all right to go out soon?"

"Yes, of course." I dabbed the handkerchief against my eyes and gave it back to him. "Where are we going?"

"To see Barratt."

I looked away. "Oh."

"I want to know what business he had with Coyle. You don't have to come if you don't feel up to it."

"I want to go. What about Coyle himself? Shall we confront him about the man he sent?"

"We certainly will, but we'll see what Barratt knows first. He may know nothing at all. Like you said, he could be innocent."

He was being diplomatic for my sake. I wished he wouldn't. He seemed to think I liked Oscar Barratt in *that* way, and that certainly wasn't the message I wanted to send him. I wasn't interested in Barratt at all. I found him charming, and it was nice to discuss magic with another magician. But I couldn't tell Matt any of that without giving away too much of my heart's secrets.

I headed to my rooms but paused in the doorway. Miss Glass sat at my dressing table, rearranging my trinkets and combs.

"Miss Glass! Is everything all right?"

"I thought we were friends, India," she said without looking up.

"We are." I crouched beside her. She spoke evenly, with a strong voice, yet she did not seem like herself. "What's wrong?"

"Friends do not betray one another."

I blinked. "How have I betrayed you?" The moment I said it, I knew she'd seen Matt and me together through his open door. We hadn't noticed her.

"You know how."

I sat on the end of the bed. "I was upset and Matt was consoling me. Actually, he made me upset, so I suppose he felt guilty. That's all it was, Miss Glass, nothing more."

Finally she met my gaze with her cool one. "It didn't

appear to be nothing to me, India, nor would it appear that way to any of the servants if they saw."

"It won't happen again."

"Are you quite sure?"

"Yes. There is nothing of that nature between us."

Her lips thinned. She didn't believe me. "The thing is, India, as much as I like you, I love my nephew even more. He's my family and the Rycroft heir. He has duties to consider, and chief among those duties is to marry well and produce an heir. His wife must be from a proper family."

"Why?" I blurted out. "What difference does it make?"

She seemed surprised by my outburst. I couldn't blame her. It was a little out of character for me. "A marriage is an alliance between two families," she went on. "Each partner brings something to the marriage, whether that be money, land, influence or a title. If a gentleman marries a girl who brings none of that, he risks his estate being whittled away over time as well as becoming a laughing stock among his peers. No one will take him seriously. Is that what you want? For Matthew to be treated like an outcast?"

"He already is an outcast," I said. "He's not even English."

"He most certainly is!"

I put my hands up, in no mood for her prejudices. "His father ran away from his responsibilities and yet you don't seem to blame *him* for marrying a poor American girl."

"Don't bring Harry into it," she snapped. "He was not the heir, and he had his reasons for leaving. Our father did not treat him well." This last she slurred into her chin as her shoulders slumped. "Poor Harry. My poor dear brother, when are you coming home? I'm so alone without you."

I went to her side and gently helped her to stand. "Come, Miss Glass, it's time you rested." As much as I hated seeing her descend so quickly into her addled state, it was a blessing in this instance. I didn't want to battle with her over something that did not exist and could never be.

She clung to me as I steered her to the door, her fingers surprisingly strong. "You understand, don't you, India?"

Her clear voice surprised me. She seemed to remember our exchange.

"I do, Miss Glass. You only want what's best for the Rycroft name."

"And for Matthew. Always, and only, for him. The Rycroft estate will one day be his, as it should be. Every door will open to him and every opportunity will be laid at his feet, as long as he steps carefully and does not repeat Harry's mistake and marry an unsuitable girl. But we are still friends, are we not, India?" Her voice shook and her fingers tightened on my arm. "Please say we are still friends."

"We're still friends, Miss Glass. I've always known Matt is far beyond me and that hasn't changed. You have nothing to fear on that score."

"I knew I could trust you."

Matt walked past as we exited my room. "Aunt? Are you feeling unwell?"

"A little light in the head," she said.

"Allow me to escort you to your rooms while India gets ready."

"Does she have to go out with you?"

He looked to me.

"I do," I told them both. "I'll send Polly up. As to the other matter, Miss Glass, you have my word."

She gave me a weak smile. "Thank you, India. You're a good girl."

They walked off and I heard Miss Glass ask him about the bruise on his cheek. I did not hear Matt's response but I doubted he mentioned sparring with Cyclops.

I finished freshening up and found Polly in the servants'

sitting room, mending Miss Glass's dress hem. I sent her upstairs and waited for Matt in the entrance hall. He joined me a few minutes later, frowning.

"She's all right," he said when I asked. "Frail, but aware of who everyone is."

"I'm glad to hear it. She did turn very suddenly that time."

"Why was she in your room? And what is the other matter you two had been discussing?"

"It's something between us. She wouldn't want you to know."

His frown deepened but he didn't press me for an answer.

Bryce drove us to the office of *The Weekly Gazette* where we found Oscar Barratt writing in a notebook. He snapped it shut upon seeing us and welcomed us in.

"This is a pleasant surprise," he said, smiling, "and fortu-itous, too. You've saved me a walk to Mayfair to see you both." He held a chair out for me then returned to the other side of the desk. "Nasty bruise you've got, Glass."

"I walked into a door," Matt said.

"Of course you did. So how may I help you?"

"How do you know Lord Coyle?" Matt asked.

"Coyle?" Mr. Barratt's gaze shifted between us. "I don't know him beyond an initial meeting I had with him only this morning. I'm guessing from your expression you already know this, Mr. Glass. May I ask why the interest?"

"One question at a time," Matt said calmly. "What was your meeting about?"

Mr. Barratt sat back in his chair and steepled his fingers. "He summoned me, as it happens. Apparently men like Coyle expect you to visit them when they want to talk with you, not the other way around. His world works differently to mine." He laughed without humor. "He told me he has read some of my articles and was curious if I was alluding to magic in them."

"He asked you that outright?" I said.

He nodded. "It was rather bold, but he seemed to think I would answer in the affirmative. I suppose when one is aware of magic and looking for it, one can tell from my articles that I believe."

"Then what did he say?" Matt went on.

"He asked me how much I knew. I told him I'd heard about magic and said that some of the subjects in my articles claimed to be magicians, Dr. Hale among them."

"Did he ask a lot of questions about Hale, or his death?"

"He asked none. He didn't mention Hale specifically after I told him the doctor claimed to be an apothecary magician. If I had to guess, I would say he wasn't overly interested in Dr. Hale or his murder."

"That's odd," I said. "You would think a man with Coyle's interests would be wildly curious."

"Unless he knew everything he needed to know about Hale already," Matt said, "and his death."

Could Coyle be behind the murder? But why? What would he gain?

"What do you mean, a man with his interests would be curious?" Mr. Barratt asked.

He addressed me but I waited for Matt to answer. I no longer trusted my own instincts when it came to Barratt, or how much to tell him.

"Miss Steele?"

I looked to Matt but he simply frowned back at me. It would seem he wasn't going to guide me. So be it. It was on his head if he didn't like what I was going to say.

"We're quite certain Lord Coyle knows about magic," I said.

"Do you think he's a magician?"

"We don't know. He collects magical objects but we're not certain if *he* put the magic into any of them."

"He collects them? Whatever for?"

"There seems to be no reason behind it. Most of the magic in his collection would have disappeared—many years ago, in some cases. He kept the collection hidden and only brings it out on special occasions for select guests."

"Perhaps he's merely an eccentric." He tapped his fingers together in thought. "It explains his interest in my articles. If he's collecting magical objects, he'll want to know of any magicians who can provide him with artifacts to add to his collection."

"Did you tell him you're an ink magician?" Matt asked.

"No. I probably would have, if he had asked directly, but he didn't. I got the feeling he suspected, however. It was a strange sort of standoff. I was waiting for him to tell me he was a magician, and he was waiting for me."

"You think he is?"

"I did at the time, merely to explain his interest in my articles, but in light of what you've said about his collection, I'm no longer sure. An artless man may like to collect magic objects as much as a man who can't paint likes to collect paintings."

"Did you see a man arrive at Coyle's house a few minutes before you left?" I described the stranger to him, but he shook his head.

"Sorry," he said. "The butler let me in and out. A footman took me up to Coyle's office and I met with Coyle. I saw no one else. Why? Who is he?"

"We're assuming he's Coyle's man," Matt said. "He ordered us to cease our investigation into Hale's murder."

"Good lord. That's brazen. In broad daylight?"

"In Matt's house," I said. "Miss Glass and I had just returned from a walk and he came right up to the door and threatened me."

Mr. Barratt's brows flew up his forehead. "You were alone?"

"The butler was there."

"But Mr. Glass was not?"

Matt drew in a deep breath and let it out slowly. I got the feeling he was keeping his temper in check and his response to himself.

"Matt can't be home all the time," I said, "and he can't know when someone plans on threatening us. To be fair, he was threatened too."

"You're a very reasonable woman, Miss Steele. I know ladies who would berate their menfolk for not being around for such an event, rightly or wrongly."

"Mr. Glass is my employer, not my *folk*," I said icily. Honestly, I'd had enough of men and their overbearing notions for one day.

Mr. Barratt surprised me with a genuine smile. "Thank you for clarifying that for me."

I got the feeling he'd done some fishing and I'd gobbled up the bait and hook in one gulp.

Both men regarded one another over the desk, one smiling and the other scowling. It was a thrilling feeling to be the object of their silent battle, until I remembered that my instincts could be completely off. It was more likely that Matt didn't trust Mr. Barratt and Mr. Barratt...actually I could not think of a reason for him to dislike Matt.

"You said you were coming to visit me today," Matt said. "Why?"

"Not you," Mr. Barratt said. "I wanted to see Miss Steele."

"Me?" I blinked at him. "Why?"

"Ever since we spoke about your grandparents, I decided to do a little investigation of my own."

Matt sat forward. "You did *what*?"

Mr. Barratt put up his hands. "Whoa, calm down. Why

are you angry, Mr. Glass?"

"You've been spying on India, that's why."

"Not at all. I'm helping her find the missing pieces of her background. I want her to understand where her magic came from."

"I see," I said before Matt could interrupt. While I saw his point, and it was odd that Mr. Barratt would investigate my background without asking me first, he was telling me now. And I was wildly curious about what he'd found. "And?" I prompted.

"And I learned two things. First of all, you may not have inherited your magic from your paternal grandfather but your paternal *grandmother*."

"Well, that's interesting, and could explain why my grand-father was granted a license from the Watchmaker's Guild. He was artless and harmless in their eyes. My grandmother may have assisted him, but the guild probably didn't know about her."

"She died before you were born?" Matt asked.

I nodded. "My father spoke fondly of her, but not so fondly of my grandfather. Their marriage wasn't a happy one. Apparently my grandfather was a selfish man and his neglect drove my grandmother to an early grave. I always thought it sad."

"Unhappy marriages are common," Matt said quietly. "I've certainly seen enough of them."

"Amen," Mr. Barratt muttered.

"How did you find out about my grandmother's magic?" I asked him.

"I asked a retired watchmaker I know in passing if he knew the Steeles of St. Martins Lane. His son now owns the shop around the corner from here, but the elderly man remembered your father and grandparents. After a few perti-nent questions about your grandfather's skill, he said that his work deteriorated after your grandmother died. That got me thinking that *he* wasn't the magician, but *she* was. A few more questions and I became certain of it. He'd once seen her fix an extremely old clock with mechanisms that had stumped him."

"Did you mention magic to the retired watchmaker?" Matt asked.

"Of course not." Mr. Barratt pulled his chair forward and leaned his elbows on the desk. His blue eyes sparkled. "That's not all I learned from the old watchmaker. As we were talking, he said it was odd that I was asking him about your grandfather now, of all times."

"Why?" I asked.

"Because he thought he saw him recently."

"That's impossible. He's dead."

"That's what I told him, but he insisted he passed him in the street a few weeks ago. He called out but the other man kept going."

"Your source must have been mistaken."

"I thought so too, but I decided to follow it up." Mr. Barratt smiled an odd little smile. "I checked at the General Register Office. His birth and marriage details are recorded, but not his death."

"It must be an oversight," I said. "He is dead. My father told me."

Mr. Barratt and Matt exchanged glances. "Unless your father lied," Matt said. "If he didn't like him and wanted nothing to do with him…" He shrugged, almost as if offering me an apology for suggesting it.

"It's possible," I muttered.

"Separately, the two pieces of evidence amount to no more than speculation," Mr. Barratt said. "But together, I think there's a very real possibility that your grandfather is alive and living in London."

CHAPTER 11

"*I* think we should change our plans," I said as Matt opened the carriage door for me outside the *Gazette's* office. "Instead of confronting Lord Coyle, I think we should spy on him. He's unlikely to admit to sending his man to threaten us, and spying on him might give us more evidence against him."

"I've been thinking the same thing myself," Matt said. He ordered Bryce to take us to Scotland Yard.

"You want to speak to Munro about Coyle?" I asked as he settled on the seat opposite me.

"Brockwell, not Munro."

"But he wants to arrest you!"

"All the more reason to keep him informed. I don't have the greatest faith in the police force coming to the right conclusion on their own, so we need to feed them as much evidence as we can."

"You may have to convince him not to confront Coyle and ruin our spying efforts."

"Or I may need to convince him to believe me in the first place."

That was as much a concern as anything. If Brockwell was in Payne's pocket, we might have to go over his head and speak to Munro again. I knew it galled Matt to even consider it, but we may have no other choice.

I was about to say as much and looked up to see Matt watching me.

"Are you thinking about your grandfather?" he asked.

Barratt's suggestion that my grandfather could be alive had rocked me, but now that the initial shock had passed, I wasn't convinced.

"You're frowning," he said, leaning forward. "Are you all right?"

I nodded. "I never knew the man, so the news isn't upsetting. But don't you think my grandfather would have tried to make contact with me if he was in London?"

"Perhaps he didn't know where to look. He may have gone to the shop and found it renamed Hardacre's and given up."

"If so, then he gave up too easily. He could have asked Eddie where to find me."

"Unless he didn't want anyone to know he was still alive. India…" He scrubbed a hand over his jaw. "India, have you considered that your grandfather may be Chronos, hiding out in London under the name DuPont?"

"It crossed my mind. But he isn't a magician so he can't be Chronos. Mr. Barratt says my grandmother was the magical one."

"Barratt could be wrong. He based his assumption on the observations of one source—and an elderly man, at that. If your grandfather is Chronos, it would explain why he hasn't come looking for you—he wants to keep his identity a secret."

"For reasons we do not yet know." I sighed, feeling rather exhausted by it all, and by our lack of progress in finding

Chronos. Time was running out for Matt, and every step forward was followed by another step back.

He must be heartily sick of getting nowhere.

Matt's hand closed over mine on my lap. "It'll be all right, India. We'll find him."

"Do you mean my grandfather or Chronos?"

"Both." His crooked smile told me he still supposed them to be one and the same.

We had to wait thirty-five minutes for Detective Inspector Brockwell. One of his men brought us tea that we drank in the outer office. Matt could hardly sit still, however, and frequently got up to pace the room or look out the window. I, on the other hand, occupied myself with the small mantel clock which was a full minute behind. I had it working perfectly by the time Brockwell finally entered.

He removed his coat and hat and hung them on the stand near the door. He did not seem surprised to see us, so he must have been warned. "Come through," he said and indicated the two guest chairs near the desk in his office.

"We have another suspect for you," Matt said as he sat. "You need to investigate him."

Brockwell undid the buttons on his jacket, taking his time with each one before moving on to the next. He kept his gaze on Matt but did not speak. It was as if he could only focus on one task at a time. Or he was deliberately trying to rile Matt by stirring up his simmering frustration? "Do I now? And who might that be?"

"Lord Coyle."

Brockwell scratched his sideburns. "And why would Lord Coyle murder a doctor from the London Hospital?"

"We don't know, but he's involved somehow. He sent a man to my house to order us to stop the investigation. He threatened Miss Steele in my absence."

"Threatened you? Miss Steele, were you harmed?"

"No," I said.

"When was this?"

"Before lunch."

The detective tugged his watch by its chain and checked the time. "It's almost four now. Why did you take so long to report it?"

"We're reporting it to you now," Matt growled.

"I was overwrought," I said. "I needed time to recover."

The poor, delicate female act seemed to work on Brockwell. He nodded in sympathy. "So tell me, Mr. Glass, how did you connect the man to Coyle?"

"Miss Steele followed him," Matt said.

Brockwell turned to me. "*You* followed him? Despite being overwrought?"

"That came later," I said quickly. "He went to Lord Coyle's house. I've been there before and recognized it."

"So you assume the man works for Coyle."

"We do," Matt said. "There's no other conclusion to make."

"He could be a friend or acquaintance."

"Then Lord Coyle keeps strange company," I said. "The man was a thug with a Cockney accent."

"Perhaps Lord Coyle isn't too particular who he calls friend."

Matt drew in a deep breath and let it out slowly. "You sound as if you have no intention of investigating him."

Brockwell scratched his other sideburn and took his time answering. I had to clutch the chair arm to stop myself from shouting at him to say something. "I can't accuse Lord Coyle of murder based on your account," he finally said. "The connection is tenuous."

"The connection is very real," Matt snapped.

"The evidence is flimsy."

"Even flimsy evidence should be followed up. You forget, Brockwell, that I am well aware of what a man in your position should do at this juncture. My job in America was much the same as yours."

"That's not what I heard," Brockwell said with bland indifference, as if he didn't care. But his eyes gave him away. They may be half hidden beneath lazily lowered lids, but they were intently focused on Matt.

"I've already told you," Matt said, his jaw set hard, "Payne is lying. Do you have fresh evidence against me or are you merely his puppet, repeating his nonsense?"

Brockwell tensed. It may not have been a good idea to call him a puppet. "I have a list of all your family's misdeeds." He rifled through some papers on his desk and pulled one out. He handed it to Matt. "Every crime and misdemeanor committed by every member of your extended family is on there."

Matt gave it a cursory glance then handed it back. "None of those are news to me, Munro, or any American lawman worth his salt."

"That list wouldn't be half as long if Matt didn't work for the American police," I said since Matt didn't elaborate. "It's precisely because of his connection to the Johnson clan that he has been so successful in bringing outlaws to justice."

Brockwell dipped his chin in a slight nod. "Your devotion to your employer is admirable, Miss Steele."

"It isn't devotion. It's the truth. Kindly refrain from pre-judging me as you have done Mr. Glass."

"Pre-judging?" It was the most rapid response he'd given yet, coming before I'd even finished speaking.

"Yes, Detective, you have pre-judged Matt, taking one man's word as gospel. I may not be a policeman, but even I know that is not the best way to approach an investigation. Now, are you going to speak to Lord Coyle or not?"

Brockwell considered his answer. "Not without more

evidence. I can't accuse a man in his position of being involved in murder. There will be consequences for me."

"If anyone else had come to you with this information," Matt said, "would you investigate?"

Again, Brockwell thought through his answer before finally speaking. "You are a suspect, Mr. Glass. It's possible that you are trying to lead me astray. So I would have to say yes."

"If we wanted to lead you astray, we would not have chosen someone like Lord Coyle, previously unrelated to this crime. Further, you may cast doubts on my character to your heart's content, but do not accuse Miss Steele of deliberately trying to mislead you." Matt stood and held his hand out to me.

"If I have offended Miss Steele then I am deeply sorry." Brockwell rose and bowed to me. "It's not my intention. As to your accusation, Mr. Glass, I am merely being cautious. To be fair, I trust very few people, but in your case, I have even less reason to believe you, considering what I know." He tapped the sheet of paper listing the Johnson family's crimes.

"You have no difficulty trusting Sheriff Payne," I shot back.

"Do I, Miss Steele?"

I strode toward the door, my skirts swishing violently around my legs. I assumed Matt followed me but when I turned at the door, he was still with Brockwell at the desk.

"You should make up your mind who to trust soon," he told Brockwell. "Or you may find yourself with enemies."

"And you, Mr. Glass, ought to be careful not to go about accusing noblemen like Lord Coyle without very solid evidence of guilt. Your English family will not be able to save you if you make a mistake, nor will Commissioner Munro."

"I am well aware of that."

"I believe your man, the one with the eye patch, is watching the premises of Mr. Pitt today," he went on.

"Is he?" Matt asked idly.

"Don't play me for a fool, Glass. You know he is. I first saw him that day at your house. He's very distinctive. Kindly tell him not to return. Pitt is a suspect. If he notices him, it could ruin the investigation."

"Why is Pitt a suspect?"

Brockwell smirked. "Nice try. Good day, Mr. Glass, Miss Steele."

"I don't like that man," I grumbled as we headed out of the building into a rain shower. "He believes everything Payne told him."

"Home, Bryce," Matt said before climbing into the cabin after me. "I don't know," he said. "I'm beginning to see him a little differently. He didn't like me calling him Payne's puppet."

"Oh," I murmured. "You think I'm wrong about him too?"

He looked pained. "Perhaps. I don't know. But you're not wrong about everyone. You *are* a good judge of character, India. The only people you misjudged are those deliberately trying to dupe you."

"Brockwell isn't?"

"To be honest, I don't know what Brockwell's up to either."

I turned to the window with a sigh and said nothing. I found it hard to believe that Brockwell wasn't in Payne's pocket. He certainly didn't like us interfering and he didn't believe his own commissioner when it came to Matt's innocence.

"I wish I could eat my words," Matt said softly. "I'm sorry, India."

"For what?"

"For making you doubt yourself."

I kept my mouth shut and stared out the window for the remainder of the journey. Not because I didn't appreciate his apology, but because I didn't want to think about our little spat over Barratt anymore. I didn't want to argue with Matt over anything, least of all Oscar Barratt.

* * *

MATT USED his watch before dinner but did not retire for a rest. Cyclops was the first to arrive home, followed by Duke, then Willie. Miss Glass ate in her rooms so we were able to talk in the dining room after Matt dismissed the servants. We told the others about our eventful day, stopping frequently as Willie interjected with cuss words, exclamations or declarations that she should have been there with her Colt.

"I admit," I told her, "your presence and your gun would have been welcome when Coyle's man was here. I might have even allowed you to shoot off his little toe, if it meant he would tell us who employed him and why."

"It would have been my pleasure, India," she said, saluting me with her knife.

"That's precisely why we're lucky you weren't here," Duke grumbled.

"You learned that he worked for Lord Coyle on your own," Matt said to me. "Congratulations, India, by the way. I'm very impressed."

"She could have been caught!" Duke protested. "You want her to follow everyone who threatens you when you're not here?"

"India's capable of deciding for herself if it's safe enough to do so."

I narrowed my eyes. Matt's praise was highly suspicious. He must still feel guilty over the argument we'd had earlier.

"Tell us what you three discovered today," I said, eager to change the topic. "Cyclops, you first. You went to Pitt's, didn't you?"

Cyclops had been busy piling his plate with enough sliced meats, boiled potatoes, and vegetables to feed all of us, but stopped when I asked my question. "Pitt's shop wasn't busy," he said. "Only a handful of customers came and went."

"Anyone you recognized?" Matt asked. "Or might recognize again if you saw them?

He shook his head. "They weren't distinctive."

I glanced at Matt. Was he going to tell Cyclops that Brockwell had used the same term to describe him?

"None wore particularly fine clothing," Cyclops went on. "All entered the shop alone, all came out carrying a small package. It was odd, though. None of them looked ill."

"Perhaps they were purchasing the medicine for an ill family member," I said.

Cyclops shrugged his shoulders then tucked into his meal. "I'll go back tomorrow."

"You should lay low for a while," Matt said. "Brockwell spotted you there."

"Damn it," Cyclops muttered with a particularly severe stab of his fork into a potato.

"I've got news," Duke announced.

"So do I," Willie cut in.

"Ladies first."

"No." She plucked her wine glass off the table and swirled the contents until a drop fell over the rim and splashed onto the tablecloth. "Mine's the biggest news, so I'll go last. Go on, Duke. You tell 'em your little story."

"It ain't a little story, I'll have you know. I followed Clark to Abercrombie's shop today and saw 'em arguing."

"Go on," Matt said when Duke paused to shoot a smug look at Willie. "What did they argue about?"

"I didn't hear every word, but I definitely heard them say Hale, and also India's name, and magic. The argument was one-sided. Clark did all the shouting and Abercrombie mostly tried to calm him down."

My gaze connected with Matt's. "Anything else?" I asked.

Duke shook his head and concentrated on his food.

"That weren't much." Willie pushed her plate away and shot a smug look at Duke. "Listen to this. Dr. Ritter sold Hale's medicines today. You know, the ones he kept in his office."

"Sold them!" I said. "To whom?"

"I don't know. I didn't see it happen. One of the nurses told me about it later."

"It would've been more helpful if you followed the buyer," Duke muttered.

Willie rolled her eyes but he didn't see, too intent was he on his beans.

"It must be Coyle," I said. "He got wind of Hale's magic, perhaps after his discussion with Barratt, and bought the medicines to add to his collection."

Matt nodded. "I think so too. Good work, Willie."

"That ain't everything," she said. "Dr. Wiley exploded like a firecracker at the widow of one of his patients. Right in front of other patients, too."

"The widow?" Matt echoed. "So the patient died."

"According to my new nurse friend, the patient had been Hale's before he died. Wiley disagreed with Hale's diagnosis and changed the treatment. Well, the patient up and died this morning. The widow was no weeping violet, though. No, sir. She marched up to Wiley when he was doing his rounds and shouted at him. I could hear her clear at the other end of the ward, calling Wiley a bad doctor and wishing Hale was still there because her husband had been getting better under his care. By then, I reached that ward, and just in time, too. That's when Wiley snapped. He ranted and raved about how poor a doctor Hale had been, and that it was only luck her husband hadn't died under Hale's care, not good doctoring. He went on and on about Hale's mistakes and how some patients just up and die for no good reason, but maybe because they ain't got the will to live no more. That's when he accused her of being a bad wife and said her husband died to escape her."

I gasped. "That's awful! What a horrid man."

"If I were her, I'd have thumped him," Cyclops said.

Duke nodded. "You win, Willie."

"She does," Matt said. "And now I know where to go first thing in the morning."

* * *

Miss Glass tried to get Matt and me to remain home the next morning, but he refused. "I'm sorry, Aunt, but we have to go out. Urgent business."

"To do with that doctor's murder?" she asked, handing him his glove.

He blinked at her.

"I'm not a complete fool, Matthew," she said. "I know I lose my wits sometimes, but I do see things."

"Yes, it's to do with Dr. Hale's murder. We're helping the police with their investigation."

She did up his jacket button for him then patted his lapels. "I wish you wouldn't get involved in such a vulgar thing as police work."

"I'm sorry you find murder vulgar, Aunt Letitia. Believe me, you're not the only one."

"It's not just the murder but the police themselves. I do like knowing they're protecting us from criminals, or trying to, but I wonder what sort of person wants to go about chasing down murderers and thieves and other undesirable characters."

"The active sort." He kissed her forehead. "Did you have plans for India and me today?"

"You, yes. I wanted to take you to lunch with me. Lady Abbington is going, and Oriel Haviland, and your cousins, too."

"Another time, Aunt. When this is over."

"Promise me?"

He clasped her hands in his. "Promise. You can throw as many eligible women at me as you can possibly find. I just can't promise to like any of them."

"That is entirely the wrong attitude, Matthew."

He smiled. "Ready, India?"

"Oh, and India, before you go," Miss Glass said. "Wait there." She disappeared into the adjoining sitting room and came out again a moment later carrying a piece of folded soft green fabric. "I bought this for you."

"For me?" I said, accepting it.

"It's a shawl. It will look lovely with your coloring." She helped me adjust the shawl around my shoulders then stepped back and smiled. "I was right. It does."

"That's very kind of you, Miss Glass, but you didn't have to."

"It's a token of how much I value your friendship." She stepped in and fussed with the shawl near my throat. When it dragged on too long, I touched her elbows. She stepped back again, and that's when I saw her damp eyes. "You're very special to me," she said quietly. "Very special indeed."

"Thank you," I said, not quite sure how to react. Was it an apology gift because she felt guilty for forbidding me from being with Matt, or did she genuinely consider me a close friend? Perhaps it was both.

I removed the wrap and handed it to Bristow. "Please take it to my room."

"My aunt is behaving very oddly lately," Matt said as we drove off. "More so than usual, and mostly with you. Is everything all right between you?"

I nodded. I would not tell him that his aunt forbade a *tendre* between us. It would only embarrass me and make things awkward. I couldn't bear that. "Perhaps she's lonely. We are out of the house an awful lot. I should be home with her more."

"She's been doing quite a lot of visiting herself, lately. I don't think it's loneliness. And you're busy, anyway. I have need of you too."

The coach slowed as we approached the London Hospital. My reticule, which I'd been holding loosely, throbbed. Startled, I let it go and it fell off my lap and landed on the floor at my feet.

Matt picked it up. "Is everything all right?"

"It moved."

He held up the reticule by its ribbon. The little pouch twirled slowly until it settled, but it did not throb again. "It's not moving now," he said.

"The watch inside pulsed, like it did that day the Dark Rider attacked me. Matt, I think—"

The coach door wrenched open and a figure wearing a billowing black hooded cloak jumped in. I swallowed a scream and crowded against the far side of the cabin. Matt grabbed the man by his cloak and shook him. The hood fell back.

It was Coyle's thug!

"How dare you," Matt snarled, rising off the seat. The cabin seemed too small all of a sudden, the ceiling too low. Both men filled it, trapping me in the corner.

My watch chimed. Matt no longer held my reticule but I couldn't see it.

"Let me go, Mr. Glass, or you'll regret it," the man said to Matt in his thick cockney accent. Yet it was his calm, sinister tone that made the hairs on the back of my neck rise, not the threat itself.

Matt twisted his fist, tightening the cloak at the man's throat, forcing him to lift his chin. "You're coming with us to Scotland Yard," Matt growled.

"No, Mr. Glass, I ain't." The click of a gun cocking stopped my heart dead. "Let me go or I'll shoot."

CHAPTER 12

*M*att uncurled his fingers and eased his fist out of the man's cloak. "There's a lady present," he said through clenched teeth.

"I ain't blind," Coyle's thug shot back.

"Let her go then we'll talk."

"We're past the point of talk, Mr. Glass, and your woman ain't going nowhere. She's a part of this. Now, put your hands in the air, both of you."

I did but Matt hesitated. "Matt!" My whispered voice trembled.

He slowly raised his hands. "Are you all right, India?"

I nodded and tried not to look terrified out of my wits.

The man jerked the gun at Matt. "Order your driver to move on."

"Bryce!" Matt called. "Drive off!"

"Where to, sir?" Bryce called back.

"Just drive around," the man said.

"Anywhere!" Matt shouted. "And go as fast as you can!"

"Fast, eh?" The thug's dry chuckle hung in the cloying air

of the cabin. "You think you can overpower me without this going off?" He turned the gun on me. "Think again."

The coach rolled forward and the thug settled on the seat where I'd been sitting moments ago. I perched at the other end with Matt occupying the opposite seat. He didn't take his gaze off Coyle's man.

"You didn't heed my last warning," the man said. "I told you not to continue your investigation, and yet you were about to go to the hospital where Hale worked."

"You followed us," Matt said.

The man shrugged. "Since you didn't listen to me, I have to punish you so you know I'm serious."

"Punish?" I whispered. "What are you going to do?"

My watch chimed, a sharp sound that punctured the tense air.

"Let me show you," the man said. "Remove your glove, Miss Steele, and give me your right hand."

"Don't, India," Matt snapped.

The watch chimed again, louder.

"Either you give me your hand, Miss Steele, or I shoot you."

The watch chimed again, and I hesitated. It was warning me. Against giving him my hand or against inaction? "What will you do?" I asked.

"Since you're such a pretty lady, I'll kiss it first." He smiled, revealing a chipped front tooth and several crooked ones. "Then I'll snap every bone in every finger."

I recoiled. My stomach rebelled and bile burned my throat.

Again, my watch chimed, louder than before. The thug glanced around, annoyed, but his gaze quickly settled on me again.

"You touch her and I'll kill you." Matt's harsh voice filled the cabin over the rumble of wheels.

"Either I break your hand or I shoot you, Miss Steele. It's your choice."

"Why?" I whispered.

"Because you didn't take my first threat seriously. Maybe a broken hand will remind you the next time you decide to continue with the investigation. Now, put out those pretty, fine fingers and let me kiss them first. If you don't, I put a bullet through you. I reckon your shoulder. What do you think, Mr. Glass?"

Matt's ragged breaths expanded his chest. "You won't get out of this coach alive if you hurt her."

My watch's chime clanged like a bell.

The thug flinched. "Where is that bleeding racket coming from?"

"It's my watch," I said. "It's in my reticule. I dropped it when you ambushed us."

"Pick it up and hand it to me. Do it slowly."

I reached down and my hand touched the reticule's fabric. I passed it to the thug and he squeezed the pouch, feeling for a pistol or other weapon perhaps. Then he suddenly let it go.

The reticule bounced on his lap, leaping inches into the air, and the watch clanged over and over with deafening relentlessness. Coyle's man stared at it, his eyes huge. "What the devil—?"

Matt lunged at the hand holding the gun. It went off.

"Matt!" I screamed.

Oh God, was he hurt? Had he been shot?

Strips of leather, wool and wood rained down on me. The leather-clad ceiling sported a large hole, exposing its woolen padding. Matt hadn't been hit. I half sighed, half sobbed in relief.

Matt wrestled the man in the corner, causing the cabin to rock violently. He pinned down the hand that clutched the gun and dug his knee into the man's chest. His other hand circled his throat. The thug's eyes bulged, and his face turned a dangerous shade of purple.

"Don't kill him!" I cried.

My reticule had fallen to the floor again. I picked it up and opened the drawstring mouth. My watch had fallen silent and no longer leapt about. I pulled it out and checked it. It seemed to be in perfect order and even warmed to my touch. I didn't return it to my reticule but kept it in my hand.

"India, order Bryce to drive to Coyle's house," Matt said, taking the gun off the man.

"Not Scotland Yard?" I asked.

"Not yet." He sat back on the seat and pointed the gun at the thug.

I opened the window and gave Bryce new orders then closed it again.

Coyle's man rubbed his red throat and scowled at Matt. "I'll gut you when I get free," he rasped.

"You won't get free," Matt said.

He barked a laugh that made him cough.

"Lord Coyle won't save you," Matt said. "You've just become a liability."

We drove in silence to Belgravia. Bryce must have remembered which house was Lord Coyle's from a previous visit, because he pulled up outside its grand entrance.

"Everything all right, sir?" the coachman asked as we alighted. "I thought I heard a…" He trailed off when he saw Matt pointing a gun at the thug's head.

"Wait here," I directed him then followed Matt up the steps.

The butler opened the door and fell back a step. Matt didn't wait to be invited inside but shoved the thug across the threshold despite the butler's protests.

"Your master," Matt snapped. "Now!"

"I-I'll see if h-he's in," the butler said.

"He better damn well be in."

The next two minutes were excruciating on my nerves. Matt held the back of the thug's collar in his left hand and the gun at his temple with his right. Both men had lost their hats in the coach.

Finally Lord Coyle trudged down the stairs, flanked by two young, wide-eyed footmen and the butler, who'd regained his composure and now looked down his nose at us.

"What is the meaning of this?" Coyle demanded in a voice as robust as his stout body.

Matt hustled the thug forward. "Your man attacked us. He threatened to break Miss Steele's fingers if we didn't stop investigating Hale's murder."

"My man?" Coyle looked the brute up and down and wrinkled his nose as if he smelled something foul. "I've never seen him before."

"Don't play me for a fool, Coyle. He was seen coming here."

Coyle looked to his butler.

"Er...a delivery of some sort, if I recall, sir. Nothing important."

"He came to the front door," I pointed out, "not the service entrance."

"It is hardly my master's fault if that fellow doesn't know the proper order of things." The butler straightened and placed his hands at his back. He looked entirely too smug for my liking.

"There you have it, Glass," Coyle said, stroking his thumb and forefinger along his drooping white mustache. "This man has nothing to do with me. Now if you'll kindly remove him from my premises, I would be most grateful."

Matt pulled hard on the man's collar and he made a choking sound. "Threatening me is one thing, Coyle, but you do not threaten Miss Steele and get away with it."

"My dear fellow, I have not threatened anyone. He has. Now, if you'll excuse me."

Matt looked as if he would protest, but instead he swung the thug around and marched him out the door. The man tripped down the steps but Matt managed to keep him on his feet.

"Coyle has thrown you to the wolves," Matt growled at the man. "Care to admit that you work for him now?"

The man didn't speak. He looked angry, but at Coyle or Matt?

"He doesn't care what happens to you," Matt said. "He's saving his own skin at your expense."

Still, the man said nothing.

"Don't you care what will happen to you?"

"The law will do what it wants with me. Ain't nothing going to change that."

With a grunt of frustration, Matt shoved him into the cabin. "India, you'll ride alongside Bryce. Bryce, take us to Scotland Yard."

Bryce helped me up to the driver's seat then waited until Matt shut the cabin door. I sat with my heart in my throat the entire journey, jumping at every shout from other coachmen or loud noise. Matt seemed to have everything under control, but the disappointment of Coyle's unruffled reaction must be eating at him. Perhaps he'd got the thug to confess by now.

The cabin door flew open before the coach came to a complete stop outside the Victoria Embankment police headquarters. Matt pushed the man ahead of him. He still held his collar and the gun at his temple, but the man now sported a bloody nose and bruised cheek.

I eyed Matt but made no comment. I didn't dare. Fury hardened his face and clouded his eyes so that I hardly recognized him. He didn't seem to see me as he marched the thug toward the New Scotland Yard building. I followed a few paces behind.

Inside, constables rushed over. Matt briefly explained that the thug had threatened me and pulled a gun on us. They took him and his gun away, then led us to a windowless room that seemed to be used as a sitting room but had more in common with a cell it was so airless and sparsely furnished.

"Get me Brockwell," Matt demanded. He paced for five minutes until Brockwell came, then he stopped pacing. He did not sit.

Brockwell walked into the room in his slow, deliberate gait that wound my already fraught nerves even tighter. Matt was just as tense, if his rigid shoulders and stony silence were anything to go by. He had not spoken to me since ordering me to sit alongside Bryce.

"My constable tells me you brought someone in after he threatened you," Brockwell said. "Poor Miss Steele! What an ordeal for you. Constable, bring tea for Miss Steele."

"He's linked to Hale's murder," Matt said before Brockwell addressed him. "He's the man who threatened Miss Steele yesterday. Today, he held us at gunpoint in my conveyance. If I hadn't overpowered him, he would have broken Miss Steele's fingers or shot her to get his point across."

"Perhaps you should have stopped investigating after the first threat."

Matt sucked in a sharp breath and looked as if he would explode in fury. I caught his hand and squeezed so hard it must have hurt. He merely blinked but at least he no longer looked like he wanted to punch Brockwell.

"When you question him," I said, "you must ask him about Lord Coyle."

"Thank you, Miss Steele," Brockwell said. "I am aware of what I must ask him."

"He won't admit anything," Matt bit off. "Coyle has somehow managed to convince him not to speak. Perhaps he has threatened the man's family or promised them money if something happens to him." He lowered his head and swore under his breath.

"Thank you for bringing him to me," Brockwell said, standing. "Please, stay for tea. Miss Steele looks as if she could do with a cup. You both do." He headed out, passing the constable carrying a tray.

Matt dragged his hands through his hair and shook his head when the man offered him tea.

"I think we'll go," I said to the constable. "I'm sorry for your trouble."

"No trouble, ma'am." He eyed Matt who was once again pacing.

I grabbed Matt's arm and forced him to stand with me. "We have work to do," I said. "Remember?"

We followed the constable back through the warren of offices and cubicles then saw ourselves out. "The London Hospital," I said to Bryce.

"We should go home," Matt said. "Brockwell's right. You've had an ordeal."

"We both have, but I seem to have calmed down. You have not. I think you need to focus on work for a little while, and then we'll return to Park Street. If we go home now, you'll sit there and stew in your own anger."

"I am not angry," he said, settling beside me.

I took his hand in both of mine and rubbed it. After a minute, I felt the tension leach away and his body relax. He caught my hand and tugged the fingertips of my glove, removing it completely. He stroked his thumb across my knuckles, giving the motion his full attention. He breathed deeply, expanding his chest, and let it out slowly.

"India, I'm sorry for all of this. You shouldn't have gone through that."

"It's hardly your fault. There's no need for you to apologize."

"If I'd left you home, you would not have endured that."

"Therein lies the problem. I would not allow you to leave me at home." I curled my other hand around his arm above the elbow. "Matt, do not blame yourself. And anyway, you saved us."

He merely grunted.

"Although my watch would have managed once I let it out of my reticule."

His faced lifted, although he didn't quite smile. "I'm not yet confident in your watch's abilities to put our lives in its hands."

I rolled my eyes. "Very amusing."

"Pardon?"

"Hands. Watches have hands. You made a pun."

He smiled, sort of. I counted it as a small victory and smiled back, but his features quickly settled into a frown again. He concentrated on my fingers, perhaps thinking about what would have happened if he hadn't stopped Coyle's man from breaking the bones.

A shiver threatened to wrack me, only to be stopped in its tracks when he kissed my hand. My breath stopped too as his warm lips pressed against the knuckles.

I stared at the top of his head, then, without really thinking, went to stroke his hair.

But he pulled away and caught my hand. He tucked it between both of his, cradling it. "We're stopping the investigation," he said.

"No! Matt, you can't stop now."

"We have to put our faith in Brockwell."

"And wait and see if he arrests you for Hale's murder?" I

withdrew my hand and thrust it back into my glove. "Unlike you, I have little faith in our constabulary. We're going to continue until the murderer is caught, and that's that."

"India—"

"No, Matt. I insist. Besides, Coyle now knows we're aware of his involvement, and he knows the police are aware, too. He'd be a fool to send a second man after us."

"Perhaps he is a fool. We don't know enough about him to say for certain. India, I'm not placing your life in unnecessary danger."

"If you won't help, then I'll continue the investigation on my own."

"Now you're just being stubborn and unreasonable."

I crossed my arms. "I suspect Willie will help me."

He threw his hands in the air. "Of course she will! She's one card short of a full deck, and I'm beginning to think you are too." He shook his head. "I can't believe you're going to defy me on this."

"I'm glad you realize that I will."

He crossed his arms too, matching my pose. "I don't see that I have a choice if I want to protect you."

We sat side by side without speaking the rest of the way to the hospital.

* * *

UNFORTUNATELY, Dr. Ritter and Dr. Wiley were in surgery and were expected to remain there for some time. We decided to go home and return later. Matt had looked tired ever since the incident with Coyle's man, so it was perhaps for the best that he would be forced to rest now and use his watch in the privacy of his own house. It wasn't yet midday, however. It worried me that he needed his watch already.

He refused to retire to his rooms until after he'd spoken

with the others. Miss Glass was out making calls so the rest of us assembled in the sitting room with cups of tea. Matt told them what had happened when we'd first arrived at the hospital and then went on to confront Lord Coyle. It wasn't easy with Willie interjecting every few seconds.

"That God damn pig swill," she muttered when he finally finished. "He should be tied and gutted like the hog he is. Wish I'd been there, Matt. I'd have helped you get Coyle to talk."

"Matt handled the situation as well as could be expected," I said. "No one could have gotten Lord Coyle to admit any wrongdoing. He's much too clever."

"And he'd know he can't be touched," Cyclops added. "No one would dare accuse a lord of being involved in a murder."

"He's not above the law," Matt said. "We just have to find enough evidence against him that would convince the police and a jury."

"You're going to continue?" Cyclops glanced sideways at me. "Is that a good idea?"

Matt's lips flattened. "I have been given no other option."

I lifted my chin. "I told him I'm going to investigate with or without him."

Willie slapped me on the shoulder. Some of my tea splashed over the rim of my cup and pooled in the saucer. "Good for you, India. We don't let men like Coyle scare us."

"His man tried to shoot her!" Duke cried. "A wise person would be scared of Coyle."

"You calling me an idiot?"

He lifted his cup to his lips and sipped.

"This is nothing to do with foolhardiness," I told them, "and everything to do with making sure Matt's neck doesn't end up in a noose."

My pronouncement was met with silence from the men and an "Amen," from Willie. "You think he killed Hale because the doctor refused to sell him his magic medicine, don't you?" she asked.

Matt nodded and pressed his finger against his temple, as if he could dig out the ache there. "We think Coyle found out that Hale is an apothecary magician. He approached Hale to purchase some of his magic medicine, but Hale refused. So he had him killed then offered to buy Hale's private bottles from the hospital."

"It's a good theory," Duke said, nodding.

"Sounds too drastic to me," Cyclops said from where he stood by the fireplace. "Why not just steal the bottles from Hale's office? Why kill Hale?"

"Because Coyle's mad." Willie drew little circles at her ear with her finger. "Mad folk don't think like the rest of us. They go straight for the throat. Or the poison, in this case."

"It means Coyle put a spell on Hale's personal bottle of Cure-All," I said with a shake of my head. "I think it's too much of a coincidence for him to be an apothecary magician when he has nothing to do with the industry."

"He could have colluded with an apothecary magician," Matt said. "Which brings us back to our original suspects."

The others went over old ground, tossing out theories and suppositions. I did not join in. I'd had a thought, and when Matt asked me what was on my mind, I told them.

"What if Hale infused the poison spell into his own medicine, not intending to take it himself but give it to someone else?"

"And then he took it by accident?" Matt asked.

"Or someone swapped the poisoned bottle with his regular one in his desk drawer. It means they would have seen him place the spell on the medicine and seen where he put the bottle."

"Ritter or Wiley," Duke suggested. "Someone from the hospital."

"Not necessarily an employee," I said. "It's quite easy to get in and walk through the building. It could have been any of our suspects."

Matt squeezed the bridge of his nose. "It would mean there is no other apothecary magician and we're barking up the wrong tree by looking for one."

Several sighs filled the sitting room, followed by silence. Matt closed his eyes. He looked done in.

"Matt," I said gently, "your watch."

He pulled the watch out of his inside jacket pocket. He flipped the case open and closed his eyes again as the magic flowed along his veins. I watched, fascinated by the effect. It made him seem otherworldly and not quite human, the way I imagined fairy folk appeared.

A movement near the door startled me. Hope Glass stood there, her lips forming a perfect O, her wide gaze on Matt as the magic lit up his face and disappeared into his hair.

CHAPTER 13

"*H*ope!" I leapt to my feet and rushed to stand between her and Matt, blocking her line of sight.

Duke and Cyclops sprang into action, too, flanking either side of me to form a shield.

"But…Matthew!" Hope blurted out. "Your skin!"

"Ain't nothing to see." Willie grabbed her by the shoulders, turned her around and marched her out.

Hope glanced back, but Willie kicked the door closed with her foot. I could hear Hope's excited voice questioning her on the other side, and Willie getting crosser and crosser.

"Damn it," Matt muttered, slipping his watch back into his pocket. "I'd better talk to her."

"And say what?" Duke asked.

"I'll think of something." He strode to the door and turned on a charming smile as he opened it. "Hope! What a pleasant surprise." He held out his hand and she hesitated before placing hers in it.

"Is everything all right, Matt?" she asked.

"Of course," he said cheerfully. "It's wonderful to see you, and without the others, too." He beamed one of his dashing smiles and her face glowed, thanks to the sheer brightness of it.

It was a genuine smile, and why wouldn't it be? He admitted he liked her, perhaps more than he let on. The familiar knot of jealousy tied my insides together.

"Excuse me," I said and headed to the stairs, only to have Willie catch up to me and block my path.

She gripped my arm hard and bent her head to mine. "You can't leave now, India," she whispered. "Someone has to stay and make sure she doesn't get him into a compromising position."

"Willie! He wouldn't do that."

"I said *she'd* do it to *him*. Not all ladies are prim and proper like you. Some are devious. And anyway, if they're alone, she'll ask him about what she saw and he might tell her. Someone has to stop him from confiding in her."

"You do it."

"Polite talk makes me want to gouge my own eyes out. You're good at it."

"At being dull?" I picked up my skirts and forced my way past her. "Send Duke or Cyclops in. I've got better things to do."

"Like what?"

"Like…see to the clock in the drawing room. It's running a little slow."

"Coward."

"India?" Matt called after me. "Won't you join us for tea?"

I paused on the step and smiled back at him. Hope, now holding on to Matt's arm, inspected his profile, perhaps looking for signs of the magic. "I'll be in the drawing room," I said. "The clock needs fixing."

He narrowed his gaze.

"Come, Cousin," Hope said. "It'll just be us. We can discuss private family matters."

Willie sighed heavily. "Then I better come too, since I'm family." She turned her back to them and glared at me so hard her eyeballs looked in danger of popping out of their sockets. "You owe me," she mouthed.

* * *

MATT JOINED me in the drawing room a half hour later. I checked behind him but he was alone.

"Found the problem?" he asked, nodding at the mantel clock in front of me on the table, its housing open and the mechanisms exposed.

"Not yet," I said.

"Perhaps that's because there is no problem."

I ignored him and inspected the wheel, barrel and spiral spring under my magnifier. All pieces were, in fact, in good working order, but I wasn't going to tell him that. "Has Hope left already?"

"She grew tired of Willie making her presence known with yawns, coughs and sniffs. I got the distinct impression Willie doesn't want me to be left alone with Hope."

"She's worried you're going to fall in love with her and want to remain here in England."

He hiked up his trouser legs and sat. "She has a point."

I dropped the spring and it rolled off the table.

Matt picked it up. "As always, Willie has her own interests at heart. Pay her no mind."

"I-I'm not." I accepted the spring and used my tweezers to insert it back into the clock's housing. "Did Hope ask you about what she'd seen?"

"She asked to see my watch, so I showed it to her. That reminds me, we still need to buy me a new artless one."

"Stop trying to change the subject. What did Hope say about your watch and the magic?"

"She gave the watch a good inspection and handed it back to me. She then asked why my skin had changed color while I was clutching the watch. I told her she'd been mistaken as I was holding the watch at that moment and my skin was perfectly normal."

"She won't believe that. Hope is not the sort of girl who is easily led to believe the opposite of what she saw. Her curiosity must be piqued even further."

"Speaking from your own experience?"

"This is not a laughing matter, Matt."

He held up his hands in surrender. "I'm not laughing."

"You were smiling." I closed the housing on the back of the clock and gave the glass dome a clean with my cloth. "Hope won't give up until she learns the truth. She's clever, tenacious and devious. She'll find out about your watch somehow."

"Then perhaps I should just tell her."

I stopped cleaning and stared at him. "You're joking again."

"To be honest, I don't know. Sometimes I think it would be easier if she just knew what was wrong with me. She and my Aunt Beatrice would give up on marrying me then."

"I wouldn't be so sure. Your Aunt Letitia still thinks you're a prize, and she knows you're ill." I inspected the clock dome for smudges. "Anyway, we will find Chronos, and he will fix your watch, so your point is not relevant."

He continued to watch me as I polished the glass case, my strokes getting more and more vigorous as my nerves stretched tighter with each tick of the clock. "You're going to polish a hole through that glass," he eventually said.

When I continued, he leaned forward and laid his hand over mine, stilling it.

"What's wrong, India?"

"I'm worried. First Payne sees you using your watch and now Hope."

He stroked my hand with his thumb then pulled away. "Hope is hardly like Payne."

"But what if she confides in someone and they use the information against you in some way? Her father, for instance. Lord Rycroft may be your uncle but I don't like him."

"I don't like him either, but, as you say, he is my uncle and he ultimately wants what's best for me. He's on my side simply because I'm the Rycroft heir. The family title must continue and all that."

"You have more faith in him than I do. I agree that family and the title are very important to him, but you are not the lord yet, and he seems to resent the title going to his brother's American son."

He looked pained, and I instantly regretted my directness. I don't know what had come over me lately. I'd turned into quite the opinionated mule. "I doubt Hope will tell him anything about what she saw today," he said. "It's not like anyone would believe her if she claimed to witness my watch glow and my veins turn purple."

True, but my fears were not allayed. His secret was best kept among ourselves. I picked up the clock, my arms straining under its weight.

"Allow me." Matt took it off me. The clock made a whirring sound then silenced. He stared at it. "Should it be making that noise?"

"No." I checked that it still kept correct time against my watch. It seemed fine and didn't whir again. "Perhaps it likes you."

"Or perhaps it's protesting leaving your hands," he said with a wicked gleam in his eyes. He set the clock on the mantel and centered it beneath the painting of a Glass ancestor above. "I think this clock is now my favorite in the entire house."

"Because it made a whirring sound?"

"Because we understand one another."

"It's a clock, Matt. It doesn't understand anything."

The clock whirred again and chimed once. I hurried from the room, not because of the clock, but because I didn't want Matt to see how his flirting made me blush.

* * *

WE MANAGED to be shown in to Dr. Ritter's office by lying to the nurse at the front desk. We claimed to be relatives of the man who'd died under Dr. Wiley's care. Dr. Ritter agreed to see us immediately.

"You!" he snapped when we walked in. "Get out at once!" He attempted to shut the door, but Matt wedged himself into the gap and forced it open.

"Dr. Ritter, we just have a quick, discreet question," he said. "Who did you sell Dr. Hale's medicines to?"

Dr. Ritter shrank back then, sighing, retreated behind his desk. "I don't know what you're talking about."

"You sold Dr. Hale's personal medicine collection to someone. Who?"

He collected a stack of papers and shuffled them. "You're mistaken."

"So if we enter Dr. Hale's office now, we'll still find jars and bottles on the shelves?"

"Of course not. Everything in his office was sent down to the storeroom or dispensary. His personal effects were returned to his business partner, Mr. Pitt."

Matt leaned over the desk. "You're lying."

Dr. Ritter scooted his chair back as far as it would go.

"Mr. Glass, if you don't leave now, I'll report you to Detective Inspector Brockwell. He assured me that your investigation was not sanctioned by him and that you are not working with him. I suspect he would happily arrest you." He shot Matt a triumphant look from his distant position.

I wrapped my hand around Matt's arm but didn't have to say anything. He turned and marched off, waiting for me to catch up at the door.

"That's your idea of discreet?" I said as we headed back along the corridor.

"If you think sweetness will lure him into answering, then be my guest and try."

We found Dr. Wiley in his office down the hallway, his head in his hands and an open medical text in front of him on the desk. I felt a little sorry for him. He'd not had a good week, what with pronouncing one patient dead only to have him brought back to life by a rival, then having another patient die under his care and the widow accuse him of negligence.

"Dr. Wiley," I said gently before Matt could fire questions at him. "Are you all right?"

Dr. Wiley lowered his hands. He looked awful. Indeed, he looked like Matt did when he needed a rest. His thin gray hair was disheveled, his eyes red-rimmed and the wrinkles across his forehead had multiplied and deepened. He groaned upon seeing us. "Miss Steele, Mr. Glass, what are you doing here?"

"We came to speak to Dr. Ritter," I said. It wasn't a complete lie but I thought it might make him relax enough to talk to us if he thought we weren't interested in him.

His shoulders did lose some of their tension. "Ritter," he said with a bitter twist of his mouth.

I waited for him to go on, or for Matt to ask his questions, but neither spoke. "Has something happened between you and Dr. Ritter?" I prompted. "You seem a little...upset."

"And rightly so!" He tapped his chest. "I have been a surgeon for over thirty years, Miss Steele. Thirty! Ten of those at this hospital. I ought to be respected." He opened his desk drawer and pulled out a silver flask. "If I'd been made principal surgeon, this hospital would never have employed the likes of that jumped up pharmacist in the first place."

"You mean Dr. Hale?" I asked, all innocence.

He took a sip from his flask but it mustn't have been enough to fortify him, because he drank more. "Of course I mean Hale. Everything began to unravel after he came here. Everything!"

"It seems to me that you've been treated most unfairly, Dr. Wiley," I said, approaching him. "Anyone can see that you work hard. And if it's any consolation, I think most of the staff appreciate you."

"Not Ritter," he muttered into the flask. "Not after...after my patient died and his widow...well, I won't bore you with the details."

"I did hear about it," I said, resting my hand on his arm. Out of the corner of my eye I saw Matt nod for me to go on, so I followed my instincts and perched on the edge of Wiley's desk. "And I believe that patient used to be Dr. Hale's?"

Wiley nodded. "Hale misdiagnosed him, not me. The odd thing is, despite the misdiagnosis, Hale managed to keep him alive. According to the chart, the medicine Hale prescribed shouldn't have worked on either the condition Hale thought he had, or the one he actually died of. And yet the fellow hung on."

I did not look at Matt for fear that my face would give me away to Wiley. But I was sure now that Hale had prescribed magical medicine to his patient, enough to alleviate his symptoms and pain as his condition deteriorated.

Wiley sipped from his flask again, but finding it empty, tossed it on the desk with a click of his tongue. "Try telling any of that to Ritter. Since the patient died under my care, I must be responsible, so he says."

"And the widow didn't believe you either," I said.

"That old dragon. It's her fault I'm in an even bigger hole than I would have been. Have you ever noticed, Miss Steele, how some women become crosser and fiercer as they get older? Don't get old, Miss Steele. Stay young and pretty and kind." He patted my hand and his eyes turned watery.

"Dr. Ritter will forgive you in time," I assured him. "Speaking of Dr. Ritter, do you know who he sold Dr. Hale's personal medicine collection to?"

He lifted one shoulder. "I don't know, and I don't care. Ask him."

"We did and he wouldn't say."

He frowned. "Why wouldn't he tell you? There's no reason for that sort of thing to be kept private."

"He said all of Dr. Hale's things were taken to the dispensary or store room. He claims not to have sold anything."

He frowned harder. "Dr. Hale's collection was so large, there wouldn't be room for all of those bottles in the store room. I wonder why he refuses to admit he sold them."

"Dr. Wiley," Matt said, speaking for the first time.

Dr. Wiley blinked slowly at him, as if he'd just realized he was present. "Yes?"

"Cast your mind back to the afternoon Dr. Hale died."

Dr. Wiley picked up his flask and shook it. Finding it still empty, he set it down on his desk again. "If I have to."

"You checked on a patient in your ward then went home. Do you remember that?"

"I think so," he hedged. "Why?"

"You wrote the time as five fifty-five on the patient's chart, but one of the nurses who came after you wrote the time as five forty-five. How can that happen if you were first? And before you attempt to lie to us, let me warn you that we've spoken to the nurse and she's adamant that she wrote the correct time and that you had already left the hospital."

Dr. Wiley swallowed. "I-I can't recall. I suppose I simply made a mistake."

"You seem to make a lot of them."

Dr. Wiley folded his arms over his chest. "Your point?"

"My point is, you could have killed Dr. Hale or you could have simply lied in order to leave early."

"I didn't kill him! My god, man, I know I've made mistakes lately, but I haven't deliberately killed anyone in my life! What do you take me for?"

"For a man who is skating on thin ice. If Dr. Ritter finds out you lied on a patient's chart, that'll be another strike against your name."

Dr. Wiley half rose from the chair, only to fall back heavily, as if he didn't have the energy to confront Matt face to face. "Don't tell him," he said. "Please. I can't afford to look for another job at my age. I'm tired, and I just wanted to go home a few minutes early that evening. That's all."

Matt nodded, and I thought that was the end of it. I rejoined him on the other side of the desk and headed toward the door. He did not follow.

"If you want me to keep your secret," Matt said to Wiley, "then find out who Dr. Ritter sold Dr. Hale's medicines to."

Dr. Wiley stared at Matt. Matt glared back at him, his face as uncompromising as I'd ever seen. Like Dr. Wiley, he too was at the end of his tether, but it manifested in anger, not resignation.

For a moment, I thought Dr. Wiley would refuse, but then he nodded. "I'll do my best."

"Send word to me at sixteen Park Street, Mayfair, when you learn something," Matt said.

We made our way through the hospital and outside. Matt insisted on exiting first and making sure no one accosted him before allowing me to follow. Until this investigation was over, he would remain cautious.

"You were very severe with poor Dr. Wiley," I said as we drove off.

"We need answers and we need them quickly to get this investigation over with. If that means pushing harder and stepping on toes, then so be it. Besides, he is still a suspect."

"I believe him when he said he didn't do it."

I half expected Matt to tell me I was too trusting or not a very good judge of character, but he said nothing. Perhaps he didn't want to hurt my feelings again.

* * *

MATT DINED with his aunt at her friend's house, and I retired before they returned home. He slept late the next morning. So late, in fact, that Duke went to check on him at ten.

"He just woke," he announced upon his return to the sitting room.

I breathed a sigh of relief. Willie muttered a prayer under her breath.

"He's getting worse," Cyclops said from his position by the window. "He tires quicker and he's got that look about him like he had after Doc Parsons stitched him up and before he believed in the watch's power."

They'd told me the story of those days after Dr. Parsons and Chronos combined their magic into Matt's watch, and how he refused to consider that it could keep him alive. He became terribly ill and would have died if Willie, who'd witnessed the surgery and initial magic, hadn't pressed the watch into his palm as he lay dying.

Willie buried her face in her hands, her fingers digging into her hair. "We've got to find Chronos."

"We're waiting for him to return to the Cross Keys," I reminded her.

"All this waiting! It makes me want to stab myself in the eye with a fork."

Duke pushed up from the chair where he'd thrown himself and marched to the door. "I'm going to Worthey's factory in Clerkenwell. Maybe Chronos will show up again."

"And I'm going to the Cross Keys," Cyclops said.

Willie followed them out. "I ain't sitting here doing nothing, either."

I was tempted to join them, but the investigation needed to continue.

Matt finally came down and apologized for his tardiness. "It was a late night," he said.

"Was the dinner enjoyable?"

"It was, surprisingly. Aunt Letitia has an eclectic circle. I find there's usually someone interesting to talk to, and last night was no exception. I discussed archaeology with a gentleman who funds digs and collects Egyptian artifacts."

I smiled despite the hollowness that opened up inside me. It wasn't jealousy. He hadn't even mentioned speaking to any women. No, it was the emptiness that came from being left out, of wishing I'd heard what the gentleman had to say, too, and of not being at Matt's side. I'd grown so used to investigating alongside him, traveling everywhere together, and discovering new things with him, that I felt the exclusion keenly.

"I wish you could have been there, India," he said. "You would have found him interesting too."

I concentrated on the papers I'd been staring at most of

the morning. It was a contract for a small house on the edge of London that I was considering purchasing. The papers had arrived in the morning's post, but the legal jargon was so complicated that I couldn't make heads or tails of it. I gave up and glanced at Matt, catching him trying to sneak a look at the papers.

"It's for that house," I told him. "The one in Willesden."

"You really are considering purchasing it? Good for you, India. It's in a great location, near the station and in a quiet street. It'll be easy to rent out to a family where the husband works in the city. I think it's a solid investment for your reward money."

I didn't tell him I was thinking about living in it myself. I could still commute to Mayfair every day to work with him or be with his aunt, and it would provide me with an income if he returned to America, as I could rent out the spare room. I had to think about my future, and the house was far too good to let go. I had to think about the present too, and how awkward it was living in the same house as him, particularly in the evenings when his aunt had gone to bed and we spent quiet moments together or happened upon each other in a dark corridor. The longer I remained at number sixteen Park Street, the more danger I was of falling further in love with him. So much further, in fact, that I worried I could not untangle myself when he found himself a wife or…or died.

"Will you look over these papers with me later?" I asked. "I feel as though I need a law degree to understand them."

"Of course. And if it's all in order, I'll have my lawyer finalize arrangements for you."

"Thank you, Matt. That's very generous of you."

"Generous?" He frowned. "India, it's nothing."

Peter the footman entered and announced the arrival of a visitor. "There's a Dr. Wiley to see you, sir. Shall I escort him to your study?"

"I'll see him in here," Matt said. Once Peter left, Matt addressed me again. "If ever you need anything, just ask. I'm happy to help you. In fact, I need to help you."

Need? That was an odd thing to say. He must have thought so too, because his frown deepened and did not disappear until Dr. Wiley entered. The doctor clutched his hat in both hands and gave me a nervous little bow.

"G-good morning," he said. "Lovely day today."

"It does seem pleasant," I said with a glance at the window.

"You have something for me?" Matt asked.

Dr. Wiley cleared his throat. "Y-yes."

"Then please sit," I said, shooting Matt a stern glare at his inhospitable behavior.

Matt settled his feet a little apart and his hands behind his back. When I realized he wasn't going to sit too, I glared even harder at him. He finally relented and sat.

"Go on, Dr. Wiley," I prompted.

"I had to wait for Dr. Ritter to leave his office and look through his papers," the doctor said. "I didn't like doing it, mind, but you left me no choice, Mr. Glass."

Matt didn't bat an eyelid at the accusation. If his form of blackmail bothered him, he didn't show it. "To whom did he sell the medicines?" Matt asked.

"To Mr. Clark from the Apothecary's Guild."

Clark! Oh my.

"Why did Clark want them?" Matt asked.

"I don't know, and I don't care. I *do* care that the documents for the sale were hidden and not on official hospital letter-headed paper. One must assume that Dr. Ritter profited personally. Now, if you'll excuse me, I have a meeting with members of the hospital board."

"You're going to inform them of Dr. Ritter's activities?" I asked.

He slapped his hat on his head and smiled. "I'm glad we were able to help one another out, Mr. Glass."

"So am I." Matt shook his hand.

I tugged on the bell pull, and Bristow arrived to escort Dr. Wiley back down the stairs. "Good luck with the meeting," I said.

Dr. Wiley smiled and bowed. "Good day, Miss Steele."

"Well," I said, turning to Matt after the doctor left. "That turned out rather well for him in the end."

"And you doubted my methods." Matt clicked his tongue and a playful smile flirted with his mouth. "Have a little more faith in your partner, India. Sometimes I even know what I'm doing."

"Don't pretend that the outcome was according to plan, Matt. You didn't care a whit for Dr. Wiley's predicament."

"That's not true. I cared, I just didn't do anything about it. To be honest, I didn't think he'd go through with spying for us. I'm surprised that he did and found what we needed. I'm even more surprised that he's going to use the information for his own benefit. I didn't think he had it in him."

I settled my hand in the crook of his arm and walked with him to the staircase. "You're admitting that you misjudged someone? Well, well, this is a day to mark in our calendars."

He chuckled. "Are you ready to visit Clark now?"

"I certainly am. I want to know why he's interested in those bottles since his guild is against magic."

CHAPTER 14

$\mathcal{T}$he porter at the Apothecary's Guild hall must have been told not to let us in if we visited again. He slammed the door in Matt's face.

Matt hammered it with his fist. "Inform Mr. Clark that if he doesn't speak to us, we will take our information to the police!" he called out. "I'm sure they'll be very interested to know he bought a murder victim's medicine collection."

His threat was followed by several seconds of silence, then: "If you'll wait there, sir."

Matt leaned one shoulder against a column and crossed his arms and ankles. He looked as if he were waiting for a friend, not someone he needed to interrogate.

I checked my watch. It was five minutes past eleven. A minute later, I checked again.

"Time won't go faster, no matter how much you look at it," Matt said with a smirk.

I snapped the case closed and slipped the watch back into my reticule. "You're in a cheerful mood this morning."

"I had a good sleep and, more importantly, I feel as if

we're finally getting somewhere. There's a piece of the puzzle still missing but perhaps Clark holds it."

"I hope so." I checked along the street, looking for someone who may threaten us, but none presented themselves. "Coyle seems to have given up."

"Nobody followed us from home," he agreed. "That's a good sign, but it pays to remain vigilant."

I pulled my watch out of my reticule again and hung the chain around my neck. Matt nodded his approval.

The door finally opened and Mr. Clark stepped out. "What do you want?" he snapped. "I'm busy."

"You wish to discuss this here on the street?" Matt asked.

"I have nothing to hide."

"Then why tell your porter to keep us out?"

"Because you're a liar, and I don't trust you. I know your name is not Wild. You're Glass and Steele."

"Did you learn that from Abercrombie after you told him that an American and Englishwoman came to your guild hall asking about magic?"

Mr. Clark bristled. "What do you want?"

"We want to ask you some questions about the medicine bottles you bought from the London Hospital."

Mr. Clark smoothed the side of his head with his palm, although his hair was already in place thanks to the oil slicked through it. "It's not a crime to purchase the belongings of the deceased."

"Not if sold by the heir, no, but you bought those from Dr. Ritter. They were part of Dr. Hale's private collection and didn't belong to the hospital. He sold them to you illegally."

"Then the police ought to speak to him, not me!"

Matt lifted his hand to warn Clark to lower his voice as a passerby eyed him warily then hurried on his way. "Are you sure you want to remain out here for the rest of this discussion?"

"I'd rather be in a public place where there are witnesses."

"What *has* Mr. Abercrombie told you about us?" I asked.

"Everything, Miss Steele."

I smiled but it was hard and bitter. "I doubt that very much, since Mr. Abercrombie doesn't know us at all. He made his mind up about me before he even met me. I'm not a villain, Mr. Clark. If Abercrombie has told you I am, then perhaps *he* is the villain."

Two men wearing woolen caps walked toward us and Matt stiffened. He edged closer to me. "What do you want with Hale's medicines?" he asked Clark.

"That is none of your affair." Mr. Clark backed toward the door. "Now, if that's all—"

"You want to test them," Matt went on. "Am I right? You want to know what ingredients he has used to make them so good."

"If you say so."

Matt waited until the two men were out of earshot before speaking again. "You won't find the secret ingredient, Mr. Clark. Magic cannot be seen, smelled, touched or extracted."

Mr. Clark glanced nervously at the men's backs. "Are you mad?" he hissed, stepping toward Matt. "They could have overheard you."

"Magic is bound to the medicine," Matt said. "The spell makes it part of the medicine, but it fades in time. It's likely the magic infused into the medicines in your possession has dispersed and lost effectiveness. Even if that is not the case, an artless apothecary will learn nothing from testing them. A magician can, perhaps. I don't know. I'm no expert."

Mr. Clark's nostrils flared, but I didn't know if it was in anger or disappointment. "Is that what you came for? To tell me my efforts are wasted?"

"And to ask you to tell us what you and Abercrombie argued about the other day." Matt held up his finger when

Mr. Clark opened his mouth to speak. "Before you deny it, I'll point out that you were seen. Oh, and if you refuse to tell us, I'll go to the police about the stolen medicine bottles."

"They're not stolen! I bought them!"

"I doubt the police will care how you acquired them, only that you did."

Mr. Clark appealed to me, but I merely shrugged. "We could send the police to Mr. Abercrombie's shop, if you like," I said, "and have them question him."

"Our discussion had nothing to do with Hale's murder," he whispered harshly as two women walked by.

"A visit from the police will be terribly inconvenient for Mr. Abercrombie," I went on. "They might frighten his customers away."

His expelled breath hissed between his teeth. "We argued about what to do with magicians. There. Satisfied?"

"And what did you decide ought to be done?" Matt growled. "Burning at the stake? Hanging?"

Mr. Clark screwed up his face. "Don't be absurd. What do you take us for? We simply argued about whether banning them from their respective guilds was enough. I say yes, he thinks not. He used you as an example, Miss Steele."

"Me?"

He nodded. "He thinks if nothing is done about the problem, magicians will begin to see themselves as…as invincible."

"Invincible? Is that the word he used?"

"Not quite." His gaze drifted away. "He said you would see yourselves as gods, far above the rest of us mortals."

"We are mortal, Mr. Clark, like you." Good lord. The misinformation was bordering on the ridiculous. "Perhaps Mr. Abercrombie ought to actually speak to a magician about their powers rather than read medieval stories designed to scare people."

"India doesn't think she is invincible," Matt said. "You can tell Abercrombie that."

"According to him, she has become rather a...difficult woman since learning of her ability."

"She has come out of her shell, that's all."

"Abercrombie says she used to be a good, agreeable sort of girl, and now she speaks her mind and doesn't listen to her betters."

Matt grunted. "Abercrombie is *not* her better. Be sure to tell him that too when next you see him. And add that she *should* speak her mind since she's an intelligent woman with interesting things to say. Perhaps if he, or you, got to know her, you'd see that. Good day, Mr. Clark."

Matt stepped away and waited for me, but I didn't move. "Mr. Clark," I said, "what did Mr. Abercrombie propose should be done with magicians if banning them from the guilds is not enough?"

He backed up and rapped sharply on the door. "Dear me," he said, hands in the air. "I can't recall."

The porter opened the door and Clark slipped inside. The door slammed shut.

Matt took my hand. "India, you're shaking."

"With fury."

His hand tightened. "You need a treat. Would you like a bun? Scone? Pie?"

I spluttered a laugh. Of all the things I expected him to say, that was not one of them. "What I need is to pay Abercrombie a visit and turn him into a toad. Since my magic isn't that useful, I'll settle for confectionery. There's an excellent shop on Piccadilly."

He did not let my hand go as we drove off, and I felt grateful for the contact. I stopped shaking after a few minutes and thought over the discussion again. Mr. Clark had not told us anything that we didn't already know, including Abercrombie's thoughts on the matter of magicians. It had been a wasted effort that had only served to fluster me.

Matt kept his gaze locked on the street out the window and announced that we had not been followed when we reached Piccadilly. He sent Bryce home and bought a selection of petit fours from The Family Confectioner. We sat at a table in the corner with the delicacies and I quite forgot to speak as I devoured my share of the little cakes and tarts.

"You enjoyed that," Matt said when I finished.

I touched my napkin to the corners of my mouth. "I did, thank you. These haven't changed since I was last here, quite some time ago."

"You came regularly?"

"With my mother."

"Ah, yes, the daughter of a confectioner."

"You remembered."

"Of course. Your maternal grandfather had a shop and your father used to buy sweets every day just so he could see your mother."

I smiled. "She worked as my grandfather's assistant, mostly in the shop front, while my grandfather made his confectionery out the back. He didn't sell buns, petit fours and other pastries like this place, but his sweets were very popular with the local children."

The Family Confectioner catered to a more well-to-do class of customer, particularly ladies wanting to pass the time with a friend over a cup of tea and a pastry. Nothing had changed since my mother used to bring me before her death, some ten years ago. The rose pink and white striped curtains matched the cushions, and little cakes were set out in enticing displays under glass domes on the counter. A boy no more than four years old ogled the glass jars filled to the brim with colorful hard sweets and pointed out his selection to the shopkeeper while his mother or nanny withdrew coins from her reticule.

"You don't talk about her much," Matt said quietly.

"Don't I? I suppose it's been so long now since she died. I'm ashamed to say I don't think of her as much as I ought."

"I'm sure she'd want it that way. No parent would want their child to mourn them for long. Your parents would want you to get on with your life and live for the future, not the past. Mine would be the same."

"You're probably right." Even so, I must visit my parents' graves as soon as Matt could spare me from the investigation.

We handed our plates and cups back at the counter and were about to leave when Matt changed his mind and bought a bag of bonbons. I suspected it was because I'd been eyeing them.

He offered me one as we exited but I refused. "I couldn't possibly fit another thing in."

"Not even one?" He shook the bag.

I caught a whiff of the chocolate and breathed it into my lungs. "Perhaps just one."

He watched me eat it. "Feel better?"

"Infinitely. But put those away or I'll eat the entire bag before we get home."

He stuffed them into his jacket pocket and smiled at me. "I've noticed that sweets seem to ease your anger."

"One can't possibly be angry when one is eating chocolate or a sweet. That's why confectioners are in demand. And anyway, I wasn't angry with you, Matt."

"For once."

"Matthew Glass, I am never angry with you. Not truly."

He narrowed his gaze. "Ever?"

"Sometimes you vex me, but you never anger me. You couldn't possibly anger anyone."

"Except Clark and Abercrombie."

"And Doctors Ritter and Wiley," I added. "Detective Inspector Brockwell, too, and Lord Coyle."

"And quite a few people from the Mapmaker's Guild. You're building up an impressive list."

"I think I spoke out of turn." I clutched his arm tighter. "Let's change the topic."

"Very well." He looked to the sky. "It looks like rain is on the way."

I studied the gray pall hanging so low it seemed as if the church spire pierced it. "Those aren't rain clouds but merely London's miasmic air."

"Why do the authorities not do something about it? Surely it must spread disease."

"All the more reason for me to purchase that cottage in Willesden," I said. "Did you notice how clean the air was there? I think it'll be a lovely place to live, and not too far to travel to the city."

"The family who rents it will no doubt think the same way." He chose his words carefully, his gaze on me. He seemed to have guessed that I was considering living in the cottage myself.

"You must be eager to return to California," I said quickly. "Away from London and our putrid air."

We walked on a few paces before he answered. "I find I'm in no hurry."

"You must miss it."

"Only the weather." He smiled. "Certainly not my Johnson relatives."

"Surely they're no worse than your Glass ones. Or do you have cousins over there who want to marry you too?"

He laughed. "My Johnson cousins are made in the same mold as Willie, except most of them hate me since I became a turncoat. They'd rather kill me than marry me."

"Then you must stay here." My tone was more serious than I intended. It was hard not to be serious when talking about his death. "Don't ever go home, Matt."

His step slowed and he looked down at me with smoky eyes. "London is my home at the moment."

Until I move on, his unspoken words said. Matt had traveled extensively as a child before his parents died. He'd lived much of his life in various European countries. After their deaths, he'd returned to America at age fifteen. It was understandable that he considered himself a citizen of no single country. He was a man with wandering in his veins. After Chronos was found, and his watch fixed, he may not return to America, but he wouldn't remain in England either.

That cottage was looking more and more attractive.

* * *

MATT APPROACHED PARK STREET CAUTIOUSLY, walking in front of me until he was sure that no one waited to jump out at us. Someone *was* waiting for us to return, as it happened, but inside the house. Detective Inspector Brockwell sat in the drawing room.

"He insisted on waiting, sir," Bristow whispered as he took our hats and the bag of bonbons.

"Is he alone?" I asked. "Or are there constables with him?"

"Alone, ma'am. I put him in the drawing room."

He hadn't come to arrest Matt then, thank goodness.

"It's more likely he's here to warn us off his investigation again," Matt told me.

He was correct, as it turned out, but only in part. "I've had another complaint from Dr. Ritter." Brockwell pronounced the T in complaint with crisp precision. "He claims you've been badgering him with questions and that he had to throw you out of his hospital."

"I asked him one question," Matt said, "and he did not have to throw us out of anything. By the way, do you know he's been tampering with the scene of the crime?"

Brockwell cocked his head to the side, the movement quite jerky for a fellow who favored slow, deliberate words and actions that always seemed carefully thought out first. "Go on."

"He sold off Hale's medicine bottles."

Brockwell seemed to have recovered his composure because he took his time answering. "Then he is a thief unless Mr. Pitt, Dr. Hale's heir, gave his consent."

"Not only that, Dr. Ritter sold them without the hospital's knowledge and pocketed the money. The hospital board is most likely aware of the situation now."

"Ah. That explains why Dr. Ritter visited me in an agitated state early this morning blaming you for his ill luck. He wouldn't elaborate, however, merely ordered me to 'put my dog on a leash.' Those are his words."

"I've been called worse," Matt said.

Brockwell's mouth stretched into a flat smile. "I don't doubt it."

"Consider me chastised," Matt said, standing.

"That's not all."

Matt huffed out a breath and sat again.

"Thank you for the information about Dr. Ritter," Brockwell said. "Is there anything else you'd like to pass on? Anything about Mr. Oakshot, for example?"

"Nothing," Matt said. "Why? What do you know?"

The inspector scratched first one sideburn then the other. The seconds ticked by, stretching my nerves thin. Matt did a remarkable job of looking unruffled, but I suspected he was as frustrated as me with Brockwell's delaying tactics.

"Oakshot's company bought all remaining stock of Hale's Cure-All from Mr. Pitt."

"He moved quickly," Matt said.

That was all he had to say? "We can guess why Mr. Pitt sold it," I said. "The Cure-All's reputation has been damaged for its role in Hale's death. But why would Mr. Oakshot buy it? He'll be stuck with something he can't sell."

"He didn't say," Brockwell intoned. "I wondered if you'd learned anything."

Matt shook his head. "As to why he'd do it, I suspect he'll simply change the label and market it as something else. It might be cheaper to buy the stock than make his own."

"That must be it." Brockwell stood and buttoned up his jacket, an ill-fitting garment that looked as old as the man himself. "Good day, Miss Steele, Mr. Glass. Please inform me of any progress you make."

"You actually seem amenable to us continuing with our investigation," Matt said. "Indeed, you shared something of your own investigation with us. Why?"

"I've come to the conclusion that it's best if we pool our knowledge. We both want the killer caught, and three heads are better than two or one. Besides, I cannot force you to stop. Not while you have the commissioner's favor and I suspect you'll have that for some time. He did seem very grateful to you both for finding Daniel Gibbons's killer. Very grateful indeed."

Did he know Daniel was the illegitimate son of Commissioner Munro or was he guessing and trying to gauge from our reactions if it were true? I studiously kept my gaze on him, trying hard not to blink or glance at Matt and give anything away.

"As he was grateful that Miss Steele captured the Dark Rider," Matt said lightly. "Indeed, our success doesn't make his force look particularly competent. Perhaps that will all change with this investigation, now that you are on board, Detective."

Brockwell linked his hands behind him. "And now that we are sharing information."

Matt tugged on the bell pull and Bristow appeared to show Brockwell out. Matt stifled a yawn.

"Perhaps you ought to ask Mr. Pitt or Mr. Oakshot for a medicine for your condition," Brockwell said.

"My condition?"

"You look unwell." Brockwell put up his hands in surrender. "My apologies if I am mistaken. Perhaps you're merely showing the effects of a late night and early morning."

So Commissioner Munro hadn't told his detective that our reason for visiting Dr. Hale in the first place had been to find a miraculous cure for Matt's illness. He was a decent man, the commissioner, and knew how to keep a secret.

Matt gave Brockwell a tight smile. "We gentleman of leisure tend to burn the candle at both ends."

"Indeed."

Bristow indicated Brockwell should walk ahead of him and, a moment later, we heard the front door open and close. Matt sat and rested his elbows on his knees. He raked his hands through his hair then down his face. He caught me watching and dropped his hands away.

"I know, I know," he muttered, unbuttoning his inside jacket pocket. "I'm getting it."

I closed the drawing room door and stood by it as his watch's magic soaked into his skin and his coloring returned to a more healthful hue. His eyes, however, remained shadowed, the bruise inflicted by Cyclops darker than ever. He returned his watch to his pocket and I stepped away from the door.

"Shall we visit Oakshot after you've rested?" I asked.

He nodded. "Hopefully he'll tell us more than he told Brockwell."

"I'm sure he will, particularly once we inform him we

know that Hale was a magician and that the Cure-All might still hold some magic." I shot him a smile.

He did not return it. "And what if he asks how we know that?"

"We'll make something up. You're good at that, Matt, thinking up things as you go."

He tipped his head back and closed his eyes. "High praise indeed."

I smiled and picked up a book. He slept in that position for an hour. He would have slept longer but his aunt woke him when she entered.

"There you are, India," she declared. "I've come to ask you to read to me."

"Not this afternoon," I said. "We've got too much to do."

She clicked her tongue. "You're working her too hard, Matthew. And yourself. Look at you! You ought to be abed."

"I just rested," he said.

"It did nothing for you. Tell him, India."

I did not tell him anything. Matt wouldn't want to hear it. Besides, he was well aware that his watch wasn't working as efficiently as it used to. "I'll make sure he doesn't exert himself too much this afternoon, Miss Glass," I assured her.

"Good girl. If you weren't so sensible I would worry more." She turned her back to Matt and rested a hand on my shoulder. "But I trust you to do the right thing by my nephew." She squeezed my shoulder before letting go and walking out of the room.

I caught Matt watching me out of the corner of my eye, a frown disturbing his handsome features. "I don't need luncheon after those petit fours," I said. "I'm ready to leave when you are."

"Then we'll go now."

* * *

"THAT IS NO BUSINESS OF YOURS," Mr. Oakshot snapped in response to Matt's question about the purchase of the Cure-All. He turned away and marched back to his desk. "See yourselves out."

Matt strolled to the window overlooking the factory floor. The occasional shouted order or clinking of glass bottles could be heard over the grind and whir of the machinery. Mr. Oakshot's office provided no sanctuary from the incessant noise and I wondered how he could concentrate on his paperwork. There seemed to be more of it than the last time we visited.

"Are you removing Pitt's labels and replacing them with your own?" Matt pressed.

Mr. Oakshot glared at him. "Did you not hear me? Get out!"

"Did you purchase the remaining stock of Dr. Hale's Cure-All because you think its magical properties will make it a success for your company?"

The color drained from Mr. Oakshot's face, along with his temper. He slumped in his chair, suddenly looking like a man floundering in the depths of misery. "Pardon?" His whisper could barely be heard over the machinery. "Magic?"

"You heard me," Matt said. "And don't pretend you know nothing about magic. You're on the Court of Assistants at the Apothecary's Guild and the guilds are well aware that magic exists. Are *you* a magician, Mr. Oakshot?"

"Pardon?" he said again, his voice trembling. "No, of course not. I know nothing about magic." He did not meet our gazes and pretended to take great interest in his paperwork.

"You have a flourishing business here." Matt indicated the factory through the window. "You're considered the most successful apothecary in London. A singular trait of magicians is the exceptional quality of their work. Even I, who knows nothing about medicine, would assume you're a magician."

"Your logic is lacking, Mr. Glass." Mr. Oakshot thrust out his chin. "You accuse me of being a magician and yet assume that I bought the remaining stock of Hale's Cure-All because it contains magic. Wouldn't I be able to put magic into my own medicine if I were a magician?"

"Perhaps the particular spell in the Cure-All eludes you and you wish to study it."

Mr. Oakshot dropped the papers back onto the desk. They scattered, some falling to the floor. He scrubbed his hand across his jaw where gray whiskers had begun to sprout. The brief flare of defiance in his eyes extinguished, and he looked miserable again. "Don't spread those sort of rumors, Mr. Glass. I beg you. If the guild so much as *think* I'm a magician, they'll set out to ruin me."

"I won't tell the guild if you tell us the truth. You have my word. Why did you buy the remaining stock of Cure-All from Mr. Pitt if not to place your own label on it?"

He smacked his palm on his desk, knocking more papers off. "I don't want to sell it," he hissed. "I don't want that doctor's medicine here, or anywhere! Pitt is ceasing production since sales have all but stopped, so I bought the remaining stock off his hands and crushed every last bottle, burned every label, and tipped that bloody medicine into the sewers."

Matt paused, apparently as surprised by Oakshot's admission as me. "But why?" he asked. "You deliberately lost money on it."

"Because that so-called doctor—that bloody *murderer*—killed my wife. His name doesn't deserve to live on in his Cure-All. He doesn't deserve to be remembered, not even on a label. He doesn't have children; he left behind no family, and I rejoice, because that makes it easier to obliterate his name forever. He took away the one thing I cared about…" He choked back a sob and his mouth twisted as he fought to control himself. "So I took away the thing he cared about— his legacy. Now he is truly, unequivocally, gone."

He sat back in his chair again, all the fight gone out of him. He was nothing more than a middle-aged man staring into the pit of despair.

Matt thanked him for his time and we hurried down the stairs and out to the street.

"That poor man," I said once we settled into the carriage.

"That poor man just climbed to the top of my suspect list," Matt said. "There is a lot of hate in his heart. That much hate can drive a man to murder."

"Destroying a few hundred bottles is not the same thing as taking a life, Matt. It takes quite a different man to kill." But I didn't speak with much conviction. What if I was wrong about Mr. Oakshot? What if my sympathy for him affected my judgment? "Perhaps you're right," I muttered to the window. "I don't know."

"Or I might be wrong," Matt said.

I met his gaze in the reflection. It looked troubled.

"You're doubting your instincts again," he said.

And with good reason. I didn't tell him so, however. It would only make him feel guilty for the argument over Oscar Barratt again. "So why are we going to Mr. Pitt's shop now?" He'd directed Bryce to drive there before assisting me into the carriage. "What do you hope to learn?"

"I have no idea." He sighed. "But I don't know where else to turn. Perhaps he'll know if Oakshot lied about destroying the Cure-All."

"You really do think Oakshot's a magician and wishes to study it?"

"I'm not discarding any possibility yet."

* * *

"I WANTED to get rid of it," Mr. Pitt said without looking up from the brass and timber scales he was using. "I've ended the Cure-All's production and couldn't move the remaining stock. Mr. Oakshot offered to buy it, and I was keen to sell. We both benefit."

"Do you know what he did with it?" Matt asked.

Mr. Pitt tipped a small amount of brown powder onto the scales then added another spoonful. "No. You'd have to ask him."

"He destroyed every last bottle and label."

"So he's going to sell it as his own, eh?" He tipped more powder onto the scales, balancing them. "That's typical of him. Oakshot believes in quantity not quality. He sells his medicines cheaply but because he makes so much of it, he still makes a handsome profit. He was able to buy the Cure-All at a vastly reduced sum. Even with the cost of putting it into his own bottles with his own labels, he'll still save on production."

"He emptied the medicine into the sewer."

He glanced up from the scales. "Why?"

"Because he hated Dr. Hale and wants there to be nothing left of him."

Mr. Pitt blinked. "Good lord. I knew he was upset over his wife's death, but I always thought business came first with him. It appears I was wrong." He swept the powder off the scales with a piece of thin wood and into a bowl that he set aside.

I wandered around the shop. It was rather an interesting place, with its colored bottles, jars and sleek polished wooden counter and drawers. It also smelled divine. Matt didn't ask any more questions so I glanced back at them to see why. Mr. Pitt watched me and Matt watched him. I felt my face heat so turned back to the stack of face cream pots forming a pyramid on the table in the middle of the shop.

"Do you have any plans to replace the Cure-All?" I asked. "It was such a success that it would be a shame not to try and make something just as successful."

"It was a success because it had Jonathon's name on it," Mr. Pitt said. "He's gone and I can't use his name again."

"He's gone and so is his magic," Matt said with a sigh. "No doubt that had something to do with the Cure-All's success."

"You can assume all you want, but I don't know for certain. The only person who could tell you if he put magic in some of the Cure-All bottles is Jonathon himself. As to any plans to replace it with something else, the answer is no. You might find this hard to believe, in this day and age of businesses seeking profits at any cost, but I want to keep my operation small. I have my loyal customers and that's all I need. I don't need the fame that Jonathon craved or the profits Oakshot strives for. I just want to live a quiet, content life here, serving my customers."

"Then that makes you a unique businessman," Matt said.

"Indeed." Mr. Pitt picked up the mortar and pestle and began grinding the contents. "Did Oakshot tell you he offered to buy the shop from me?"

"You're not selling?" I asked.

"Not to anyone. What would I do with myself, Miss Steele?" He smiled but it faded quickly. "I wonder why Oakshot didn't mention it."

Perhaps because he thought it might incriminate him further. Buying the rest of the Cure-All was one thing, but buying out a rival's business was quite another.

Matt inspected the medicine chest near his elbow. He opened the lid and drawers, and inspected the medicine bottles placed there for display. "Perhaps you should have considered it," he said to Mr. Pitt. "Without the Cure-All, and the damage Hale's death has done to your reputation, you might find your profits dwindling." He pulled a powder packet from one of the drawers and read the label.

Mr. Pitt snatched it off him and gave Matt such a fierce glare that Matt put up his hands and backed away.

The little bell above the door tinkled and a woman dressed in a simple black and white dress walked in. She paused just inside the doorway, her startled gaze on Matt. Then she bobbed her head and performed a shallow curtsy.

"Good afternoon, Mr. Glass," she said.

"Good afternoon," he said as he passed her. "You don't need that, India," he said to me.

"Pardon?" I had been concentrating on the woman and forgotten I'd picked up a pot of the cream until he pointed to a line on the label that read IMPROVES THE COMPLEXION.

"Your complexion doesn't need improving." He took the pot from me and returned it to the top of the pyramid. "Good day, Mr. Pitt."

Mr. Pitt waved at us from the counter where the woman now stood, inspecting a cluster of blue bottles. The bell above the door chimed as we exited.

"Who was she?" I asked.

Matt frowned at the closed door. "I can't recall but she does seem familiar."

"She certainly knew you. Perhaps she's one of your past liaisons," I said, knowing perfectly well it wasn't. I was quite sure Matt had not had so much as a dalliance since I'd met him, which was almost the entire time he'd been in London.

My teasing had little effect, however. He continued to frown. "I usually remember those," he said, sounding distracted.

"Usually?"

His cheeks pinked. "I mean always. I always remember my past liaisons."

"What? *All* of them? My, my, you must have an excellent memory."

He opened the carriage door and put out his hand to assist me up the step. "Very amusing, India. There aren't *that* many. In fact, hardly any, and not all that serious."

"I think the gentleman doth protest too much."

He folded up the step and climbed in. His face drew close enough to mine that I could see the wicked gleam in his eyes. "And I think the lady is trying to trick me into discussing my past when all she has to do is ask." He sat opposite and tossed me a smile. "I'll tell you anything you want to know."

I tried to affect the same devil-may-care air as him, but I suspected I failed. "Of course I don't want to know. Why would I?"

His smile widened.

Bryce drove into Park Street and Matt turned to the window and scanned the vicinity. My watch chimed.

We both stared at it, hanging from its chain around my neck. It chimed again and throbbed.

Matt thumped on the ceiling. "Don't stop!" he shouted.

But Bryce couldn't have heard him with the window up. The coach began to slow as we approached number sixteen. Matt went to open the window, but I caught his arm.

"It's too dangerous," I said.

As if it agreed with me, my watch chimed. I clutched it tightly. Its pulse warmed my palm, the regular beat counting out the seconds.

"I'm not getting out," Matt said. "Just telling him to drive on so we can see who's there. You keep watch through—"

A gun fired.

Wood splintered, and the horses squealed.

"Get down!" Matt went to dive across me but the frightened horses took off and the coach hurtled forward. He fell back and I tumbled onto the seat beside him.

Bryce shouted orders at the horses but our speed only picked up. Matt helped me to sit then looped his arm around my waist, anchoring me. Bryce's shouts became more frantic, his panic doing nothing to calm the animals. The end of the street must be near. *Oh God.*

"Brace yourself!" Even as Matt said it, the coach lurched to the right.

The cabin tipped. It happened so fast that I hardly registered Matt pulling me across his lap so that our positions swapped. He took the full force of the impact, using his body to cushion my fall.

But his body was hard and the impact profound. My right side took the brunt of it, slamming into Matt, the seat, walls. Pain pierced my shoulder and hip, and my heart felt as if it would burst out of my chest. I couldn't breathe.

The deafening crash of the coach hitting the road rang in my ears, drowning out my cries and Matt's groans. Glass shattered, wood splintered. And then the awful, relentless grind as the carriage was dragged on its side, the horses still trying to flee. Bryce... Oh God.

Someone outside screamed.

I pushed up and collapsed again as pain spiked from my shoulder across my back and down my arm. Matt lay beneath me, his eyes closed. He didn't move.

"Matt?" I managed to roll off him despite the shuddering movement of the cabin. I bent my ear to his lips. Nothing. He wasn't breathing. "Matt!" I pressed my hand to his chest over his heart. It was utterly still.

"MATT!" I clasped his face, turning it to me.

Blood oozed out from behind his head, smearing the broken shards of window glass underneath.

CHAPTER 15

*S*omething dripped down my face. Blood? Tears?

I stared at Matt's lifeless form and a well of sorrow opened up inside me. It swallowed me whole, taking all my courage and hope and even my soul into its depths.

The carriage slowed and came to a stop. I lost my balance and found myself on top of Matt again. I sobbed into his chest.

My watch chimed, then chimed again. It still hung around my neck where it now burned so hot I could feel it through the layers of clothing. Another warning? Had the killer come back to make sure his work was done?

And then I felt another warmth, not from my watch, but beneath me. It came from the inside pocket of Matt's jacket. My watch chimed again and again, so loud that I could hear it clear above the shouts outside.

Matt's watch! I scrabbled at his jacket and waistcoat, but my shaking fingers couldn't manipulate the buttons. I wrenched the clothes open and the buttons scattered. The heat from both his watch and mine combined within me, raging like a furnace as if they were communicating through me.

I felt the carriage rock and heard someone inquire if anyone was inside, but I didn't answer as I flipped open the watch case, removed Matt's glove and pressed the watch into his hand. The purple glow flowed from the watch into his skin, racing along his veins, shooting out again above his collar, up his throat and over his face.

His chest expanded with his gasped breath. His eyes flew open and stared wildly back at me.

I burst into tears and clasped his hand in mine so that he did not let go of the watch too soon.

"Ma'am?" a man behind me said. "Ma'am, are you all right?"

I shielded Matt and smiled down at him through my tears. It must have looked crooked and wobbly but I didn't care. I laid my hand over his chest and silently thanked God, Chronos and Dr. Parsons that his heart beat steadily.

He lifted a hand to my face. "You're bleeding," he said.

His first words after coming back from death were concern for me? I cried even harder.

"Ma'am, let me help you." I felt a hand on my shoulder and hissed in pain.

"India?" Matt snapped his watch case closed and his veins cleared. He sat up and that's when I realized I was still sitting on him. "India, you're hurt."

I peered up at the two men perched on the carriage's side, the door open between them. I took their hands and they helped me through and passed me down to someone standing on the road.

"Come with me, Miss Steele," said the familiar voice of Bristow. "We'll go home and call the doctor. Is Mr. Glass...?"

"He's all right," I said, clutching the butler to stop myself falling. "He saved my life."

Bristow looked past me and then I was handed to someone else. Someone with familiar arms and smell. Someone who felt strong and capable, and not at all near death. Matt scooped me into his arms and I nestled into him, my head beneath his chin.

"Bristow, see to things here." Matt's voice rumbled through me, calming me a little. He was alive, thank God. "Bryce?" he added.

"Peter is with him now," Bristow said. "I don't know his condition yet, sir."

"Make sure he has all the care he needs. And my aunt?"

"Miss Glass is out."

"A small mercy," Matt muttered.

A wave of nausea threatened to overwhelm me. I concentrated on breathing evenly and steadying my nerves, but it was an impossible task. I stopped crying, only to find that I'd begun to shake. I couldn't stop.

Matt carried me back to the house and Mrs. Bristow took charge, directing her daughter the maid to fetch clean cloths.

"Polly has already gone to fetch the doctor in anticipation," she assured Matt. "Take Miss Steele to her room and I'll be there— Sir! Your head. There's a lot of blood at the back. Are you injured badly?"

"I'm fine," he said.

He carried me up the stairs then laid me gently on my bed. He sat on the mattress beside me. "India, say something. You're too quiet."

I opened my eyes and blinked up at him. He was a marvelously wonderful sight, despite the blood, the disheveled hair and the deep worry lines scoring his forehead. "Am I not usually this quiet?"

He lifted my hand to his lips and smiled against my knuckles. "That's better."

I tried to sit up and, despite the pain in my right side,

managed it with his help. The nausea had vanished, thank goodness, and I felt as though I had all my wits about me once again. "Your watch," I began. "It...saved you."

"That's what it's for."

"Yes, but—"

Mrs. Bristow entered carrying tea, her daughter behind her with an armful of towels. She ordered Matt to leave, and for a moment I thought he'd refuse but as Mrs. Bristow undid the buttons on my jacket, he bowed out and closed the door.

The housekeeper cleaned away some blood from a cut on my cheek and inspected my injuries. The doctor arrived some time later and inspected me all over again. He declared nothing to be broken but my hip and shoulder would sport bruises for a few weeks. The pain ought to lessen in a day or two.

He went in search of Matt, and I was left alone to rest. But I couldn't rest. My mind whirled with questions about Matt, Bryce and the horses, not to mention the shooter.

I gave up trying after an hour and dressed in a skirt, chemise and a waistcoat, without a corset. It seemed a little too difficult to manipulate my body into one with all the aches and pains. I threw my new shawl around my shoulders to hide my state of *dishabille* and went downstairs. I found Matt with Willie, Duke, Cyclops and his aunt in the sitting room.

"India!" Miss Glass held her hands out to me but Willie intercepted me before I could take them.

"I'm a little sore," I warned her before she could embrace me.

She looked me over, her hands hovering, searching for somewhere to touch me. I clasped them in mine and smiled at her. She smiled back, only for it to wobble. Tears filled her eyes. She pulled away and dashed the tears against her sleeve. To my surprise, she said nothing.

Miss Glass patted the sofa beside her. "Come sit by me, India. You look terrible. Your poor face." She inspected the cut on my cheek with a frown. "It will heal without a scar, so the doctor told Matthew."

"You saw the doctor?" I asked him.

He nodded. "Are you in pain?"

"Not overmuch," I lied.

Duke handed me a cup of tea and Cyclops offered me a scone. I accepted both and nibbled and sipped before setting them down.

"Can you please all stop staring?" I said. "And fussing," I added when Miss Glass removed the cushion at her back and passed it to me.

"You've had an ordeal," she said briskly. "And so have we. You must allow us to fuss or…" Her voice cracked and she sucked in her lower lip.

I leaned forward and she settled the cushion at my back.

"Are you injured?" I asked Matt, knowing full well that he'd suffered grave wounds. He seemed unaffected, however. He moved easily and didn't so much as wince.

"I appear to be unharmed," he said. "A slight scratch on the back of the head that gives me no trouble."

A slight scratch indeed.

"Matthew has a strong constitution," Miss Glass said with pride. "It takes more than an accident or illness to knock him off his feet."

"Aunt," he chided gently. "That's enough."

"India, too," she said, patting my arm. "Look at her! She's up and about already. Your cousins take to their beds for a week if they get so much as a sniffle."

"And Bryce?" I asked.

Matt lowered his head and dragged both hands through

his hair. "He died at the scene. I paid a call to his family while you rested. The other servants are upset but refused to take the rest of the day off. Mrs. Bristow says they'd rather be here for us during this difficult time."

I pressed a hand to my chest as a lump clogged my throat. There was nothing to say that could ease anyone's sorrow. Poor Bryce.

"Why did the horses startle like that?" Miss Glass asked after a weighty silence. "The neighbors claim they heard a loud noise. What do you think it was?"

Matt and I both sipped our tea.

"I heard someone say a gunshot," she went on. Cyclops, Duke and Willie all turned to her. "You must be careful, Harry," Miss Glass went on, her voice thin. "It's the Wild West, you know. Be sure to come back to England soon. It's much safer."

"I think you should rest, Aunt," Matt said, taking her arm.

Cyclops fetched Bristow and Polly.

"Thank you, Harry. Veronica? Where's my maid?" Miss Glass spied me and smiled. "There you are."

"I'll be with you soon," I told her gently.

Matt escorted her out and came back a few minutes later. He took the seat she'd vacated beside me. "Perhaps you should retire too," he said. "You look pale."

"As do you, although considering you died in that carriage, you could look much worse."

My response brought down a barrage of questions from his three friends. He scowled at me, but I didn't regret informing them. They ought to know.

He finally held up his hand for them to cease. "I used my watch," he said. "Or India put it in my hand, I suppose."

I told them what had happened in the carriage, not leaving out any of the details. "You seem to suffer no ill effects, Matt," I finished. "I didn't realize the watch would work on other injuries and illnesses."

"Neither did I, at first," he said. "Dr. Parsons suspected it would cure me of anything, but this is the first real test."

I touched his chin and turned his face away so I could inspect the back of his head. The wound had completely closed, leaving only a scar. He cleaned away some but not all of the blood. "It would seem he was right," I murmured. "Thank God."

"Amen," Willie added.

"But..." I bit my lip. I felt odd asking him my next question.

He arched his brows at me. "I know what you're going to say. Am I immortal? The answer is no. Dr. Parsons said I'll die one day. The watch won't stop my organs from aging. My body will change with time, as is natural."

"But until then...you will continue to live no matter what illness or accident befalls you."

"Unless the watch stops working or I can't get to it in time. There is only so long I can survive without blood pumping through my veins or air reaching my lungs."

The pronouncement weighed heavily on my shoulders. I couldn't help thinking of what might have happened if I hadn't got him to hold the watch in time, or if it had broken in the accident. I lifted a shaky hand to my lips and blinked back tears.

"It's a miracle," Willie murmured.

"It's magic," Cyclops said. "Rare magic."

"What do you think startled the horses?" Duke asked. "A gunshot, like Miss Glass reckoned?"

Matt nodded. "There'll be a bullet lodged in the coach. I didn't see the shooter. India?"

I shook my head. "Coyle, again, I suppose."

"Most likely, considering our previous experience with his man."

"He's gone too far." Willie shot to her feet and pulled a small pistol from her waistband, much smaller than her usual Colt. Better to hide, I suspected. "Who's coming with me to pay him a visit?"

"Sit down," Matt ordered. "No one will confront Coyle. There's no point. He'll deny it, and without solid evidence, the police will do nothing. Besides, there's always the chance that it wasn't him."

"Who else could it be?" she asked, tucking the pistol away.

"Any of our suspects who turns out to be Hale's murderer. We've questioned them all again lately. This attack was a little different to the first one," he went on. "It's more cowardly, carried out from a distance. Perhaps that's Coyle's new man's style, or perhaps it's what a poisoner would do."

"So the net widens," Duke said with disgust. "We ain't getting closer."

"Nor are we going to get any closer," Matt said. "Our involvement in the investigation ends. Coyle, or whoever shot at us, has won. It's up to the police to catch the murderer now." He looked up at me and drew in a deep breath. "The risks are too great."

Nobody disagreed with him.

I set aside my teacup. "I need something stronger."

"Brandy," Duke said. "For all of us."

* * *

We ate an informal dinner in the dining room, a somber air pressing down on everyone. Matt spoke quietly of his intention to set up an annuity for Bryce's family, and we arranged to visit his lawyer in two days' time, when I was hopefully moving more freely, so that the lawyer could arrange the annuity and the purchase of the Willesden cottage on my behalf too.

Cyclops, Duke and Willie played cards in the drawing room after dinner, while I sat and read, Matt beside me. At least, I intended to read. I couldn't concentrate, and then Matt spoke.

"I haven't had a chance to thank you," he said. "You saved my life, India, and I don't know how to repay you."

"You saved mine by taking the brunt of the impact. And besides, your watch saved your life, not me."

"I didn't get it out of my pocket. You did. Did you guess it might work?"

"My watch told me, in a way. In fact, I think it communicated with yours." I shrugged. "I don't know. It's all rather a blur now."

He lowered his head and pinched the bridge of his nose. "I should have stopped after the first threat. This is my fault."

"No, it's not. I wanted to continue, too. Indeed, I wanted to continue more than you."

He rubbed his forehead as if a headache hammered away at it. "I'll report this incident to Brockwell tomorrow. He probably can't do anything about it, but he needs to know."

"Your head aches, doesn't it?"

He lowered his hand. "A little."

"I'd say it's more than a little. You ought to go to bed."

"I will if you will."

"This is hardly the time for a childish game of one-upmanship, Matt. But since I think I'm ready to rest, then I'll retire too. It's been a long day."

He escorted me up the stairs, despite my insistence that I was quite capable. My hip troubled me, but it was nothing compared to the trouble my heart caused. It flipped wildly in my chest when we stopped at my door. There was something about Matt tonight, something in his quiet manner, his intense gaze. I didn't know quite what to make of it.

"Goodnight," I said without turning to look at him.

He reached past me and took hold of the doorknob. "India." The whisper fanned my cheek and my heart stuttered again. He swept my hair back, brushing it over my shoulder.

I held my breath and waited for his kiss on my neck. It did not come.

I half turned, only to wish I hadn't. His smoky eyes fixed intently on me, and I felt as if he could see into my heart, mind and soul, and he knew what I felt for him. And yet he did not kiss me.

"Today was...an ordeal," he said. "When you were in here and I waited downstairs for the doctor's report...it's not a feeling I wish to experience again."

"It wasn't exactly a joy watching you die in the carriage either," I choked out.

He cupped my jaw and stroked his thumb along my cheek. My heart stopped its rapid rhythm only to swell to ten times its size. I tried hard to think of all the reasons I should push him away, but I could think of none. My mind blanked.

And then it was too late. He kissed me.

It was gentle and kind, and a little tentative. Not quite a lover's kiss, but then, how should a lover's kiss feel? I was no expert. This was my first real kiss and it was with someone very special to me. Someone I admired and liked, perhaps even loved. Someone forbidden and so far above me that he should *not* be kissing me like this.

And yet I did not pull away. Propriety and principles be damned. I wanted this kiss, this man, and I wanted to know how it felt to be desired. It was almost impossible to consider that Matt desired me, and yet here he was kissing me as thoroughly as I kissed him.

All the emotion of the afternoon surged through me like a

tide, drowning out the voice of reason. There was just Matt and me, and the kiss that I wished would progress from gentle to passionate.

I stretched my arms around his neck, pressing my body against his. My shawl slipped down and I felt wanton, brazen, with only my chemise and a waistcoat covering my breasts. He must be able to feel them, and my rapidly beating heart.

He laid a hand on my hip and I gasped in pain against his mouth.

He broke the kiss. "Christ. I forgot. Did I hurt you?"

"No."

"I must have or you wouldn't have gasped like that."

"It's nothing. I'm fine."

I was not fine, but it wasn't my hip that hurt. My soul felt bruised as I stood there, his kiss lingering on my lips, and the gap between us widening. I could see the desire fading from his eyes and the disbelief and regret replacing it with every passing second. He did not speak for some time, but he didn't need to for my confidence to slowly recede. I folded my arms over my chest, tucking the ends of the shawl away.

"India, I'm sorry." He raked his fingers through his hair. "I don't know what came over me."

I shrugged off his concern, searching for words to serve back at him. But I couldn't find any. I didn't know what I wanted to say. Should I tell him I wanted to resume the kiss or pretend I did not? Pretend that all would be well between us in the morning? Or tell him that everything had changed now?

"Goodnight, Matt." I opened my door and rushed inside. I closed it without glancing back.

* * *

MATT and the others had gone out before I rose in the morning. I ate a light breakfast with Miss Glass in her rooms then read the newspaper to her. She didn't appear to be listening, however. I couldn't concentrate and skipped words and, once, an entire paragraph. She made no comment, but continued to stare out the window at the street below. Perhaps the events of the day before troubled her so much that she couldn't take her mind off them.

I knew how she felt. Between Bryce's death, my injuries, Matt's resurrection, and the kiss, my own mind spun like a top. Thank goodness Miss Glass didn't know about that kiss. I couldn't sit through a lecture about the importance of Matt marrying well. I must ask him not to mention it to her. Or to anyone, for that matter.

Perhaps he'd already come to the same conclusion, hence his absence. I hoped so. The shorter that conversation, the better.

Miss Glass sat forward on the chair and peered straight down at the street below. "Someone comes," she said. "A gentleman."

"Someone for Matt," I said.

But a moment later, Peter announced that Oscar Barratt wished to speak to me in the drawing room.

"Did you tell him Mr. Glass wasn't at home?" I asked.

"Yes, ma'am. He insisted that you would do just as well."

"Come, India." Miss Glass rose and held out her hand to me. "I'll chaperone you."

"I hardly need a chaperone to speak to Mr. Barratt."

She touched my chin and inspected the cut on my cheek. "You'll do."

"Do? For what purpose?"

"For the purpose of catching his eye."

"Miss Glass!"

"Don't play coy with me, India. I know you too well. This fellow may be perfect for you."

"You've never met him," I said, following her out.

"I am about to." She marched on, a formidable erectness to her spine. She would not deviate from her matchmaking mission.

"Miss Steele!" Mr. Barratt rose from the armchair by the fire and smiled broadly. "I am beside myself with relief at seeing you looking well. I read about the accident in this morning's papers. I hoped the reports of your good health were correct and that your condition did not deteriorate overnight. I am very happy to see you unharmed, aside from the scratch."

"Thank you, Mr. Barratt. As you can see, I am quite well. The scratch is minor." I introduced him to Miss Glass. After a brief exchange, she sat on the sofa and proceeded not to say another word.

"The papers said your coachman died," Mr. Barratt went on once settled again in the armchair. "It must have been a terrible accident.

"It was."

"And yet here you are, mostly uninjured. Remarkable."

"I do sport some bruises," I told him tightly. "Nothing of concern, however."

He winced and gave me a sheepish shrug. "I'm sorry, Miss Steele. I don't mean to sound like a journalist fishing for information. It's a terrible habit of mine. I want us to be friends, considering our…" His gaze flicked to Miss Glass. "… our similarities."

"Your friendship is most welcome," I said. "I'd like that too."

His face flushed ever so slightly. It made him seem vulnerable, and I liked him a little more for it. "Tell me about the accident," he said. "The papers mentioned the horses were startled but did not say how. They claimed Mr. Glass also walked away unscathed. I hope that's true."

"He's unharmed," I said.

"Good to hear."

"As to the horses being startled, we heard a gunshot."

"Someone *shot* at you?"

"Most likely, considering our recent encounter with Lord Coyle's man. We're not entirely convinced that the gunman is connected to Coyle, however it does seem to be someone who wants us to stop investigating Dr. Hale's murder."

"I see the connection." He scrubbed a hand over his jaw, slowly shaking his head as if he couldn't quite believe it. "You are stopping now, aren't you?"

I nodded. "Matt insisted."

He cocked his head to the side, his handsome brow furrowed. "You don't seem as though you agree."

I felt Miss Glass's glare bore into the side of my head. I didn't dare turn to her and experience its full force. "I do agree," I said quickly. "But we were getting close. This attack proves how close. The problem is, we can't untangle our evidence. It's a giant mess of leads and lies."

"Talk it through with me," he said. "It may help you sort it out."

The prospect of such grim discussion must have been too much for Miss Glass. She finally spoke up. "I'll leave you two to talk among yourselves," she said, rising. "Ah, here's Bristow with tea. I'll take mine in my rooms, Bristow. Goodbye, Mr. Barratt. It was a pleasure to meet you. Do come again. India speaks so fondly of you. Now I see why."

He looked utterly shocked. Perhaps as shocked as I felt. He managed to recover and bid her farewell. He didn't speak as Bristow poured tea for us then followed Miss Glass out with her cup. I was beginning to think it was Miss Glass's intention to leave me alone with Mr. Barratt all along, but only if he met with her approval first. Clearly, he'd passed whatever test she'd set for him.

Perhaps I shouldn't have been so surprised. The best way to keep Matt and me apart was to find a suitor for me. She need not have bothered. I had enough willpower to resist Matt on my own, but Mr. Barratt was a welcome companion, nevertheless.

"Now that she's gone," I said, "we can discuss magic freely."

"She's not aware of yours?"

I shook my head. "Are you ready to hear everything we learned?"

"Most eagerly."

I told him about Mr. Oakshot's purchase of the remaining bottles of Dr. Hale's Cure-All as well as Mr. Clark's purchase of Hale's personal medicine collection. "The transaction was done without the hospital's knowledge, or that of Mr. Pitt, Hale's heir. It was quite illegal."

"You suspect Clark or Ritter of killing Hale?"

I sighed into my teacup. "Neither motive seems strong enough. If Mr. Clark wanted to study Dr. Hale's medicines for magic, he could have simply stolen them. Killing Hale so he could purchase the medicines is an extreme measure. And I think Dr. Ritter is merely taking advantage of Hale's death to profit."

"So Oakshot is your main suspect. He certainly seems to have hated Hale enough to commit murder."

"As does Dr. Wiley." I told him about Wiley's resentment of Hale, and how he blamed him for his ill luck.

He sat back and regarded me, a smile on his lips. It was not the response I expected in the midst of a discussion about murder. "You are remarkable, Miss Steele."

"I didn't come up with this on my own," I said. "Matt and I have worked together."

"Yes, but few women of my acquaintance would be so comfortable talking about murder, particularly when their own life is in danger. It's a shame you have to give it all up after getting so far. But I do agree that you must stop. Leave it to the police, now."

"We will."

Mr. Barratt cleared his throat then concentrated on his teacup as if he could see something of immense importance in there. "Miss Steele..."

"Yes?"

He set down the cup and fixed me with his pleasant blue eyes. "Miss Steele, I wonder if you'll do me the honor of attending the theater with me on Friday evening."

"What's showing?"

"I...I don't know." He picked up his cup again. "I probably should have found out before inviting you."

For some reason, I found his awkwardness amusing. I giggled then, a little ashamed, tried to smother it. I ended up making an unladylike noise through my nose.

He grinned and we both began to laugh.

The front door opened and I heard Bristow greet Matt, but not Matt's response. A moment later he strode in. He lifted his eyebrows at me and I instantly sobered. He looked tired and damp from the drizzling rain.

"Mr. Barratt," he intoned.

"Mr. Glass."

They exchanged nods but nothing more. One of those awful silences ensued where seconds felt like minutes. It was as if each man were waiting for the other to give in and break the silence first. I was not prepared to do it for them.

The clock in the entrance hall struck the hour, and finally Mr. Barratt spoke. "I'm glad to see you looking well after your ordeal yesterday." He nodded at me. "Miss Steele was just telling me about it. Nasty affair."

"It was." Matt accepted the teacup I handed to him and sat beside me on the sofa, rather closer than appropriate. If Mr. Barratt noticed, he gave no sign.

"The others aren't with you?" I asked Matt.

"They're at the Cross Keys."

"Have you spoken to Inspector Brockwell?" I asked.

Matt nodded. "I told him everything I could. He'll send some men out to question the neighbors, but if no one has come forward yet, it's unlikely the gunman was seen." He seemed to be waiting for someone to speak next, but when no one did, he added, "You came to see me, Mr. Barratt?"

"Not particularly," Mr. Barratt said. "I was concerned for Miss Steele after reading about the accident. I was concerned about you too, of course."

Matt grunted. "Of course."

"I'm relieved to see her looking as pretty and healthy as ever."

"She's not."

Mr. Barratt and I both stared at him.

"I mean, she does look as pretty as ever, but she's not altogether unharmed," Matt said.

Mr. Barratt's eyes narrowed as he studied me anew. "She mentioned bruising. Miss Steele, is there something you didn't tell me?"

"She's not your concern," Matt cut in before I could answer. "I'll see to her health and wellbeing."

"Matt!" I instantly regretted my outburst when he turned his glare onto me. Why was he in such a foul temper this morning?

He looked away and passed a hand over his eyes. "My apologies, Mr. Barratt. It was good of you to call on her. Yesterday was a trying day. I can't speak for Miss Steele, but I'm still recovering from the shock. It's too easy to imagine what might have happened."

The frankness of his admission set my heart racing. There was no doubting his sincerity. The rawness of his voice could not be faked. I stretched out my smallest finger on the sofa to touch his, either to thank him or reassure him, or...I didn't know why. I just wanted to connect with him.

But my finger didn't reach, and Mr. Barratt spoke. I tucked my fingers away.

"I must go," he said, checking the clock. "I have a meeting. Thank you for the tea. I'll be writing some articles about Hale's murder, so if you learn anything else, do pass it on to me."

"We won't learn anything more," Matt said. "Our involvement has ended."

We walked with him to the front door and I got the feeling from Mr. Barratt's hesitant goodbye that he wanted to say something more. Matt must have sensed it too.

"Is there anything else?" he pressed.

Mr. Barratt rocked on his feet and glanced through his lashes at me. "The theater, Miss Steele?"

"Oh," I said. "Yes, of course."

"Friday night, then."

Oh dear. I had only acknowledged the invitation, but he'd taken it as agreement and it seemed we were now off to the theater together. I felt Matt watching me and didn't dare glance his way.

"I'll send word about a time when I've looked at the program." Mr. Barratt said his farewells and exited.

I headed back to the drawing room but regretted my decision when Matt followed me. He did not resume his seat but remained in the doorway, filling it with his presence. I felt trapped.

"Is something wrong?" I asked, deciding to remain standing too.

"You're going to the theater," he said. "With Barratt."

"Yes."

"Why?"

"Because he asked me."

He folded his arms and regarded me down his nose. "Why didn't you tell me you wanted to go to the theater? I would have taken you."

"Because I didn't specifically want to go to the theater. He asked and I found myself accepting. There's nothing more to it."

"Nothing more to it?" He advanced into the room.

I stepped to the side, eyeing the door. I had the awful feeling this conversation was heading down a path I didn't want it to go. I wasn't prepared.

Fortunately a fierce rap on the front door distracted us both. I went to step around Matt, but he caught my elbow.

"We need to have this conversation, India," he said. "You can't run from it forever."

He let me go as his Aunt, Lady Rycroft, entered the drawing room, her three daughters in tow. I groaned, wishing I'd escaped faster. Perhaps I could plead soreness and retire.

I bobbed a curtsy but Lady Rycroft barely even looked at me. She wore a turban of bright turquoise that covered all her hair. Her striped jacket matched its color. It would have been a smart outfit if not for the alternating pink stripes. The bright colors made her complexion even more sallow.

"I have a bone to pick with you, Matthew." She swept past him and descended onto the sofa as if it were a throne and she had every right to sit on it. "Come, girls."

The girls followed her like puppets on strings, obediently doing her bidding. Only Hope rolled her eyes at Matt then winked as she passed him. He offered no smile in return.

"Is something the matter, Aunt?" he asked with thinly disguised patience.

"Something most certainly is the matter." She glared at the chair but he did not take the hint. "Sit down, Matthew. Looking up at you is giving my neck an ache."

A muscle in his jaw pulsed but he sat. "Tea?"

"This is not a social call."

"If it's about the accident, I want to reassure you that India and I are both fine."

"What accident?"

"There's been an accident?" Hope asked. Clearly they did not read the papers.

"Never mind," Matt muttered.

"I'm here to tell you to stop interrogating our pharmacist," Lady Rycroft said, her vowels plummier than ever. "He told me what you've been doing and I don't like it. You must cease immediately."

"And who is your pharmacist?"

"Mr. Pitt."

Matt frowned. "His business partner was murdered, and he is a suspect in the murder."

"Don't be ridiculous. Mr. Pitt is above suspicion."

"Why?"

"Because he is my pharmacist and the pharmacist to almost all of my friends. His medicines are highly sought after, but your presence at his shop is causing problems."

"Why?"

"Because no person of consequence wants to be seen coming and going from Pitt's shop if he is a suspect! Good lord, Matthew, do you not think about others before you go charging in, accusing him of this, that and the other? Have a little respect for the way things are done here in England."

"I have not accused Mr. Pitt of anything. I have merely questioned him." Matt didn't try to hide the steel in his voice. The only person who did not seem to notice it was his aunt. The two older Glass girls stared down at their laps, their shoulders tense. Hope tried to catch her mother's eye but failed.

"Then you will cease your questioning," Lady Rycroft demanded. "Understand me? That is an order."

Matt went still. A beat passed. Two. "An order?" His ominously quiet voice did not bode well. "And who are you to order me?"

She blinked rapidly at him, as if such a question had never occurred to her so she had never had to think of an answer. "I am your aunt! Your better! Your—"

"You are nobody to me. Do you understand? Get out. All of you."

"I beg your pardon!"

Matt looked as if he would manhandle her out of the drawing room.

"May I suggest a solution?" I said before he did anything he would regret later.

"Yes, please do, Miss Steele," Patience said quickly. Her mother did not turn my way. She looked as if she were rallying and preparing to take Matt to task again.

"Why not send your servants to Mr. Pitt's shop instead?" I asked. "Won't that be more discreet?"

"We already do," Hope said heavily.

Matt frowned. He leaned forward and rested his elbows on his knees. The storm cloud he'd brought in with him had dispersed somewhat, but some of the thunder lingered in his eyes. "Your maid…we saw her at Pitt's shop yesterday. I knew I recognized her."

"Sending her, or any other servant, won't solve the problem, though," Hope went on since her mother seemed far too angry to continue and her sisters too shy or stupid. "You see, if Mr. Pitt is found guilty—which I am sure he is not, but the police have been known to arrest innocent men before. But if he is, we will be without a pharmacist. And he really is the best in London. His special medicines work wonders on all sorts of ailments."

"Special medicines?" both Matt and I echoed. He looked at me at the same moment that I looked at him.

Did she mean special *magical* medicines? But Dr. Hale had told us he'd only cast spells on his own medicines not the Cure-Alls. If the medicines in Pitt's shop contained magic, he must have put it in the bottles himself.

He'd lied to us. He was a magician after all.

CHAPTER 16

"M r. Pitt doesn't sell them to his regular customers," Hope went on. "Only to his favorites, like us. Only to the elite."

"Like Lord Coyle," I said to no one in particular.

"Matt, you ought to ask Mr. Pitt if he has something for you," Hope said. "Tell him you're our relation and that Mama sent you."

Matt stared at her but didn't seem to see her. His mind was probably trying to fit all the pieces of the puzzle together, as was mine.

"Your illness," Hope pressed, sounding bemused by his lack of response. "Perhaps he has something for your condition. Mr. Pitt says he can't cure disease, but he can alleviate the symptoms, at least for a while. Everyone in our circle swears by his special medicines."

"Tell me about these special medicines," Matt said.

"He keeps them under the counter or in the back room. They're not on display. They're far too precious, so Mr. Pitt says, and reserved for only his best customers."

That's why I didn't feel any warmth in any of the bottles

on his shelves. The magic ones were kept elsewhere and sold only to his most exclusive customers, whom he no doubt charged an exorbitant price. If Pitt was an apothecary magician, then it *had* to be him who put the poison into Dr. Hale's personal bottle of Cure-All. The question was, why kill his business partner? They weren't rivals. Pitt may have inherited Hale's wealth, but he was already well off, and putting the poison into the Cure-All actually caused his business harm.

"You should visit Mr. Pitt yourself, Matt," Hope said again. "For medicine, I mean, not to question him. The medicine you take now doesn't seem to work all that well. You look more ill than ever today."

"I don't take medicine," Matt said, absently.

"The stuff that makes your skin glow purple."

Matt looked sharply at her.

"Don't be ridiculous," Lady Rycroft scoffed. "No medicine turns anyone purple. You're making things up again, Hope."

"Typical," Charity said with a click of her tongue. "Always so dramatic."

Hope clenched her jaw and waited for Matt to tell them she spoke the truth.

"Excuse me," he said, rising. "I have to go out."

He shepherded his aunt and cousins toward the front door where Bristow took over. Matt stalked off, much to Lady Rycroft's disgust. "Ill-bred American," she muttered. "I don't know why we come here."

"So one of us can catch his interest." Hope didn't even bother to speak quietly or hide the bitterness in her voice. "I'm afraid your plan is a resounding failure, Mama. Cousin Matthew barely even knows we exist. He's much too preoccupied with another matter. Wouldn't you agree, Miss Steele?"

"Good day," I said, picking up my skirts and following

Matt. I caught up to him on the landing between the first and second floor, but only after exerting myself more than my corset allowed. "Slow down, Matt," I puffed out.

He did, but did not stop.

"This is not the sort of information we can pass on to Brockwell," I said to his broad back.

"No."

"Then what do you plan on doing?"

"Confronting Pitt."

"Isn't that too dangerous?"

"That's why you're not going."

"I most certainly am if you are."

He finally stopped and rounded on me. "Stay here," he growled.

I straightened my spine. "If I hadn't been with you in the carriage, you would be dead. If you hadn't been in the carriage, I would be dead. It seems we make a good team. Teams should not split up or they become weaker."

He *humphed*, turned again and marched off to his room.

"Where are you going?" I called after him.

"To use my watch. Then we're going to see Pitt."

We? So he had relented. But dear lord, if his temper got any worse he'd explode. I just hoped he held it in check until we confronted Pitt. If not, the nearest person would be in his line of fire—me.

* * *

WITHOUT A COACHMAN TO DRIVE US, we decided to catch a hackney to Pitt's shop. Yesterday's attack must have been as fresh in Matt's mind as mine because he bundled me into the cab with unceremonious haste. I only managed to stay upright because he caught me.

"I can't believe you talked me into bringing you," he said, pulling the curtains closed.

He seemed to be spoiling for an argument so I did not respond. He edged aside the curtain and peered through the gap. His fingers drummed on his knee and then his knee itself jiggled. The plodding horses weren't fast enough for him.

I couldn't stand it for more than a few seconds. "Calm down, Matt."

His icy gaze slid to me. "I am calm." His knee stopped jiggling, but only for a moment before it resumed.

I tried to ignore it. I tried looking out of my window but he growled at me to keep the curtain closed. Well! It was fine for him to peer through a gap but not me, it seemed. I checked my watch, and checked it again five minutes later. It felt like a very long drive.

"We need to discuss what happened," he finally said.

I let out my pent up breath. "Thank goodness! I agree. So Pitt is the magician we've been looking for all along. His exclusive customers don't know he's using magic in his medicines, of course, although Coyle probably does. I suppose the magic lasts long enough in some bottles to have an effect on headaches and the like. But why would Mr. Pitt murder his business partner? His motive eludes me. Any thoughts?"

His dry laugh held no humor. "You win, India."

"Win?"

"We'll discuss the case." He squared his shoulders and sat up straighter. The cabin felt smaller, the air close. "Pitt's weapon of choice may be magic poison, but he might not be averse to using more violent means if we confront him. We need to approach this very carefully and gently."

"I'm quite capable of being gentle, but are you, at the moment?"

"I'm fine," he said, part pout, part defiance.

"You'll need to be at your most charming. Your present state is a little fierce. It wouldn't do to get angry with him and blurt out our suspicions. We need to trick him into confessing."

"I can manage," he ground out.

"See what I mean? Fierce."

The coach stopped and I took my watch out of my reticule and clutched it tightly.

"Wait here," Matt ordered the coachman as he alighted. He scanned the vicinity then kept me close as we traversed the few steps from the carriage to the shop door.

It was locked. A sign on the door said Mr. Pitt would be back soon. Matt knocked but there was no answer. He swore under his breath.

"Cover me," he said.

"Pardon?"

"Stand there and shield me from view. I'm breaking in."

"Matt!"

But he was already fidgeting with the door, inserting two slender tools like needles into the lock. It clicked open. He entered, tucking the tool back into his pocket.

"You must teach me how to do that," I said, following.

I shut the door behind us. The shop was dim but not completely dark, and once my eyes adjusted, I could walk through it without bumping into things.

"Check the medicines behind the counter for magic," Matt said. He inspected the countertop then bent to look in the drawers and cupboards underneath.

I rounded the counter and skimmed my hands across the bottles and jars on the rear wall. They all felt normal, not warm. I opened the back door and peered into the work-shop. The scent wafting out was even stronger than in the shop. It clung to the roof of my mouth and clogged my throat. The tight space of the workshop contained a bench, stool, and dozens of small drawers stretching almost to the ceiling down one length of wall. Shelves on the other wall held bottles, pots and jars of all sizes and shapes. Their magical warmth drifted toward me as if on a breeze and my watch pulsed in response. I touched a dozen or so bottles to make sure.

I returned to Matt in the shop. "There's magic in the back room," I told him.

He didn't look up from the ledger opened in front of him. No, not a ledger, a dated diary. His finger tapped on the entry for today that read: *Barratt, Gazette, 12:30.*

My knees buckled. I clutched the countertop for balance.

"India?" Matt caught my elbow. "Are you all right?"

"I was wrong," I whispered, "and you were right. Barratt and Pitt are working together." I'd been a silly fool, believing a man who flattered and flirted with me over my own common sense. I was making a bad habit of it. "Clearly they know one another. It's not a great leap from there."

Matt shut the diary and slipped it back onto the shelf under the counter. "This doesn't prove anything. It could just be an innocent meeting. There are no other entries in recent weeks mentioning Barratt."

He was defending Barratt? So that I didn't feel too awful? I sniffed and blinked back hot tears.

"Don't presume until we know for sure." He pressed his hand to my lower back and steered me out of the shop. "Let's find out, shall we?"

He gave orders to the driver to take us to the office of *The Weekly Gazette*, post-haste.

* * *

THE RHYTHMIC CLANK *clank* of machinery grew louder upon entering the *Gazette's* building. They must be printing the latest edition.

No one met us in the front reception room so we headed through the door to the main room. Two men, one young, the other ancient, bent over a newspaper spread out on the desk before them. Neither had heard our entry over the press.

Matt inquired after Oscar Barratt and was told he'd taken a friend down to see the machines working. "May we see them too?" Matt asked.

"Be our guest," said the young man. "Just don't touch anything and tell the foreman you're friends of Oscar's."

Matt went to open the door the man pointed out to us, but it was locked. The younger of the two men frowned and tried the handle himself.

"It shouldn't be locked now," he said. "Not during a press run and hardly ever from the other side."

"Do you have a key?" Matt asked.

The man shook his head. "The foreman has it."

The older fellow joined us, trying the handle too. "Blast it. What's going on?"

"Go to Scotland Yard," Matt urged. "Ask for Detective Inspector Brockwell and tell him Matthew Glass sent you. He needs to come here immediately. Go!"

The young man nodded quickly and ran off. The older one tried the handle again and thumped his fist on the door. "Open up!"

No one could have heard him above the din. It seemed to me as if the presses grew even louder, the rumble and grind rising from the depths like a mechanical monster.

Matt reached into his pocket for his tools. "Who else is in there?" he asked.

"Just Jones, the foreman, and a packer," the elderly man

said. "Once the presses start, only the two of them are required. Why? What are you going to do?"

Matt had the door unlocked in seconds but he didn't open it. He put his tools away and unbuttoned his jacket. He removed two pistols from the waistband of his trousers and handed one to the whiskered man. The old man hesitated then took it, holding it in his gnarled and knotted fingers.

"Stay here," Matt directed us both. "Use that if you need to."

The old man stared at the pistol. It shook in his hands. "Why? Who's down there with Oscar?"

Matt didn't answer but opened the door a fraction. Heat blasted through the gap as if it had been waiting for the opportunity to escape. I caught a glimpse of reams of paper slipping along a conveyer belt and a giant metal mouth opening and closing. Steam hissed and spat from the pipes, mushrooming in the air. The noise was too loud to speak over.

Matt gave me a weighty glance then disappeared inside. He shut the door.

I hadn't even told him to be careful.

The old man and I watched the door. I didn't want to look away, afraid that if I did, something bad would happen. After a moment, he lowered the gun as if it were too heavy to hold.

"Name's Baggley," he said. "I'm the editor."

"Miss Steele," I said. "I'm a friend of Mr. Barratt's."

"I saw you the last time you were here. He spoke about you afterward, and again this morning."

"He did?"

He gave me a wan smile. "He asked if anyone knew what was playing at the Savoy this Friday night as you'd agreed to see a show with him."

"Oh." Tears burned my eyes again, but this time I couldn't be sure why.

My watch, hanging on its chain around my neck, chimed.

"What is all this about anyway?" Mr. Baggley asked.

I removed my watch just as it chimed again. I stared at it, wishing I understood it better. The door suddenly burst open and crashed back on its hinges. Mr. Pitt stumbled out then stopped. He pointed a gun at my head.

I swallowed my scream but it escaped as a whimper.

"I say!" the editor said, raising his gun, but only half way.

"I knew you wouldn't be far away, Miss Steele!" Mr. Pitt shouted above the machines. He edged away from the door just as Matt raced up behind him.

He halted too as he spotted me at gunpoint. His face drained of color.

"Put your weapons down!" Mr. Pitt shouted. "Both of you!"

Mr. Baggley set the pistol on the desk to his side and put his hands in the air. He begged me to do the same. "Please, sir, let us go," he said. "Or at least allow the lady to walk free."

Pitt ignored him—or perhaps didn't hear him, such was his focus. He shuffled to the side, keeping us and Matt in his sights. Matt lowered his weapon to the floor without taking his eyes off Pitt. Cold fury banked in their depths and kept his body rigid. He looked ready to spring at the first opportunity.

But Pitt gave him none. "Come with me, Miss Steele," he commanded. "Walk in front of me to the door. Anyone come after us, or try any heroics, I'll shoot her dead. Understand?" He pushed my sore shoulder. Pain from my bruises flared and I hissed air between my teeth.

Matt stepped toward us. "Let her go!"

Pitt pressed the gun to my temple and Matt stilled. His chest heaved with deep breaths and his nostrils flared. But he did not come after us. I stumbled forward, uncertainty gripping me. Was Pitt bluffing? Would he really kill me? Why didn't my watch do something more than merely chime? Perhaps I wasn't holding it right.

And where was Oscar Barratt, the foreman and packer? I didn't dare wonder.

"This is madness." Matt's words could be heard clear across the room. "Let her go!"

"And allow you to catch me? Not a chance, Glass." Pitt urged me forward, through to the front reception room then outside. Our hack driver gasped and gathered up the reins.

"Belgrave Square," Pitt ordered, pushing me into the carriage. "And fast."

Belgrave Square! Did he mean to visit Lord Coyle?

I landed awkwardly across the bench seat, almost letting go of my watch. Pain ratcheted up my side, momentarily distracting me from thoughts of escape. The door slammed shut and the hack sped off. For one brief moment, Pitt lost his balance and fell on the other seat. He sat up quickly, however, and trained the gun on me again.

I glanced behind me through the rear window, just in time to see Baggley, the editor, watching us, looking desperate and in despair. Matt was nowhere to be seen. My stomach rose to my throat, and I choked out a sob.

"He won't risk coming after us." Pitt wiped the back of his hand across his mouth. His forehead glistened with sweat. "I'm sorry about this, Miss Steele, but it's necessary. If you hadn't stuck your noses in, none of this would have happened. You should have left well enough alone."

I loosened my grip on my watch and smoothed my thumb over the warm silver instead. It throbbed to my touch, but did not leap out and wrap itself around Mr. Pitt. I silently willed it to choke him. "The police accused Mr. Glass of murdering Dr. Hale," I told him. "We had to intervene or he could have been arrested."

The cabin rocked as we slowed, the traffic ahead thickening. "Blast it," Pitt snarled. He thumped the cabin roof. "Move!"

"What have you done to Mr. Barratt and the other newspaper men?"

"The two workers are simply knocked out and tied up. I had no beef with them. Barratt, however, is a fool. He wanted to interview me today, about Jonathon, for an article that will reveal the existence of magic. Can you believe the stupidity of the man? I was prepared to let him go if he agreed not to write it, but he refused." He shook his head. "He had to be silenced or the whole bloody world will find out, and then where would we be? Chaos, Miss Steele, that's where."

My mouth went dry. "You killed him?"

"I don't even know if I hit him, to be honest. He fell, I know that much. The machines were too loud to hear his reaction. That's why I took him down there. That hellish noise even drowns out gunshots. I would have checked his condition if Glass hadn't surprised me."

I closed my eyes and prayed Mr. Barratt was all right. But he had not followed Matt out of the printing room. Bone-chilling cold crept through me. Mr. Pitt was far more ruthless than we imagined.

"Why did you kill Dr. Hale?" I asked.

He relaxed his grip on the gun a little. Perhaps it was my trembling voice that put him at ease, or the fact that no one followed us and we'd picked up speed again. Belgrave Square couldn't be far away. "He was also a fool. The world is full of them, Miss Steele. We'd known about each other's magic for years, and one day we got to talking about combining our magic into a medicine in the hope that a double dose of spell casting would make it last longer. It did not. Still, the magic lasted a little while in some bottles of Cure-All and we managed to do quite well out of those so that the medicine's reputation quickly spread. I wanted to leave it at that and end our experiment. He did not. He grew greedy, not for the money but the attention. With his name attached to the Cure-All, he became the public's darling. He got the job at the hospital on the back of it, I suspect. And then *Barratt* came sniffing around." He sneered at the name, as if he could hardly bear to speak it. "He wanted to write about Jonathon. He showered praise upon him, flattering him, and Jonathon lapped up every word. And then, when that patient seemed to come back to life, both Barratt and Jonathon had their angle for the article. It was the opening Barratt needed to get his editor to print it."

"But the article only alluded to magic. Only people who are aware of magic would have read anything into it, not the general public. The article didn't share any secrets. Why did it make you fear exposure?"

"You forget that the guild is aware of the existence of magic. Mr. Clark read the article and he too came sniffing around Hale. It is only a short leap from Jonathon to me. Too short."

"You were worried they would discover you were a magician." I understood now. It wasn't greed that had driven him to kill Hale but fear. Fear of having his apothecary's license revoked, at the very least.

"I would never work again," he said. "All my hard work, all the years of building up a reputation among London's elite....gone. I could not allow it. I could not let Jonathon's greed and stupidity ruin me."

"And yet here you are, running from the law, and all that you feared would come to pass is about to. If you are caught, you will be hanged. If you are not caught, you still cannot return to London and keep shop. You've become a wanted man."

"I'll start again, elsewhere. This is England, Miss Steele. There are other cities where London's guilds don't reach.

Cities large enough where a fellow can disappear without the police noticing." His words may have sounded brave, but his thin voice told the real story—the thought of starting again overwhelmed him.

"And what will you do to me?" I asked.

"That depends on how easily I get away. I have no qualms about shooting you if it helps me escape."

"Shooting me will achieve nothing. It will only anger Mr. Glass. With me gone, you'll have no leverage, no bargaining chip with him. He'll see you are arrested for your crimes."

He merely lifted one shoulder and tightened his grip on the gun.

"Did you shoot at us yesterday and frighten the horses?" I asked.

"I haven't been anywhere near you."

"Coyle, then?"

"Lord Coyle is his own man. I have no influence over him. If he decided to protect me from scandal and suspicion, then that is not my affair."

"Why would he want to protect you?"

"I am a magician, and he likes magic things, particularly my medicine. It eases his biliousness for a few days."

"Is that why you're going to him now? For protection?"

He did not answer.

The coach slowed. We had arrived at Belgrave Square. Pitt thumped on the roof. "Stop here!" He pushed open the door and ordered me out. "Act normal. If you make a sound, I'll shoot." He wrapped the flap of his jacket over his hand and the gun.

He threw some coins at the driver as we exited the hack. The driver didn't even check them before driving off at speed. Pitt marched me up the steps to Lord Coyle's residence, the gun barrel pressed against my spine. A cold sweat trickled down the back of my neck.

"Knock," he ordered me.

The butler opened the door, saving me the trouble. He lifted woolly eyebrows, first at me then at Pitt. "Yes?"

Pitt ushered me past the butler then kicked the door closed. "Get me Coyle," he demanded.

"Sir!" The butler's face turned an unhealthy shade of puce. "This is an outrage."

"Get Coyle *now*." Pitt whipped his jacket back, revealing the gun.

My lower lip wobbled. I caught it between my teeth and tried to convey urgency with my eyes.

The butler nodded and hurried away. A moment later, Lord Coyle emerged from the library, where he kept his magic collection hidden behind a false wall. His butler did not reappear, but another fellow, just as substantial in girth as Coyle with an equally impressive mustache, followed him out. He gasped when he saw Pitt's gun and backed up to the library door again, although he didn't disappear altogether.

"What is the meaning of this?" Coyle demanded. "Who are you and why are you pointing a gun at that girl?"

"Sir," Mr. Pitt said, licking his lips. "I'm your pharmacist. Pitt. Remember? You usually send your man but you've been to my shop once."

Lord Coyle merely grunted. I suspected that was an acknowledgement because he didn't look confused by Pitt's claim. "Answer my other questions."

"I need your protection, my lord." Pitt's voice rose an octave and sweat beaded on his brow again. He wasn't certain of this part. He was gambling with his life and the odds were not yet clear.

"Who is this man, Coyle?" the other gentleman asked. "What's going on here?" He spoke with a measure of authority and an unmistakable haughty tilt of his chin. He must be Coyle's equal, not another servant. Unlike Lord

Coyle, he kept a wary eye on the gun. Coyle paid it no mind, keeping his steady gaze on Pitt.

"A good question," Coyle said. "What do you mean you need my protection?"

"From the police," Pitt said. "They want to arrest me for murdering my business partner."

"My god," the gentleman muttered. "Murder!"

"And did you kill him?" Coyle demanded of Pitt.

Pitt wiped his sweaty top lip on his shoulder, leaving a smear on his jacket. "I had to." I suspected if anyone else had asked, he would not have answered. But with Lord Coyle, he was like a naughty child, eager to make up for his mistake beneath the critical gaze of his father. "He was going to reveal everything about magic to a reporter. *My* magic."

Coyle's snowy mustache twitched. His sharp eyes flicked to me. Behind him, his friend looked uncertain how he ought to react. "Magic?" Coyle bellowed. "What rot is this?"

"Fairy stories," the other gentleman scoffed. "He's mad."

"My lord, you know I'm not," Pitt cried. "Please." Sweat dripped down his face and he licked his lips again. "You have to help me so that I can continue to provide you with your magic—"

"Enough!" Coyle bellowed. "You are trespassing on my property! Get out!"

Pitt's gun pressed into the side of my head, the cold, hard steel shocking against my hot skin. The gun no longer shook. It would seem a kind of calmness had descended over Pitt. Had he sensed the inevitability of the end, as I had? Lord Coyle would not give in. He was not the sort to be bullied, nor did he want his friend to know of his interest in magic, it seemed. When people like Lord Coyle wanted to keep secrets, they kept them at all costs. Even if the cost was my life.

"I want transportation out of the city, money and a letter

of recommendation," Pitt demanded with an evenness that hadn't been in his voice until now. "Or her death will be on your conscience."

I closed my eyes and my lashes dampened from my tears. My watch chimed, as if in sympathy for my plight. It chimed again, louder, and I opened my eyes. Movement in the shadows at the top of the grand staircase caught my attention. Someone lurked there behind the large potted palm, watching, but I could not make out a figure.

"Give him what he wants, Coyle!" the other gentleman begged. "He's going to kill her, for God's sake."

Coyle said nothing.

And Pitt's patience had worn out. He adjusted his grip on the handle. "It seems you and I are both expendable, Miss Steele," he murmured in my ear. "I am sorry."

The click of the cocking gun was drowned out only by the chime of my watch.

I let my watch fall from my hand. Its chain slipped through my fingers. But not down. Sideways.

And then the gun went off.

CHAPTER 17

$\mathcal{I}$t felt as if my insides dropped away. Black spots danced in front of my eyes but quickly cleared. My first thought was that death didn't hurt like I expected it to. And why was it snowing inside Lord Coyle's house?

"India! India!" Matt's voice. Here. Why?

I spun around, searching for him, but only managed to make myself dizzy. I lost my balance and fell, but he caught me. His arms enveloped me. He pressed my cheek to his chest so I could hear the rapid, erratic beat of his heart. He'd forgotten my injuries, however, and the sharp pain in my shoulder snapped me out of my stupor.

I pulled away and blinked. It was definitely Matt, and he was unharmed, although the wretched look in his eyes, coupled with the exhaustion, made my heart ache. But how did he know to come here?

Questions would have to wait. Lord Coyle, the other gentleman and the butler knelt over Mr. Pitt, jerking and writhing on the floor, his face distorted into a grimace. My watch was wrapped tightly around his wrist and Lord Coyle now held the gun.

"What's he doing?" the butler asked.

"A fit," the gentleman said. "Timely."

Coyle's hand hovered above my watch. He reached out a finger to touch it but withdrew it quickly without doing so. He glanced up at me, his wide eyes full of wonder and an odd little smile on his lips.

I pulled away from Matt, bent and unwrapped my watch from Pitt's wrist. I looped the chain around my neck since I'd left my reticule behind in the hack. Coyle's gaze followed my every move.

"Send for the police," Matt ordered the butler. "We can be found at sixteen Park Street if we're required for questioning."

"Wait." Lord Coyle struggled to his feet. "Miss Steele, may I look at that watch of yours?" He reached for it, but I shook my head.

Matt put his arm around me and escorted me outside into a dull day, the sky a monotonous shade of gray. We walked home, since it wasn't far, and I was glad. I needed the air and the exercise to help clear my head. Matt let go of my waist when we reached Hyde Park Corner but gave me his arm to hold. It rippled with taut muscle and an anger that shooting the ceiling had not assuaged. He probably would have preferred to shoot Pitt but his proximity to me had meant he could not.

"It was you who fired?" I clarified.

"Yes." It was a full four minutes before he spoke again. "Are you all right?"

"I think so." My bruises from the day before ached like the devil, but I hadn't acquired any more injuries from this ordeal. "Did you follow the hack to Coyle's house?"

"I climbed onto the back and rode with you."

"You did? I didn't see you."

"Nor did Pitt, it seems. I wasn't entirely sure until we reached our destination."

He must have managed it while the coach moved off and Pitt lost his balance.

"I entered Coyle's house via the service entrance and convinced the footmen who accosted me to let me go. Once he realized what was happening above stairs, he obliged. I took the service stairs to the first floor and bided my time. Almost too damned long," he ended with a growl. "There was no clear shot."

"Hence the distraction of shooting the ceiling."

"I'm not sure whether that provided the biggest distraction or your watch did." He ushered me along the Hyde Park path, his pace much faster than the stroll of other pedestrians. "In the end, I wasn't really needed."

"You were needed," I said, quietly. "You were—and are—needed very much, Matt." I leaned into his arm and was gratified to feel the tension leave him along with a deep sigh.

He slowed his pace. "I'm sorry. I'm walking too fast. I just want to get you home."

"We're safe now. Pitt is either dead or under arrest." I looked up suddenly. "What about Oscar Barratt? Is he…"

"Alive but injured. Pitt shot him in the shoulder. It's unclear whether he wanted to kill Barratt or merely hurt him."

"Kill him," I said heavily. "He admitted as much to me."

I told him what Pitt had said, finishing when we arrived home. I was immensely glad that everyone else was out. I couldn't face explaining the events of the afternoon to them all. It suddenly felt overwhelming, coming on top of the coach accident and Bryce's death.

He steered me into the library and poured me a brandy. He wrapped my fingers around the glass with gentle, sure hands, and poured another for himself. Finally he sat in an armchair and expelled a slow, measured breath.

"If Brockwell comes this afternoon, I'll put him off until tomorrow," he said. "You're in no state to speak to him."

"I'm fine."

"You're still shaking."

I clutched the glass tighter but that only made the brandy ripple more so I set the glass down on the table beside me. I touched my hair, only to realize it had come loose from its pins. It must have happened when Pitt pushed me into the hackney. I removed the rest of the pins then teased it out with my fingers.

Matt swallowed then drank deeply.

"What do you think Coyle's involvement was in all this?" I asked.

Matt watched me from beneath hooded eyes, his finger skimming his top lip. He took a moment to answer, then said, "I think he's a customer of Pitt's, with a keen interest in keeping Pitt out of jail but not enough interest to want to get tangled up directly. Pitt crossed a line by begging Coyle for help in his house. Helping anonymously is one thing, but doing it in front of a friend and us? Coyle's not the sort of man to declare his hand."

"Pitt must have realized Coyle was keen to protect him, even to the point of sending someone to scare us off, and assumed he could turn to him now. But he overestimated his worth to Coyle."

"No doubt Coyle will come away from this looking like a victim."

I touched the watch hanging around my neck and closed my eyes, allowing its familiar warmth to seep into my skin.

A moment later—or was it longer?—Matt's voice filled my head. "India. India, wake up."

I sat up and smothered a yawn. "I'm not asleep."

His mouth lifted at the corner in that half smile I liked so much. He crouched at my side, his hand over mine, his thumb caressing. It was a reassuring gesture and just what I needed. "Mrs. Bristow ran a bath for you," he said. "It's ready."

"Oh. That was kind of her."

He helped me out of the armchair, drawing me close. His hands gently steadied me at my elbows. He smiled down at me and my insides melted. Did it really matter that he was too far above my station? Did it really matter if his aunt would never speak to me again if I begged him to lie with me? I could live with myself if I disappointed her, if I had Matt's affections.

No. I could not. I was a fool for even contemplating going against her wishes. I had too much to lose here, too many friends who'd become dear to me. I didn't dare risk the loss of their friendship over an infatuation with a handsome man who was not mine for the taking and never could be. I was a shop girl, and he the heir to the Rycroft title. Gaps that wide were never closed with marriage. *Affaires de coeur*, yes, but not a wedding.

I pulled away and thanked him, although I wasn't really sure what for.

He smiled. "Enjoy your bath."

* * *

DETECTIVE INSPECTOR BROCKWELL peeled back a page of his notebook and read the small, neat writing. "Hmmm," he said, then lifted the next page slowly, as if he wanted to savor the anticipation and prolong the moment. He read that page too, top to bottom, and repeated the act of page-turning and reading another three times.

It set my teeth on edge. How Matt sat there, one leg casually crossed over the other, and watched Brockwell without batting an eye, I couldn't fathom. Yesterday, he would have torn the notebook from Brockwell's hands, ripped out the pages and flung them back at him. Today, he accepted Brockwell's snail's pace as if he had all the time in the world to wait for the detective to get to his questions.

Willie cracked a moment before I did. "You going to sit there all day like a sorry drunk nursing his bourbon, or you going to ask what you came to ask?"

Brockwell closed his notebook and regarded her. "What do you have to do with any of this again? Please remind me. I seem to have forgotten."

Air hissed between her clenched teeth. "I'm Matt's cousin. I ain't got nothing to do with nothing. I'm just interested."

She wasn't the only interested party in the drawing room. Aside from her, Matt, and myself, Cyclops and Duke had come to hear what Brockwell had to say. The only member of the household missing was Miss Glass. She'd taken a turn after we gave them all a brief account of the previous day's events.

Brockwell had arrived mid-morning. We'd expected him the evening before, to question us, but in keeping with his nature, he'd waited until today.

Fortunately his delay wasn't a sign of his reluctance to arrest Pitt. He'd informed us that Pitt was indeed alive and had been detained at Lord Coyle's house by the servants until the constables and Brockwell arrived. Having been summoned to the office of *The Weekly Gazette*, it had taken a little longer for word to reach Brockwell, but he'd soon taken the situation in hand and arrested Pitt, on Lord Coyle's urging. My watch's involvement was not mentioned.

I had already established that Oscar Barratt was going to fully recover, despite a bullet wound to the shoulder, and the other newspapermen in the printing room had not been harmed. Lord Coyle had given his account of events, but he'd been vague on the particulars leading up to Pitt's arrival at his house with me at gunpoint.

"Mr. Pitt has confessed to the murder of Dr. Hale," Brockwell told us. "But he has not told us why."

"Does the reason matter?" Matt asked. "He has confessed. It's enough for a jury to convict him."

"True." Brockwell pocketed his pencil and notebook, the slow movement driving Willie to mutter under her breath. "But I would like to know, nevertheless."

"Then you must question Mr. Pitt more thoroughly," Matt said. "I cannot provide the answer for you."

"You see, he had no reason that I can see to murder Dr. Hale."

"The inheritance?" Matt said with a shrug.

"But Hale was worth more to him alive than dead. His name helped him make a fortune with the Cure-All. Poisoning the bottle of Cure-All sabotaged his own product. So again, I wonder why."

Willie threw her hands in the air. "People kill each other all the time because they rub the wrong way."

"Usually in fits of anger or frustration, with fists, knives or guns. Poison is far more calculating."

"Murdering someone out of frustration I can believe."

"I'm afraid I cannot give you the answer," Matt said.

"Then how did you know Pitt was guilty?"

"We didn't, not until we arrived at the office of the *Gazette* and learned that he attacked Barratt." The lie rolled smoothly off his tongue and I could see from Brockwell's face that he believed him. Matt was back to his old, assured self, in full control of his temper and emotions once again. Looking at him now, with his smooth forehead and easy manner, it was almost impossible to fathom that he had another side lurking beneath the charming façade. "It was merely our ill fortune that we were there at that time," he went on. "As I informed you after the accident, Miss Steele and I had given up the investigation. The risks were too great."

"Did Pitt confess that it was he who shot at your carriage, or threatened Miss Steele?" Brockwell asked.

"No." Matt said nothing more. It would seem he wasn't going to tell Brockwell about Coyle's involvement. I wasn't entirely sure it was a good idea to withhold the information. Coyle ought to face the repercussions of his actions, but I knew that pinning them on him would be almost impossible.

"It must have been him." Brockwell shook his head as if he couldn't quite believe Pitt had it in him. "Must say, I am surprised. I can see him attempting to bribe me to overlook evidence, but not shoot at you."

Matt leaned forward, the first sign of interest he'd shown in the conversation since Brockwell arrived. "Bribe you?"

Brockwell gave him a flat smile. "Now that it's over, I can tell you that he did. An anonymous letter arrived at Scotland Yard, addressed to me, urging me to find no guilty party in the case of Dr. Hale's murder. It must have been Pitt who sent it."

More likely it had been Coyle.

"You were offered money?" Matt asked.

"A considerable sum," Brockwell said.

"And you didn't take it?" Willie sounded as if she couldn't quite believe someone would walk away from easy money.

"No, Miss Johnson, I did not. I'm not a rich man, but my income is enough for a bachelor to live comfortably."

She nodded her appreciation and studied him again as if she were seeing him anew.

"Solving the puzzle is what drives me," Brockwell went on. "That and the satisfaction of seeing people like Pitt pay for their crimes." He stood and patted his pocket containing his notebook and pencil. "I have everything I need, for now."

Matt rose and put out his hand. "We haven't always seen

eye to eye but I think I have a better understanding of your process now."

Brockwell shook his hand. "I hope so."

Bristow arrived after Duke pulled the bell and escorted Brockwell out.

"Maybe he ain't so bad," Cyclops said, resuming his seat.

"He's only doing his job," Willie agreed. "Ain't his fault if Sheriff Payne is trying to pull the wool over his eyes. Just as long as he does his duty and investigates proper, you ain't got nothing to worry about there, Matt."

Matt watched the doorway through which Brockwell had exited. Then he turned to me. "What do you think, India?"

"Me?" I looked at him aghast. "I don't think I'm the best person to ask about someone's integrity."

"I disagree. And anyway," he added, cutting off my protest, "I'd like your opinion."

He'd said just the right thing to draw it out of me, and he knew it too, if his small smile was an indication. "Well," I began. All four sets of eyes watched me. I cleared my throat and met Matt's gaze dead-on. "Just because Brockwell can't be corrupted doesn't mean he always gets to the truth and arrests the right man."

"Precisely." He slapped his hand down on the chair arm and pushed himself up. "India, are you feeling up to a shopping expedition?"

Every time we went shopping, he bought me sweets, dresses, hats or trinkets. And every time, I fell a little bit more in love with him. Not because of the sweets, dresses, hats or trinkets, but because it was time spent alone together, just the two of us, and we were able to simply talk. The more we talked, the more I realized I liked him beyond his good looks. I liked him because he was amusing and kind, clever and curious, and interested in what I had to say. An intoxicating combination for any woman, and that was without throwing his fortune and position into the mix.

"I think I'll stay home," I said, ignoring the regret pinching my gut.

"Pity." He shrugged, as if it made no difference to him. "I hope I don't choose the wrong watch." Damn him for always knowing the right thing to say. He held out his hand to me, his eyes sparkling.

I placed my hand in his. "Unlike Inspector Brockwell, it seems I can be bribed."

* * *

"WOULD you like to visit Mr. Barratt?" Matt asked, handing me back into the carriage.

I paused on the step and stared at him. He was still taller than me, despite the step, and with the hazy sun behind his head, I had to squint to see him properly. I could almost hear Catherine's voice telling me I'd get wrinkles so I tried to widen my eyes. I ended up blinking furiously in order to see him at all.

"I... I don't know," I said. "Why?"

"Because he's injured and I suspect you have things you want to talk about." He leaned closer. "Magic things. And your appointment for this Friday night."

A bubble of laughter escaped my lips. "Appointment?"

"You know what I mean. Well? Do you want to see him or not?"

I shook my head and climbed into the cabin. "Not yet. He'll need time to recover. I imagine he's still in some pain. I'll write him a note freeing him of his obligation to take me to the theater. He can't possibly go yet."

"Home, Duke," Matt said to his friend, sitting on the coachman's seat. We'd taken out the second carriage, and

Duke had offered to drive us. He and Cyclops would share coachman duties until another could be employed. Nobody pressed Matt to interview replacements. Bryce's death was still a sensitive topic.

We'd purchased a handsome gold double hunter case watch from Catherine's father. It wasn't the most expensive watch in the shop, but it was the best. I couldn't wait to get it home and make sure it was in perfect working order. Mr. Mason assured me that it was, but I ought to check. Indeed, it had been Matt's idea.

"You said yet," Matt said as we drove off. His grin was nowhere to be seen, replaced by a scowl. I missed the smile.

"Pardon?"

"You said that Barratt can't possibly go to the theater with you *yet*." His fingers tapped his thigh and the wall behind my left ear drew his gaze. "You still plan on going with him?"

"I don't know. I haven't thought about it. I've had other things on my mind."

His gaze flew to mine. "Such as?"

"So many things." His kisses and kindnesses, mostly, but that discussion could not be borne now. "Such as the notion of bringing magic into the open."

He blinked slowly. "Ah."

"I've been thinking about Mr. Barratt's notion of writing articles about magic. They couldn't be overt, at first, but a subtle and slow introduction to the art of magic would bring it into the public consciousness. Newspapers are powerful, Matt. They can affect public opinion on a grand scale. Look at Dr. Hale's Cure-All. Its reputation made it into the newspapers and sales rocketed, then plummeted again after reports of Hale's death. Imagine harnessing that power on the side of magic. With Barratt reporting on the good it can do, the public will surely become favorable to us. With the public on our side, governments will change their policies and the guilds would become less effective. They're only powerful now because successive governments let them become powerful, but public opinion would change that in our favor." The more I spoke, the more the idea excited me. It had excited Oscar Barratt too, and I could see why. "If we want to keep magicians safe, then bringing magic into the open is the only way to do it."

Matt didn't interrupt me, but I could see from his face that he didn't share my enthusiasm. While I felt as if I would bounce off the seat, he sat like an imposing statue, his brow furrowed in thought.

"Newspapers *are* powerful," he finally said. "I agree with you there. But it's a gamble to think the public would come down on the side of magic, not against it."

"You're a gambler."

"I used to be. And you, India, are definitely not the risk-taking sort. Not on this scale."

He leaned forward and rested his clasped hands on my knees. The intimate gesture did just as much to scramble my nerves as his kiss had.

"I think it best if we keep magic a secret," he said.

"We can't control Mr. Barratt. If he writes about it, then there's nothing we can do."

"If he writes about you specifically, I'll wring his neck."

"Thank you, Matt, but I can wring it myself." I wriggled my fingers. "I have big hands and his neck is not so thick."

He laughed. "So…about the theater."

"Yes?" I asked, finding it hard to catch my breath.

"May I take you instead?"

"Only if the others come with us." I said it before I could change my mind, before my resolve melted beneath his intense gaze.

He sat back slowly. His hands fell away and gripped the

seat on either side of him. "You don't wish to be alone with me."

"We're alone now."

"Don't trifle with me, India." The flat, dull edge of his voice gave way to a hardness that I hated.

I swallowed and forged on. "We need to discuss the kiss, Matt."

"Apparently so."

"It happened in the heat of the moment, after a trying, emotional day. We were both glad that the other was alive. That's all."

He turned to the window and for a moment, I thought he would ignore me completely. "You have feelings for Barratt," he finally said.

"No! This is nothing to do with him."

"You seemed to like the kiss at the time."

My face flamed, forcing me to look down at my lap. Even so, I felt his gaze on me.

"You responded to it, India. Don't deny it."

My fingers twined and untwined. I scrambled to find something to say to end this conversation before he managed to extract my true feelings and expose my lie. But I could think of nothing and the silence dragged on. I watched his rigid profile as we drove home through the streets. No, not *my* home. Not for much longer.

Slowly, with each passing minute, his jaw softened. The veins in his neck didn't throb quite so much, and he unclenched his fist.

"I see," he said so quietly I almost didn't hear him.

"See what?"

"Sometimes it's easy to forget that I'm ill," he said to his reflection. "Sometimes I allow myself to plan for the future. And then I remember that the future is not mine to plan for. Not until my watch is fixed."

The ache in his voice squeezed my heart. My eyelids fluttered closed. I couldn't bear to look at him anymore.

"I have no right to say what I said to you just now," he went on. "No right to assume. I have no claim over you because of one kiss. You must do what's best for you, India, and for your future. You're not a gambling woman, and it's unfair of me to expect you to gamble on me having a future at all."

My throat closed and my eyes burned. It was both unbearably painful and thrilling at the same time. He sounded miserable, and yet to think that he cared enough for me to want to share more than a kiss…

Somehow I managed to murmur an agreement and we spent the remainder of the journey to Park Street in uncomfortable silence. I did not regret withholding the real reason for my rejection. Matt, with his American ideals of equality, would dismiss the obstacles set by his aunt—and of England as a whole. He would see them as surmountable, and use his own parents as an example. But his father had not been the heir, and his mother didn't owe someone a debt of gratitude.

Miss Glass wanted her nephew to have the sort of life a man in his position should have, and I wanted him to have the life he deserved. He'd not had a settled home in any single country as a child, and his adulthood had been fraught with danger. England could provide him with a family that didn't feel as though he'd betrayed them, and a home that no one could take away from him. A home where he was the master. A wife with the proper connections would help him become a powerful force in any field he chose.

But with me, he'd never be more than the American upstart whose mother's family were outlaws. I could not help him rise above that like a woman of Hope Glass's or Lady Abbington's stature could.

"As soon as the Willesden house is settled, I'll move there," I told him.

He turned sharply to face me.

"It's for the best," I went on, unable to look at him.

* * *

"Good, you're here, India, and she's not," Willie said, bursting in on me in the sitting room.

I'd taken luncheon in there with Miss Glass but she'd gone out afterward to make calls. She'd wanted Matt to go with her but he'd declined. They'd argued about it until Matt refused to discuss it any further. She'd left, her steps a little heavier as she walked up Park Street.

I worried that Matt would seek me out to talk to me. I wasn't ready for another discussion about his future—our future—so soon after the last one. It was draining. He hadn't, however, but I was far from glad. Relieved, yes, but not glad.

"I'm alone, if that's what you mean," I said to Willie.

She poured herself a cup of tea and, finding it cold, screwed up her nose and set the cup down. She threw herself into a chair. Her hair fell out of its loose knot and tumbled around her shoulders in waves.

"You look very pretty this afternoon," I said.

"What?"

"Miss Glass would think your hair is a mess, but I think it suits you. It frames your face nicely."

She snorted and wiped her hand across her nose. "Don't be a ninny."

"I know you think you're proving a point by behaving like a man, and an uncouth one at that, but I'm not fooled. Nor is Duke."

"What's he got to do with anything?"

"You ought to give him a chance. Don't be so cruel to him when he's only trying to be nice to you."

"Nice to me! He lectures me and tells me what to do all the time. He gets on my nerves."

I smiled down at Matt's new watch, its inner workings laid out on the table before me.

She planted both feet on the floor and stood. "Wait here. I need to get Matt."

She left before I could stop her. I busied myself with the watch, returning parts to the housing while I waited, only to find it took longer than expected. My mind was not on the task this afternoon.

"Right," Willie announced upon re-entering. "Sit down, both of you. I've got something to say."

Matt stood by the hearth, his cool gaze on his cousin. He hadn't so much as looked my way.

"I went for a walk alone," Willie said. She hadn't sat either, preferring to pace. Her agitated state had me intrigued. I set down my tools. "I wanted to think," she went on. "And I've realized something. Something about you, India."

"Me?" I blinked at her. "You'd better go on."

"We made the mistake of assuming Dr. Hale was the only magical one in the business partnership with Mr. Pitt."

"We shouldn't have," Matt agreed. "So? What's that got to do with India?"

"What if she's the product of *two* magicians, not one?"

"By product, you mean child," I said.

"Grandchild. That journalist reckons your grandmother was the magician, but we know Chronos is."

"You're jumping to the conclusion that Chronos *is* my grandfather. I don't think he is. He hasn't sought me out since he's been in London, and he didn't come to his own son's funeral." My voice trembled, catching me unawares. Why was I so emotional about a man I never knew?

Matt touched my shoulder. His thumb brushed the underside of my jaw.

And then he withdrew it and sat on a chair. "Both your grandparents being magicians would explain why your magic is strong," he said.

"It's not that strong."

"It is. Mr. Gibbons thought so. I think so."

"There's no reason why two timepiece magicians couldn't have married," Willie said. "It's likely, when you think about it. Their families would have known each other. They both had an interest in watches and clocks." She brushed her hands together and headed to the door. "That's my work done for the day, then. I'm off to meet Cyclops and Duke at the Cross Keys for a drink. Care to join me, India? I can teach you some drinking games."

"Not today," I said.

I watched her go and almost wished Matt would go with her to avoid the inevitable awkwardness. He didn't get up, and I found I was grateful for his company. The sooner we worked through this phase and became comfortable with one another again, the better.

I closed the watch's case and handed it to Matt, only to regret giving it up. Now I had nothing to hold. I clasped my hands in my lap instead. "Matt," I began. "I want us to remain friends."

"As do I." If he was as nervous as me, he didn't show it. He looked as calm and assured as ever. It was grossly unfair.

"I want things to be the way they were between us," I said.

"They will be, India. I promise. Although it'll be harder with you living elsewhere."

"I'll be here every day that I'm required."

"Then you might as well stay. You'll be here more than you'll be at the cottage."

I smiled at him and he smiled back. It was a good start.

"Have you told my aunt yet?" he asked.

I shook my head. "I'm summoning the courage."

"Speak to her in my presence. I'll be an ally if you need it."

"You will?" I must have looked utterly stunned because he chuckled.

"India, I'll always be on your side, no matter what."

"Even when I want to do something you don't agree with?"

"You mean like move away and live elsewhere? Yes, even then. I'll grumble to myself in the quiet of my own room, but outwardly, I'll support you. It's the best I can do."

"It's enough, Matt. Thank you."

His smile turned wistful, sad. I blinked back tears and looked down at my linked hands.

"Matt!" Willie's screech filled the entire house, making it difficult to tell where it came from. "Matt, come quick!"

He sprang from the chair and sprinted out the door. I followed, but could not keep up.

"Willie!" he shouted back. "What's wrong?"

I did not hear her response. I caught up to them at the top of the stairs, looking down at the entrance hall below. Bristow stood by the front door, removing the coat and hat of the white haired visitor. The visitor seemed not to hear him. He stared up at us.

"Pierre DuPont," I said on a rush of breath. I recognized him from the brief moment I'd seen him at Worthey's factory before he'd run off.

"It's him," Willie said, grinning broadly. "It's him, Matt."

"Chronos," Matt whispered.

Thank God. We'd found him. We'd found the man who could repair Matt's watch. He was here and he could not run away with Cyclops standing behind him, blocking the exit.

Chronos did not look like he wanted to run off. His gaze

swept over Matt, then he nodded in recognition. Matt returned it.

Finally Chronos's gaze settled on me. He didn't even blink as Matt and I headed downstairs, side by side. It unnerved me.

The closer we got, the clearer the lines on the man's face became. He was certainly old, the pattern of wrinkles telling a long and convoluted story. His snowy beard was full but the hair on his head light and wispy. He had clear eyes, however. Clear and clever.

Matt extended his hand. "My name is Matthew Glass," he said. "You saved my life in Broken Creek, New Mexico, five years ago. I've been looking for you."

Chronos hesitated then shook his hand. "You've found me." He once again looked at me. I wanted to shrink into Matt's side, but stood my ground. Chronos—DuPont—had an unnerving stare. He also had no French accent. It was utterly English.

"This is Miss Steele," Matt said. "Miss India Steele, daughter of Elliot Steele."

Chronos nodded, unsurprised. "So your friend told me on the way here." He extended his hand to me. I took it. He did not wear gloves and his hand was cool and rough; a working man's hands. "The last time I saw you, India, you were a babe in your mother's arms."

I blinked back at him. My eyes felt huge in my head and my hand small in his. "You're my grandfather."

It felt so right that I knew it must be true, even before he said, "Yes, I am."

THE END

LOOK OUT FOR

THE MAGICIAN'S DIARY
The 4th book in the Glass and Steele series by C.J. Archer.
To fix Matt's magic watch, Matt and India must find a diary that once belonged to a doctor magician murdered decades ago. The hunt drags them into a sordid mystery as long-held secrets are unearthed.

Sign up to C.J.'s newsletter through her website to be notified when she releases the next Glass and Steele novel. Subscribers also get access to a FREE Glass and Steele short story.

A MESSAGE FROM THE AUTHOR

I hope you enjoyed reading THE APOTHECARY'S POISON as much as I enjoyed writing it. As an independent author, getting the word out about my book is vital to its success, so if you liked this book please consider telling your friends and writing a review at the store where you purchased it. If you would like to be contacted when I release a new book, subscribe to my newsletter at http://cjarcher.com/contact-cj/newsletter/. You will only be contacted when I have a new book out.

GET A FREE SHORT STORY

I wrote a short story for the Glass and Steele series that is set before THE WATCHMAKER'S DAUGHTER. Titled THE TRAITOR'S GAMBLE it features Matt and his friends in the Wild West town of Broken Creek. It contains spoilers from THE WATCHMAKER'S DAUGHTER, so you must read that first. The best part is, the short story is FREE, but only to my newsletter subscribers. So subscribe now via my website if you haven't already.

ALSO BY C.J. ARCHER

SERIES WITH 2 OR MORE BOOKS

The Glass Library

Cleopatra Fox Mysteries

After The Rift

Glass and Steele

The Ministry of Curiosities Series

The Emily Chambers Spirit Medium Trilogy

The 1st Freak House Trilogy

The 2nd Freak House Trilogy

The 3rd Freak House Trilogy

The Assassins Guild Series

Lord Hawkesbury's Players Series

Witch Born

SINGLE TITLES NOT IN A SERIES

Courting His Countess

Surrender

Redemption

The Mercenary's Price

ABOUT THE AUTHOR

C.J. Archer has loved history and books for as long as she can remember and feels fortunate that she found a way to combine the two. She spent her early childhood in the dramatic beauty of outback Queensland, Australia, but now lives in suburban Melbourne with her husband, two children and a mischievous black & white cat named Coco.

Subscribe to C.J.'s newsletter through her website to be notified when she releases a new book, as well as get access to exclusive content and subscriber-only giveaways. Her website also contains up to date details on all her books: http://cjarcher.com She loves to hear from readers. You can contact her through email cj@cjarcher.com or follow her on social media to get the latest updates on her books:

facebook.com/CJArcherAuthorPage

twitter.com/cj_archer

instagram.com/authorcjarcher

Made in the USA
Monee, IL
28 June 2023

37959099R00187